MASTERS OF WAR

Also by Chris Ryan

Non-fiction

The One That Got Away
Chris Ryan's SAS Fitness Book
Chris Ryan's Ultimate Survival Guide
Fight to Win

Fiction

Stand By, Stand By
Zero Option
The Kremlin Device
Tenth Man Down
Hit List
The Watchman
Land of Fire
Greed
The Increment
Blackout
Ultimate Weapon
Strike Back
Firefight
Who Dares Wins
The Kill Zone
Killing for the Company
Osama

Chris Ryan Extreme: Hard Target

Mission 1: Redeemer
Mission 2: The Rock
Mission 3: Die Trying
Mission 4: Fallout

Chris Ryan Extreme: Night Strike

Mission 1: Avenger
Mission 2: Armed and Dangerous
Mission 3: The Enemy
Mission 4: Lone Wolf

Chris Ryan Extreme: Most Wanted

Mission 1: Protector
Mission 2: The Specialist
Mission 3: Hard to Kill
Mission 4: The Feared

CHRIS RYAN
MASTERS OF WAR

CORONET

First published in Great Britain in 2013 by Coronet
An imprint of Hodder & Stoughton
An Hachette UK company

First published in paperback in 2014

2

A CIP catalogue record for this title is available from the British Library

ISBN 978 1 444 70649 9
Export ISBN 978 1 444 74143 8

Printed and bound by Clays Ltd, St Ives plc

Hodder & Stoughton policy is to use papers that are natural, renewable
and recyclable products and made from wood grown in sustainable
forests. The logging and manufacturing processes are expected to
conform to the environmental regulations of the country of origin.

Hodder & Stoughton Ltd
338 Euston Road
London NW1 3BH

www.hodder.co.uk

AUTHOR'S NOTE

On Thursday, 31 January 1991, a week after the ill-fated Bravo Two Zero patrol had been compromised, I crossed the Iraqi border into Syria. I was the only member of the unit to escape capture alive, but I was in a bad way. I'd been on the run for seven days and nights. I hadn't eaten for six days, or drunk any water for three. My toenails had fallen off and my blistered feet had become infected and were oozing pus. I'd been exposed to nuclear waste and I was hallucinating. But at least, here in Syria, I was safe.

Or so I thought.

The first Syrian people I encountered were villagers living so simply that they were cooking breakfast on a fire outside their little house of whitewashed stone. They gave me cool water. Without their kindness I doubt I could have survived much longer.

We did not speak each other's language, but I managed to make them understand that I needed to get to the nearest town. A young man helped me get there, but in the hours that followed I saw a very different side to life in Syria. I had to escape an angry mob who seemed determined to kill me. I found myself in the custody of three low-ranking Syrian police officers who performed a mock execution on me. Having covered about two hundred miles on foot in Iraq, I crossed most of Syria by car before reaching the capital, Damascus. There I ended up in the headquarters of the feared *Mukhabarat* secret police. The very name was enough to terrify the ordinary citizens of Syria, as the *Mukhabarat*'s tortures were notoriously cruel and they had a nasty habit of 'disappearing' anyone who displeased them.

Syria was a complex, dangerous place for me back in 1991. But now, more than twenty years on, one thing strikes me: it was not nearly so dangerous then as it is now. I got out alive. Tens of thousands of victims of the present Syrian civil war haven't been so lucky.

The story that follows is drawn from experience, and from first-hand knowledge of a country which, as I write these words, has become one of the most dangerous and war-torn places on earth. Some of it might make uncomfortable reading. I make no apology for that. Conflict is not a glamorous business. It's ugly and violent, and those who suffer the worst are not the politicians, for whom death tolls are little more than statistics. They are the ordinary people, stuck in the middle, and the soldiers sent to do the bidding of the masters of war.

Chris Ryan
London, 2013

In time of war, when truth is so precious, it must be attended by a bodyguard of lies.

Winston Churchill

PROLOGUE

The maternity ward, the Ulster Hospital, Dundonald, Northern Ireland. 1989.

If Susan Black had not been quite so brave, she might have got away with it. But bravery is always a gamble. You never know how it will turn out.

She lay in a hospital bed, propped up by pillows, her pale face exhausted. It was a plain room, about ten metres by ten, basic but not unpleasant. There was a blood-pressure machine to Susan's right and, on the wall behind the bedside table on her left, a laminated poster. It showed a suckling baby and stated: 'Breast is Best.' At the end of the bed was an empty cot. Susan softly hummed 'Rock-a-bye Baby' as she cradled her warmly wrapped newborn in the crook of her right arm. The little boy's few wisps of hair were matted with dried amniotic fluid. It was a bright spring morning, and the smell of newly mown grass wafted in through the open ground-floor window, where a lazy bee buzzed a counterpoint to Susan's humming. She looked over to the corner of the hospital room. Her husband Simon was there, cross-legged on the floor with their eldest, Kyle. The five-year-old was colouring – the excitement of his baby brother's arrival had already worn off, and Simon was doing what he could to keep the boy occupied.

Susan loved looking at her family. It gave her hope. Kyle had inherited her reddish-blond hair and his father's grey eyes. A perfect mixture of Irish and British. She had no time for the

1

sectarian rubbish that had surrounded her all her life. Never had, and nor had her family. She'd met Simon at New Forge rugby club, where he'd played for the RUC, and hadn't thought twice about making eyes at him. The Troubles were for other people. Sure, if she walked along the wrong side of the Falls Road she could, having married a member of the British Army, expect some insults she wouldn't want her children to hear. But living in Aldershot, as she now did, that stuff was just a memory. She had only come back to the Province for a quick visit with her parents – and of course with Simon himself, in the middle of his second six-month tour of duty with the Parachute Regiment – before the baby arrived. But the baby had decided to put in an early appearance.

Susan had expected to give birth in England, without the support of her husband. But sometimes, she thought to herself, things work out for the best. She hugged the bundle in her arms a little harder as Kyle bossily told his dad which crayon to use to colour in his He-Man and Skeletor picture. There weren't many people who could boss Simon Black around, but their lad was one of them.

Simon seemed distracted, though. Worried. There were frown lines on his face and he was absent-mindedly sparking the Zippo lighter carved with his initials that she'd bought him for Christmas – a clear sign that he was on edge. In a corner of her mind Susan supposed that she should be anxious about this. Why was he not more excited about the arrival of their baby? But the pethidine the doctors had given her hadn't yet worn off, and she had other things to occupy her, like the precious, fragile beauty of the child in her arms.

She caught her husband looking at her. 'You want some water?' he asked.

Susan gave him a smile and nodded. She wasn't really thirsty, but she knew how Simon hated having nothing to do. He walked over to her bedside table, where there was a jug of water and a glass. As he stretched out his right arm to lift the jug she watched his muscles flex and caught sight of the tattoo on the underside of his forearm. The motto of the Parachute Regiment, in Gothic letters: *Utrinque Paratus*. Ready for Anything. She always joked that he needed to be, having got together with a good Catholic girl like her. *He* always joked back that there was nothing Catholic about her once the lights were out.

A clinking sound as jug touched glass. Scribbling from the corner of the room. And, as Simon handed her the water and took the baby from her so she could drink, the sound of the door opening.

'Nurses can't keep away, can they?' Simon said, his Newcastle accent very soft. 'It's because he's got his ma's good looks, eh? Better hope he's got her brains, and all.'

He flashed a smile at Susan, but then frowned as he saw the look on her face. Still holding the baby, he spun round.

He'd been expecting to see a nurse or a midwife. They'd been in and out of the room ever since the baby had been born. This newcomer was dressed in the standard green scrubs of a hospital orderly. Unlike a hospital orderly, however, he wore a black balaclava and tan leather gloves and brandished an evil-looking handgun with a cylindrical suppressor fitted to the barrel.

The bee buzzed near the open window. Kyle, unaware of what was happening, continued to scribble. Susan opened her mouth to scream, but no noise came.

The intruder strode towards them, his gun raised, silently closing the five-metre gap between the door and the bed. As he drew alongside the bed, he seemed uncertain where to fire. His preference was clearly for Simon's chest – a wider target – but the baby was in the way and so his weapon drifted up towards the father's head.

Down to the chest.

Up to the head.

3

Had the gunman not hesitated before firing, Simon Black would have died instantly. But Susan, although very weak, had pushed herself up from her reclining position and hurled herself at him. She wasn't strong enough to knock the gunman down, but she bashed into him just the same. 'Provo cunt!' Simon hissed, just as the round intended for the centre of his forehead clipped the edge of his left temple. Its trajectory altered, it smashed the water jug behind him. Simon fell backwards as a spray of blood and a small shard of bone flew from the side of his head, spattering the 'Breast is Best' poster with a flat, slapping sound. Still holding the child, he slouched against the bedside table, water streaming over his bloody head. The gunman took aim again, ready to finish the job.

Susan had once heard a story, an urban myth, of a mother whose child was stuck under a car and who managed, thanks to the adrenalin surging through her veins, to lift the car and rescue the child. She had never believed it. Now, though, she found herself filled with a similar strength. As the gunman prepared to take his second shot, she threw herself at him, screaming at last – an animal mixture of fury and fear. Her body slammed against the gunman's, and they became a knot of limbs.

They were already tumbling to the ground when the second round was discharged.

It was quieter than the first, muffled not only by the suppressor but also by the soft, post-natal flesh of Susan's belly.

There was a moment of silence. The gunman lay quite still under Susan's body. The bee had fled from the open window. And then, after five seconds, there was a horrific retching sound as a torrent of foam and blood erupted from Susan's mouth.

The gunman heaved Susan's body away from his. The baby started wailing, a thin but persistent sound that was mostly drowned out by the sudden screaming of the five-year-old boy. As the gunman pushed himself to his feet, Susan rolled on to her back. She was clutching the wound to her stomach but it was useless: blood gushed over and between her hands, pooling stickily on the floor around her. She tried to say something, but simply spewed more blood as her lungs and other vital organs failed.

Then the door flew open. Two nurses stood frozen in the doorway. The gunman looked around at his handiwork. It was impossible to tell through the balaclava what he was thinking as, in another moment of hesitation, he stared first at the bleeding woman on the floor and then at her husband. Simon Black was still slumped by the bedside table. He still held his baby. But one side of his face was smeared with blood, his left foot was twitching and his eyes stared straight ahead without blinking.

The nurses screamed. There was a commotion in the corridor outside. The gunman – his green scrubs stained dark – ran to the open window and climbed through it, into the gardens outside.

By the time, forty-five seconds later, three security men burst into the room, he was gone.

In the minutes that followed, the chaos of the maternity ward increased tenfold. Doctors sprinted down the corridor to the room where the botched hit had taken place, barking instructions. Stretcher beds arrived. A nurse with trembling hands took the screaming baby from his wounded father. The midwife who had delivered him gave his five-year-old brother Kyle a hug so he wouldn't have to watch his mother and father being lifted on to the stretcher beds and rushed into the operating theatre. And when they had gone, she buried his face in her ample chest so he wouldn't have to see how closely the room now resembled an abattoir. She tried hard not to retch as she glanced at the poster above the bedside table, now gruesomely defaced with red spots.

In theatre number one, Susan Black lay under the bright overhead lights, an oxygen mask pressed to her face, her sheets saturated by an oozing continent of her blood. A container of fresh rhesus negative hung on a drip stand next to the bed, but it was clear to the seven-strong medical team trying to save her life that she was losing blood faster than they could transfuse it. A surgeon shouted through his canvas mask: 'Haemodynamically unstable, we need a laparotomy.' Moments later he was making a lower midline incision, the scalpel passing an inch to the right of the catastrophic entrance wound in the patient's abdomen. As his scalpel cut through skin and a layer of subcutaneous fat, the rate of beeping from the ECG machine rapidly increased. To the shock of everybody in the room, the patient's eyes pinged open. Her abdomen arched upward. Her body stiffened. The screen on the ECG machine flatlined.

'Vasopressin!' the surgeon shouted. '*Vasopressin!*' Seconds later a nurse handed the surgeon a syringe full of a clear liquid, which he injected immediately in an attempt to revert the cardiac arrest.

There was no response.

He started to administer chest compressions, pumping rapidly and firmly down on the breastbone, just above the butchered abdomen. But after twenty compressions there was still no sign of electrical activity on the ECG. No pulse. Nothing.

The surgeon stepped back, his scrubs as bloody as the gunman's had been. From somewhere in the distance, beyond the walls of the operating theatre, came the sound of police sirens. The surgeon looked at his watch. 'Time of death, nine fifty-six a.m.,' he said. Then, unable to hide his anger at his failure to keep the young woman alive, he ripped off his mask and threw it to the floor, before storming out of the theatre.

Outside in the corridor a man was waiting. He looked scruffy. He was a head taller than the surgeon, and had shoulder-length hair and a straggly beard that were as dark as his eyes and the look on his face. His cheekbones were pronounced, his nose slightly out of joint. 'What's happening in there?' he demanded.

'You'll have to speak to the hospital administrators,' the surgeon said, not even stopping to say it.

The man grabbed him by one arm. A firm, vice-like grip. The surgeon stopped, looked meaningfully at the hand restraining him, and then up at its owner.

'Sorry,' said the man. 'I'm . . . the name's Taff Davies. I'm a friend of the family. I need to know . . .' His voice had the faintest trace of a Welsh accent. It dripped with anxiety.

The surgeon bowed his head. 'I'm sorry,' he said. 'We did everything we could. It was a terrible wound. The worst I've seen.' He looked up and down the hospital corridor. 'And I've seen some bad ones.'

Three British Army soldiers appeared at one end of the corridor. They wore camouflage gear, and as they approached, the surgeon – who had made a study of such things – recognised the red shoulder flash of the Parachute Regiment. One of the Paras walked straight up to the man who had introduced himself as Taff Davies, who immediately held out a small military ID card. 'I'm with the mob,' he told the soldier quietly. 'Don't make a play of it, eh?'

The grim-faced soldier looked surprised. 'The Regiment's here?'

Taff shook his head. 'They're friends of mine. I came to visit the kid. They know what's happened up at Palace Barracks?'

The Paras nodded grimly.

Taff loosened his grip on the surgeon, to whom this conversation meant nothing. 'Where's Simon?' he asked.

'The husband?'

He nodded.

'Theatre number two. I wouldn't get your hopes up.' With a respectful nod, the surgeon continued down the corridor. Seconds later a noise made him look back over his shoulder. Taff Davies had picked up one of the plastic chairs lining the corridor and slammed it down on the floor, while the soldiers, clearly alarmed, stood at a safe distance of a few metres. Now he was clutching his hair, and looking around with a helpless, anguished expression. The surgeon had seen many people who had lost loved ones. He could tell instantly that Taff Davies was one of their number.

The corridor was spinning. Taff could barely stand. The doors to operating theatre number one swung open. A sombre collection of hospital staff emerged, wheeling a stretcher bed. A blue sheet covered the body on the bed. He heard one of the Paras swear under his breath. The sheet had a dark stain where it had come in contact with the corpse's abdomen. In his time Taff had seen more dead bodies than he could easily count. He'd added to them. But not all dead bodies are the same. The sight of some leave you as cold as the corpse itself.

Taff watched the bed disappear. Then he moved his substantial frame past the soldiers, in the direction the surgeon had indicated. A minute later he was outside operating theatre number two. Two nurses were standing about five metres beyond the door, talking in hushed voices, but fell silent as Taff approached. Standing by the door itself was a uniformed member of the RUC.

'News?' Taff asked.

The police officer shook his head.

Breathing deeply, Taff removed his wallet. His army ID was not on display, but hidden inside. He flashed the ID, which bore his name, photograph, army number and blood group, at the police officer. 'Family friend,' he explained.

The officer nodded.

'Anyone asks, the nurses or anything, just tell them that.'

They stood in silence outside the operating theatre. Time passed.

*　　*　　*

8

At 13.24 another exhausted-looking surgeon emerged from the operating theatre. He gave the RUC man a respectful nod, then cast Taff an enquiring look. 'Next of kin?'

'Good as,' Taff said.

'He's critical but stable. The gunshot affected part of his temporal lobe. We've managed to stop the internal bleeding, but there's substantial damage to the brain. He'll survive, but . . .' The surgeon's voice tailed off.

'But what?' Taff said.

'The temporal lobe regulates memory, emotions, language, learning . . . We can expect full amnesia, maybe profound mental deficiency going forward. Sometimes I think it would be kinder to let patients like this . . .' The surgeon stopped himself. 'Maybe the amnesia's for the best,' he continued. 'I hear the wife didn't make it?'

Taff nodded.

'Bastard Provos,' said the surgeon with a sudden burst of anger. 'I sometimes think they should spend a few hours on the wards, see exactly what they're doing to people.' He passed a tired hand over his eyes. 'I apologise,' he said.

'Don't apologise to me,' Taff replied, his voice flat and dead. 'The only good Provo is a dead one as far as I'm concerned. When can I see him?'

'Not yet, I'm afraid. They'll be moving him to intensive care at some point in the next hour or so. Speak to the ward sister. I'm sorry for your loss.'

The surgeon moved away, massaging the back of his neck as he went.

'Kyle. *Kyle?* It's me. It's your uncle Taff.'

He wasn't really Kyle's uncle, of course, but he was as close as made no difference. Kyle was in a brightly coloured children's room with snakes and ladders painted on the floor and puzzle boxes with Sellotaped corners on the shelves against one side.

On the floor in front of him lay a selection of Action Man characters. In the corner of the room a uniformed female police officer and a social worker in a grey A-line skirt observed them silently.

'How you doing, kiddo?' Taff asked. But it was obvious that Kyle was doing shit. The kid's eyes were bloodshot and there were scratches down his face where he'd dug into them with his nails. Ordinarily the boy would be excited to see Taff, who always gave him fifty pence for some sweets. But not now. He picked up an Action Man and slowly started smashing it against the floor. Taff put one hand on his wrist to stop him ruining the toy, but Kyle snatched it away and went on banging it on the floor. Harder and harder. Quicker and quicker. One arm split away from its body. Its head cracked. The social worker hurried forwards and gave Taff a look that suggested now would be a good time to leave. He stood up and made for the exit. When he looked back, the social worker had her arm around Kyle, but he was still destroying the toy.

The room to which they'd moved Simon was now guarded by two RUC officers, both armed and wearing body armour. The original officer was accompanying Taff. 'This is the guy I was telling you about, fellas.'

They gave Taff a respectful nod and let him in. Taff closed the door gently behind him and turned to look at Simon. 'Jesus,' he breathed. 'You look like shit.'

And he did. His bed was surrounded by medical equipment. A plastic tube emerged from his nose and cannulas sprouted from both hands. But it wasn't the beeping of the equipment, or the drip stands, or the sinister bandaging around his head that made Simon appear so desperate. It was the look on his face. His eyes were open, but whether they saw anything was impossible to tell. His mouth was open too, and his tongue lolled to one side, a patch of white spittle just visible along one edge.

Although he was conscious, he gave no indication that he was aware of Taff's presence.

Taff leaned over the bed and looked straight into his friend's eyes. There was nothing. No hint of recognition. The machines around the bed displayed his vital signs. Even so, Taff checked for a pulse. It was faint, but it was there. He looked down at his friend's wrist. The letters of the regimental motto looked darker than usual against his pale skin.

Taff realised he was breathing in time with the patient. Slowly. The door opened. A female police officer who had been watching over Kyle appeared. She was holding the little boy's hand and stood respectfully by the door while Taff finished his visit.

'I don't know if you can understand me, mucker,' Taff said, loud enough for Kyle and the policewoman to hear, 'but I hope you can. One of these days we're going to find the bastard who did this to you. And when that happens, he'll pay. That's all. He'll *fucking* pay.'

But Simon was in no state to answer. He continued to stare straight ahead of him. The machines keeping him alive continued to ping.

The newborn baby lay in a Perspex cot. He was tightly swaddled and fast asleep. Taff looked down at him. He remembered someone saying that babies always looked like their dads – nature's way of stopping the father from running away. As far as Taff could see, the kid looked like neither his mother nor his father. He looked like a newborn baby, and they all looked the same.

Taff remembered the kid's mother and his face darkened. He thought of Simon, lying there in a near-vegetative state. The image of his tattoo popped into Taff's head. *Utrinque Paratus*.

'You'll need to be, kiddo,' he murmured. 'You'll need to be.'

TWENTY-THREE YEARS LATER

ONE

'*J'ai l'impression qu'on nous regarde,*' Fatima said. *I feel like someone's watching us.*

At six o'clock on weekday evenings the old tenement building on rue du Faubourg Saint-Antoine in Paris always smelled the same. It was the pungent stink of cheap cuts of meat, boiled long and slow so even the bones could be mashed with a fork, then mixed with North African spices. The meat itself was barely fit for animals, let alone humans. The spices went some way to masking the taste, and their aroma seemed engrained in the dirty brick walls. The building always *sounded* the same, too. Babies wailing. TVs blaring. Couples arguing. This evening was no exception.

Fatima looked around the single room that she shared with her husband Hakim and their twin daughters. It was about six metres by four and contained a double mattress on the floor, a wooden cot and a rickety Formica-topped table with two chairs. At one end was a kitchenette – little more than a sink, a water heater and a two-ring electric hob. To the right of the kitchenette, in an alcove, were a poky bath-cum-shower and a toilet. Neither worked properly, and both stank. Through some quirk of the plumbing, whatever went down the kitchen sink reappeared in the bath, where it festered. The babies were crying. They were always crying. From hunger, mostly. Sometimes Fatima felt like joining in. Hakim, in boxer shorts and a white vest, lay on the mattress staring at the ceiling. He made no attempt to acknowledge what she'd just said. Fatima wasn't even sure he'd heard her.

She walked to the window. It looked on to a lightwell, open to the sky and about ten metres square. On each side of this were more cramped bedsits. The concrete walls were stained by years of exposure to the elements. All the grimy windows were open on account of the suffocating summer heat.

All except one. She stared at it carefully. Had she just seen a strange dot of red light in the darkness of the flat?

She pulled her threadbare cardigan a little tighter so it covered more of her breasts, then felt the heat of Hakim's body behind her. His hands on her shoulders. She turned and managed to smile at him. He smiled back.

'*Je pense que j'ai peut-être trouvé un boulot,*' he said over the sound of the twins' crying. *I think I might have found a job.*

'Really?' Fatima asked, her voice neutral and her French tinged, like her husband's, with an Algerian accent. She stepped back to the hob, on which she was boiling up meat and bones for the family. It was a conversation they had three times a week, and she was running out of ways to make it sound like she believed him.

'Yeah, this guy . . . sells old phones in the marketplace . . . said he maybe wanted . . .' Hakim's voice petered out.

'That's great!' she said as she stirred the contents of the pot. She drew a deep breath. 'Hakim, maybe we should go back.'

'What do you mean?'

'To Algiers. We have family there, and—'

'Don't be *stupid*. You *know* I can't go back there.'

Fatima turned to face him. 'Maybe we can change our identities . . .'

But she could tell that Hakim was somewhere between panic and anger. 'You want me to go to prison? Is that what you want? You know what they *do* to people in prison? Life has fucked me up the arse enough already.'

The babies' wailing became louder. In one corner of her mind Fatima was aware that this evening *they* were at risk of becoming the arguing couple whose voices echoed around the whole block. She didn't want that, and so she stepped across the room to her husband, took him by the hand and looked at him sincerely. 'Of course not,' she whispered. With a glance over at the steaming pot, she said, 'I'm not so hungry tonight. We'll feed the little ones, and then you have the . . .'

She stopped. Out of the corner of her eye she saw the red dot again, and inhaled sharply. 'Did you see that?'

But Hakim was lying back down on the mattress, his chest rising and falling quickly as he calmed himself. 'Nobody's watching us,' he said. 'Nobody even knows we're here. Give the kids some food. Their crying's getting on my nerves.'

Fatima nodded. He was right. Of course he was.

So why had she just shivered, when it was so hot?

She turned her attention to her babies while her husband went back to staring at the ceiling.

The bedsit on the opposite side of the lightwell from Hakim and Fatima's was in darkness, and almost unbearably hot since the window was closed. Two men occupied it, a squat, blond guy called Hector with a Union Jack tattoo on his forearm, and his lean, muscular companion, whose nickname was Skinner and whose real name even he himself had almost forgotten. Standing motionless, Hector was peering through binoculars mounted on a tripod into the bedsit opposite. 'Fuckin' Ada,' he said. 'I'm sweating like Jimmy Savile in a playground.'

There was a short silence, only broken by the faint crackling of Skinner's Gitane as he dragged deeply on it.

'Can't you put that fucking cigarette out, mucker?' Hector asked irritably. 'It's like waving a torch at them. I'm sure the bird just looked straight at us.'

Skinner sniffed, then took another drag before he answered. 'We're wasting our time here anyway,' he said, his cockney accent strong, though not quite as strong as Hector's. 'We can sort this Algerian fuck-knuckles in our sleep.'

Hector pulled back from the binos and inclined his head. Skinner had a point. As far as terrorists went, the Algerian kid they had under surveillance was hardly Carlos the Jackal. Carlos the Jackass more like.

'The sooner we make contact,' Skinner said, 'the sooner we can be out of this shithole. I say we do it in the morning.'

Hector looked over his shoulder. He could just make out Skinner's silhouette slumped lazily in a chair by the door, and the red dot of his cigarette as he put it to his mouth. As he dragged on the cigarette, the glow illuminated his features. Shaved head, pronounced Adam's apple, tattoos above the neckline of his T-shirt.

Skinner was right. The job was straightforward. And Hector sure as hell wouldn't miss being cooped up in the sweltering room. Surveillance was always the worst part. He stepped back from the binoculars again. 'Chuck us a tab,' he said. Skinner threw him a cigarette. 'We'll do it tomorrow,' Hector announced. 'Happy now?'

Skinner sniffed for a second time, and dragged once more on his cigarette.

At a quarter past eight the following morning, Hakim left his wife and children in the bedsit. The kids were still crying; they had been all night. He had to get out of there. He descended one flight of stairs and paid a visit to the communal toilet. It was just a tiny cubicle with a hole in the floor and there was no light. A good thing too, because it was never cleaned, and the walls and floor were covered with dried excrement. He added to it before heading down to the ground floor and out into rue du Faubourg Saint-Antoine.

The morning was already hot, but the crowded pavements and traffic made it feel even hotter. He headed towards Bastille, not because he had any business in that direction, but because he had to walk somewhere. It was a tired part of Paris, full of immigrant stores and faces. For that reason he liked it. It meant his Algerian features were unremarkable. He passed a little café where his countrymen were in the habit of gathering to drink small cups of strong coffee and talk about the old days. Maybe in time he could make friends here. For now, he had to remain anonymous.

So instead he stepped into another café, where the coffee was cheap so long as he stood at the bar. He handed over a single euro – the last of the money he had hidden from Fatima. He was halfway through his drink before he sensed the man standing behind him.

Hakim stared over the brim of his cup into the window behind the bar. The man was squat and tanned, with bleached blond hair, freckles and the remnants of a cut on his lower lip. He carried a grey rucksack over his right shoulder. He placed a gentle hand on Hakim's left shoulder. Hakim jabbed it away, as if he'd been electrified. His coffee sloshed over his hand.

'Hakim?' the man said. His voice had an accent. British? Hakim wasn't sure.

He turned round slowly.

And then he bolted for the door.

He might have made it out into the street had a second man sitting by the door not been waiting for him to run. This man had a shaved head, sunburned skin and a pronounced Adam's apple. As he grabbed hold of Hakim's arm with a tattooed hand, his strength was apparent. Hakim wasn't going anywhere so long as this guy held on to him.

'We're not going to hurt you,' said the blond man in service-able French. 'Not unless you try to run away – in which case my friend Skinner here will break both your fucking legs.'

Skinner said nothing. He just looked at Hakim with unconcealed contempt.

'Let's walk,' said the blond man. He nodded at Skinner, who manhandled Hakim out of the café and into the street. They turned right, back up towards, and then past, Hakim's block. Skinner didn't let go of his arm and although they attracted a few strange looks, nobody tried to help him. After a couple of hundred metres they came to a small park. Two tramps sat over on the far side sharing a bottle of unlabelled alcohol. The remaining wooden benches were vacant. Skinner forced Hakim on to one of them and, still gripping his arm, sat down to his right. The blond man sat on Hakim's left. He rested his rucksack on his lap and, staring straight ahead, continued speaking in French.

'Your name is Hakim al-Ashaba. Algerian. You entered France illegally with your wife Fatima and your two daughters via Marseilles three months ago. A week prior to that you were arrested parking a Toyota Corolla in front of a government building in Algiers with a boot full of plastic explosive. When an intelligence officer tried to restrain you, you punched him. He fell and hit his head on the kerb. Fatally, as it turned out, but giving you the opportunity to escape.'

The blond man's words were sledgehammers. Each one of them was true. Hakim realised that his skin had gone clammy. He started to shake. 'I didn't *mean* to kill him,' he said.

'Ah,' said the blond man. 'You hear that, Skinner? He didn't *mean* to kill him. So that's all right.' A pause. 'Don't worry, Hakim, we're not here to turn you in. Not unless . . .' His voice trailed away and he turned his attention back to the rucksack. He opened it.

The rucksack's contents caused Hakim to catch his breath. It was filled to the brim with fifty-euro notes. The man lifted one of the bundles, to reveal more below.

'Can't be easy,' he said. 'You're damaged goods for your

terrorist mates back in Algiers, so they don't want anything to do with you. You've got no job. A family.'

Hakim stared into the middle distance.

The man slowly closed the rucksack. 'This is yours,' he said. 'But only if you do something for us.'

Hakim blinked.

'What?' he asked. His voice was hoarse. '*What?*'

The blond man looked straight ahead again. 'Do you know how to use a handgun?' he asked.

Hakim shook his head.

'It's very easy. You'll only need one shot. And then, all this' – he patted the rucksack again – 'is yours.'

'I'm not a killer,' Hakim whispered.

'Yes you are, Hakim. That's why you're stuck in a stinking room with a starving family. But if you're not interested . . .' The man shrugged and stood up. 'Come on,' he said to his companion in English. 'Let's go.'

For the first time since the café, Skinner let go of Hakim's arm. He stood up and the two men walked away.

'Wait,' Hakim called after them. And when they didn't stop, he said it louder. '*Wait!*'

When they were fifteen metres away, the men turned. With a slow, lazy arrogance, they walked back to the bench.

Hakim licked his dry lips. 'Who?' he asked.

'There's an old man. You don't need to know his name. He goes for a walk every morning at seven a.m. It will be easy to get close to him, and easy to run away. And you already know how easy it is to hide.'

The sweat on Hakim's skin had grown warm again. 'If it's so easy,' he asked, 'why don't you kill him?'

'For the same reason I don't clean my own toilet. I can afford to pay someone to do it for me.'

'You have to give me the money first.' Hakim's voice cracked again as he spoke.

'No, my friend. That's not the way it works. You meet me tomorrow morning, you walk away 10,000 euros richer. If not . . .' He spread out his hands in a show of regret.

There was a silence. Hakim felt as if someone had switched off the volume. He couldn't hear the cars in the nearby streets, or the birds in the trees, or the passenger jet overhead. All he could hear was the grinding of his teeth. And the beating of his heart. It was faster than usual.

'Ten thousand?' he asked. His voice sounded like it was separated from his body.

The blond man nodded. 'Cash,' he said. 'Untraceable.'

Hakim inhaled. He clenched his fists to conceal their shaking.

'OK,' he heard himself saying. 'OK. I'll do it.'

The following morning brought rain. A thin, persistent drizzle that failed to relieve the humidity. Hector's expression was bleak as he walked in the half light of dawn along rue Berger towards the RV point. He had already recced the area to check there were no cameras on the street, no CCTV to link him to the Algerian. Just to be sure, the rucksack had a bright orange waterproof cover, which he'd remove when the time came to hand it over, so he couldn't be linked to the bag either. But there were other things that could go wrong. If the rain continued, the target might break his regular habit and decide not to take his daily seven o'clock walk that morning, and that would royally fuck things up. It would mean staying longer in Paris, and Skinner was getting restless. They needed to get the job done and get out of there before he did something stupid.

By 06.40 hrs, however, the drizzle had eased off. And as Hector approached the Café des Amis, its glass doors closed and red awning retracted, he saw Hakim leaning against a nearby tree. The young Algerian saw him and stood up straight.

Hector nodded in greeting. His mobile phone buzzed in the pocket of his jeans, but he didn't bother to look at the message. He knew what it was.

Hakim nodded back.

Foaming water gushed from an outlet by the kerb. Fifty metres down the road, a green cleaning truck with spinning brushes at the front trundled slowly towards them. Two street cleaners, also in green, swept debris from the pavement into the water channel. Otherwise, there was nobody else in rue Berger. This part of the seedy Châtelet district had not yet awoken.

'Who knows you're here?'

'Nobody.'

Hector observed the dark patches of sweat around Hakim's armpits, spreading through his rough shirt and circled with salt.

'Your wife?'

'I told her I had a job . . . there's this guy in the market who sells mobile phones—'

'When I give you the weapon,' Hector interrupted, 'it will be already cocked. That means all you'll need to do is point and fire. It's an automatic pistol, so you can keep firing until you're certain he's dead simply by squeezing the trigger. The important thing is to get close to him. If you're not used to firearms, it's easy to miss if you're not at point-blank range. Do you understand?'

'Yeah,' replied the Algerian. Hector noticed how his eyes darted up and down the road, resting briefly on a narrow street twenty metres to the north-west. No doubt this was the way he intended to escape. Hakim returned his gaze to Hector's rucksack. 'You got the money there?'

'Of course.'

Hector made to hand the rucksack to Hakim, but at the last moment snatched it away again. 'One small thing,' he said, pulling his phone from his pocket. 'You're a clever guy. I can tell that. You're not the type to do anything stupid. But just in case you were thinking of, ah, I don't know, running away with the money before the job's complete, or warning the target, or anything like that, perhaps you'd better look at this.' He pulled his phone from his pocket, unlocked it and swiped to his recent message. There was no text. Just a picture. He tapped on it so it filled the screen.

The two men examined the picture together. It showed a small bedsit. In one corner, crouched on the floor, was Hakim's wife. Her face was gaunt with terror, and she was clutching the two babies, whose little faces were blurred, though it was clear they were screaming. In the foreground of the picture, also slightly blurred but clearly pointing at Fatima and her children, was the barrel of a gun.

'They're perfectly safe,' Hector said quietly, 'just so long as you keep your side of the bargain. Of course, if you don't . . .' He returned the phone to his pocket and gave the dumbstruck Hakim a bland smile. 'If you *don't*, Skinner can be unpleasant.'

Hakim gave Hector a look of helpless hatred, which he ignored. He checked his watch. 'Eight minutes,' he said. 'Is that your stomach rumbling? You should have eaten. It settles things down. At least, it always does for me.'

Hector checked his watch again. 06.55 hrs. He noticed Hakim was sweating even more now.

Then Hector looked up at a window on the third floor of the apartment building on the other side of the street, immediately opposite their position. Somebody inside opened the curtains. Bang on schedule. Hector looked up and down the street. The cleaning truck was twenty metres away. He could hear its engine turning over and the whirr and hiss of its brushes. The two street cleaners were alongside it. They were concentrating on their job, and not on the two men loitering outside the Café des Amis.

Coming from the opposite end of rue Berger, an elegantly dressed woman walked briskly in their direction. She was about thirty metres away and talking on her mobile phone. Seconds later, as she passed, Hector caught the scent of her perfume. He felt himself frowning as the smell drifted away, to be replaced by Hakim's stinking breath. 'Any minute now,' he murmured. He took the rucksack from his shoulder and removed the coloured waterproof covering. 'This is yours.'

Trembling, Hakim slung the rucksack awkwardly over his own shoulder. 'It's heavy,' he said.

'Lot of money, my friend. Lot of money.' From inside his jacket Hector pulled out a Browning Hi-Power semi-automatic pistol. Hakim stared at it. Hidden by the tree from the gaze of the truck driver and the street cleaners, Hector cocked the weapon, before carefully handing it over. 'Thirteen rounds,' he said over the noise of the brushes. 'You should only need one if you fire it close enough.'

Hakim accepted the weapon like an amateur, holding it lightly in his fingertips. Hector had to move the Algerian's arm out of the way so that the weapon was not pointing in his direction. He could feel the kid trembling.

'Remember,' he said. 'Skinner's with your family. Nobody wants them to get hurt.'

Hakim swallowed hard and a trickle of sweat slid down his face.

06.59 hrs. The door of the apartment block opened. For a tense few seconds, nobody appeared. And then, very slowly, an old man, clearly Middle Eastern, stepped out into the street, accompanied by a much younger woman. The man's shoulders were stooped, and he walked with the aid of a stick. He had a short grey beard and his head was wrapped in a red and white keffiyeh. The young woman was also Middle Eastern, but she was dressed in Western clothes – jeans and a scarlet jumper – and was strikingly beautiful. She gently held the old man's free arm and helped him as he tottered along.

Distance between Hakim and the target: twenty-five metres.

'That's him,' Hector said. 'Do it now.'

Hakim hesitated and Hector felt a moment of anxiety as the couple disappeared behind a parked Transit van. Surely they weren't going to get into the vehicle and disappear? He took out his phone again and waved Skinner's photograph in front of Hakim's face. That was enough. As the old man and his companion reappeared from behind the Transit, at Hakim's eleven o'clock, the Algerian moved nervously forwards, the rucksack firmly on his back, the Browning hanging by his side. He stepped into the stream of water gushing from the outlet, soaking his shoes. As he crossed the street he left wet footprints.

Hakim approached the target. Hector walked along the pavement in the opposite direction, looking repeatedly over his shoulder. He could see the cleaning truck getting nearer. He was not concentrating specifically on the Algerian or the old man, but on the distance between the two. Twenty metres. Fifteen metres. Ten.

Hector slipped his left hand into the pocket of his trousers and felt for its contents: a simple switch, fitted to a radio transmitter and a battery, the whole device no bigger than an ordinary house key. He continued to hurry along rue Berger, and to estimate the distance between Hakim and the target.

Seven metres.

Five.

Three.

Suddenly the elderly man stopped and looked at Hakim with alarm. With surprising vigour, he grabbed his young companion and manhandled her in between himself and Hakim.

Hakim stopped too. He looked around wildly as he raised his gun. He held it inexpertly with two hands and Hector could tell, even from this distance, that his chances of nailing the guy with that kind of technique were close to zero.

Not that it mattered, of course, because the Browning wasn't loaded.

There was just enough time, before the cleaning truck obscured Hector's line of sight, for him to see Hakim pull the trigger. When nothing happened, the look of astonishment on the faces of both the would-be assassin and his target was almost comical. The truck edged closer. Hector could no longer see them. He braced himself and flicked the switch.

The sound of the rucksack exploding was immense. Even Hector, who had been expecting it, felt an electric jolt through his body and winced at the pain in his eardrums. He heard glass shatter and the thunder of shrapnel and body parts hammering on the side of the truck. Even before the remaining shrapnel had settled, several car alarms burst into life. He could hear screaming too. Having packed the explosives into the rucksack himself, he knew it couldn't be Hakim, the young woman or the old man. They were already dead. Probably just one of the street cleaners. Wrong place at the wrong time. Bad luck, son.

He picked up his pace and, having reached the end of rue Berger, turned right before taking out his phone, dialling a number and holding the phone to his ear as he walked. It rang just twice before Skinner answered.

'Done?'

'Done,' Hector confirmed. 'Fucking muppet didn't even try to check the money. We could have saved ourselves a few euros on a cheaper copying machine to do the notes and pocketed the difference.' A pause. 'Everything OK at your end, mucker? What the hell's that banging noise?'

A pause. Long enough to make Hector uneasy.

'Nothing,' Skinner said. 'I'm leaving now.' He hung up.

Hector stopped and looked at the screen of his phone for a moment. Then he heard the sound of sirens. He removed the battery from the phone, ripped out the SIM card and bent it in two, then stuffed both down a drain. With the phone dealt with, he put his head down and headed to

Châtelet–Les Halles Métro station. An hour from now he'd be on a train out of Paris, and on to the next job, wherever that might take him.

Skinner shoved his phone into his pocket and looked around the room. What a fucking dump, he thought to himself. At least the brats were silent. He'd ripped a dirty dishcloth in two and shoved one half in each of their mouths. Shame he couldn't say the same for their bitch of a mother. She was whimpering like a child despite the scouring pad he'd shoved in her mouth to shut her up. He looked at her. She was naked and tied face down to the table, her thighs and torso bound so tightly with the sturdy duct tape he had brought with him that the flesh around the indentations was already swollen. Skinner's eyes passed over the area around her anus and genitals, bleeding from where he had violated her, and looked with contempt at her head, which she was rhythmically banging against the table as she wept.

That fucking banging. It got on his nerves. 'Shut up!' he told her. He couldn't speak French, but that was her problem, not his. '*Shut . . . the fuck . . . up . . .*'

The whimpering became more desperate. The banging a little faster.

Skinner spat. Then he grabbed his suppressed handgun from the drainer beside the sink and pressed the barrel against the woman's cheek. She opened her eyes and, for a moment, the banging stopped.

'*Mes enfants . . .*' she whispered. '*Elles sont trop petites . . .*'

The words meant nothing to Skinner. He muttered one of his own – 'Bitch' – before turning his head to one side and squeezing the trigger.

The woman's head thudded against the table for a final time.

Skinner's hand and weapon were covered with blood. He rinsed his fingers briefly under the tap, shook them dry, then walked over to the little cot where the two newly orphaned babies were lying, the pieces of dishcloth still stuffed in their mouths. He raised his gun and pressed the butt of the suppressor against the cheek of one of them. A rectangular smear of their mother's blood transferred itself to the child's skin. Both babies lay very still. It was as if they knew their lives were in the balance.

They were hardly worth a bullet. He had another idea. There was enough duct tape left on the roll for him to bind the two of them together, like Siamese twins joined at the belly. They screamed as he did it, but this was the sort of place where the screams of children went unheard. He picked up the monstrously swaddled bundle and carried it over to the little bath. It was stained yellow, and encrusted with limescale around the plug-hole. He put the plug in, then laid the wailing babies in the bath.

He turned on the taps, leaving the babies to their watery death. He didn't even glance at their mother's corpse as he left the bedsit, closing the door silently behind him.

TWO

The MoD policeman at the entrance to RAF Credenhill approached the black car with a neutral expression on his face, neither welcoming nor threatening. He waited while the rear-right passenger window slid silently down, then accepted two identity cards from a hand with neatly trimmed nails and a gold signet ring. He examined the cards, then bent down to peer into the back of the car.

'Mr Carrington?' he asked.

The man nearest him nodded. Steel-grey hair, black-rimmed glasses. His face matched his photo.

'And Mr Buckingham?' The policeman turned his attention to the man next to him. Much younger, thirty maybe. Absurdly handsome, with a pleasant, open expression, a thick head of black, slightly floppy hair and a healthy tan. Hugo Buckingham nodded respectfully. The MoD policeman handed back the identity cards and waved the vehicle through the gates.

Hugo would never have admitted it to anybody, but he'd been rather looking forward to today. SAS headquarters. Not everyone got to see inside this place. In the five years he'd been with the Foreign Office he'd had to acknowledge privately that, for the most part, intelligence work was dull. Oh, he'd had the opportunity to travel, no doubt about it. There was barely a British embassy in the Middle East he hadn't set foot inside, and he'd had his share of contact with agents on the ground. In reality, however, he was little more than a glorified secretary, filing the correct bits of information in the correct place in the hope that the analysts back in London could use them to join up some dots. Whenever his old school friends – bankers, most of them, already planning to retire and spend a bit more time with their money – tried to get him drunk in the hope that he could be persuaded into some juicy indiscretion, Hugo Buckingham would always touch the side of his nose slyly and deliver his favourite line: 'It's government business, my friend. That's all you need to know.' A useful phrase. It sounded at once good-natured and jokey, made it sound as though he might know a great deal, and hid his ignorance of anything remotely resembling a state secret.

But a visit to SAS headquarters? Now *that* was something to dine out on.

The car slid to a halt outside the main Regiment building, which was disappointingly bland and utilitarian. The driver turned off the engine and remained seated, discreet and silent. 'Shall we?' Carrington said. These were the first two words the old fart had spoken to Buckingham for the entire journey from London.

'Righto,' Buckingham replied. He exited the car, then walked round the back to open the other rear door. Carrington climbed out without a word, removed a leather attaché case from the back seat, dusted the lapels of his suit and walked towards the building, where a simple brass plaque bore the inscription '22 SAS HQ'.

As the two visitors reached the door, a couple of soldiers were coming out of the building. Their hair was longer than the average soldier's, and although they were in camouflage gear, they looked very casual – sleeves rolled up, no berets, unconventional Salomon Quest boots. Like they were wearing uniform but not *really*. Army, but not *really* army. One of them held the door open. Carrington, in one movement, pointed at the soldier, winked and made a friendly clicking noise with the side of his tongue as he entered. Hugo cringed and felt himself offering the soldier an apologetic look that evidently only compounded the offence. He hurried to keep up with Carrington as he walked deeper into the building.

The older spook knew where he was going. He strode purposefully along anonymous corridors, past doors indicating RSM, Adjutant, Training Adjutant, Training Officer, Ops Officer. Finally they stopped outside one marked 'Lieutenant-Colonel J. Cartwright, Commanding Officer'. Carrington knocked three times and entered without waiting for a response. Buckingham followed rather more diffidently, and closed the door behind him. He found himself in a plain room, about five metres by five, furnished with just a desk and three chairs. On one of the walls hung old photographs, some black and white, of men wearing berets bearing the familiar winged dagger. On another was a large, laminated map of the world. Behind the desk sat a man so tall and broad of shoulder that the desk looked comically small. He didn't stand, but nodded respectfully at Carrington. 'Oliver,' he said. He had a rasping voice, as if he was recovering from laryngitis.

'Johnny. How goes it?'

'Badly, since you ask.' He had a posh voice, not unlike Carrington's. 'These bloody cuts are hitting us hard. I'm bleeding guys left, right and centre to the private sector, and most of the kids putting themselves up for selection wouldn't make it round *The Krypton Factor*.'

'I'm sure your training wing haven't lost the knack of applying boot to arse, Johnny.'

The CO shrugged, then, looking in Buckingham's direction, raised an enquiring eyebrow. 'Who's this? Hugh Grant?'

'Hugo Buckingham,' Carrington said. 'Buckingham, this is Johnny Cartwright, Commanding Officer of 22 SAS. Johnny, Hugo here's the chap I told you about. Had a desk at our Saudi station until a couple of weeks ago. Went to the Other Place, I'm afraid, but we try not to hold that against him.'

Cartwright blinked. 'The Other Place?'

'Harrow.' Carrington mouthed it silently like it was a dirty word. Cartwright gave Buckingham an uninterested nod. Buckingham tried to return it with a smile, but flushed when he realised Cartwright's attention was already back on his senior colleague.

Carrington placed his attaché case on the CO's desk, opened it and removed four green foolscap files. 'Sit down, Hugo,' he said as he did so. 'This concerns you rather intimately, after all.' He handed the files to Cartwright. 'These are the men we've selected. Personal vetting has in each case come up positive.'

'I hope GCHQ haven't been tapping my men's phones again?'

'Your men. Their wives and girlfriends. Their parents. Their bank managers . . .'

The CO held up his palm. 'I don't want to know, Oliver,' he said. Cartwright flicked through the files, reciting the name of the Regiment member to whom each pertained. 'Jack Dodds . . . Greg Murray – good man, Greg – Spud Glover . . .'

A frown crossed his face as he opened the last file. 'Danny Black?' He looked up. 'You don't want him, fellas. He's out of town anyway.'

'I'm afraid I might have to insist, Johnny.'

Cartwright stared at his MI6 sparring partner, then exhaled with the air of a defeated man. 'Do me a favour, Oliver. Take someone else. Give Black a break.' The CO glanced at Buckingham as he said this – not, Buckingham noted, without a hint of resentment. 'The lad's been on ops for six months solid. And he doesn't know it yet, but he's got a bastard of a homecoming to look forward to. He needs some down time. Compassionate problems to sort out.'

'What problems, exactly?' Buckingham asked, careful to keep his voice respectful.

'You've read his file,' the CO snapped without even looking at the younger man.

Chastened, Buckingham looked at his knees.

'Hugo has had other matters to occupy him,' Carrington said.

'Look,' Cartwright went on, 'the lad comes from a military family. Father was in the Parachute Regiment, took a bullet to the head in Northern Ireland from an IRA hit team. Been in a wheelchair ever since. Can't even answer a call of nature without the help of a nurse, so I've heard. Astonishing the kid isn't messed up himself. His brother certainly is – mental health issues ever since he was a child, in and out of prison since sixteen. Just reaching the end of six months for GBH. Ever heard of a Hereford Spanner?'

'Can't say I have,' Carrington said.

'Nasty little cocktail of ketamine, MDMA and cocaine.'

'More of a brandy and soda man myself.'

'Why's it called a Hereford Spanner?' asked Buckingham.

'Because it looks like you've been hit in the face with one. If I had my way, we'd send the little buggers who think that kind of stuff is a good idea on ops to Colombia, let them see exactly where their recreational drugs come from.' He shrugged. 'Kyle Black saw fit to beat some kid to a pulp when he was high on one of these cocktails, then knock his dad out of his chair when the old boy tried to calm him down. Poor sod broke his arm – last thing he needed. I want to give Danny time to sort all this out.' The CO squeezed the bridge of his nose and suddenly looked very tired. 'Seriously, Oliver, choose someone else. Black's off limits for now.'

Hugo turned to his colleague and gave an apologetic little cough. 'Sounds to me like the poor fellow has enough on his plate already,' he said. 'I'm sure we can find a suitable—'

'*Let's*,' Carrington interrupted, a withering look on his face, 'speak when we're spoken to, shall we, Hugo?' Hugo felt himself flushing for a second time, and fell silent.

Turning his attention back to Cartwright, Carrington asked, 'Do you know where the lad is now?'

'I'm his commanding officer. Of course I know where he is.'

'Good,' said Carrington, resting his hands on his stomach. 'Where?'

THREE

Fifty nautical miles north of the Libyan coastline, six billion dollars' worth of US Navy aircraft carrier stood watch in the failing light. The USS *George Bush* was a long way from home. So was Danny Black.

He checked his watch. 21.45 hrs, Eastern European Time. The green light had come through from COBRA at 17.00 hrs GMT on the dot. Danny had a picture in his mind of the decision-makers hurriedly wrapping up their discussions before the end of working hours. Wouldn't do for them to be late for their dinner appointments. Gordon Ramsay for the suits, meals ready-to-eat for the troops they were sending into action. Which was just fine by Danny. Thirty minutes from now it would be fully dark, and he and his patrol would be airborne. He glanced up, past the air traffic control radars, at the moon's state: full, rising from the west, clear sky. There would be light to see by tonight, but also light to be seen by.

The Sea Knight that would ferry them off the aircraft carrier, over the southern Mediterranean and into the Libyan desert, was in a state of readiness. Tailgate down, rotors slowly spinning. Beyond it, parked to the side of the runway, were two F-16s. Beyond them, a whole fleet of aircraft. This *Nimitz*-class supercarrier could portage ninety fixed-wing aircraft and helicopters, and tonight it had a full complement. Danny had been on the *George Bush* for twenty-four hours already, having arrived with his unit from a staging post in Malta. He had spent most of that time below decks in the SF quarters, a spartan collection of rooms that held little more than bunks for the guys to sleep in, an operations room with co-ax points for their radios, mapping areas and satellite comms, and a briefing room where they could plug in their laptops. They only ventured out for meals, taken with the rest of the ship's crew, at a table set aside for their use. Below decks, only the lull of the ship and the boom of fast air taking off and landing gave any hint that they were at sea. Now though, up here, he was surrounded by sea, a saline mist and the deafening industrial grind of the vessel's steam turbines and nuclear reactors. It resembled not so much a ship as a floating city.

Like any city, the *George Bush* took a lot of running. With a ship's company of more than three thousand, just keeping everyone fed – not to mention dealing with their sewage – was a round-the-clock enterprise. The aircraft carrier even had its own naval police force. Crime was far from unheard of. These ships hosted muggings, rapes, even murders – the usual depravities to be found among a population of this size. But the most dangerous place to be, by far, was here on the flight deck. It only took a pilot to misjudge his position by a few metres to turn this seaborne airfield into a disaster area. So the US Navy personnel running the show were strict. Nobody was on deck who didn't have a legitimate reason to be there. Marshals with different coloured luminous jackets and hand-held signalling beacons conducted their business around the grounded aircraft. Aircraft-handling officers in yellow, ordnancemen in red, fuel handlers in purple, inspectors in black. The flight crew of the Sea Knight were loading up, along with the two US army shooters who would take the roles of door-gunner and rear-gunner for the next three hours.

And Danny. He stood twenty metres from the chopper, his pack on his back, his personal weapon slung low, his Kevlar helmet in his hands. The US military personnel all but ignored him as they swarmed round the Sea Knight, readying it for take-off, even though they were doing so for the benefit of Danny and his mates. The wind blew his blond hair all over the place and salty spray stung his skin. On the southern horizon he could see lights twinkling. Tripoli, he figured from his mental map. Amazing how some of the world's worst shitholes could look all Thomas Cook from a distance. Something nudged him in the back. He turned round to see Boyd, their patrol leader. Like Danny, he was dressed in Crye multicam, belt kit fitted and M4 slung low and attached to his body with a short halyard. Unlike Danny, he already had his helmet on, complete with NV goggles – disengaged for now – and a small torch attachment. The helmet itself was cut away around the ears to make space for his earpiece, and a thin boom mike hung just below his lower lip.

'Hey, Snapper!' he shouted over the noise of the deck in his thick Northern Irish accent. Danny didn't mind the nickname. Snapper was Irish slang for a kid, and at twenty-three Danny was the youngest in the patrol. Boydie was well known for stamping his authority on an op, and anyway, a bit of ribbing came with the territory.

'Aye?'

'What d'youse call a Libyan militant with no arms and no legs?'

'A good start?'

Double thumbs up from Boydie and a grin that revealed the worst set of teeth in the Regiment. 'We're loading in five,' he yelled back. 'Ready to rumble?'

'Roger that.' Danny fitted his helmet and NV as Boydie went off to round up the others. The patrol leader always cracked the same joke before an op. Taliban commander with no arms and no legs? Ba'athist scumbag with no arms and no legs? Always a good start, in Boydie's take on the world. Nobody in the Regiment would ever disagree with him, and certainly not tonight. The militants that Danny and his mates were heading in country to locate deserved everything they were about to get.

Three days previously, a group of four UN peacekeepers – all British – had been kidnapped in Benghazi. For twenty-four ominous hours there had been no news, until a tape had arrived at the offices of Al-Jazeera TV in the time-honoured fashion. The grainy footage showed the peacekeepers first bound and beaten, then hooded and dead, hanging by the neck from a wooden ceiling beam. A balaclava'd figure, speaking in Sulaimitian Arabic, claimed responsibility for the atrocity on behalf of a rebel group still loyal to the memory of the ousted Gaddafi regime. To add insult to injury, he was wearing one of the peacekeepers' camouflage jackets, complete with the bright blue armbands of the UN. It had taken about twenty minutes for the footage to go viral – which meant the families of the deceased got the good news via YouTube rather than the traditional knock on the door – and thirty minutes for two of the bodies to show up in a street two blocks from the British Embassy in Tripoli, not only dead but horrifically mutilated, a pro-Gaddafi slogan carved on the torsos with a razor or the point of a knife.

Intelligence operations on the ground in Libya had gone into overdrive. Who were these militants? More to the point, *where* were they? There was no doubt in Danny's mind that a fair few Libyan nationals had had their arms twisted – literally – to reveal what they knew, or suspected, about the location of the militants. The limb-twisting had come up trumps. Word had reached British intelligence officers of a tiny Ruwallah Bedouin village in the Libyan desert 150 klicks due south of Benghazi. Two independent sources had verified that the inhabitants had been evicted from their encampment there by a group of pro-Gaddafi militia. Evidence that these militia were the same individuals who had captured and killed the four UN personnel was sketchier, but, so far as Danny could tell, the powers didn't give a shit about that. And he was right behind them: the only good militant was a dead one, and his patrol had direct orders to help the bastards on their way.

Their objective was straightforward. Insert under cover of night into a wadi five klicks to the south-west of the target area. Tab along the wadi and set up an OP at a pre-determined location with a visual on the Bedouin village. Conduct surveillance on the village to confirm the absence of Bedouin and the presence of militia. Then laser-mark the location so that an RAF Tornado could bomb the living shit out of the place and send a message loud and clear that anyone who harmed British nationals could expect a swift and brutal reprisal. Job done.

The rotors of the Sea Knight increased in speed. Boydie reappeared on deck with Tommo and Five Bellies, the other two members of their four-man patrol. Tommo was posher than tea at the Ritz, but his healthy disdain for the Ruperts meant the lads in the Regiment accepted him as one of their own. Five Bellies' nickname had nothing to do with his girth – on the contrary, he was one of the fittest men Danny had ever met – but commemorated one particularly blood-soaked afternoon in Lashkar Gah when a group of heavily armed Taliban had cropped up out of nowhere and the advance to contact was faster than anyone wanted. He'd taken a shot with a .50-cal machine gun, and through sheer good luck it had ripped straight through five of them. A nickname, and a little piece of Regimental history, had been born. This evening, though, the guys looked almost identical, in their multicam and helmets with NV goggles perched on top. The five-klick tab was long enough that they didn't want to be wearing plate hangers, though their CamelBaks full of fresh water were essential.

The loadmaster appeared at the tailgate of the Sea Knight, bulky headphones covering his ears and a mike at his mouth. With a wide sweep of his arms he indicated that Danny's patrol should embark.

'Let's go, fellas,' Boydie yelled over the noise. The four men jogged up the tailgate as the marshals cleared the deck ready for take-off. Danny nodded a greeting as he passed the rear-gunner on his way into the belly of the Sea Knight. Each member of the patrol removed his bergen and stowed it at his feet. Danny took a seat with his back to the side wall – Tommo to his left, the door-gunner to his right – and lightly clutched the webbing behind him while connecting his radio to the aircraft comms system. Five Bellies and Boydie, sitting directly opposite on the other side of the black cylindrical long-range fuel tank – it looked like nothing so much as a massive rubber sausage – did the same. The loadie's voice came over Danny's earpiece, a gravelly Midwestern drawl. 'We have thirty seconds till take-off . . . three-zero seconds till take-off.'

The tailgate remained open. The rear-gunner was hunkered over his Minigun looking like he was about to lay down fire on the aircraft carrier itself. Through the opening, Danny could just make out a marshal in a yellow jacket receding from the LZ. The pitch of the Sea Knight's engines rose, and with a low judder the chopper lifted slowly up from the carrier. It made a forty-five-degree turn so that it was heading towards land, and then gained speed.

With each member of the patrol hooked into the comms system, ordinary conversation was out of the question. The flight would be conducted largely in silence as each man prepared himself mentally for the op. Danny had other preparations to make too. He bent down and removed a small GPS unit from the top of his pack, along with a roll of gaffer tape. Boydie had designated him lead scout. They'd already entered into the GPS units the coordinates of their expected LUP and OP as waypoints, as well as two emergency RV locations in case they were bumped. If the guys got into a contact and scattered, each man would know where to head: make your way to the first RV, wait out for an hour and, if no one arrives, head for the second RV and wait out for another hour, before walking back on a bearing for the original drop point.

Hope for the best, plan for the worst.

Now Danny took the opportunity to tape the GPS unit securely to the body of his M4 – easy to locate without having to fumble for it in the darkness, and easy to read even while holding your weapon. He double-checked the rest of his gear. His Sig 9mm was clipped across his chest and his belt kit contained extra ammunition – he'd elected to stock up on this at the expense of full rations as they didn't intend to be on the ground for more than twenty-four hours. Two flashbangs, two frags. A black-handled utility knife. Also a couple of personal items: a dented, burnished Zippo lighter with the letters 'SB' engraved in fussy copperplate. And a second knife, its five-inch blade narrower than that of the utility knife but just as sharp, its handle fashioned from ivory. There weren't many kids who'd receive a gift like that on their thirteenth birthday, but there weren't many kids who had Taff Davies as a godfather. 'A man always has need of a good knife, kiddo,' he'd said. Danny remembered it like it was yesterday.

He looked through a small window just to his right. It was almost fully dark now, but the reflection of the moon on the water, combined with the lights from the Sea Knight itself, showed how close to sea level they were flying. There couldn't be more than ten feet between the chopper and the water. The Med remained undisturbed despite the proximity of the skimming aircraft, but it was a reminder of how bright the moon was that he could make out a faint shadow of the Sea Knight on the flat surface.

Danny's earpiece crackled into life. A member of the flight crew communicating with the SF ops room on the aircraft carrier. 'Zero, this is Desert Wanderer. Requesting permission to cross from water on to land. Repeat, requesting permission to cross from water on to land.' They'd already had a briefing with the pilot so he could explain their flight plan. Danny pictured their location on the mapping, near the southernmost point of the Gulf of Sirte, fifty klicks west of Brega.

A five-second pause. And then, as clearly as if he were on the Sea Knight with them, he heard the familiar voice of the ops officer – a broad-shouldered American major who was also liaising with the ops room back at Hereford. '*Desert Wanderer, that's an affirmative. The op is still a go.*'

Ten seconds later they made land. A deserted beach where the flight crew extinguished the chopper's lights and started flying blind. Through the window, the ground beneath them resembled a fast-moving photographic negative. 'Welcome to the dark continent, gentlemen,' the pilot's voice came over the comms. 'That's twenty minutes till target.'

Danny turned his eyes back to the inside of the chopper. Boydie, Tommo and Five Bellies were still sitting in silence, their faces calm as they mentally prepared themselves for their insertion. Danny was doing the same, reminding himself in simple terms of their objective: insert by helicopter, tab to a predetermined location in view of the deserted encampment where the militants were thought to be, set up an OP about a kilometre from the encampment and try to get a visual on the militants themselves. If they did, they were to laser-mark so fast air could come in and bomb the place to hell.

Theirs was a non-offensive role. The real violence would be done by the bombs of the RAF Tornado squadron once the patrol had marked the target and given the go-ahead. That didn't mean it was safe. You could stare at a patch of satellite mapping till you were cross-eyed, but it wouldn't tell you half of what you needed to know about the terrain of an insertion zone. You'd be an idiot to think any time spent on the ground in a country like Libya wasn't a risk. Eighteen months earlier an SAS patrol had been compromised by a group of farmers. It had sounded comical to everyone back home, and the papers had enjoyed a good laugh at the Regiment's expense. To Danny it had simply highlighted one thing: on unfamiliar ground you had to expect the unexpected. Sometimes a stray farmer could fuck your mission just as surely as a landmine. And although Gaddafi might have assumed a horizontal position while the rebels who ousted him were scrabbling around to form a government, the situation on the ground was still extremely volatile – not to mention the international news crews crawling round the place, sniffing for stories.

The pilot's voice again. 'Patrol commander, we've flown over the main highway. One vehicle, heading east.'

'Roger that,' Boydie replied in a flat voice, his face betraying no emotion.

The loadie was holding up the fingers of one hand. 'Five minutes till target.' Danny checked his watch. 23.08 hrs. On schedule. Each member of the patrol disconnected his radio from the Sea Knight's comms system, before picking up their packs and settling them on their shoulders. Through the open tailgate, Danny could just make out the dark shadow of the desert floor zooming past ten feet below.

The loadie had moved to the tailgate end of the fuselage, where he was holding up three fingers. Three minutes till target.

Two minutes.

One.

Danny engaged his NV. The world changed. The four apertures of his fifth-generation goggles – two for each eye – afforded him a wide field of view and excellent peripheral vision. He had a full panorama of the chopper's interior, both the tailgate and the sides of the fuselage to left and right cast clearly in green and black. There had been a time when wearing NV meant you could only see what was directly in front of you, like looking through a Smarties tube. Not any more.

A sudden change in the pitch of the Sea Knight's engines. A lurch as it lost speed quickly. A shudder as it made land. The loadie's voice, urgent, shouting over the engine noise. '*You're on the ground! Go!*'

The flight crew wanted to be airborne and out of Libyan airspace as soon as possible, and the patrol wanted the same. The longer the Sea Knight was on the ground, the higher their risk of being compromised. Boydie led them down the tailgate, and Danny felt the crunch of hard-baked earth under his feet. They were surrounded by a brown-out of dust. Above him there was a neon glow where the particles of sand sparked against the spinning rotors, causing a double halo over the chopper. Even though Danny was expecting it, he had to control a moment of anxiety. Those halos were always brighter than you expected them to be. If everything had gone according to plan, they'd set down in a deep wadi. But the desert was dark and flat, and glows such as this could be seen from several kilometres away.

Instinctively, and in a matter of seconds, the patrol formed a defensive position, fanning out in a semicircle in the dust cloud around the tailgate, about five metres apart and with Danny at the leading edge. He threw himself flat on the ground, his bergen to one side, aware that the other three were doing the same, and lay there, his weapon engaged. Visibility was zero in the brown-out. He was aware simply of a dusty glow all around him. But as the chopper took to the air again, the glow faded, along with the sound of the engines, as the rotors rose clear of the dust. The brown-out settled. Through it, Danny saw the Sea Knight silhouetted against the full moon, before its massive black body angled northwards and it headed back towards the coast.

Silence fell gradually.

Clarity returned.

The men neither moved nor spoke.

Danny's eyes probed and scanned the landscape. They had a ten-minute window during which they could recall the Sea

Knight if there was any hint that they'd inserted into a hot LZ. After that, they were on their own.

The wadi was about twenty metres wide, its jagged walls some ten metres high. In the winter this dried-up river bed would be quite an oasis. Even though Danny was lying parallel with the length of the wadi – a direction he knew to be facing almost precisely due west – the wide field of vision of his NV goggles revealed fissures in the walls. About wide enough for a man to hide in, he estimated, but not if he was wearing a bergen. No matter. Their expected lying-up point was five klicks from here, where the topography of the land would afford them a place to hide, if their intel was correct.

Rocks littered the bed of the wadi. Vegetation was very sparse, but the occasional plant had managed to force itself up through the earth. Danny scanned for movement, paying particular attention to any rock sufficiently large to act as a hiding place. His ears were as alert as his eyes. Now that the Sea Knight was no longer in earshot, he knew that he could very well hear an enemy threat before he could see it: the crunch of footsteps, the telltale sound of a weapon being cocked. But the desert air was silent. Not even the sound of wind in this channel that could easily act as a—

Movement. Thirty metres to his eleven o'clock. There was a large rock, strangely similar in shape to a smart car, with one flattened, weathered end. Danny had seen its outline change. Only momentarily, but perceptibly. There was definitely something – or someone – behind that rock.

Slowly, silently, he shifted the direction of his weapon.

He was on the point of breathing a warning to the others into his boom mike when a shrill scream cut through the air. It sounded almost human, and for a split second he thought it was. But then he saw a four-legged creature, about the size of a fox, scamper from behind the rock. It ran five metres towards the edge of the wadi, then stopped suddenly and looked back towards where the patrol was lying in the dirt. Its eyes glowed brightly in Danny's NV, and for a moment he had the impression that this desert creature was staring right at him. But then it scampered off again, quickly covering the remaining three metres to the edge of the wadi, where it disappeared into a fissure.

The patrol relaxed as one. They continued to lie still, scanning for movement, for another minute before Danny heard Boydie's voice in his earpiece. 'Zero, this is Charlie Alpha Five. We're good to go.'

A pause, and then the voice of the American ops officer back on the ship. '*Charlie Alpha Five, this is Zero. Message understood.*'

And then silence once more.

Boydie was the first to get to his feet. The other three followed suit. Danny disengaged his NV and gave his eyes thirty seconds to readjust. He tightened the straps of his bergen, then switched on the GPS unit taped to his personal weapon. Under the clear open skies, the device quickly triangulated itself, confirming that they had inserted at the correct location. Danny switched it off to kill the light from the screen, then looked over his shoulder and gave Boydie a thumbs up.

They tabbed in single file, Danny at the front, then Boydie, followed by Tommo and Five Bellies. The moon was bright enough to cast shadows on the bed of the wadi. Hardly ideal – cloud cover would have concealed them more effectively – but they could only work with what they had. They kept a distance of ten metres between them. Enough to stop them being a single, bunched-up target in the event of a contact, not so much that they could lose sight of each other in the darkness, or miss a hand signal from the guy in front. Weapons at the ready, all senses alive to the possibility of the tiniest threat, they started to tab west along the wadi.

Average walking speed with full pack and personal weapon, two klicks per hour. The terrain around them barely changed, except for a six-foot-deep ditch running at right angles across the wadi two klicks from their insertion point, which they boxed around rather than try to negotiate in the dark. After ninety minutes Danny held up one hand to bring the company to a halt and checked their location on the GPS. The first way-point was 300 metres farther up the wadi. Time check: 00.47 hrs. Another hand gesture, like a forward karate chop, and the patrol moved on.

They found it five minutes later. From above, the satellite imagery had indicated a triangular cavity cut away from the wadi's southern edge, approximately seven metres wide at the opening and extending ten metres from the wadi. As an LUP it was adequate – enough space to leave their packs and neatly concealed from the desert floor above by overhanging rock. All four members of the patrol wordlessly entered the crevice and set about removing from their packs everything they'd need for the next stage of the operation: two Claymore mines, the laser target designator, a padded case with the necessary optics, a collapsible steel entrenching tool and a hessian sheet. One side of the hessian sheet was sprayed in the sandy brown of the desert, the other fixed to a sheet of chicken wire to allow it to be fashioned into whatever shape was required. Right now it was folded into a neat, rigid square.

Once they'd gathered all their equipment, Danny ventured back out into the wadi with his utility knife. It took about five minutes to locate and cut sufficient vegetation to cover their packs. When he returned, the others had lined them up at the end of the crevice, in reverse order of march and with the straps facing outwards. If they had to leave in a hurry, they didn't want to be fumbling around for the right pack. Danny layered the foliage over the bags. It wouldn't stand up to detailed scrutiny, but it was better than nothing. 'OK, fellas,' Boydie told them, keeping his voice low. 'We've got four hours till sunrise. Let's recce and set up the OP.'

They continued along the wadi for 400 metres. Then the depth of the side walls decreased rather suddenly. By the time Danny's GPS indicated that they were at their second waypoint, the walls were little more than three metres high. They found an area of wall that was sufficiently sloping for them to climb up it, then hunkered down on the flat desert plain. Five Bellies was carrying the optics pack. He lay down flat, removed a kite sight and scanned the horizon to the south. 'I've got a visual,' he said almost immediately. 'Bedouin village, about one klick.' He lowered the kite sight and looked round at his companions. 'Let's dig,' he said.

The ditch that would serve as an OP didn't need to be very big – six foot by four, and about a foot deep, enough for two guys to lie side by side. The most important thing was that it offered line of sight on the village – that, rather than distance, was the crucial factor when it came to laser-marking a target. The hard ground was tough to penetrate. Danny unfolded the entrenching tool and used the pointed metal shovel to hack into the ground while Five Bellies kept stag, leaving Boydie and Tommo to lay the Claymores. They unwound the detonation wires, laying the mines in opposite directions along the wadi, the first two at 100 metres either side of the OP and the rest at 100-metre intervals. By the time they'd returned, Danny, sweating and dust-covered, had loosened the earth and was digging out the trench. The guys spread the displaced earth on the desert floor, and in half an hour they had a trench deep enough for two of them to lie in. Boydie unfolded the reinforced hessian and moulded a few random undulations into it before laying it on top of the trench and appraising it critically.

'Good work,' he said. As he spoke, a lone cloud drifted across the moon, wiping out their shadows for the first time that night. 'Great fucking timing,' Boydie muttered. He looked at his watch – 02.13 hrs – before addressing Tommo and Five Bellies. 'We've got three and a half hours till sunrise,' he said. 'Tommo, take the

LUP and set up comms. Five, find somewhere to keep watch on me and Snapper. We'll lase the target as soon as we have visual confirmation of the militants.'

The two guys nodded wordlessly. Tommo picked up the entrenching tool and folded it, then both he and Five Bellies melted silently away into the darkness of the wadi.

'Let's get comfy,' Boydie said. 'Could be a long one. If you need to curl one out, do it now. We'll try and keep the trench a turd-free zone, eh?'

'Roger that,' Danny replied. Neither of them much wanted to hold the plastic bag while the other took a shit, but his bowels were empty. He lifted the hessian from over the trench, moved their equipment into the trench and lay on his front on the left side with his M4 alongside him on the right. Boydie settled down next to him and refitted the hessian cover.

It was cramped in the little trench, almost impossible to move without disturbing their camouflage. It made sense, though, to get everything prepared under cover of night. Boydie laid a selection of foil-packed MREs in the six-inch gap between them, while Danny erected a small tripod and fitted the LTD on it. Taking the kite sight, he looked in the direction of the village. The night-vision scope revealed a hotchpotch of buildings, some permanent, some temporary. He counted four domed roofs, roughly rendered with some kind of daub. They were, he estimated, no more than five metres high. A collection of single-storey, flat-roofed buildings surrounded them. The whole settlement was no more than fifty metres in width, and Danny knew from satellite imagery that it extended the same distance in depth. About twenty metres in front of the village, to eleven o'clock of the OP, there was a parked vehicle. Danny thought he recognised the outline of a Land Rover. There was no sign of movement. It figured that there might not be any humans moving around at this time of night, but a Bedouin village normally meant animals. So far as Danny could see, there were none. Hardly proof positive that the villagers had been driven away, but a pretty good indicator nonetheless. Still, it didn't mean a thing until they had a positive ID of the militants.

'What you got?' Boydie asked quietly.

'Nothing,' Danny said.

'Anyone keeping stag?'

'It's a ghost town.'

A pause.

'Fucking will be soon,' Boydie said.

05.00 hrs.

Dawn crept slowly upon them. The desert grew imperceptibly lighter. Danny and Boydie lay silently in the OP, barely moving. They were facing due south, which meant they couldn't see the sun rising, but the new day was barely twenty minutes old before Danny felt the sun growing hot on his left side and sweat started to seep from his skin. He sipped a ration of water from his CamelBak, then changed the kite sight for a new Leica spotting scope more suited to daytime use. Already the whole area was shimmering in a heat haze. There was no sign of Bedouin. No animals. No nothing.

Danny lowered the optic, grabbed one of the MREs and ripped it open. The contents were supposed to be heated through – boiled in the bag – but Danny simply squeezed the salty brown stew straight into his mouth. It was fuel, nothing more. Surveillance like this could take a very long time, and it was important to keep his energy levels up. 'Tastes like shit,' he murmured, more to himself than to Boydie.

'Course it tastes like shit,' Boydie replied. 'How else they gonna keep us angry enough to kill people?' He cut himself short. 'Movement,' he said. His voice was terse. Business-like.

Danny had barely swallowed a mouthful, but he dropped the MRE and looked through the scope again. Sure enough, he saw a vehicle trundling round the eastern side of the village. A

Bedouin truck? Like hell. This wasn't a dirty, run-down van used to transport animal feed. It was an open-topped pick-up, a technical with a top-mounted machine gun and five armed men surrounding it. They were all dressed exactly the same: keffiyehs, bandoliers of ammo strapped round their chests and assault rifles slung around their necks. Kalashnikovs, Danny reckoned, though from this distance it was hard to be sure. Not that it mattered either way. One thing was for sure: these were *not* ordinary Bedouin.

'Don't know about you,' Boydie said as the pick-up passed between the village and the Land Rover, 'but I think we just caught ourselves some militants with a .50-cal.'

'Where do they get hardware like that from?'

'We probably sold it to the gobshites, Snapper.'

Danny didn't have time to reply. Boydie was already on the radio back to the *George Bush* ops room. 'Zero, this is Charlie Alpha Five.'

Five seconds.

'*Go ahead, Charlie Alpha Five.*'

'We've got a visual on five tangos. Heavily armed. No sign of locals. Awaiting instructions.'

'*Roger that, Charlie Alpha Five. Wait out, figures five.*'

The radio fell silent. Danny and Boydie kept the militants in their sights. The technical stopped almost directly to their twelve o'clock. Two of the guys climbed down and the vehicle continued back round the opposite side of the village and disappeared from sight. The men lit cigarettes and stood there, looking out across the desert. Even from a kilometre away, Danny could discern their arrogant slouch. One of them put binoculars to his eyes and scanned round. Danny felt himself tense up slightly as the binoculars aligned with their location, but the militant didn't even pause before moving on. Their cover was good.

Activity on the radio. '*Charlie Alpha Five, this is Zero. We have a green light. Repeat, we have a green light.*'

'OK, Snapper,' Boydie said. 'Lase the target.'

Danny focused the cross hairs of the LTD on to the closest building, a single-storey breeze-block house against which the second Libyan militant was leaning. Moments later the device was firing an invisible beam directly at the building. When the ordnance came in, it would follow that beam to make a direct hit.

'Done,' Danny said.

'Target lit,' Boydie confirmed over his headset. 'Repeat, target lit.'

A pause. A crackle. Then: '*Fast air on target at 06.25. Wait out, Charlie Alpha Five. Over.*'

Silence. Danny checked his watch. 05.32 hrs. The two militants lit fresh cigarettes, unaware that they were getting a wake-up call, RAF style, in fifty-three minutes.

They waited. Somewhere above the Mediterranean, Danny knew, an RAF Tornado squadron would be thundering towards the North African coast. The Libyan skies were no stranger to fast air, of course, but the average local probably wouldn't know a Tornado from a twin-prop. Not that they'd have much chance to check these aircraft out. By the time the boom of their jets hit anybody's ears, the Tornados themselves would be out of sight. And the militants in the Bedouin village probably wouldn't hear a thing anyway: by the time the sonic boom hit their location, the Tornados would be gone and their bombs would have hit.

'Looks like Dumb and Dumber got bored,' Boydie said. Danny took a look on target. The two militants had disappeared.

'With half of NATO after them, you'd think they'd at least keep stag.'

'Don't get cocky, Snapper,' Boyd said in his frustratingly patronising way. 'No telling what we can't see. They might have covert OPs.'

Before Danny could reply, the radio crackled again. '*Fast air, fifteen minutes out.*'

'Gonna get noisy,' Boydie warned. Danny felt a flash of irritation. Boyd was a good guy, but he sure had a way about him sometimes. I might be young, Danny thought, but I'm not some wet-behind-the-ears newbie fresh out of jungle training . . . Keep your pie-hole shut, he told himself. Now wasn't the time to give Boydie a rundown of his character failings. Instead he just grunted in agreement and went back to watching.

And waiting.

'*Fast air, five minutes from target.*'

Danny sipped water from his CamelBak. His multicam was soaked with sweat. It would be good to get the hell out of this sweltering OP.

'*Fast air, two minutes from target.*'

Through the scope Danny saw the technical return, this time along the western perimeter of the village. It stopped in almost exactly the same position as earlier, but this time the make-up of its passengers had changed. There were now three militants standing round the .50-cal, while two others sat along the side of the vehicle, the backs of their heads facing the OP. Unlike the others, these two weren't wearing keffiyehs.

'*Fast air, one minute from target.*'

'Something's wrong,' Danny said.

'What's up?'

Before Danny could answer, the two new arrivals stood up. In an instant he saw that their jackets bore the UN's blue armband.

'Call it off,' he said, his voice terse.

'Easy, Snapper . . .'

'There's two UN personnel in that vehicle. Call off the strike!'

'*Fast air, thirty seconds from target.*'

'The peacekeepers are dead,' Boydie said. He was angry now. 'The militants were wearing their fucking jackets, remember?'

'We don't know for sure *all* the peacekeepers are dead. They've only recovered two out of four bodies. What if two of them are still alive? *Call it off!*'

'*Fast air, fifteen seconds from target.*'

Boydie had lowered his optic and was hunkering down ready for the blast. Danny, however, kept his eyes on the target. Was his mate right? Maybe the figures in the UN jackets *were* just more militants. He watched carefully as they dismounted from the back of the technical. Two of the armed militants joined them.

'*Fast air, ten seconds from target.*'

'Turn around,' Danny willed the figures. 'Turn—'

He took a sharp intake of breath. A militant had just raised his fist and dealt one of the jacketed figures a massive blow to the stomach. The figure bent double and collapsed to the ground.

'*Fast air, five seconds from target.*'

Danny quickly shifted himself closer to Boydie's side of the OP. With his right hand he forcibly grabbed his mate's boom mike and twisted it round. '*ABORT! ABORT! ABORT!*' he shouted. From somewhere behind them, Danny heard the distant roar of jets. It faded as soon he'd heard it, and in his mind he saw Tornados pulling away at the last moment. The militants clearly heard it too. A couple of them looked up into the air, but then made dismissive gestures as they evidently decided that the distant fast air was nothing to do with them. Danny's earpiece burst into life. '*Strike aborted. Strike aborted. Charlie Alpha Five, you'd better have a damn good reason for this.*'

Boydie was staring at Danny with a mixture of fury and shock. Danny was breathing heavily. He jabbed a finger in the direction of the village. 'Look!' he hissed.

Boydie looked.

The two figures in UN jackets were both on the ground now, being kicked and beaten by the three militants. One of them produced two hoods, knelt down and slipped them over the hostages' heads. Danny felt Boydie readying his weapon and was about to do the same when another militant fired a shot in the air. The three militants laughed, removed the hoods and started kicking their captives again. Boydie lowered his optic and twisted his boom mike back into position.

'Zero, this is Charlie Alpha Five. We have eyes on two UN hostages. Awaiting instructions. Out.'

The silence in the OP was as oppressive as the increasing heat as Danny and Boydie waited for further instructions from base. They watched from a distance as the militants laid into the hostages – more, Danny sensed, out of boredom than for any strategic reason.

'Good call, fella,' Boydie said finally. There was reluctance in his voice, but respect too. Boydie was a big enough man to admit that he'd been wrong.

'Charlie Alpha Five, this is Zero. We have a green light for a hostage rescue. All militants to be killed or captured. Over.'

Boydie and Danny exchanged a glance. 'Wilco,' Boydie replied, before turning back to his mate. His eyes were searching. Testing. 'So, Snapper,' he said. 'We've got a klick of open ground and an enemy armed with AKs and a .50-cal. If those poor sods whose bellies they're using for footy practice die, they die badly. Ready to get them out?'

Danny looked towards the village again. The militants had had their fun and were loading the hostages back on to the technical, which then started up and soon disappeared from view. All that was left was the barren desert, the low buildings of the Bedouin village and the Land Rover.

'Ready,' he said.

FOUR

The plan was simple. Wait for nightfall, when darkness gave them a good chance of approaching the village unseen. Cause a diversion to draw out as many militants as possible – that was Danny's job, and he had it all worked out. Then go in hard and fast to take out the remainder and release the hostages. The headshed wanted to send in reinforcements, but Boydie stamped on that idea with a curt radio communication. If the militants had any idea they were being watched, there was a strong possibility they'd drive away and the whole thing would be over. The team were the ones who were on the ground, and the ops room were letting them call the shots.

It meant waiting out in the OP for the rest of the day. Danny and Boydie took it in turns to sleep, two hours on, two hours off. Danny's sleep was fitful. Whenever Boydie started to doze, he would sort of whistle, a gentle buzzing between his tongue and the roof of his mouth that he probably wasn't even aware of. The tune sounded mournful. Strangely familiar, though Danny couldn't put his finger on it. An old Irish song maybe? He didn't know. He distracted himself by recalling everything he knew about the village from the aerial photography they'd studied back at base. It was about fifty metres by fifty. In addition to the four domed buildings at the front, and the single-storey structures that surrounded them, there was a central square, about ten metres by ten. The photography had shown this square surrounded by tents. Whether these were still there, or the Bedouin had taken them with them when they left, the unit couldn't say. Nor did they know where the hostages were being kept. They'd have to work that out on the job.

Around midday the weather suddenly, and unexpectedly, changed. Cloud cover rolled in, but the heat was still dry and intense. Covered by the hessian camouflage, Danny felt like he was lying in a puddle of sweat. His muscles ached from lack of movement, and the pressure points where his flesh pressed against the ground throbbed. It was a relief when the light started to fail. They had seen no movement during all that time. Danny realised he was anxious – not on his own behalf, but for the hostages.

'You don't curse much, eh, Snapper?' Boydie said out of the blue.

Danny said nothing.

'I noticed it, that's all. Don't know how you manage it. All those gaps in talking where you have to put a "fuck" in.' He sniffed. 'Or a "cunt".'

Danny ignored this and asked, 'Why do you think they pretended they'd killed all four UN guys?'

Boydie thought for a moment. 'They'll be pumping these two survivors for intel. My guess is they thought that, if we had them all down as dead, we wouldn't send in a rescue mission.' A pause. 'I reckon our UN friends are having a pretty ugly day. That little mock execution we saw was a way of shitting them up. The PIRA boys used to do it back home. Nothing like the prospect of a bit of lead in your skull to get the old tongue wagging.' Danny felt Boydie giving him a piercing look. 'I heard you had a bit of family history in the Province.'

'Aye,' Danny said. It wasn't something he liked to talk about. But Boydie kept up his gaze. 'My dad was 1 Para,' Danny said. 'Took an IRA round to the side of the head during the Troubles. Total amnesia. Forgot everything.'

'Jesus,' Boydie sighed.

'I was just a baby.'

'How'd your ma take it?'

Danny stared resolutely through the optic. 'She didn't have to,' he said. 'She died just after I was born.'

Silence in the OP. Danny didn't feel like discussing it any more. He checked his watch. 'Seventeen hundred hours. It'll be dark in a couple of hours,' he said.

And that ended the conversation.

It was 22.00 hrs before they emerged gingerly from the OP. Keeping low, they collected up their Claymores before ducking back down into the wadi. The cloud cover rendered it darker than the previous night, so Danny engaged his NV as they picked their way back to the lying-up point to RV with Tommo and Five Bellies. Having kept radio contact to a minimum during the day, they filled their patrol mates in on the events of that morning. 'We've counted five militants, all armed, plus the two hostages,' Boydie explained. 'But there may be more. We're going to take out as many as we can in one hit.' He looked over at the packs. 'Only take what you need,' he said. 'We don't know what to expect up there. We don't want anything slowing us down.'

It took them five minutes to prep. Each man checked his personal weapon and the contents of his belt kit: spare ammo, frags, flashbangs. Danny carried the Claymores as well as a small, hand-held cutting tool. Then, on a word of instruction from Boydie, they commenced their sortie. The patrol reassumed single-file formation. But this time Danny, weighed down by the Claymores, ceded the role of lead scout to Tommo, and instead took third position in the line-up. The four tabbed along the wadi back towards the OP, climbed up on to the desert plain and started to jog across open ground.

Three hundred metres from the village, Tommo held up one hand and the patrol came to a halt and went to ground. Danny scanned the area ahead, preparing to cause his diversion. No sign of the militants. The parked Land Rover was to his eleven o'clock, approximately twenty metres shy of the village. At a thumbs up from Boydie, Danny pushed himself to his feet again and trod quietly towards the vehicle. He didn't look back. He didn't need to. He knew the others would be stealthily putting themselves into position, surrounding the village, ready to strike at the given moment.

Fifty metres to the Land Rover. Danny went to ground again. Waited. No sound. No movement. He pushed on. Now that he was close to the Land Rover, Danny flipped up his NV goggles. It was old, creamy beige in colour and had certainly seen better days. The bodywork was dented and rusted. The rear windscreen had a jagged crack along the centre and it stank of oil and petrol. Bizarrely, one of the side windows had a peeling Arsenal sticker on the inside. The vehicle was facing away from the village. Danny positioned himself at its front, where he kneeled down and unfurled the detonation wire from each Claymore. The mines were about twenty centimetres by ten and slightly curved at one end. This convex face was embossed with the words 'Front Toward Enemy'. Claymores being directional, you wanted to be very sure you were orientating them correctly, hence the kindergarten-style instruction. As every training officer he'd ever come across was so keen on saying: keep it simple, stupid. Not that this was a guarantee of success. Danny had heard stories of American troops in Vietnam laying Claymores to snare the enemy, only for the Vietcong to creep out under cover of night and reverse the direction of the mines. Being peppered by 700 steel balls moving at 1200 metres per second was a bad way to go.

Danny placed the Claymores two metres in front of the Land Rover, their convex sides facing it. He unwound each detonation wire, held the clacker at each end and moved these into position 100 metres to the north-east of the village. After laying them carefully on the ground, he returned to the vehicle.

Moment of truth.

Danny removed his cutting tool from his belt kit and crouched down to feel under the Land Rover's engine. It took him less than ten seconds to locate the fuel line. The tool cut through the metal tube like it wasn't even there. Danny felt petrol drip on to his hand and the fumes immediately hit his nose. He returned the cutting tool to his belt kit and swapped it for his dad's old Zippo. He sparked it up and touched the flame to the dripping fuel. And then he ran.

Danny followed the Claymores' det wires. He'd run fifty metres by the time he heard an explosion behind him. He glanced once over his shoulder – flames were already licking from the Land Rover's engine – before reaching the clackers ten seconds later and throwing himself to the ground. He pulled his spotting scope from his belt kit and quickly got a visual on his diversion.

It took half a minute for the militants to emerge. Two of them, to start with. They looked perplexed and loitered for a moment some five metres from the blazing vehicle, their AKs strapped across their bodies, before one of them turned towards the village, put his hand to his mouth and shouted something. Thirty seconds later three more men emerged. Although Danny couldn't hear them, he could tell they were shouting at each other. Arguing.

And all the time moving closer to the Land Rover.

With one hand he felt for the clackers. The militant closest to the vehicle was two metres from it. The furthest about seven, and getting nearer.

Just a little closer, Danny thought.

Five metres.

They were bunched up.

One of them pushed another in the chest. They were definitely arguing. No point waiting for the row to split them up. If he could take out all five in one hit, the rest of the job would be a lot more straightforward.

61

He squeezed the clackers.

The sound of the Claymores erupting echoed across the desert. The Land Rover exploded and a flurry of body parts showered around it, but Danny had already panned his scope to the right. It took just a few seconds for him to see three hunched silhouettes, about thirty metres from the edge of the village, sprinting towards it now that the signal to advance – the detonation of the Claymores – had been given. Danny got to his feet, flicked the selector switch of his M4 to automatic and sprinted towards the village to join his mates.

They had to move fast. As soon as the militants realised they were under attack, the hostages would be in even greater danger than they were already. When he was twenty-five metres from the main building, Danny saw a figure at the entrance. He raised his weapon and lined up the scope. AK-47. Bandolier. Danny lined the weapon up with the militant's chest and squeezed a short burst. The target hit the ground and Danny picked up pace again.

He reached the building ten seconds later. Boydie was waiting for him, standing to the right of the entrance, his back against the wall, a flashbang in his hand. Danny took up position on the opposite side of the open door and held up three fingers.

Two.

One.

Boydie threw the flashbang into the building. Danny steeled himself for the explosion. It came within a split second – a burst of light and a deafening crack that would disorientate anybody in there. Boydie entered first, NV in place, weapon engaged. Danny did the same.

The building comprised a single room some ten metres by fifteen. Beds along one side, otherwise empty of furniture. It was full of smoke from the flashbang, but through his NV Danny counted three militants, all of them crouched on the ground, hands over their ears. They were in a neat little row, three metres apart and about eight metres from Danny's position. 'Go left!' Boydie shouted, and Danny knew what he meant. He directed his weapon at the crouching figure on the left and delivered a second burst of fire. The figure shuddered with the impact of the rounds, then fell still. Boydie had gone right, nailing a second militant just as quickly. Which left only one.

Boydie strode towards him, his weapon aimed directly at his head.

'*Kam antun?*' he asked. *How many men are you?*

The militant didn't answer. There was a harsh, arrogant look on his face.

'*Kam antun?*'

Still no reply.

Danny loosened the ivory-handled knife in his belt.

A man always has need of a good knife, kiddo.

He strode towards the militant, whose attention was all on Boydie, and grabbed his right hand. With a sudden, brutal thrust, he slammed the exquisitely sharp point of the knife between the tendons that led to the man's third and fourth fingers. At first the militant only gasped. When Danny twisted the knife forty-five degrees, hitting the nerve endings, the man screamed.

'*Kam antun?*' Danny hissed.

'*Hamastash . . .*' the man squealed. *Fifteen.*

That was all they needed. Boydie fired a single shot into the militant's head and he slumped to the floor. Then he turned to Danny, saying, 'Those MREs did their job. Quite the fucking psycho tonight, aren't we?'

'We didn't seem to be getting very far. That's eight men down by my count.'

Boydie spoke over the radio. 'Seven men still standing,' he reported to Tommo and Five Bellies.

From outside the building came four more bursts of fire. 'Make that three,' Tommo reported.

'Any sign of the hostages?'

'Negative.'

Boydie and Danny stepped outside, panning their weapons left and right. A terrible silence had fallen on the encampment, broken only by the crackle of the burning Land Rover. Boydie jabbed one finger eastwards, indicating that Danny should take that side of the building. Danny followed the patrol leader's instruction, feeling the heat from the vehicle just ten metres to his left. He covered the five metres to the corner of the building. To his right there was a passageway, two metres wide, formed by the wall of the building and a smaller outhouse. Danny swung round, his weapon aimed down the passageway, his trigger finger ready. The passageway extended eight or nine metres, but it was empty.

Suddenly, to Danny's eight o'clock, somewhere behind him on the other side of the outhouse, he heard the coughing of a car engine. He heard Five Bellies' voice in his ear: 'They're doing a runner!'

The sound of the car moved south, towards the burning Land Rover. 'I got it,' Danny said. He spun round 180 degrees and, using the wall of the outhouse for cover, looked out towards the conflagration. He was just in time to see the open-topped technical speed away from the eastern side of the village. High acceleration – he had just two seconds before it disappeared behind the cover of the Land Rover. Four figures in the back. Silhouettes only. Insufficient time to verify, if he was about to open fire on the hostages. He lowered his rifle and discharged a long burst towards the technical's rear left tyre. The vehicle skidded badly on the desert earth, then came to a halt.

Danny threw himself back into the passageway. Just in time. The response from the .50-cal was thunderous, the rounds blasting a chunk from the corner of the building he and Boydie had just left. Sweating profusely, Danny pressed his back to the wall.

'Tyre's out,' he reported into his boom mike. His voice sounded high-pitched. Wired.

'Tommo, Five, draw their fire,' Boydie ordered.

Almost immediately Danny heard a burst of rifle fire from the other side of the encampment. He didn't need to ask what Boydie had in mind. It was obvious. He ran along the passageway to find himself on the edge of the central square. It was still surrounded by canvas tents. Boydie was running towards Danny from the right. He nodded at him and they headed east, past a particularly threadbare tent and ten metres out into the open desert. Another burst from the .50-cal confirmed that Tommo and Five Bellies' decoy fire was taking all the militants' attention. Which gave Danny and Boydie the opportunity to approach the technical unseen. It was twenty metres away, a distinct black shadow against the burning Land Rover just a few metres beyond it. The headlamps were off – clearly the driver had calculated they were a less easy target that way – but the result was that the Regiment men had the cover of darkness with which to approach.

Another burst of rifle fire. The .50-cal replied in kind. Danny saw the silhouette of a figure being hustled down from the back of the technical by a single armed figure and taken round to the far side of the vehicle, leaving two other figures in the back. The driver had his door open and was climbing out, rifle in hand. The militants' attention was fully on Tommo and Five Bellies' incoming fire. None of them noticed Boydie and Danny until it was too late.

The driver was Danny's. The burst from his M4, from a distance of five metres, coincided with the roar of the .50-cal, rendering it barely audible but no less deadly for that. The driver had just put his feet on the ground when the rounds hit his torso, throwing him violently against the cab of the pick-up. Boydie ran towards the rear of the vehicle, firing on the militant manning the .50-cal when he was five metres distant. A new silhouette of blood and brain matter showered down in front of the burning Land Rover.

The firing ceased. There was whimpering from the back of the pick-up. At least one of the hostages was still alive.

By Danny's calculation there was a single militant remaining: the one who had taken the other hostage round to the far side of the technical. Now the Libyan started shouting – desperate words, threats, in Arabic that Danny couldn't make out, but their meaning was clear enough. He had only one play to make: I've got the hostage. Come any closer and he dies.

Danny and Boydie were up against the technical now, crouching low to stay out of the sight of the surviving militant. 'Hold his attention,' Danny said. Boydie nodded and they separated, creeping around opposite ends of the vehicle. Peering round by the headlamps, Danny took in the scene. The militant and his hostage were standing five metres away. They were facing the opposite direction, the militant standing behind the hostage, left arm around his neck and a pistol in his right, pressed up against the captive's head. Danny couldn't risk a shot. A round from the M4 or even the Sig could go straight through the militant's body and into the hostage.

Boydie appeared from the far side of the technical. He had his weapon engaged and trained directly on the two figures. The militant started screaming incomprehensible threats again. His whole body was shaking, his weapon aimed at the hostage's head. Boydie didn't move. He just stood there, relentless, threatening, maintaining the stalemate.

Keeping the militant's attention very firmly on him, while Danny emerged from the cover of the Land Rover.

As silent as smoke.

Danny stood very still, his sights lined up with the back of the target's head. He was aware that the blazing Land Rover made his shadow unnaturally huge on the technical. He ignored it. All attention on the target. There was no scope for error. The bastard had to be put down before he fired out of nerves.

Slowly, Boydie lowered his weapon. He let it hang by its halyard while he raised his hands, palms outward in a gesture of surrender.

The militant swallowed it. In a single movement he threw the hostage to one side and aimed his gun at Boydie. He barely had time to straighten his arm. Danny fired a single shot. The round slammed into the back of the Libyan's head and he flew forwards, landing face down on the hard-baked earth with a dull slam.

'Nice shot,' Boydie said.

There is a special kind of silence that falls in the wake of a contact. The silence of the dead. Danny was only half aware of the man he'd just killed, half his skull blown away, hair matted over what remained of it, blood oozing thickly from the wound like a tiny oil slick. His attention had already moved on. Were all the enemy down? Were there any more threats? The hostage staggered back, clearly struck dumb by the sudden brutality he had just witnessed. Danny pulled him roughly to the ground while Boydie kept his weapon engaged and started scanning the area, looking out for any more enemy targets. The other hostage was still whimpering in the back of the pick-up, but at least he was keeping out of sight.

Five minutes passed before Tommo's posh voice came over the headset.

'All enemy down,' he said. 'We're clear.'

The militants were dead, but there was still work to do.

It was Boydie's decision to round up the bodies. 'Too many news crews crawling round this country, sniffing for a story,' he said. 'They'll fucking find one too if they stumble over these stiffs with rounds in their heads.' He was right. If a story started with fourteen dead insurgents and a NATO hit squad nowhere to be seen, there was no way of telling how it would end up once the Chinese whispers had finished. Danny recalled a story he'd heard about A Squadron during the First Gulf War. A few of the lads had got into a contact and captured a handful of Iraqis. The red mist was down, and one of the SAS lads had executed them. The guys didn't know what to do with the bodies, so they piled them into one of the Iraqis' vehicles and took them out into the desert, where they placed a couple of anti-tank mines on a timer under the vehicle. The A Squadron boys had driven off into the night and let the fearsome mines do their work. They'd all known that what they were doing was on the edge, but, at the end of the day, if there were no bodies there was no story. *End of story.*

Boydie was clearly thinking along the same lines. After a brief radio conversation with the headshed, he announced their next move. 'We'll relight the target,' he said. 'Do the original job. There'll be fuck all left of them if anyone decides to come nosing around.'

Tommo and Five Bellies were given the job of looking after the hostages. Once Tommo had changed the wheel that Danny had shot out on the technical, he and Five Bellies loaded the quivering UN personnel into the cab. The hostages couldn't even speak: they just trembled and stared into the middle distance. 'Get them out of here,' Boydie said. 'Their nerves are shot already. They don't need to see this. Four klicks should do it. We'll meet you back at the LUP once you've heard the strike.' Danny and Boydie watched the technical disappear, then got to work.

It took about twenty minutes to locate all of the dead bodies and carry them into the main building at the front of the village. The corpses were already starting to stiffen, and it was grisly work: the fatal wounds the Regiment's rounds had inflicted were diabolical. As soon as a body was moved just an inch, blood oozed from the entrance and exit wounds. By the time they had unceremoniously dumped them all in a pile in the centre of the room, both Danny and Boydie looked like they'd been bathing in gore. It was sticky on Danny's face, and filled his nostrils with an unpleasant, iron-like smell. He wasn't sorry to leave the village and start trekking back towards the wadi.

They moved quickly. Fifteen minutes to cross the open ground. Once they had regained their gear from the LUP, they reinserted themselves into the narrow trench, where Danny set up the LTD once more. He directed the device's cross hairs directly at the building in which they'd piled the militants, then Boydie made the call for fast air for the second time in twenty-four hours.

And this time there was no reason to abort the air strike.

The Tornado arrived twenty minutes later. The boom of its jet engines was enough to make Danny's body rattle as he lay in the trench. But it was nothing compared to the force of the bomb as it hit. Guided by the laser, it slammed directly into the militants' makeshift tomb. Danny saw a flash of light. A fraction of a second later the shock wave rolled out across the desert and vibrated in their ears, knocking the LTD from its little tripod. For a horrible, irrational moment, Danny wondered if he'd lit the target badly and the bomb had landed too close. He needn't have worried. Through a sudden mushroom of smoke, and amid the shock wave, he saw flames licking up to the sky. By now the bodies would have been blasted to pieces, and anything that remained of them would be consumed by the fire.

They stayed in the OP, scanning the desert night, watching for anybody coming to investigate the site of the air strike. But the only vehicle they saw was the technical, driven by Tommo with Five Bellies beside him, headlamps off, trundling towards them from the west.

Boydie got on the radio. 'Zero, this is Charlie Alpha Five,' he said. 'Target destroyed. Hostages safe. Request pick-up. Repeat, request pick-up.'

FIVE

The two hostages were in a bad way. Physically weak, mentally fucked.

One of them was in his mid-thirties, a tall, rather ungainly man with cracked round glasses. He had been badly beaten on one side of his head. His skin was bruised and his cheekbone had a slight indentation which suggested to Danny that it had been smashed. The other man was older, probably in his fifties. He had three teeth missing: two canines and a molar. It looked like each tooth had been individually removed. There was dried blood on his chin as a souvenir of that little dental surgery. The two men could barely walk. They certainly still couldn't speak, so although Danny knew they were British, there was no way of confirming this. It was as if the terror of the previous few days had wiped everything from their minds. They could do nothing but stare ahead and tremble. If any of the guys tried to talk to them, they would flinch as if someone had prodded an open wound. It didn't seem to register that they'd been rescued by British Army personnel who were going to get them home safely.

They left the hostages to Tommo's care. As patrol medic, he dealt with their superficial injuries, though there was little he could do other than get fluids inside them, bandage their cuts and feed them some DF118 painkillers. The remaining three members of the patrol took up defensive positions and scanned the surrounding desert for suspicious movement. The burning village was like a massive beacon in the middle of this vast expanse of open ground. Smoke drifted low across the desert towards the wadi, compromising their vision. Not good. It wasn't a matter of if someone approached the conflagration, but when. Their luck held, however. Their location was sufficiently remote for them to remain unobserved for now.

The Sea Knight arrived just before midnight. The dust halos were no less bright out here in the open desert, but they were less of a threat than they had been the previous night. Tommo and Five Bellies helped the hostages up the tailgate. Danny and Boydie followed immediately after with their packs. The chopper rose from the ground before they'd even sat down. A couple of US Army medics were waiting to take care of the hostages. As Danny took a seat and plugged himself once more into the aircraft's comms, he was happy that someone else had taken delivery of them. A sudden wave of exhaustion crashed over him, and he could sense the same of the other members of the patrol. They'd only been airborne a couple of minutes before he felt his eyes closing despite the thunderous grind of the chopper and the occasional status report over the cans.

It was neither of these sounds that woke him suddenly, but a sudden lurch by the Sea Knight. Danny's eyes pinged open. His hands automatically felt for his weapon, and he could see similar signs of readiness in the other guys. The aircraft immediately steadied itself, but Danny could tell they had shifted direction slightly. He looked out of the window. They were over water. One patch of sea looked the same as another. It took a communication from the pilot thirty seconds later to explain what was happening. 'OK, gentlemen, we've had an instruction to re-route.'

'Where to?' Boydie demanded.

No answer. And equally, no more chance of sleep. Danny's senses were on high alert again. Where were they going? What was happening? The Sea Knight gained height. Looking out of the window, Danny caught sight of the *George Bush* several

71

hundred feet below. He used its position and the movement of the aircraft to calculate their direction. North-west. He relaxed a little. Everything suggested they were heading back to their staging post in Malta.

He was right. An hour later the Sea Knight made ground again. This time the rotors powered down. The grinding of the engine came to a halt. A reception party of four green army lads ran up the tailgate carrying stretchers. Their eyes flickered over towards the special forces unit, but they were professional enough not to let their curiosity interfere with the more important business of ferrying the hostages off the aircraft. His body once more heavy with fatigue, Danny disconnected himself from the comms system. Thirty seconds later he and the rest of his patrol were walking down the tailgate into the heavy, humid air of Malta International Airport.

An ambulance was waiting on the airfield, thirty metres from the Sea Knight, its neon light flashing. The green army boys were loading up the second of the two hostages. A hundred metres beyond it, Danny saw the familiar hulking outline of a Hercules. On the runway to his two o'clock, a Ryanair flight was coming in to land. Holidaymakers arriving in the Med for sun, sand and sex. As though reading his thoughts, Boydie said, 'I wouldn't mind a bit of that myself.' Danny didn't have a chance to answer. Just as his feet hit the tarmac, his attention snapped back to the area between the Sea Knight and the ambulance. An unmarked van had pulled up ten metres in front of them. Two men climbed out. Danny recognised them at once. Eddie Anderson, OC B Squadron, and ops sergeant Ben Powell. Anderson nodded briefly at the advancing patrol. 'Fucking good work,' he said gruffly. 'Sorry, lads, but we'll need a debrief for government in twenty minutes over the satcom. Danny, you're needed back at HQ asap. Don't worry, son. Nothing to worry about. Ben will sort you out with anything you need.'

Danny's stomach felt leaden. Ben Powell had the blank expression of a man about to deliver bad news. Danny strode over to the ops sergeant, who immediately started walking away from the Sea Knight in the direction of the Hercules. Danny fell in beside him. 'What's wrong?' And before Powell could answer, he fired more questions. 'My dad all right? Something happen to my brother?'

'Relax, Danny,' Powell said. 'As far as I know it's nothing personal.'

A wave of relief. 'Then what?'

'Your guess is as good as mine. All I know is they want you back in the UK. This morning.'

Regiment guys being plucked out of theatre like this was seldom good news. He quickly made a mental list of anything he might have done wrong. Were the MoD about to screw him over? 'What the hell's going on, Ben?' he demanded.

'I told you,' the ops sergeant replied. 'I don't know.' Powell seemed slightly annoyed by his own ignorance. 'All I know is it must be important.' He held up an airline boarding card. 'BA flight to Heathrow. Supposed to leave two hours ago. They've delayed it for you, but you need to get cleaned up first – you smell like a dog's arse. Fucking look like one too, so shake a leg, mate. Somebody clearly doesn't want to be kept waiting.'

The hours that followed were a blur. Powell led Danny to a small shower room, where his North Face drop bag was waiting for him. He showered off the dirt, using the tub of Swarfega that he always packed for this purpose to strip off the blood smeared over his head, face and hands. Then he got dressed into blue jeans, black Converse, white shirt and leather jacket. As he walked out of the shower room there was not a hint of his profession, or the way he'd spent the past twenty-four hours.

The BA jet was sitting on the tarmac, fully loaded. Nobody asked Danny for any ID as a refuelling vehicle drove him directly to the front, where a mobile stairway was waiting for him. As he boarded, an attractive air hostess with a little upturned nose escorted him to his seat in business class. Danny wondered what bullshit the airport authorities had fed the other passengers to explain the delay of their flight. As he took his seat he felt eyes on him that suggested some of them had twigged from his late arrival and damp hair that they hadn't been told the whole truth.

The plane was a hell of a sight more comfortable than the Sea Knight. Once they were airborne, the pretty air hostess offered him champagne. She looked almost disappointed when he asked for coffee instead, and he noticed the way her hand brushed against his as she handed it to him. 'Let me know if you need anything at all,' she almost purred at him. Danny just nodded. Ordinarily he'd have played the game, but he was too dog-tired even to think about that. He was asleep before the aircraft reached its cruising altitude.

He dozed fitfully. Even though Powell had assured him that everything was OK back home, in some corner of his exhausted mind he couldn't shake the suspicion that something was wrong. He saw his dad, limp in his wheelchair, a look of fear on the face that had grown fat through lack of exercise. He'd been stuck in that damn thing in a tiny bungalow in Hereford for the past thirty years, stubbornly rearing his children and refusing any help that was offered to him. Danny had never once heard him complain about his lot. Even when Danny's brother Kyle had started getting into trouble with the police – just as all his teachers had predicted he would – their dad had been philosophical. You can only shit with the arse you've got, he always said – one of Taff's favourite sayings – and Danny privately knew that his disappointment with Kyle's behaviour was more than balanced by his pride when Danny had passed selection. Even so, the thought of life throwing anything more at his father made Danny nauseous.

The plane touched down at Heathrow at 06.00 hrs GMT. Dawn had broken, but although the sky was clear the air had a bite to it that Danny had not experienced farther south. Even with his eyes shut, he'd have known this was the UK. The desert just smelled different. Waiting on the tarmac for him was an anonymous black Land Cruiser. The driver – he wore jeans, a sports jacket and brown leather driving gloves – opened the rear door for him. Ignoring the bleary-eyed and suspicious looks from the other passengers on the tarmac, Danny climbed into the back. Without a word, the chauffeur drove off the airfield.

'Where we headed, mucker?' Danny asked.

'Acton,' the driver said.

'Lucky me. Do I need my military ID?'

'Not necessary.' Thirty metres up ahead, an orange barrier rose automatically and the Land Cruiser passed through it. Moments later it had slipped into the early-morning traffic on the M4.

'You with the Firm?' Danny asked.

No reply, which was as good as a yes.

They travelled in silence. Now and then Danny felt the driver's eyes on him in the rear-view mirror. He didn't blame the guy. No doubt he was as much an enigma as the driver was to him. After twenty minutes they found themselves on the Uxbridge Road. Danny looked at his watch – 06.37 hrs – as they turned left. Five minutes later they entered the Park Royal industrial estate, where the Land Cruiser approached a large brick unit, about the size of an aircraft hangar and surrounded by a three-metre-high metal fence. A warehouse of some kind. Danny spotted a notice on the fence that said: 'Ronson Logistics – A Better Service To You'. The driver stopped at a wide, sturdy gate set into the fence, wound down the window and punched a number into a keypad to the right. The gate opened and the Land Cruiser slipped in. It came to a halt by a door in the side of the warehouse. Danny jumped out, looking around warily.

'What is this place?' he demanded.

The driver didn't answer. He simply jutted his chin towards the side door. Danny suppressed a moment of frustration that made him want to grab the guy and drag some more concrete information out of him. Instead he nodded briefly and entered the building.

He found himself in a bleak little office. A desk, a chair, a lamp and nothing else. No occupants, but in the far wall was another door. He opened it, walked through and found himself in the main part of the warehouse. It was a vast space, about fifty metres long, thirty wide and fifteen high. A radio was playing at the far end – Danny thought he recognised a Snow Patrol song that some of the lads back in Bastion had listened to. There was a cold, concrete floor, and strip lighting hung from the ceiling. The warehouse was filled with vehicles. They were parked in five neat lines, like in a car showroom. Unlike a car showroom, however, these vehicles looked anything but new. Danny counted thirteen black cabs. One of them had an advertisement for *Mamma Mia: The Musical* plastered across its side. A few others had the odd dent in their bodywork. There were VWs, Minis, a couple of Transits, even a battered old Royal Mail van whose rear doors were open and the interior filled with grey mail sacks. Notable by their absence in what Danny immediately took to be a vehicle pool for the Security Services was anything remotely flash. No Porsches, no Range Rovers, nothing convertible. These vehicles were supposed to be invisible – there was, after all, nothing so commonplace as a black cab on the streets of London. One of them had its bonnet up and a mechanic – the only other person present that Danny could see – peered round from one side on hearing footsteps. He didn't look surprised to see Danny standing there. He just pointed towards the far side of the warehouse where there was an anonymous Portakabin. A box within a box. Danny strode up to it, knocked firmly on the door and then stepped inside.

There were six men inside. Three of them were standing drinking coffee from polystyrene cups. The others stood a few metres apart, clearly in conference. Danny recognised one of them as Johnny Cartwright, the CO of 22. Cartwright was the first to notice Danny. He beckoned him to come and join them. As Danny grew nearer, he realised he recognised each of the three guys drinking coffee. He'd seen them around Hereford HQ but didn't know them by name. The two men Cartwright was speaking with, Danny didn't know at all.

Cartwright made a curt string of introductions, starting with the Regiment boys. 'Jack Ward.' A lean, wiry guy with a pronounced mole on his left cheek. 'Greg Murray.' Shaved head, piercing blue eyes. 'Spud Glover.' A head shorter than Danny, but with squat, broad shoulders so solid they looked like they'd stop a green-tipped round at point-blank range, and a round face and balding head that, weirdly, reminded him of Phil Collins. Danny shook each soldier's hand before the CO directed him towards the two suits. 'Oliver Carrington.' The older of the two, Carrington had steel-grey hair and wore old-fashioned black-rimmed glasses. The lenses were very thick and the eyes behind them seemed wary as he shook hands with Danny.

'I appreciate you joining us at such short notice,' he said.

'I was at a loose end anyway, pal,' replied Danny.

Carrington smiled blandly. Danny had the impression of a man well used to hiding his emotions.

'And Hugo Buckingham,' Cartwright continued. Danny nodded at this younger man. He was slender, almost girlishly so – the dead spit of Hugh Grant. His floppy brown hair was a bit scruffy, but he had a friendly face.

'Very good to meet you,' Buckingham said. His voice was posh but not unpleasant. Danny nodded noncommittally at him, before throwing his CO a questioning glance.

'Six,' Cartwright said, as if that explained everything. Which, in a way, it did.

Carrington cleared his throat and then took charge of the meeting. 'May I suggest we get started, gentlemen? Find a seat where you can.'

'Yeah, I heard you were pushed for space up at MI6,' Spud said. Good point. Danny wondered what he was about to hear that made this spook so keen to banish unwanted ears. But that strand of conversation was over. A cautious respect existed between the men of 22 and the MI6 personnel whose dirty work they were so often brought in to do. The guys sat down on plastic stackable chairs and listened.

'You'll be aware of the current situation in Syria,' Carrington said. None of the Regiment men gave any indication that this was so, but it almost went without saying. When you know there's a chance of your superiors ordering an insertion into any of the world's hot spots at any given moment, you tend to keep one eye on the news. Even in the forward operating bases of Helmand, word had reached the men of the bloodshed and violence the Syrian government was inflicting on its own people.

'The anti-government rebels are fragmented,' Carrington went on. 'Different groups, different agendas. Some of them have a genuine political focus, some are simply opportunists taking advantage of the civilian unrest. The usual story. The PM has made it perfectly clear that the UK would welcome an orderly transfer of power. He's even gone so far as to offer senior members of the Syrian administration safe passage out of the country should they decide to stand down.'

'Give them a seat next to me,' Spud said. 'I don't have much use for kid-killers.'

'Quite,' Carrington murmured. 'In any case, it may or may not surprise you to learn that we have opened up lines of communication with certain rebel factions. All completely under the radar, of course. Our intelligence networks have identified

78

the faction most likely to come to power in the event of a regime change. Clearly, the British government would like to be on good terms with whoever succeeds the current Syrian regime.'

Carrington held up an A4 photograph. It was taken with a long-distance lens and showed an elderly Middle Eastern-looking man wearing a red and white keffiyeh. Danny was put in mind of pictures of Yasser Arafat he'd seen on TV when he was growing up. 'This is Baltasar Farhad,' Carrington explained. 'He is the patriarch of a rebel family most likely to have a leading role in any future Syrian administration. Or perhaps I should say, he *was*. Two weeks ago Farhad was assassinated in a suicide attack. You probably heard the news at the time.'

Danny hadn't. He squinted at the picture. In the background, a little blurred, he saw the arch of a Métro station. 'Paris?'

Carrington nodded. 'Farhad was in exile. The French had given him asylum. He himself had always been sympathetic to French interests in Syria. That made him a very valuable asset to the French. They were vexed, to say the least, when he met his maker.'

'Who did it?' Jack Ward asked.

'The intelligence points towards a young Algerian man wanted on terrorism charges.'

'Kids today,' Spud muttered. 'They blow up so quickly.'

Carrington ignored that. 'To be frank,' he said, 'who did it isn't our biggest problem. Our concern now is to deal with the aftermath. Farhad was more than just a figurehead. Even in his absence, he was the glue that stopped his own family from falling apart. He has two sons. Chalk and cheese: one by the name of Sorgen, the other called Asu. Sorgen is a chip off the old block. Like his father, he is mostly sympathetic to French interests. Asu, on the other hand, has spent a good deal of time in London. Our intelligence tells us that he has a penchant for British women – we've located four separate prostitutes who claim to have been regular clients of his during his time in the

UK. He even had a season ticket for . . . Tottenham Hotspur, was it, Hugo?'

Buckingham nodded.

'Footy and hookers,' Greg Murray said. 'Makes you proud to be British, don't it?'

'Yes, well, football isn't really my cup of tea. Whatever the reason, though, Asu is something of an Anglophile. He and Sorgen loathe each other. Always have done. Their father was the only person who could keep them from each other's throats. Out of respect for him, they avoided open hostilities. Now that Farhad has gone, they clearly see no reason to keep up the pretence. The family has split into two distinct factions. This is, of course, good news for the Syrian administration, as it means that their most significant rebel threat has been weakened. However, our analysts remain convinced that one or other of these brothers will lead the new administration when the time comes. It goes without saying that the British government would prefer to see Asu in that role, rather than Sorgen.'

There was a moment of silence while Carrington allowed that information to sink in.

'The government has made it quite clear that, while it supports the notion of regime change in Syria, it is pursuing a non-interventionist policy. After Iraq and Afghanistan, there just isn't the stomach for it. However, *if* one of these two factions is to come to power in Syria, we want to make sure it's Asu's side of the family, not Sorgen's. There was a time when we'd have been happy to put a Regiment unit on the ground in order to coordinate a training package for the rebels. Having assured the international community that we are taking a non-combative role in Syria, you can see, I'm sure, how it would be diplomatically awkward for us to do so now.'

Danny thought back to Libya. His paymasters hadn't been so squeamish about 'non-combative' roles out there. He put that thought from his mind. He'd long since stopped trying to work out the politics. He was there to do a job of work, not to think about the consequences.

'Nevertheless,' Carrington said, 'we're keen to extend the hand of friendship to Asu. You're all aware of International Solutions Ltd?'

Damn right they were all aware of it. International Solutions were private military contractors. They had half the Regiment on their books – guys who'd got sick of risking their necks for Queen and Country and wanted to exercise their skills for a proper paycheck. There wasn't a hot spot in the world without someone spying a chance to make some money, and that meant private close-protection work was easy to come by. International Solutions supplied the muscle for a good proportion of those kinds of jobs. Word on the streets of Hereford was that they did a whole lot more besides. Stick a few private military contractors in a war zone and you've got yourself a fighting force that isn't bound by the Geneva Convention. Amazing how many problems disappear when you throw away the rules of engagement.

'International Solutions successfully tendered for a government contract – strictly on the QT, you understand – to deploy a small team of private military contractors to help train Asu's men. A hand of friendship from the British government, but at one step removed – if anybody follows the money trail, they will be under the impression that Asu himself is employing the PMCs. There are, however, certain elements among the upper echelons of government who are nervous about using the private sector in this way.' He gave another of his meaningless smiles. 'Which is where Hugo comes in. He comes to us fresh from a stint in Saudi Arabia. One of our more distinguished Arabists. He's to make contact with our contractors and ensure that they're doing the job we're paying them for. Unofficially, of course. However, we also have a second, perhaps more important, mission for Hugo.' Carrington turned to the younger man. 'Perhaps you'd care to explain, Hugo.'

Buckingham looked a little surprised at being put on the spot. Danny watched his cheeks flush as he tried – and failed – to master it. Buckingham stood up, combed the fingers of his right hand through his abundant hair and cleared his throat – to little effect, as his voice was still somewhat croaky when he spoke. 'I had the good fortune to attend the Sorbonne as a student and—'

'The sore what?' Spud interrupted.

An embarrassed pause. 'It's a French university. In Paris,' Buckingham said. 'I studied Arabic and Political Theory there. So did Sorgen, Asu's brother. We became friends. I think I can persuade him to build bridges with his brother.'

'What, just like that?' Greg sounded deeply sceptical.

'We *are* approaching the festival of Eid al-Fitr,' Buckingham said, as if that explained everything. He was met by a line of blank faces that clearly told him that it didn't. 'It's a very important Muslim holiday. It marks the end of Ramadan, the holy month of fasting. It's a time of unity, when families come together to feast and pray. Sorgen is a devout man. I think I can convince him that this is a good time for him to open up communications with Asu.'

'Which would be a win-win situation,' Carrington said. 'The rebels are far stronger united than they are divided. And if Hugo can persuade Sorgen of the British government's good intentions towards him, the endgame would be most favourable.' Another smile. 'Your role, gentlemen, is to look after Mr Buckingham on the ground. Make sure he gets to where he needs to be, safely and secretly. I'm sure I don't need to impress upon you the covert nature of this operation. If you're located, the British government will deny all knowledge of your presence in the region. The British Embassy in Damascus has been abandoned. In its absence, the Czech

Embassy might – *might* – offer you assistance if it comes to it, but you certainly shouldn't rely on that. Each one of you has been vetted at the highest level. It seems we can trust you all, and by God we'll need to.' He looked at each of the four in turn. 'The Middle East is changing,' he said. 'The Arab Spring has seen the old regimes swept away. We may not have liked them, but at least we *knew* them. Now we find ourselves in the unenviable position of having to rebuild our networks across the region. Hugo has important work to do, gentlemen. Don't let him down.'

Carrington stood up and looked over at Cartwright. 'I believe that's all you need from me, Johnny?'

The CO nodded.

'Come along then, Hugo,' Carrington said, almost as if he were talking to a dog. 'Let's leave our friends to their preparations.' Without another word, he turned on his heel and made for the door. Buckingham lingered. He still appeared embarrassed by his boss's manner, and for a moment looked as though he was going apologise for it. His eyes caught Danny's, who nodded at him. As Carrington exited, Buckingham offered Danny his hand. 'I'm very grateful,' he said. 'I do understand that I'm being chaperoned by the very best. I hope I won't be too much of a hindrance.'

Danny shook his hand. 'No worries, mate.'

Buckingham nodded respectfully, then plunged his hands into his pockets and followed Carrington at something resembling a trot.

As soon as the door was closed, Spud let out an explosion of breath. 'Fucking hell, boss,' he said. 'Couldn't they send in someone with a bit more backbone? That Buckingham looked like he'd brown his trousers if you told him boo.'

Cartwright seemed as if he was about to agree, but kept his opinion to himself. 'You'll forward mount from the eastern Mediterranean,' he said. 'Full briefing when we get to Hereford.'

He checked his watch. 'There'll be a van outside. I'll meet you there. Black, stay behind a minute.'

The other three left the Portakabin.

The CO surveyed Danny for a moment, as if weighing up his options. 'I'm assigning you unit leader,' he said.

Danny blinked. This was unusual. The other three were a good five or six years older. More experienced. Ordinarily the role would have fallen to one of them. Cartwright clearly saw the surprise on Danny's face. 'I heard about what happened in Libya,' he said. 'Sounds like those UN fellas have a lot to thank you for. I think you're ready for a bit more responsibility.'

'Yes, boss.'

Cartwright sniffed. 'Your brother got parole,' he said. 'He's been out about a week.'

Danny felt his jaw clenching. 'My dad know?'

The CO nodded.

'Shit!' Danny thumped one of the plastic chairs and sent it clattering across the floor. Then he turned back to his commanding officer. 'Boss, I need some time. Someone else can babysit the spook. They don't need me.'

'No can do, Black. I'm sorry.'

'Boss, I—'

'It's an order, Black. You insert from Brize Norton at 12.00 hrs tomorrow. There's time between this afternoon's briefing and then to sort out any personal affairs.' He approached Danny and handed him a slip of paper with a Hereford address written on it. 'Your brother's staying here,' he said. 'Do what you need to do.'

Danny took a deep breath, then nodded and stowed the slip of paper in his pocket. 'Thank you,' he murmured. He glanced over towards the door. 'Boss?'

'Yeah?'

'This is a straightforward op. They could have given it to anybody. What's all this personal-vetting shite about? Why drag me all the way from Malta when Hereford's full of men who could take my place?'

Cartwright didn't say anything, but the look that crossed his face spoke plainly: the same question had occurred to him, and he didn't know the answer either. 'Just do the job,' he said tersely, 'and get the hell out of there as quickly as you can. Got it? Syria's a dog's dinner. If it was up to me we'd leave the fuckers to it.'

'Aye,' Danny said. 'Roger that.' And with an uneasy feeling creeping through his veins, he and the CO stepped out of the Portakabin. Snow Patrol had fallen silent. The radio was off. The mechanic was leaning against a Mini with a cigarette in his hand, watching them quietly. As they approached the door, he started to whistle.

Danny stopped. He recognised the song. It was the same one that Boydie had been whistling in the OP.

'What *is* that?' he said.

The CO gave him an impatient look. 'What is this? *Name That Fucking Tune*? Get a move on, Black.'

Danny nodded. 'Yes, boss,' he said.

They joined the others outside, where an unmarked white Transit van was waiting to transport them all to Hereford.

SIX

Hereford. 15.00 hrs.

They call it the Kremlin, because that's where all the secrets are. This secure network of corridors, deep inside Regimental headquarters, was where the unit's briefing took place. The briefing room was two doors along from the records room and bang opposite the CO's office. With a lectern and whiteboard screen at the front, and curved seating for the men, it resembled a modern university lecture hall, with one exception. The walls were so thickly soundproofed that any noise in here was immediately deadened. In that respect it was more like a sound studio, and it served as a constant reminder that whatever was spoken within these four walls was not to be repeated beyond them.

The briefing room was easily big enough for an entire squadron to sit and receive their orders. Right now there were just four men: Danny and his unit. Spud was regaling them with the story of his conquest of an American intelligence officer at Kandahar airbase. 'Cheeky cow said if I shaved off my beard and cut my hair, I wouldn't be bad-looking.' He pretended to sound outraged. 'So *I* said that if I shaved off my beard and cut my hair, I wouldn't be talking to her, I'd be talking to her fit mates.'

'You're a smooth-talking fucker, Spud,' Jack observed.

Spud shrugged. 'Not my best ever chat-up line, but it worked.' A confused look crossed his face. 'Mind you, she *was* a fucking munter, and they let themselves go in theatre, don't they? This one had a minge like Terry Waite's allotment.'

The guys laughed, but Spud was only just warming to his subject. 'Looked a lot better with her arse in the air!' he announced, just as the door opened and Major Ray Hammond, the Regiment's ops officer, walked in. The laughter instantly died away.

Major Hammond always had rings under his eyes and a slightly hangdog expression. It was well known in the Regiment that the more pronounced those rings, the shorter his temper. This afternoon they looked like they'd been painted on with boot polish. He walked up to the lectern, opened his laptop, plugged in a couple of jacks, then browsed through a sheaf of papers without looking up. The unit remained silent while Hammond organised his thoughts, tapped his papers into order on the table and cleared his throat.

'Patrol call sign Kilo Alpha Six Four,' the ops officer announced. 'You insert by sea.' He looked round the room with his chin slightly jutting out, as if daring any of the men to contradict him.

'We could get closer to Homs by air,' Jack Ward suggested.

Hammond shook his head. 'It would mean a HALO, and we're not about to stick this Buckingham character on a tandem with one of you lot. He'd shit himself before he even left the ground.'

'Fucker needs to grow a pair,' Spud observed. Even the ops officer smiled. Danny kept quiet. The bloke seemed OK to him, and if he was prepared to put himself in harm's way to serve his country, then he deserved some respect. And in any case, on the ground their little company needed to be on good terms with each other. What they said in front of the ops officer wasn't Danny's business. What they said in front of Danny once the operation had begun was. For the next few days Hugo Buckingham would be one of them.

'In any case,' Hammond was saying, 'the airspace above Syria is too crowded for an airborne insertion. And obviously it'll be no good simply flying into Damascus on a commercial flight. The spook needs to go in under the radar and it's like Checkpoint fucking Charlie there at the moment. And you don't want to be screwing around with border crossings from Lebanon.' He flicked a couple of switches on the lectern. The lights dimmed. Hammond turned and indicated a map of the region that was projected on to the wall by an OHP connected to his laptop. With one finger he traced Syria's western border with the Mediterranean. 'This coastline is porous,' he said. 'You should be able to insert without difficulty.'

'As the actress said to the bishop,' Spud muttered. Hammond tapped a key on the laptop and the image changed. A man's face appeared. Dark skin, black beard tinged with grey, a hooked nose. 'This is your fixer,' the ops officer said. 'Called Muhammad, surprise surprise. The Firm have had him on the payroll for the past six months. He'll supply you with two vehicles and enough fuel to get you in and around Homs and back again. The road from the coast to the city is about a hundred klicks. Our intelligence tells us that there are two army checkpoints along the way, but they tend not to be manned during the hours of darkness.' Hammond sniffed. 'Government troops manning them are probably too busy killing and looting. Anyway, if you don't run into any difficulties, you should reach the city in a couple of hours.'

'And if we *do* run into difficulties?' Greg asked.

The ops officer gave him a flat-eyed stare. 'Deal with them,' he said. 'Once you've entered the city, you'll need to make contact with the private sector guys. Black, you have an RV with Max Saunders, the MD of International Solutions, tomorrow at 10.00 hrs in London.'

'What for?'

'He's insisting on meeting the patrol leader. Shake your hand, look you in the eye, the usual bullshit.' A frown crossed the ops officer's face. 'Saunders is ex-Regiment. Slippery piece of shit, so mind your Ps and Qs. Just smile sweetly and don't give him cause to worry. Once you've had the meet, a car will take you to Brize Norton for 14.00 hrs. The rest of you will be bussed there from HQ at the same time, and you'll RV with Buckingham at the airport. You fly at 16.00 hrs. ETA Larnaca, Cyprus, 20.30 hrs local time. You'll be met by a Sergeant Wilkinson, who'll take you down to the port. There'll be a detachment of 42 Commando waiting with a Rigid Raider to transport you to submarine HMS *Vanguard*. You'll surface approximately two miles offshore and your Marines will escort you by RIB to your insertion point: latitude 34.705. Any questions?'

'How long are we expected to be on the ground?' asked Jack.

'Five days, max. If you need rations beyond that, the PMCs will sort you out. We've no reason to believe the Syrian authorities know you're coming, but be aware that the Russians have a vested interest in maintaining the status quo in Syria. They're backing the current administration, so it wouldn't be a surprise if they have men on the ground.'

'Spetznaz?' Danny asked.

'Probably. What we do know is it's a fucking mosh pit out there and a few more dead bodies won't even come up on the statistics. The Firm want this Buckingham fella back in one piece. Make sure they're not disappointed.' Hammond turned to Danny. 'The boss told me you've got something to sort out.' Was it Danny's imagination, or had the rings under his eyes just grown a little darker?

Danny nodded.

'Then get a move on. I want you back here to go through the mapping and predicted weather conditions at 21.00 hrs. Understood?'

'Understood.'

The slip of paper Danny's CO had handed to him gave the address of a B&B on Whitecross Road in the west of Hereford. Grandly, it called itself the Greenacres Hotel, but it wasn't the kind of place anybody would want to stay for long. Yellowed net curtains obscured all the windows of the mid-terrace house. The paintwork was peeling. A sign on the door announced that there were vacancies. Danny suspected there always were.

He rang the doorbell. No answer. He clenched his fist and hammered on the door, making it rattle in its frame. Thirty seconds later he heard the sound of a man cursing from inside. The door opened. An overweight guy in a gravy-spotted vest appeared. He squinted suspiciously at Danny.

'Evening, pal,' Danny said. 'You got a Kyle Black staying?'

The landlord appeared to consider this for a moment, then grunted, turned and, wheezing, led Danny into the hallway. 'I'll call him.'

'Don't worry, mate. He's expecting me. What room was it again?'

No hint of suspicion in the landlord's eyes now. 'Room 3. Upstairs.'

Danny heard Room 3 before he saw it. The TV was on and the opening music of *Strictly Come Dancing* seeped out on to the landing. The room itself was the second on the right, opposite a communal bathroom, with the door ajar, that needed cleaning. Danny didn't bother to knock. He simply walked right in.

Kyle was lying on the bed, propped up by pillows, drinking whisky from a toothbrush glass. There was a half-empty bottle of Famous Grouse on his bedside table and his eyes were glazed as he stared at the television. Danny stood by the closed door for a full ten seconds before his brother turned his head. He had the uncanny sensation of looking at an older version of himself. Kyle wore an unkempt beard that was going prematurely grey. His reddish-blond hair was longer than Danny's, but thinning at the crown. His face was more lined than a twenty-eight-year-old's ought to be.

Kyle sneered. 'I'm a bit upset you didn't fast-rope through the window. That's what you twats like doing, right?'

Danny ignored the slurred insult. He walked round to the other side of the bed, intending to take the whisky and empty it down the sink in the bathroom. At the last minute, Kyle realised what he was trying to do. A look of panic crossed his drunken face. He clumsily tried to grab the bottle, but knocked it over. The whisky glugged out on to the carpet.

'Fucking *hell*!' Kyle said. He set the bottle upright, but it was empty now.

'You smell like a tramp,' Danny told him.

Kyle shrugged and took a swig from the glass. There was something about the arrogant nonchalance in his expression that filled Danny with a sudden rage. He leaned over and grabbed Kyle by his sweat-stained T-shirt, which ripped slightly as he pulled his brother towards him. 'I have to leave the country,' he growled. 'If I hear that you've so much as laid a finger on Dad when I come back, I swear to God *you'll* be needing a wheelchair too, and *I'll* be the one doing time.'

Kyle made no attempt to fight. His body was floppy as Danny threw him back on to the bed. Danny had said all he'd come to say. He made for the door.

'I already went to the house,' Kyle mumbled just as Danny's hand touched the handle.

Danny turned. Kyle's face had lost none of its drunken arrogance. 'Surprised, little bro? Surprised that I talked to the old cunt without your permission?' He snorted dismissively. 'Don't worry, we kissed and made up. The prod . . . progid . . .' He tried three times to say the word 'prodigal', then gave up. 'You want to know what he told me?' he said suddenly, hoisting himself to his feet. He staggered unsteadily towards Danny.

'You're arseholed, Kyle. Why don't you just keep your pie-hole shut?'

'He told me sometimes he thought you were more like Taff's son than his.'

Something snapped. Danny shoved his brother against the wall behind the bed. Their eyes met, but even though Danny had the better of him, Kyle clearly knew he wouldn't do him any real damage. 'Stay away from him,' Danny rasped. As he said it, he felt his fist clenching the scruff of Kyle's shirt tighter, constricting his neck. Kyle's eyes bulged slightly, and for a moment he looked a little less sure of himself.

Get a grip, Danny told himself. He forced his anger to dissolve, relaxed his arms and let go of Kyle, who started to cough. There was a banging on the door, and a wheezy voice demanded to know what the hell was going on. Danny stormed out of the room, pushed past the landlord, then hurried down the stairs and out into the street, slamming the front door behind him.

He was out of breath, adrenalin throbbing, his head full of a hundred things he wanted to shout at his brother. He slammed a heavy fist against a postbox, then stalked fifty metres back down the road to where he had parked his BMW motorbike. The tyres screeched angrily as he burned off towards the centre of Hereford.

He had to be back at base. There was kit to sort out. Preparations to be made. But after driving for five minutes he stopped pretending to himself that he was heading to RAF Credenhill. And five minutes after that, he pulled up outside the tiny brick bungalow that he and Kyle had called home all their life. It stood in the heart of a housing estate in the Redhill area of Hereford that looked more run-down every time Danny saw it. It was surrounded by a wooden fence whose uprights were so rotten that it was only half standing. The tiny garden was overgrown. His father didn't have the money, or enough pride in his surroundings, to pay anyone to sort it out for him, and there was no way he could do it himself. In the road outside, a group of six kids – four guys, two girls, all about eighteen – were sitting on the kerb sharing a spliff. Faces pierced, arms inked up, tinny R&B blaring from a smartphone. They looked at Danny with wary expressions. He might not have been around for six months, but his reputation still stood up around here. At a jerk of his thumb, the kids silently stood up and slunk away.

Danny looked at the bungalow. Cream render stained by years of rain. Double glazing that had only been installed three years ago, because the council offered to pay for it. Cheaper to keep Dad in his own home than pay for sheltered accommodation. Not that Simon Black would ever accept that.

The very sight of the place gave Danny the same claustrophobic feeling that had been his constant companion when he was growing up. All he'd ever wanted to do was get out into the countryside. Track animals. Build fires. Sleep out. His father was stubborn. He insisted that his disability wasn't going to stop him leading a normal life. In reality Danny had learned from a very young age to always keep an eye on him in case he overstretched himself and fell out of his wheelchair, or worse. And, of course, his dad could never take him out into the fields and forests.

That had been left to Taff.

His dad's oldest friend visited whenever he could. It was the reason they'd moved from Newcastle to Hereford in the first place, or so Danny had always been told. Taff hadn't served with the Regiment for years, but his roots were here. Whenever he returned from one of his unexplained excursions abroad, this little bungalow would be his first port of call. Danny looked forward to those visits more than anything else. While Kyle skulked in the corner, Taff had filled Danny's head with stories of far-off places: central Africa, South America, the Middle and Far East. He'd taken him out and shown him how to build shelters, how to find his way and live off the land.

Once, they'd caught trout in the river using homemade hooks, then built a fire and cooked their catch. Another time they had stalked a deer, after going out before dawn and building a screen of fallen tree limbs from behind which to observe it. 'Remember today,' Taff had said as they crouched motionless behind that makeshift OP waiting for their quarry. 'There might come times in your life when you have to hide. If you can't hide, then run. And if you can't run' – he'd given Danny a piercing look – 'then fight.' When the deer had arrived, he had let Danny make the kill with his hunting rifle. A direct hit that Danny had put down to beginner's luck but which Taff had read more into. 'It'll be the Regiment for you, kiddo,' he'd said that day. 'You've got the hunger for it.'

And now Danny remembered what Kyle had said. 'Sometimes he thought you were more like Taff's son than his.' There was truth in that, he realised. A lot of truth.

He stepped up to the bungalow, but didn't knock on the door. Instead he went round to the side, where a window looked into the tiny front room. Danny could see his father in his wheelchair, back to the window, in front of the TV. To his right there was a small coffee table with a mug of tea. Danny could just see the steam rising from it. The TV showed some chiselled twat with high cheekbones and a spangly suit ballroom dancing with a girl dressed up like a peacock. Same thing Kyle had been watching. But Simon Black wasn't watching them. His head was slumped. He was clearly asleep.

Danny stood there for five minutes. Not moving. Just watching. Then he turned away and walked back to his motorbike. He had no desire to disturb his father. He'd checked that the old boy was OK, and that was all that mattered.

SEVEN

At 08.45 hrs the following morning, Danny was back in London. An MoD driver had dropped him at the corner of Jermyn Street and Haymarket. He'd walked along Jermyn Street and left into St James's Square, where he'd lingered for two minutes, taking everything in. Three attractive young women sat gossiping on the steps of the London Library, piles of books in their arms, casting occasional glances in his direction. Outside the East India Club, a man in a business suit climbed into a black cab. Danny walked anticlockwise round the square, and now he was standing outside one of the tall terraced houses on the south side, looking up at the imposing architecture of number 36. Black railings. Burgundy door with a black knocker in the shape of a lion's head – clearly decorative because to the right of the door was a state-of-the-art video intercom. Danny's practised eye immediately picked out a further camera, fitted to the corner of a first-floor window and angled down on to the pavement. He cheekily inclined his head at whoever was watching him on the CCTV, then approached the door. It had a burnished brass plaque on it, engraved with the words 'International Solutions Ltd'. Beneath the company name was a logo: two hands, shaking each other in a gesture of solidarity. Danny pressed the button on the intercom. A ten-second pause, and then a female voice. 'Good morning?'

'I'm here to see Max Saunders.'

'Your name, please?'

'He's expecting me.'

Another pause, and then a low hum and the door clicked open.

The offices of International Solutions were extremely plush. The reception room in which Danny found himself had a thick carpet and art on the walls. Along the left-hand side there was a large, comfortable sofa with curved wooden feet. As Danny closed the door behind him, a young woman in an elegant business suit walked in from another room at the far end. Her blonde hair was immaculately cut and straightened and her glasses looked like a fashion accessory rather than a necessity. She was about Danny's age, and walked like she would be more at home on the catwalk than here. 'Max will be with you any moment,' she said. 'Can I get you something? Coffee? Guatemalan or Colombian? Mineral water?'

'Mug of PG?' Danny suggested. 'Three sugars?'

The PA gave him a forced, thin-lipped smile. 'I can offer you Earl Grey, Assam or Lapsang Sou—'

'I'm fine, love.' Danny pointed at the sofa. 'Shall I wait here?'

'Come on through, come on through!' A new voice, male. Danny looked past the PA to see a man walking into the reception room.

Max Saunders couldn't have been taller than five foot eight, but Danny didn't let that fool him. He was a tough, wiry little guy. Although he was probably in his late forties, he clearly still kept in shape. His greying, curly hair was slicked back with gel, and he wore little round glasses propped halfway down his nose. 'Has Anastasia offered you coffee? We've got some bloody good Guatemalan stuff.' Without waiting for a reply, he strode up to Danny and shook his hand firmly. 'Max Saunders. You must be Black. Come on through.'

Danny winked at the ice queen, then followed Saunders into the room beyond and up an impressive wooden staircase.

'Bit uptight, young Anastasia,' Saunders said in a conspiratorial tone of voice as they walked up to the next floor. 'Fucking terrible secretary, but she's got a pair of titties on her like a couple of Zeppelins. Defy gravity. They should give them the once-over at CERN, see what's going on.'

The thought of Saunders' personal assistant giving this self-important little Rupert a happy ending wasn't one Danny wanted to linger on. 'Nice gaff,' he said, to change the subject.

'Comes a time in a man's life,' Saunders said, 'when he needs more than a wet tarp and a plastic bag to shit in. I did my time in Hereford, you know.'

'Yeah, I heard,' Danny replied. In fact, he'd heard a lot more. Saunders' name was well known back at HQ. He'd started International Solutions fifteen years ago. Nice little business model: let the Regiment spend hundreds of thousands training up the most ruthless fighting force in the world and then, when they get too old, or too sick of risking their neck for a pittance in the bank account at the end of the month, Saunders would welcome them with open arms. Danny knew full well that half the Regiment were banking on two pensions: the one they'd get from the government, and the one they'd get from Max Saunders. Recently he'd taken things a step further. The Regiment's L Detachment had taken to welcoming some of Saunders' personnel on training exercises on the Brecon Beacons. It meant they were fully up to date with all the latest technology, and their skills were kept razor-sharp. They were SAS in all but name. Convenient for the British government, who could swear blind they had no troops in a particular territory, when in fact they'd just contracted the job out to Saunders. And Saunders himself was a Rupert to the tips of his toes – while his men were on the ground, bodyguarding greedy businessmen in God knows what hellholes around the world, he was happy to stay in the comfort of his fancy London offices, growing fat off the profits.

'Course, back in my day we were having a crack at the Mick,' Saunders was saying as he showed Danny into his personal office. 'Bloody dirty little war that. Who's your OC?'

'Major Anderson.'

'Eddie?' Saunders said with delight. 'I knew him when he was in the Guards. Bloody good soldier. Give him my regards, won't you?'

Saunders' office was more like a trophy room. The walls were panelled with oak, and his vast wooden desk was covered with trinkets: ivory statues, wooden carvings, an elaborate gold hookah. This was clearly the room of a well-travelled man, or at least of a man who wanted to give that impression. Hanging on the wall behind the desk was an enormously blown-up image of a stretch of coastline, deep sea to the left, highly forested land to the right.

'Scene of one of my greatest triumphs,' Saunders said as he noticed Danny looking at it. 'Angola, '98. The government – democratically elected, mind you – was having a spot of bother with rebel militia. Claimed to have political motives but the reality was that they were raping and looting – the usual. Government couldn't cope, so they brought us in to help out.' He smiled at the memory. 'The rebels used to move their troops at night. Couldn't work out how it was that we always knew where they were. In the end they put it down to witchcraft. Thought we were communing with the great Ju-Ju up the mountain. Surrendered en masse.'

'And really?'

'Really, I'd bought a couple of old Russian MiGs on the black market and fitted the pilots out with NV. We were just watching the silly sods from air. Easiest five mill I ever made. Do have a seat.'

He showed Danny to an expensive-looking leather armchair, and took a seat opposite him. Between them was a scale model of a yacht, its prow white and sleek. 'Having it built,' Saunders said without any trace of self-consciousness. 'Man's got to have a hobby, eh?' He removed his glasses, looked through them at arm's length, then replaced them. 'So. Syria.'

'Syria,' Danny repeated.

'Absolute bloody shit sandwich,' Saunders said. 'We can always trust the ragheads to screw things up for themselves, eh?'

Danny didn't offer an opinion.

'How are you inserting. Air?'

Saunders dropped the question in with a forced nonchalance. When Danny didn't reply, he seemed far from embarrassed. On the contrary, he looked rather pleased, almost as if Danny had passed some kind of test. 'You'll have sat phones with you, I assume?'

Danny nodded.

'Good.' Saunders stood up and walked over to his desk. From a drawer he took a sheet of A4 letterhead, which he handed to Danny. At the top it said 'International Solutions', below which was the same motif of shaking hands Danny had noticed on the front door. At the bottom, in much smaller writing, was a list of five names: the International Solutions board. Danny picked out Saunders' name, and two others he recognised: Meryl Jackson and Bob Goodenough. One was a Labour MP, the other a Tory. Danny realised at once that, with board members sitting on both sides of the political divide, Saunders had a conduit to most of the decision-making going on in Whitehall. Useful, when you earn your money out of international conflict.

The rest of the sheet was empty apart from a twelve-digit telephone number. 'Call that number when you get to Homs,' said Saunders. 'My men will arrange an RV.'

'I'll need their names,' Danny said. 'And *I'll* decide the RV location.'

'Interesting idea,' Saunders murmured. 'But on balance I think not.' Danny was about to retort when Saunders held up one finger to stop him. When he spoke again, there was a little more gravitas to his voice, as though he had slipped back into his former role as a Regimental Rupert. 'Don't underestimate the state on the ground there, Black. It's every bit as volatile as Iraq was a couple of years ago. You've every chance of being compromised before you even reach Homs and I've no intention of risking my men's lives just because you get their names and location belted out of you.' He removed his glasses again and squinted at Danny. 'Loose lips sink ships, I'm sure you understand,' he added, his voice returning to its normal avuncular self.

Danny kept quiet, but if Saunders felt at all uneasy with the sudden silence he didn't show it. 'A word to the wise,' he said. 'I've got a bloody good team of lads out there. Can't imagine they'll be thrilled at the prospect of a spook turning up to mark their work, if you know what I mean.'

'That's between you and the Firm,' Danny said.

'Indeed it is. Just don't expect them to be rolling out the red carpet is all. Anyway, Black, bloody good to meet you. We should stay in touch. I'm always on the lookout for good men, so if the joys of Hereford ever start to lose their lustre, you know where to come. Money's not quite what it was in the glory days of Blackwater, but there's always work. Governments both side of the pond can't operate in the Middle East without us. They make cuts to the armed forces then find themselves freelancing the work out at twice the price. Can't see the sense in it myself, but I'm not complaining. And there's always the chance to earn a little extra while you're out there.'

'What do you mean, extra?'

Saunders smiled, and looked at Danny as if he was trying to work out if he was joking or not. But he didn't answer the question, and instead politely indicated the door with an outstretched palm. Danny took the hint and stood up. 'Bloody good to meet you,' Saunders repeated as he shook Danny's hand firmly, though perhaps this time he sounded a little less enthusiastic. Danny didn't return the compliment – no good lying when you don't have to, he thought as he walked to the door.

Downstairs, the PA was waiting for him rather primly. 'Leaving us so soon?' she asked, her lips pursed slightly with satisfaction.

'Aye,' Danny said. 'Wouldn't want to keep you from your sugar daddy.' The young woman's eyes narrowed at the insult. 'I'll let myself out, love,' Danny added.

Out on the street, the Land Cruiser was waiting for him. He opened the rear door of the vehicle and was about to climb inside when he looked over his shoulder up at the first-floor window. The morning sun was reflecting off the glass, but he could just see the ghost of a figure, looking down at him. Watching.

Then Max Saunders disappeared and Danny got into the vehicle.

'Brize Norton?' the driver asked.

'Brize Norton,' Danny replied.

Heading to Brize Norton was like heading home. Danny had learned static line and freefall here at No. 1 Parachute Training School, and he'd lost count of the times he'd boarded a Hercules or a Globemaster on his way to whichever part of the world the Regiment needed him. The airbase was as busy today as he'd ever seen it. As his driver pulled up outside the terminal building, it was immediately clear that his arrival had coincided with a major troop movement. There were at least a hundred green army lads, with full packs and military uniform, milling around outside, some having a fag, most simply getting a few good lungfuls of Oxfordshire air before a dirty old TriStar with its best years behind it transported them to Camp Bastion. Danny respected every one of them: the older lags with their slightly grizzled faces and the new recruits who walked with a swagger but couldn't hide the anxiety in their eyes. They had reason to feel it. If Afghanistan was their destination, there wasn't a single man who, over the next six months, wouldn't find himself in a contact that even the most hardened Regiment soldier would go out of his way to avoid. Soldiering had changed. The days of serving your time without ever firing a weapon in anger were long gone. Danny found himself picking out faces in the crowd, wondering if he was looking at the one or two who would almost certainly not make it back to British soil.

An anonymous white Transit pulled up behind them. Danny instantly knew that this would be the rest of his unit. As he climbed out of the Land Cruiser, Jack Ward, Greg Murray and Spud Glover debussed. Like Danny, they all wore civvies, but while this would ordinarily make them blend into the background, at Brize Norton it made them stand out. They approached the terminal building to the stares of some of the green army lads, while the Transit slipped away to load all their gear on the SF flight that would take them to Cyprus, without having to go through the usual security checks. They might have packed their bags themselves, but they sure as hell contained some offensive weapons that would make the average airport security officer shit himself.

The inside of the terminal building was even busier than the outside. Queues of young guys in camouflage gear snaked from the check-in desks, and the air smelled of fast food. It was noisy too, as young squaddies shouted good-natured army banter at each other and the Tannoy announced flight times and security warnings. 'How was Saunders?' Greg asked as they stepped inside the terminal.

'Like a cat with a strawberry-flavoured arse,' Danny replied, his attention elsewhere. The unit stopped by the main entrance and looked around.

It was Spud Glover who saw Buckingham first. 'What the . . . ?' he said, pointing to a figure standing thirty metres away underneath a yellow gate sign. 'Twat looks like Michael fucking Palin.'

Danny couldn't help a smile. Hugo Buckingham was dressed to travel, but he looked more like he was planning a jaunt to the Tuscan hills than a covert insertion into a war zone. He wore a white-brimmed Panama hat with a black band, a lightweight linen jacket, and at his feet stood a small suitcase. He stuck out like a turd at a picnic.

'Leave him to me,' Danny said quietly. 'Go and check in. I'll see you at the gate.'

As he walked up to Buckingham, Danny could see he was a bit flustered. When a voice from somewhere on the concourse shouted, 'EasyJet don't fly from here, mate!', the MI6 man's forehead creased as he pretended he hadn't heard. He didn't appear to notice Danny until he was standing a metre from him. A look of relief crossed his face.

'Nice hat,' Danny said.

Buckingham's eyes rolled upwards to the hat's brim. He removed it and, at a prompt from Danny, handed it over. Danny crumpled it up.

For a moment, Buckingham looked angry. Here was a man whose emotions showed plainly on his face. 'Wrong get-up?' he asked.

'You could say that.'

'I'm in your hands, of course. Only ever been to Syria on embassy business. Spot of Britishness goes a long way when you're dealing with the ambassador in Damascus . . .' He looked down at his suitcase. 'I've only got the one bag,' he said. For the briefest of moments he seemed to expect Danny to carry it, but when the SAS man didn't move he picked up the case himself. Danny pointed towards the check-in desk where the other three were waiting. As Buckingham walked in that direction, Danny dropped the scrunched-up hat on the concourse floor and followed him.

'Packed your cozzie?' Spud said as they approached. There was a slightly malicious glint in his eye, and Buckingham flushed from the neck upwards.

'Leave it,' Danny said. Spud grinned at his colleagues, but let it drop for now.

Buckingham's British passport was housed in an immaculate leather case which he handed to the RAF soldier at the check-in desk before answering the routine questions. The Regiment guys flashed their military IDs – name, photograph, blood group, religion – before being waved through to the departure lounge. Jack Ward fetched them all a cup of tasteless coffee from a machine and they settled down to wait for the moment when an RAF guy would come up to them and quietly lead them to their flight. Danny could tell that Spud had one on him. He couldn't take his eyes off Buckingham's linen jacket, and Danny could almost hear the gears in his head grinding as he worked out his next sarky comment.

'So Hugo, old boy,' Spud said finally, affecting a posh accent. 'Looking forward to a spot of sightseeing?'

Danny was about to step in, to stick up for Buckingham, who was, after all, going to be their companion for the next few days. But the MI6 man held up one hand to stop him, then turned to address Spud directly.

'Syria,' he said in a quiet voice. 'Population twenty-five million. Estimated number of internally displaced people, one point five million. Estimated number of civil-war-related deaths since the beginning of the conflict, somewhere between thirty and fifty thousand, including approximately three thousand children. Current estimate of detainees and political prisoners killed under torture, about six hundred. If you imagine, Glover, that I don't understand that we're about to travel to one of the most danger-ous parts of the world right now, let me assure you that I do. I don't have your advantages and I don't have your skills. Frankly, I'm bloody terrified, and I'll thank you not to make it any worse.'

Silence.

'I don't know why you do this job,' Buckingham continued. 'See the world? Taste for adventure? That's what soldiers usually say, isn't it? Maybe you just like killing people, I don't know. But I'd like to imagine that somewhere deep down you have a bit of loyalty to your country, and you think it's worth fighting for. I do. I entered the foreign service because I wanted to serve my country. That's what this is all about. If it means putting myself in harm's way, so be it. I don't like it, but I'll do it because, surprising though it may seem, I'm the best man for this job. I'm an Arabist and a diplomat, not a soldier. I know perfectly well that I can't do it without your help, I'm grateful to you for helping me and helping your country. But if it's all the same to you, I could do without the inverse snobbery and sarcastic comments. This isn't the school playground, and I have a feeling the next few days are going to be hard enough as it is.'

There was another moment of silence as Buckingham looked at each of the Regiment men in turn. Spud's face was unreadable. He put his coffee cup on the floor, wiped the palm of his hand on his jeans, then offered it to Buckingham. The two men shook hands. 'Thank you,' said Buckingham.

Danny could sense the men looking at the civilian with respect. In their world, standing up for yourself counted for something.

It was just as Buckingham took back his hand that the same uniformed RAF man who had checked them in approached the group. 'Time to board, gentlemen,' he said.

Buckingham was the first to stand. He removed his linen jacket, crumpled it up and threw it back down on his seat. 'Present from my mum,' he said with a grimace. 'Always hated the bloody thing. Don't know why I wear it really. Shall we go? I'm not much good with planes and waiting around makes me jolly nervous.'

EIGHT

Homs, Syria.

It was the children who made it so difficult, Clara Macleod decided. Children she would remember as long as she lived.

She was a qualified doctor. A few months of working with Médecins Sans Frontières had knocked any squeamishness out of her that still remained after five years of medical school. She had witnessed field amputations without anaesthetic. She'd held the hand of an elderly grandmother while she bled copiously to death. When she had come across a man with a split stomach, she had gently reinserted his bulging, sponge-like intestines and come away thinking he might even live. But it didn't matter how hardened you were to the sights and sounds of the Third World, or the grotesque horrors of a war zone, you never got used to the suffering of children.

Like the child in front of her now.

Clara didn't know the little girl's name. She couldn't speak. Death was so close. Clara could do nothing but make sure that the end of the child's life was as comfortable as possible.

She brushed her blonde hair off her forehead and looked around her. Nobody would ever guess that this was once a hospital. A makeshift, cobbled-together field hospital, but a hospital all the same. Now it was a bomb site. The exterior walls had crumpled into rubble. Supporting columns just about held up the ceiling, but these too were badly damaged. The breeze-blocks from which they were constructed were cracked and bare and, like everything else that remained of this building, they were streaked with soot. Inside, the open shelves that once carried scant medical supplies – now plundered – were hanging from the cracked walls at an angle. Every so often there was an ominous groan from above and the ceiling was distinctly bowed. The cautious part of Clara told her she should get out before the columns themselves collapsed. But this little girl couldn't be moved, and she didn't have the heart to leave her.

The fire damage made the whole place stink. Steel reinforcing rods jutted out of the floor, rusting and dangerous. And because the walls were no longer standing, Clara could see outside. There was blood on the road. Somebody had tried to wash it away with a hose and it had pooled in the shallow craters caused by the recent bombardment. Great puddles of pale pink liquid. The few shell-shocked locals who had remained in the area stepped around them without so much as a glance. Maybe they were used to sights like this. More likely, with the death of their loved ones and the destruction of their homes, they had other things on their minds.

The little girl groaned and Clara snapped her attention back to her. She was lying on the hard floor – there was no other place to put her – with Clara's MSF jacket as a makeshift pillow. She had a bandage round her head – not sterilised, barely even clean. It was the best Clara could find, but the wound on the child's head required more than a thin strip of gauze. It was already saturated with blood. Sodden. Clara squeezed the girl's hand. Whoever had been caring for her previously had inserted a cannula into the skin, but Clara hadn't been able to find any saline bags among the rubble to attach to it. The pouch of medical supplies that she had slung over her shoulder contained a couple of morphine shots, but there was no point administering them. The child was unconscious and unable to feel pain, and Clara knew she might need those shots later. In the absence of anything else, perhaps she could offer a little comfort.

About fifteen metres away, in one corner of this demolished room, Clara's boyfriend Bradley was hunched over four more figures. They were not moving. Bradley was a lanky Australian with a goatee beard and a ponytail. He looked more like a surfer bum than a doctor – the kind of guy Clara's parents would never have approved of. Not that they approved of much in her life. In her more self-aware moments she admitted to herself that this was the driving force behind much that she did. She was, as her father had once called her, a stubborn little madam. Before she left for Syria he had pressed a cheap, gold-plated wedding band on her. He'd read somewhere that female Western journalists always wore one when they were reporting from the Middle East. It was a way of attracting less attention. She'd given her dad a withering look and told him that the world wasn't really full of his stereotypes. Besides, rings harboured germs. Medics never wore them when they were working.

She and Bradley had watched the bombardment of this part of Homs from the Médecins Sans Frontières camp to the east of the city. As the aircraft dropped their ordnance indiscriminately over the area where they were now, Clara had wondered out loud if it really was a rebel stronghold, as the government forces carrying out the raid would undoubtedly claim, or just an ordinary part of an ordinary town populated by ordinary people.

'No way to know,' Bradley had said. 'Anyway, we've got enough patients here to keep our hands full.'

Bradley was right: their resources were limited and they already had more patients than they could adequately care for. But still, he'd gone down in her estimation a little when he'd said that. At sunrise, Clara had announced that she was going to take a vehicle and some medical supplies into the city. Bradley had tried to talk her out of it. When it had become clear that Clara was in no mood to be persuaded otherwise, he had agreed to accompany her, more out of guilt than enthusiasm, she could tell. The tension between them had disappeared when they had seen the extent of the damage. Now he was checking the pulse of these tiny bodies, verifying that they were indeed beyond anyone's help, before covering them with dirty blankets.

A yellow pick-up truck pulled over in the road ten metres from where a little girl was lying dead, its worn rubber tyres splashing in one of the rosy puddles. Two Syrian men climbed out. They couldn't have been more than twenty, but they had the worn features of much older men. One of them lowered the tailgate of the pick-up, then followed his companion into the devastated hospital. Neither of them paid Clara any attention. Their destination was the far corner of the room, where four bodies were lined up on the floor, covered in soot-stained blankets. The corpses were sufficiently small and light for the men to carry one each in their arms. Clara turned her head from the sight of a small hand, clenched tight by rigor mortis, hanging from under one of the blankets as its impromptu undertaker carried it to the pick-up and laid it in the back. Two trips each and the men had loaded the bodies. Only now did one of them look over at Clara, his expression questioning. Clara shook her head. The man shrugged, climbed into the pick-up with his companion and drove away. Clara's patient groaned again. Clara squeezed her hand a little tighter.

And then the firing started. It was the rat-tat-tat of automatic weapons. Clara didn't know how close, but near enough for it to send a physical shock through her body. She looked round. Out in the street, the few locals had quickly scampered away. Another burst of fire. Closer. She could hear shouting. It couldn't be more than thirty metres away.

Bradley hurried over to her. 'We need to get out of here,' he said. His voice had an edge of panic. 'The shooting's coming from the opposite direction to the car.' He was right. They'd had to leave their vehicle some hundred metres south of here because a bomb crater in the road had blocked their way. The gunfire sounded like it came from the north.

Clara didn't move.

'Come *on*,' Bradley said. He leaned over, grabbed her right arm and started to pull her up. She shook him away and looked back at the girl.

'I'm not leaving her,' she said quietly. The hand in which she held the girl's was trembling. She squeezed a little harder to stop this outward sign of the terror that was rising in her gut.

'For God's sake, Clara.' Bradley looked anxiously over his shoulder. 'They're running riot out there. Let's just get in the car and go.' He pointed down at the child. 'You know she's not going to make it, right? You can tell she's only got a few minutes left?'

Something snapped inside Clara. 'Fine,' she hissed. '*You* go. I'll see you back at the camp. I'm a doctor. I'm staying with her.'

'You're so bloody . . .' For a moment Bradley looked as if she had shamed him into staying with her. But then there was a third burst of automatic fire. Bradley winced, then staggered backwards as his courage deserted him. Clara was only watching him through the corner of her eye. She refused to give him his full attention as he turned and fled.

His footsteps faded as he raced up the road. Then there was a sudden, terrible silence.

It didn't last long.

Gunfire to the north *and* the south. In less than ten seconds, armed men appeared in front of the abandoned field hospital from either end of the street. Fifteen perhaps? Unlike the locals who had deserted the place minutes earlier, these gunmen were in uniform – standard military camouflage. Clara knew nothing about guns, but the weapons they were carrying looked ugly. So did the expressions on their faces. Two men looked over at the bombed-out hospital, leered and then started to amble unpleasantly in Clara's direction.

A ghastly rattle came from the little girl's chest. Her lungs were filling with fluid. She didn't have long.

Clara fumbled inside her jacket. She pulled out the ring her dad had given her and squeezed it on to the fourth finger of her left hand. Then she reached for her MSF ID card. With a fierce expression that she hoped would hide the terror pulsing through her, she held it up to the approaching gunmen when they were just a couple of metres away. One of them – he had a beard which, despite his youth, was flecked with grey – grabbed it contemptuously and tossed it into the debris.

Now they were standing over Clara. One of them bent down to pull her to her feet. She tried to wriggle free of him, as she had done with Bradley, but this bastard wasn't going to let her go so easily. He dragged her away from her patient. Clara could only watch, sickened, as the bearded soldier booted the little girl hard in the side of her bleeding head. The child's body jerked alarmingly, and then it fell still.

Clara wanted to scream, but the shock of what she had just witnessed silenced her. The two government soldiers started shouting at her in Arabic. She couldn't understand a word. The man holding her pushed her towards the street. She stumbled. He grabbed hold of her and pushed her again. Seconds later she was outside and had fallen to her knees in one of the puddles of diluted blood. She looked to her right. Farther down the street, perhaps fifty metres away, she saw a figure lying face down on the ground. Bradley's ponytail was sticking girlishly up into the air. He was surrounded by a pool of his own blood.

Bile rose in the back of Clara's throat. She bent forward to retch, but even as she did this, she felt a hand grab her and pull her to her feet. Most of the gunmen had dispersed. She was surrounded by three of them, the bearded man and two others. They were government forces all right, but she could tell at a glance they had no interest in law and order. In a country where the military had been given carte blanche, and where looting was encouraged by the administration, these three had the arrogant look of men who knew they could do what they wanted, to whom they wanted, with no comeback at all.

'Please,' Clara said. 'I just want to help people . . .' She silently cursed her lack of Arabic. How could she explain that she was simply a doctor? '*Je ne veux qu'aider des malades . . .*' she said. Maybe if she showed them the medical supplies she had in her pouch. She opened it and was about to pull out a dressing, when she felt the butt of a rifle rub between her legs.

She felt a flash of anger and swiped the rifle away. Instantly, the gunman gave her reason to regret it. He swiped the barrel brutally against the side of her face, a stunning blow that disorientated her and knocked her once more to the ground. The bearded soldier gave a harsh, barking laugh. Then Clara heard a clicking sound and although she knew little about weapons, she knew what that meant.

What happened next was a reflex action. The survival instinct.

Clara reached into her medical pouch. The first thing her fingers touched was a sterilised hypodermic needle, about four inches long, sealed in a white vacuum pack. She pulled it out, holding the blunt end of the needle like a knife. With her free hand she pushed away the barrel of the rifle that was pointing directly at her, and with the other stabbed the vacuum pack into the side of the gunman's knee. The needle slid through the packaging and pierced the gunman's trousers, before slipping easily into the tendon behind his patella. The man screamed. At the same time he fired his weapon. The rounds discharged erratically. Several of them thundered into the ribcage of one of the other soldiers, throwing him back on to the ground. Clara pushed herself to her feet, and ran.

She didn't expect to make it out of there alive. Especially when, out of nowhere, she heard a helicopter overhead. A quick glance over her shoulder, however, told her what was going on. One soldier was dead. A second was doubled over in agony, the needle protruding from his kneecap. The third – the bearded soldier who seconds previously had found the whole situation such a joke but who had now taken in the disaster around him – was anxiously looking up at the helicopter. Suddenly he turned and fled in the opposite direction. Evidently he wanted no association with what had just happened.

Clara continued to run, past walls covered with anti-government graffiti and metal security shutters that remained intact even though the buildings they protected had massive holes blasted into their facades. Her only chance was to get to their vehicle. It was 100 metres away. She looked only straight ahead as she ran. Her eyes were misty with tears and she didn't realise what she was looking at until she had covered half that distance.

Something was burning. It was just beyond the enormous bomb crater that had stopped them from continuing along the road. With a sickening twist in her stomach she realised it was their vehicle. It was surrounded by figures – five, maybe more – who were hazy in the heat and through Clara's tears. She had no doubt that they were unfriendly.

She stopped, breathless, exhaustion burning in her chest, her limbs cold with fear. She looked around. There was a street leading off to her left. A telegraph pole, damaged at the root, was swaying dangerously across the start of the street, and two of the cables it once supported were snaked messily on the ground. This street had taken the brunt of the recent bombing – the houses on either side were ruins, and it was deserted. Almost without thinking, Clara ran down it. She heard more gunfire near the hospital and, with a desperate sob, upped her pace. She was barely aware of her surroundings now, and only knew that she had to get away from the government forces who had taken Bradley's life and nearly killed her.

She ran for ten minutes, maybe more, before the build-up of lactic acid in her limbs forced her to stop. She doubled over to catch her breath, her hands shaking and her skin moist with sweat. As the burning in her legs and lungs subsided, she straightened up and looked around. She was in a narrow street. It had not been quite so heavily bombarded as the area around the hospital, but it bore the scars of war nonetheless. She saw a first-floor window with a sniper-fire hole the size of her fist, and the pavements were crammed with overflowing bags of stinking uncollected rubbish that rustled worryingly, no doubt overrun with feasting rodents.

She counted three shopfronts. Two of them had had their display windows smashed in and their contents looted. Somebody had taken the precaution of applying gaffer tape to the splintered window of the third to stop it falling in. Fifteen metres away, another car was still smouldering. Its features were burned away, with the exception of a skew-whiff Mercedes symbol that had miraculously remained fixed to the bonnet. A reek of burned fuel mingled with the stench of rotting debris. Apart from a stray dog sitting patiently in front of one of the smashed shop windows, the street was deserted – or so Clara thought. As she regained her breath, a pair of eyes peered out from behind the car.

Dark. Frightened. They belonged to a child. A little girl with a nasty cut across one cheek.

Clara couldn't stop a sob escaping her lips. She stepped towards the child, one hand outstretched. It was the worst thing she could have done. The terrified kid turned and fled, running away as fast as her little legs would go, not looking back. Clara would have run after her, but she had no energy. And in any case, her attention was suddenly elsewhere.

Two noises started at once. The first was the dog. Half a yap, half a howl. The second was the sound of machinery some-where overhead. Clara assumed it was a helicopter. She didn't quite know why, but it filled her with fear. If the chopper was about to fly over this street, she didn't want it to spot her. That single thought was enough to urge her legs back into action. She ran to the nearest of the three looted shops and climbed

114

over what remained of the window's jagged glass. Shards crunched underfoot as she stepped into the shop.

Just in time.

She turned and looked back through the broken window. The helicopter thundered overhead. She knew nothing about the machinery of war, but the glimpse of a man sitting at the open side of the aircraft with some kind of machine gun was enough to make her feel sick with fear all over again.

The chopper hovered above her for a full minute, low and threatening. Clara felt the thunder of its rotors vibrating. By the time it had moved on, she could barely move through exhaustion.

And distress. All-consuming.

It wasn't just the image of Brad's dead body, viciously seared on her mind.

It wasn't just the memory of her bruising escape from the government forces who had killed her tiny patient without a thought, and who, she was quite sure, would now want to do the same to her.

It was this. She was alone. And lost. Her only option was to try to make it back to the MSF base. She had no idea how to get there, no means of calling for help and no wish to leave the dubious protection of the abandoned shop. She didn't know what to do.

Her knees buckled underneath her and she fell to the floor, her face in her hands, overcome with the kind of desperate, racking sobs that are only ever caused by fear.

NINE

For the second time in forty-eight hours, Danny felt the warm, dry air of the Mediterranean hit his face. The light was failing, and the endless blue sky was turning indigo, with faint streaks of pink on the horizon.

Buckingham was by his side as he exited the Hercules that had transported them to Cyprus, just as he had stuck close to him for the whole journey. Danny had taken him in hand. The guys had brought their weapons and other hardware in a sturdy flight case from Hereford. Now, however, they transferred all this gear, along with their packs and the clothes they had prepared for their insertion, into two huge rubber waterproof bags. Danny had told Buckingham to open his suitcase, and had rummaged through it to find anything worth bringing along. 'Leave it here,' he'd told the MI6 man before nodding at the waterproof bags. 'We packed for you anyway.'

Since fronting up to Spud back at Brize Norton, Buckingham had barely said a word. Danny could tell it was more than a fear of flying. The guy was genuinely anxious about what they were about to do. Danny was fine with that. A bit of fear sharpened the mind. Kept you on the mark. It was the moment you started to get blasé that led to fuck-ups. And in this line of work, fuck-ups meant going home in a box, if you were lucky. He didn't mind Buckingham's puppy-dog eyes, either. If the spook felt reliant on him, he was more likely to do as he was told.

Buckingham might be the boss, but on the ground Danny would be the one calling the shots. And firing them too, if necessary. Syria was enemy territory. Increasingly lawless, increasingly dangerous. Being blasé was not an option.

As the ops officer back in Hereford had briefed them, a thin-lipped sergeant by the name of Wilkinson was waiting to lead them on to the tarmac to escort them to the docks. They moved swiftly. The RV with their Syrian fixer who was to supply them with vehicles and fuel was to take place at 01.00 hrs on the Syrian coast. If they were late, he wouldn't hang around. That would leave them stuck in-country with no onward transport. And there was a lot of ground – or rather, water – to cover yet. Wilkinson didn't say a word as he drove the unit and their gear out of the airport, although Danny did notice the way he kept glancing at them in the van's rear-view mirror. It was clear he was wondering what they were about to embark upon. It was just as clear that none of the special forces guys were going to tell him. Perhaps Buckingham was following their lead. Perhaps he was just too nervous to speak. Whatever the truth, he sat in the back, staring through the glass in absolute silence. The van stopped and Wilkinson switched off the engine. The guys alighted. Danny held back. 'You OK, pal?' he asked.

Buckingham nodded. He looked grateful that Danny had taken the trouble to ask.

The docks were crowded. A Royal Navy frigate had just docked and swarms of Navy guys were milling around the waterfront. There was a buzz about the place. The sailors were clearly looking forward to some down time, and despite every-one in the vicinity being in uniform, and the huge outline of the frigate docked just thirty metres from where Wilkinson had pulled up, there was an almost civilian atmosphere. The bars of Cyprus would be doing some good business tonight.

Two Marines were waiting for them. Danny shook hands with them, Buckingham as ever by his side, while the other lads took their waterproof holdalls from the back of Wilkinson's van. 'You need to do anything here?' one of the Marines asked.

Danny shook his head. 'Let's get moving,' he said. 'We can't hang around.'

The Marines led them to a small brick building fifty metres away, on the very edge of the dock. It was about the size of a large double garage. Inside, Danny saw that it had been constructed around a small, man-made inlet, just big enough to house the Mk1 Rigid Raider that that would transport them off shore. The assault boat was about five metres long, big enough for eight troops plus coxswain. Glass-reinforced plastic hull, 115 hp outboard motor. Simple. Utilitarian. Nothing to write home about. With the unit and their gear it would achieve about forty knots. Perfect for the job. But Buckingham looked puzzled. 'It's rather small, isn't it?' He sounded anxious. 'To get all the way to Syria, I mean?'

Danny allowed himself a smile. 'Don't worry about it, pal,' he said. 'We've got something a bit better lined up.'

To the left of the inlet, there was a rack of drysuits. The guys loaded their gear into the Rigid Raider, then got out of their civvies and into the dry suits.

The Marines and Regiment guys had changed into the tight-fitting suits long before Buckingham had even managed to ease his right leg into his. He sat on the floor, dressed in boxer shorts, his thin arms awkward as he tried to squeeze himself into the drysuit. It took him a full ten minutes, by which time all the other guys, with the exception of Danny, were sitting in the Raider, waiting for him to embark. Danny led Buckingham to the edge of the inlet and held his right arm as he gingerly stepped into the bobbing vessel. Then he embarked himself and nodded at the Marine at the helm. Within seconds the engine was purring and the boat was emerging from the end of the brick building and out into the port.

The eight-man vessel was tiny against the huge silhouette of the frigate. Even smaller against the dark night sky as the noise of its engine dissolved into the open air. The Marine navigated it expertly out into open water, then increased speed. The stern raised slightly and the Raider bounced and plunged through the inky sea, away from the safe, twinkling lights of land and into the utter blackness of the Mediterranean night. As the spray splashed Danny's face and the salt air filled his lungs, he felt a surge of exhilaration. Buckingham, sitting next to him, clearly didn't share it. He was gripping the edge of the vessel so hard that even in the darkness Danny could faintly see the whiteness of his knuckles.

The Raider continued at full pelt for ten minutes, the Marines navigating by the dim light of a small GPS unit. As the sound of the motor wound down and the vessel started to bob on the gentle swell of the Med, Danny looked back towards Cyprus. The lights of the shoreline were barely visible now.

From somewhere there came a low, rumbling sound. It seemed to be all around them. Above them, below them, coming from everywhere.

'What's that?' Buckingham whispered.

Nobody answered.

'What do we do now?' Buckingham's voice had become fearful.

'We hitch a lift,' Danny said. 'I told you we had something bigger laid on.'

Even as he spoke, the surface of the water suddenly started to tremble.

'*Shit!*' Buckingham hissed. 'What's going on?'

'Wait,' Danny said calmly. He looked around, peering into the darkness, while the coxswain spoke on his hand-held radio. 'Coming in now.' He turned to the rest of them. 'OK, lads, hold on.'

'Over there,' said one of the Marines, pointing in a direction that Danny estimated as north-west.

The sea-state grew considerably rougher. And although it was difficult to judge distances in the darkness, Danny estimated that the shape emerging from the depths was about 100 metres away. A dark shadow against the horizon, the tip of HMS *Vanguard*'s conning tower broke through the surface of the water with a resounding crash. He sensed Buckingham's breathing get faster as the tower rose higher and higher above the waves.

They were looking at it side on. As the stern of the sub appeared, twenty metres in front of the conning tower, the vast size of the vessel became clear. It was strangely whale-like in shape and perhaps one and a half football pitches long. This wasn't the first time Danny had seen a sub break water, but it never failed to astonish him how something so big could travel so silently beneath the surface of the sea.

Danny's eyes followed the sub's outline. The top of the vessel tapered down towards the stern to allow boarding by vessels such as the Rigid Raider. The coxswain started the outboard motor again, then swung the attack boat through 270 degrees so that they were travelling parallel to the sub, but towards its aft, which was still submerged. The slope of the sub's roof, however, meant that a small deck area had appeared to the rear of the conning tower. The Raider swept clockwise in a broad, 180-degree arc so that it was aligned with the sub, then headed straight for the tower. Lateral waves, caused by the emergence of the submarine, slammed against the stern of the boat, spraying its passengers and momentarily blinding them as they ploughed through them. After about five seconds there was a scraping sound beneath the Raider as it came into contact with the sub's deck. It ground to a halt five metres from the conning tower. There was a steel door in the tower, its edge defined by a series of studded rivets. As the Marines stood up in the boat, the door opened and a dull yellow light lit the deck.

Four submariners appeared. They wore heavy waterproof jackets and sturdy boots and started yelling instructions over the deafening noise of the sub's engines. Without ceremony, one of the Marines grabbed Buckingham by the arm and manhandled

him over the side of the Raider into the care of a waiting submariner, who, holding him firmly, escorted him off the deck and
into the conning tower. Danny, Spud, Jack and Greg unloaded
their waterproof holdalls and hauled them across the deck and
into the sub. There was no time to say goodbye to the Marines.
The hydraulic doors immediately hissed closed, shutting out the
sound of the sea and leaving the Raider out on the deck. It
would start floating again as the submarine submerged, and the
Marines would be back in dock fifteen minutes after that.

Danny looked around. They were in a room with a painted
steel floor, about eight metres square. The walls were covered
with pipes and hydraulics. The sub yawed, but only barely.
Buckingham looked unsteady on his feet. The four guys who
had ushered them off the deck were there, as well as one other.
He wore a greying beard, had very piercing blue eyes and looked
about forty years of age.

'Welcome aboard HMS *Vanguard*,' he said. 'I'm Commander
Flemming.'

Danny had full-on respect for members of the Silent Service,
and particularly for anyone who had passed the rigorous Submarine Command Course. Its failure rate was almost as high as
that of SAS selection, hence its nickname 'the Perisher'. He
shook Commander Flemming's hand. 'Change here, if you will,'
Flemming said. 'I've asked my men to deal with your equipment and I've had rooms set aside for you – unless you'd care to
join me on the bridge?'

Danny glanced at Buckingham, who was miserably trying to
peel off his neoprene suit. 'No, we'll go to our rooms,' he said.

'Of course,' the captain said. 'Is there anything we can do for
you? Something to eat?'

'Hot food would be good,' Danny said. With another side-
long glance at Buckingham, he added, 'And tea. Sweet.'

Flemming nodded at one of the waiting seamen. 'Aye-aye,
captain,' the man replied, then headed down a metal staircase.

'Follow me, fellas,' a second of the submariners said. He led them down below. Danny could sense the vessel submerging again as they left the staircase and passed along a series of narrow corridors.

'I don't much like enclosed spaces, old sport,' Buckingham whispered.

'Then you're in the wrong place, pal,' Danny said. 'They have to fit a couple of hundred guys on one of these things. Doesn't leave much space.'

'No chicks either,' Spud said. He looked over at the MI6 man. 'So if you were thinking of joining the mile-low club . . .' he grinned, 'you won't be fuckin' 'em, Buckingham!'

To his credit, Buckingham smiled.

The quarters to which the submariner led them comprised a single room, seven metres by four – though Danny realised this was spacious compared to the tiny berths that the *Vanguard*'s crew had to put up with. The guys stripped out of their dry-suits and changed into the all-in-one blue overalls that were waiting for them. Ten minutes later food arrived. Subs such as this were designed to be constantly at sea. It required no refuelling on account of its nuclear reactor, and it could be at sea for long stretches without being restocked. Fresh food was rare, but the cooks had a reputation for conjuring decent meals from the dried and tinned supplies at their disposal. The unit tucked into bowls of welcome, warming stew and drank mugs of hot tea in silence. When they'd finished, Danny turned to Buckingham.

'Strip off,' he told him.

Buckingham had another go at peeling off the neoprene while Danny opened one of the waterproof bags and removed a set of clothes. They were deliberately nondescript – a pair of jeans and a coarse shirt. You could wear this outfit almost anywhere, from Damascus to Dorking, without anybody batting an eyelid. The clothes smelled unpleasantly musty, and Danny was briefly reminded of his brother's B&B room. 'Put these on,' he told Buckingham once he had stripped down to his boxer shorts, 'then put the drysuit on again over them.'

The Regiment guys were stripping down too, but their preparations were a bit more exotic. The clothes they wore were similar to Buckingham's, but under his shirt each man strapped a shoulder holster and a Sig 9mm. Buckingham's eyes were wide as he watched them check over their weapons. The room filled with the dull clunk of magazines being inserted, safety switches enabled. Danny noticed how he looked rather apprehensively into the waterproof bag that contained their M4s. He zipped it shut. No point shitting the guy up more than necessary.

Once they'd put their civvies on, they pulled on the drysuits once more.

'How far down are we?' Buckingham asked.

Danny shrugged. 'Five hundred metres,' he said. 'A bit more.'

'Bloody hell. And how long until . . . ?'

Danny sensed that Buckingham was talking out of nervousness, and maybe the best thing was to *keep* him talking. 'A couple of hours,' he said. 'When they drop us off, we'll have to tab about a kilometre inland. There's a T-junction leading to the main highway. That's where we'll meet our fixer and pick up the cars.'

Buckingham looked confused. 'Wouldn't it be better for him to meet us with the cars as soon as we land? I mean, we'd rather be in vehicles than on foot, wouldn't we?'

Danny shook his head. 'We don't know this fixer from Adam. If we meet him at the T-junction, he'll assume we're approaching by road, not by sea. We can check him out before we make contact. Let's not get compromised before we've even begun.'

'Compromised? He's an MI6 agent. Surely we can trust him?'

The rest of the guys laughed.

'What?' Buckingham demanded. '*What?*'

'He's a fixer, mate,' Spud explained. 'They're the same the world over. Sneaky. Out for what they can get. He's helping us because the Firm are paying him, but he'll betray us just as quickly if someone comes along with a better offer.'

Buckingham looked a bit sick.

'Don't worry, pal,' Greg told him. 'Any problems, we'll sacrifice Spud, not you. Right, Spud?'

Spud looked down at the bulge in his chest where the dry suit was covering his handgun. Then he looked back at Buckingham. 'Yeah, right,' he said.

23.30 hrs, Eastern European Time.
A sharp rap on the door of their quarters. A bearded submariner appeared. 'Breaking the surface in ten minutes, guys. Wait here till we give you the word.' In his arms he had a pile of inflatable vests. He handed them round to Buckingham and the unit, who slipped them over their heads. Then they waited.

Danny felt the sub roll a few degrees as it broke the surface. Buckingham flinched – he'd barely spoken a word since they'd been submerged. The guys grabbed the waterproof bags. Two minutes later the door opened again. The bearded submariner nodded at them. Silently, they filed out into the narrow corridor and followed the guy back in the general direction of the conning tower. They didn't take the spiral staircase up into the tower, however, but carried on ten metres past it to a ladder that led up to an overhead hatch. Commander Flemming was waiting for them here.

'We've had a communication from Hereford HQ,' he said. 'There's been a night of heavy fighting in Homs. Two Médecins Sans Frontières doctors went missing. Reports are coming in that one of them's been found dead.' He gave Danny a piercing look. 'Watch how you go, lads. Looks like they're killing foreigners in the streets.' He glanced at Buckingham and his face was filled with distrust. Whether Buckingham noticed it or not, Danny couldn't tell. The captain pulled a red lever on the corridor wall. A hiss, and the hatch in the ceiling slid open.

A sudden rush of noise as sea air blasted down the hatch. A face appeared up above. 'Send your gear up!' it shouted. The guys passed their waterproof bags up through the hatch, then Greg, Jack and Spud climbed the ladder, leaving Danny alone with Buckingham and the captain.

'Ready?' Danny asked.

Buckingham took a deep breath. 'As I'll ever be,' he said.

'You go first. I'll be right behind. Go carefully on deck. It's not a good night for swimming.'

Buckingham nodded, then carefully climbed the ladder.

'Good luck with that one,' Flemming said quietly. Danny felt his brow furrowing as he nodded in farewell and followed the MI6 man.

On deck there was a stiff breeze. Here, two miles from the Syrian coast, the weather conditions were different to those they'd left behind in Cyprus. The moon was still bright – bright enough for the conning tower to cast a sinister shadow over the vessel – but the sea, ten metres below the deck, was rougher. The foam where the swell hit the sub was almost phosphorescent, and the spray made the deck treacherous. After the relative quiet inside HMS *Vanguard*, the steady throb of the sub's engines seemed ominously loud. But that was OK: they were two miles out to sea. Cloaked in its dull metallic black paint, *Vanguard* was out of sight and out of earshot. A black RIB was waiting for them, along with two Marines in neoprene suits and with MP5s slung around their necks. As the hatch hissed closed, Danny saw that the guys had already loaded up the RIB and were climbing in.

'Get in!' he shouted at Buckingham, before walking him five slippery metres across the deck to the stern of the RIB. With a nod at the Marines he helped Buckingham into the vessel, then climbed in too. He gave the Marine at the outboard a thumbs up. The Marine flicked the pressel of his radio twice.

'Hold on!' he shouted.

At first it seemed that nothing was happening. But then, after about twenty seconds, the massive sub juddered slightly. Slowly, it started to sink.

Five metres to sea level.

Three metres.

One.

The sea suddenly closed in over the deck. They were still in the shadow of the receding conning tower, but they were afloat. The RIB rocked precariously, caught precisely in the crash of the sea rushing in from either side. Salt water splashed over them. The coxswain waited ten seconds for the deck to submerge another few metres before swinging the hinged outboard down into the water and starting it up. As water continued to slosh over the RIB, the Marine increased its speed, heading ten metres towards the submerged aft of the *Vanguard* before turning in a wide semicircle and making directly for the shore.

Half blinded by the spray, Danny peered into the night, towards the Syrian coastline. There were lights to his ten o'clock, but in the darkness he couldn't tell how far away they were. Overhead, a commercial flight was travelling in a southerly direction. Danny wondered how many aircraft there were up there that he *couldn't* see. He remembered catching the glint of a drone when he was lying beside Boydie in the OP in Syria. Those drones were like guardian angels. You never knew if they were really there, or even if they'd help you out when you needed it most. Straight ahead, there was nothing. The deserted stretch of beach to which they were heading was five klicks from any known human habitation in any direction. He wouldn't have expected to see any lights, but that didn't mean their insertion point was safe. Far from it. If *he'd* been on the shore looking out, nobody would have seen him either.

Time check: 00.15 hrs. Forty-five minutes till RV. They were cutting this fine. If the fixer didn't hang around with their vehicles, they were screwed.

The RIB's outboard slowed down, becoming quieter: a sure sign that they were approaching land. 'Two hundred metres,' the coxswain announced. Greg and Jack, sitting on either side of the boat, raised their weapons, scanning the coast through the lenses of their IR sights. Ten seconds later they slowed again. The motor was very quiet now, barely audible above the sound of waves crashing on the beach. There, about fifty metres distant, Danny could see the humped outline of a sand dune. A sudden surge as the RIB caught a breaking wave. They glided into shallow water, where the second Marine jumped from the boat. The sea was knee-high. The coxswain killed the outboard as his colleague dragged them towards the beach.

Five metres from dry land. The unit moved quickly. This was a moment of vulnerability – anyone could be waiting for them, unfriendly eyes searching – and so they needed to be especially watchful. And fast. And quiet. Greg and Jack splashed into the shallow water and ran to shore. Ten metres up the shingle beach, they threw themselves on their bellies in the firing position, carefully scanning the area, on high alert for any sign of a threat.

'Get out,' Danny told Buckingham, who nodded and eased himself carefully into the water while Danny and Spud grabbed the waterproof bags and joined him. While the Marines grounded the RIB, Danny, Spud and Buckingham ran on to the beach. 'Get out of your drysuit,' Danny told Buckingham. The three men tore off their inflatable jackets and peeled away the dripping suits to reveal their civvies underneath. Danny stuffed the wet clothes back into the waterproof bag and picked up his weapon. He grabbed Buckingham's shirt, dragged him over to where Greg and Jack were lying and pushed him to the ground. 'Don't move,' he hissed. As he and Spud adopted the firing position, Greg and Jack returned to the Marines to hand over their wet gear.

Danny scanned the surrounding area, ignoring a sharp stone digging into his elbow. The beach was about thirty metres deep.

The sand dune that backed on to it was about fifteen metres high and had an incline of roughly forty degrees. It was high summer. Expected rainfall in western Syria was close to zero, although the winter and spring rains meant this part of the country was fertile and scrappy plants sprouted from the surface of the dune. There was no movement that he could make out. No sign that anyone had witnessed them land. No government troops. No locals.

At least, not that Danny could see.

Two minutes passed. Behind him, Danny heard the cough of the RIB's outboard. He didn't look back – he knew that Greg and Jack would by now have stuffed their wet gear into the waterproof bags and given these to the Marines, who would be on their way back to HMS *Vanguard*. There was a light crunch of footsteps as his two unit colleagues stepped past the three men on the ground and headed stealthily towards the rim of the dune.

'What's happening?' Buckingham asked.

Danny said nothing. He was too busy concentrating. Moving about ten metres apart, Greg and Jack crouched low as they approached the brow of the dune, then adopted the firing position as they reached it.

They lay there, perfectly still.

The low hum of the RIB's motor had faded. The only noise was the gentle crash and hiss of waves against the shingle.

Jack raised his right hand: the signal to advance. 'Stick close to me,' Danny whispered. He jumped up and pulled Buckingham to his feet. Then, covered by Jack and Greg up ahead and with Spud ten metres to the left, they advanced. The sand of the dune was soft. Buckingham stumbled twice and Danny had to help him up. He was already panting by the time they reached the top. Danny scanned ahead. The terrain sloped gently downward for a kilometre before it reached a road running north–south, parallel to the coastline. He could make out the distant outlines of trees and bushes, a reminder that the climate on the Mediterranean side of Syria was a good deal less harsh than the desert on the eastern side and the border with Iraq. Approximately to their two o'clock was the T-junction. Here, parked in a line facing south, were three vehicles. The lead vehicle had its headlamps on, lighting up the road.

Danny removed a night-sight from his pack. Focusing in on the lead vehicle, he could just discern the outline of a figure at the steering wheel. 'Bingo,' he said. 'We got one guy up front. I'm guessing there's at least two more as they're in three vehicles.' He lowered the sight. 'OK, everything looks as it should, but let's not take any chances. I wouldn't put it past this Muhammad bloke to do the dirty on us and set up an ambush. Spud, Greg, stay here. Keep eyes on. We'll make contact and check over the vehicles, then send Muhammad and his boys packing. If it looks like we're having any trouble, you know what to do. Jack, Buckingham, come with me.'

Jack gave him a troubled look. 'You sure about this?' he said with a glance at their companion.

Danny nodded. 'I don't want this guy to know for sure how many of us there are. If we leave Buckingham behind, they'll know we've got at least one more guy looking after him. Let's keep Muhammad in the dark if we can.'

Jack inclined his head. 'Roger that,' he said, then looked at Buckingham. 'I don't want to get your back up, mate, but when we get down there, do what we say and keep your mouth shut. We'll do the talking.'

The vehicles were at their two o'clock. Danny, Jack and Buckingham headed out to their eleven o'clock. Danny estimated that this would allow them to hit the road approximately 250 metres from the convoy. They could then approach from behind and their fixer would be none the wiser about which direction they'd really come from. Running with full pack and hindered by Buckingham's lack of fitness, it took them the best part of seven minutes to cross the open ground and reach the road. It was a good eight or nine metres wide, but its surface was potholed and stony. They walked in single file – Jack first, then Buckingham, then Danny, each man ten metres from the next. When they were twenty metres from the T-junction and the convoy, they stopped and lay on the dusty ground, surveying the site.

A car door slammed. A figure emerged from the front vehicle and walked on to the rough ground east of the road. He stood ten metres from the car, and it was perhaps five seconds before Danny realised he was taking a slash.

'Wait here,' he hissed.

Silently and in less than five seconds, Danny covered most of the twenty metres to the pissing man. The guy wasn't even aware of his presence until Danny was three metres away. He was shaking himself off as Danny wrapped his left arm around his neck and covered his mouth with his right hand. The guy tried to shout, but all that came out was a muffled whimper. Looking over his shoulder, Danny saw Jack sprinting towards the lead vehicle. Moments later he had ripped the door open and was aiming his M4 directly into the front. A babble of Arabic emerged. Jack pulled two men roughly out of the car and threw them on to the ground. Aware that Buckingham was nervously approaching, Danny pushed his man over to where the others were crouching, then beckoned to him to hurry towards them.

Danny looked at each of the three Syrian men in turn. 'Muhammad?' he asked.

One of the pair that Jack had pulled from the car looked up sharply. He looked unpleasant – the photo they'd seen back at base had massively flattered him. A big, fat, bald bastard with rotten yellow teeth and bags under his eyes. His eyes darted angrily to Jack's gun. 'What you do?' he said in broken English. 'I your friend. Put the gun down. I have cars for you. Very *good* cars. Put the gun *down*, please.'

Danny gave Jack an almost imperceptible nod. Jack lowered the M4, though Danny noticed that he kept it firmly in his grip.

Instantly, the fixer's face softened. He stood up and his two friends did the same. Muhammad opened his arms and gave them a grin that displayed his rotten teeth even more clearly. And then, in a voice that bore no trace of his previous anger, he said: 'Welcome to our poor country, my friends. Welcome to Syria!'

TEN

He was a fixer through and through. Glib, talkative, slightly nervous, slippery as a fish. He presented the two vehicles with the aplomb of a car salesman flogging a Bentley. In fact, the cars looked knackered: a dull-brown Renault and a red VW, both covered with scrapes and dents and rust. Each was decorated inside with religious icons and coloured beads, was the custom in that part of the world, and they smelled faintly of petrol and hashish.

'Very good cars!' Muhammad said.

'Yeah,' Jack muttered as he checked the vehicles over. 'Enough to give Jeremy Clarkson a lazy lob-on.'

'Jeremy?' Muhammad asked enthusiastically. 'Who is this Jeremy? A friend of yours? You have more friends coming?'

'No,' Danny stated. 'No friends coming. Just us.'

It happened in a split second. Buckingham said nothing, but his gaze darted briefly to the west, where they'd left Spud and Greg. Had the fixer noticed? Danny couldn't tell.

Jack was checking one of the cars, and got it started. Danny looked at Muhammad's two companions. 'OK, fellas,' he said. 'Time to move.'

The fixer turned to Buckingham and smiled his gruesome smile. 'Where do you travel to in our poor country?'

Danny wasn't fast enough. Before he could stop him, Buckingham had already answered. 'Aleppo,' he said.

Muhammad's eyes narrowed slightly. 'Ah,' he said. 'Aleppo. Very good—'

'You heard what the man said, guys,' Jack interrupted, deftly steering the conversation away. 'Time to make tracks.'

The fixer ignored Jack, turning back to Danny instead. 'You pay me now!' he said.

'Nice try, pal. You've had your payday. Time to go.'

An outraged expression crossed Muhammad's face. He was obviously about to escalate this argument. Danny pulled his Sig from his chest rig and pressed it against the fixer's head.

'Go,' he said quietly.

Muhammad's whole demeanour changed. He stepped back, barked a single word in Arabic to his two companions, then gave Danny an obsequious little half bow, his eyes still searching and suspicious. Moments later the three men were all in the car. The engine coughed a few times, but then the car moved off into the night.

Danny and Jack watched it disappear. Then they turned back to Buckingham. Jack's face was a storm cloud. 'I told you to leave the talking to us,' he said.

Buckingham's eyes widened in surprise. 'I said we were going to Aleppo,' he said. He looked to Danny for support. 'I thought you were trying to put him off our track.'

Danny glanced over at the departing vehicle. 'Aleppo's a hundred klicks from the Turkish border,' he said. 'If that's where we were headed, we'd never start our journey from here. Muhammad, or whatever his name is, knew you were lying.' He did everything he could to keep his voice level, even though he was as angry as Jack.

'Well, what the bloody hell was I supposed to say?' Buckingham said.

'Nothing,' Jack told him.

'We can't do anything about it now,' Danny said. 'We'll just need to keep alert.'

'Roger that,' Jack muttered. His eyes followed the lights of the fixer's vehicle. It was about 1.5 kilometres away when it turned to the left and out of sight. He removed a thin torch from his pack and pointed it back towards the coast in Greg and Spud's direction. Two quick flashes. A signal for the guys to join them.

Danny kept stag with his Sig while Jack loaded their gear into the boot of the brown Renault. He lay their M4s along the outside edge of the boot and covered them loosely with a grey travelling blanket that he'd found in the rear seat. Their packs fitted behind it. He shut the boot very quietly. Sounds could travel a long way over open ground.

'Where the fuck are the others?' Jack said.

They'd been waiting for ten minutes. Spud and Greg hadn't arrived.

An uneasy sensation crept down Danny's spine. 'Give me a kite sight,' he said. But Jack was already on it. He'd opened the boot again and was fishing a small optic out of one of the packs. Jack directed it to the west.

'Shit,' he said. 'Shit, shit, *shit!*'

'What is it?'

'They've got company.'

Jack handed him the kite sight. Danny focused in on the brow of the dune one kilometre away. He felt bile rising in his throat.

Greg and Spud's outlines were clear. They were back to back, maybe five metres apart, their weapons pointing outwards. On either side of them were people. Danny performed a quick headcount. Fourteen. Were they armed? Danny couldn't tell. If not, Spud and Greg could put them down in seconds.

And leave fourteen corpses as a calling card. Maybe the Syrian authorities would put that down as just another random massacre. Or maybe they wouldn't, and a contact now would have troops on their tail from here to Homs. Not acceptable.

'They're keeping the heat off us,' said Jack.

'Either that or they're holding off a contact.'

'That little bastard Muhammad must have shopped us.'

'We should go,' Buckingham said. 'Get in the car and go . . .'

Danny lowered the sight. He and Jack turned to look at Buckingham. Their expressions told him exactly what they thought of *that* suggestion. Danny strode quickly to the Renault and removed his and Jack's M4s from the boot. He turned to Buckingham and handed him his Sig. 'I . . . I don't know how to . . .' said the MI6 man.

'Point it at the person you want to kill, and squeeze the trigger. Stay here.'

'Can't I come with you?'

'Don't take it personally, mate, but you'd just get in the way. If everything turns pear-shaped, get on the sat phone. It's in one of the packs. *Vanguard*'s still in the vicinity. They can help you extract.'

'But . . . but we can't *do* this. We need to get to Homs.'

Danny ignored him. His mind was turning over. Whoever it was up ahead, they had to be holding the guys at gunpoint. Otherwise Spud and Greg would have nailed them. No question. It was a stand-off. Their SOP was clear. Draw the fire of these newcomers so the Regiment guys could do what needed to be done.

'What the bloody hell are you thinking of doing?' Buckingham demanded. He was clearly panicking. 'We should just get in the car—'

'Stay there,' Danny repeated. He handed Jack his weapon.

'This goes pear-shaped, it'll be front page of the fucking *Sun*,' Jack said, cocking his M4 as he spoke.

Danny kept calm. 'They don't need much. A diversion. Stay fifty metres apart. We'll get to within 500 metres and go to ground. Alternate bursts of fire. I'll go first. Wait for my signal.'

Without another word, he started to run across open ground towards the sand dune.

Five hundred metres. Over the crunching of his footsteps Danny thought he could hear voices up ahead. He stopped to listen.

Shouting. Arabic voices, he reckoned. Whatever was happening up there, it sounded ugly. They were probably nobodies, but this wouldn't be the first time some bolshie locals had screwed things up for a patrol. He silently cursed Spud and Greg for allowing them to creep up on them. Jack was right. Another bunch of farmers compromising an operation and the Regiment would be a laughing stock.

Danny went to ground and switched his M4 to automatic. He didn't want to kill any of them, but his restraint was tactical, not emotional. If one of their number went down, it would only shock them into nailing his two colleagues. He aimed his rifle a couple of metres to the left of the group.

He was on the point of firing when he heard it: the low, rhythmic thudding of a chopper, approaching from inland to his six o'clock.

When Danny looked back on it, he would identify that moment of hesitation as his mistake. There was no doubt in his mind that the chopper was unfriendly. Had Muhammad shopped them? Whatever the truth, he should have fired immediately, diverted the attention of the locals and given Spud and Greg the opportunity to escape. Because two men down within minutes of insertion meant the op was a no-go. But he didn't fire. Instead he rolled on to his back to confirm with his eyes what his ears had just told him.

The chopper was flying low and fast. Tail up, nose down, twenty feet from the ground, max. Expert flying, no question. Estimated distance: two klicks. But it would cover that ground in thirty seconds, maybe less.

Danny rolled over again, ready to fire. Through the scope of his M4, however, he saw that the situation had changed. Spud, Greg and their captors had just gone over the rim of the dune. He was in time to see their heads disappear.

The chopper was getting louder. Closer. Danny hugged the earth as it thundered past him, about thirty metres to his left.

The searchlight swept over the surrounding ground. Danny felt its bright beam sweep just a metre from where he was lying, tensed up, perfectly still. Only once the chopper had passed did he risk looking up again to see a side-gunner with a Minigun, scanning the ground. He wasn't firing. Danny supposed this meant he hadn't spotted him or Jack, but he knew he couldn't risk getting to his feet until the threat had passed.

Ten seconds. The chopper passed over the dune. Danny jumped up. To his right he saw Jack sprinting towards the dune, and he did the same. His legs burned as he forced them to cover the ground as quickly as possible. He listened hard. The sound of the chopper's rotors was constant. It had landed.

The brow of the dune was ten metres away. Danny hit the ground again. Twenty seconds later Jack joined him. They didn't speak, but crawled to the brow of the dune to check out what was happening beyond.

Danny felt his guts loosen.

The chopper had landed on the beach, maybe twenty metres from the water's edge, pretty much exactly where they'd landed. Six armed men had emerged. Danny couldn't quite make out their clothes but it was definitely military camouflage of some description. The crowd who had compromised Spud and Greg had congregated about thirty metres to Danny's ten o'clock. They were dressed in civilian clothes, though Danny counted nine of them carrying AK-47s.

But it was Spud and Greg who demanded the lion's share of Danny's attention. They were sprawled on the ground. Face down. Not moving.

'Are they . . . ?' said Jack.

No. One of the enemy troops pulled Greg to his feet and kneed him in the bollocks. Greg doubled over. His assailant pushed him towards the chopper, while another soldier yanked Spud from the ground and hustled him in the same direction, a handgun pressed firmly to his head.

'We can take them,' Danny said. He had the Minigunner in his sights. One shot would put him down. In the confusion, the remaining soldiers would be easy prey, and the civilians weren't sufficiently close to be an immediate threat.

'Hold your fire!' Jack hissed. And then, when Danny failed to lower his weapon, '*Hold your fucking fire!* Open up on these bastards, Spud and Greg are dead in a second.'

'We can *take* them,' Danny insisted. But Jack's warning stayed his trigger finger.

The moment was lost. The guys were already in the helicopter. The enemy soldiers were bundling in. Ten seconds later the chopper was in the air, its searchlight scanning the ground in long, random sweeps. Danny felt the thunder of its rotors vibrate through him. By the time the chopper was twenty metres high, it had rotated ninety degrees clockwise. Its nose dipped and it sped away, following the coastline, disappearing into the darkness.

Silence.

One of the locals, who were still standing on the beach, said something. The others laughed. Danny shifted his weapon in their direction. A couple of bursts would do it. Put them all down.

His trigger finger caressed the cold metal of his weapon.

'Easy, mucker,' Jack said softly. 'Nail the fuckers and you'll just flag up that we're here.'

Danny kept the group in his sights. Sweat trickled into his eyes.

The locals started to move. South, along the beach, away from Danny and Jack's position. Danny was breathing heavily. He wanted to take them out. But Jack was right. It was the wrong call. He moved his eye away from the sight.

'We couldn't have stopped it,' Jack said. Was it Danny's imagination, or did he sound like he was trying to persuade himself? Anger was pumping through him. They hadn't been in-country for more than an hour and already he was presiding over a cluster-fuck of epic proportions. He slammed his fist against the ground, then sucked in a massive intake of breath.

'What now?' Jack asked.

They were compromised. Two men captured. What would Taff say? 'You play the hand you're dealt, kiddo.' They'd been dealt a bad one. Or maybe they'd just made the wrong play. Either way it didn't matter. This was a hot insertion. They needed to extract.

'Let's get back to the vehicles. We'll call for a pick-up, dig in till someone can get us.'

'Roger that,' Jack agreed.

They crawled backwards ten metres, distancing themselves from the brow of the dune, before rolling on to their backs and looking back towards the road.

'What the *fuck?*' said Jack.

'What?' said Danny.

Jack pointed across the klick of open ground to the vehicles. Before their eyes, one of them – Danny thought it was the brown Renault – pulled out from where it was parked, its head-lamps on full, and started to move down the road.

'*RUN!*' Danny barked. '*GET TO THE OTHER VEHICLE!*' Jack was already on his feet. Together they sprinted across the open ground.

Different possibilities whirred through Danny's mind. Different scenarios. Had someone crept up on Buckingham while their backs were turned? Did they have him in the car now? Maybe they were opportunists and had put him down before stealing the vehicle. The sleazy face of Muhammad the fixer rose in his mind. Either way, this dog of an operation had just taken a turn for the worse, if that was possible.

There was no point chasing the moving vehicle on foot. They had to get to the stationary VW and work out their next move from there. They reached it in minutes. A cursory examination of the area told them that Buckingham wasn't there, so without a word they climbed into the car. Danny took the wheel. Their fixer had left the keys in the ignition and, despite looking like a pile of crap, the vehicle started first time. The rear wheels spun noisily in the dusty road as Danny, driving with the headlamps off and only by the light of the moon, accelerated through the gears as quickly as the tired old engine would allow.

The car rumbled and shook on the uneven road surface. Danny kept the accelerator pressed to the floor, his eyes fixed on the vehicle ahead. There was a gap between them of about a klick. A klick, and closing.

The Renault wasn't moving fast. It didn't take more than three minutes on this deserted road for Danny to close the distance to about 100 metres.

Fifty metres.

Twenty-five.

'There's only one driver,' Jack said, his voice tense.

Buckingham.

Danny slammed his palm against the steering wheel as he drove. Fifteen seconds later he was overtaking the Renault. As they passed, Danny looked over his shoulder into the other car. Sure enough, Buckingham was behind the wheel. Danny overtook, then manoeuvred the car so it was directly in front of the Renault. Gradually he slowed down, taking care to stay just in front of Buckingham. Only when they were down to 20 kph did he accelerate again, before yanking the wheel a half-turn clockwise and screeching to a halt twenty metres in front of the other car.

The moment they stopped, Jack jumped out and stalked towards the Renault. He yanked open the driver's door, pulled Buckingham out from behind the wheel as though he was made of feathers, and thumped him up against the side of the car. 'What the *fuck* are you doing?' he roared.

As Danny approached, he saw Buckingham's eyes wide with terror.

'Answer him,' he said.

'What the bloody hell do you *think* I'm doing? I saw that helicopter go overhead. I thought they'd caught you.'

'And?'

'And what? I've got to get to Homs, of course.'

The two Regiment men blinked at him.

'You were trying to do it without us?'

A vein was swelling in Buckingham's neck. He stared them down. Slowly, Jack released his grip on him. 'No offence, mate,' he said, 'but these Syrian bastards will have you for fucking breakfast before you get within sniffing distance.'

Buckingham appeared to ignore the warning. He patted down the front of his clothes rather prissily. 'Where are the others?' he asked.

'Right now, halfway to sodding Damascus,' said Jack.

Danny turned to his mate. 'Get on the blower to base. Update them. Tell them we need a pick-up.'

Jack nodded, then opened the back of the Renault and fished a sat phone out of his pack. Danny looked up and down the road. No sign of anybody in the vicinity, but they couldn't leave the cars parked across the road like this. He turned to Buckingham. 'Get to the side of the road,' he said.

Buckingham didn't move. 'We can't go back.'

'That's not your call, pal. Get to the side of the road.'

'You're annoyed with me. I understand that. But I didn't think you were coming back, and I have a job to do.'

'Me too,' said Danny. 'Keeping you alive, and you're not helping. So get to the side of the road.'

'They won't send you a pick-up, old sport,' Buckingham said quietly. 'You'd probably better prepare yourself for that.'

Calmly, Danny walked up to him. From the corner of his vision, twenty metres west, he was aware of Jack hunkering down by the side of the road, the sat phone pressed to his ear. He drew himself up face to face with Buckingham, the two of them less than half a metre apart. 'Here's the thing, old sport,' he said. 'I've got two men missing in action. I've got a fixer I don't trust and a chopper crew who knew we were here. This is a hot insertion, and unless you fancy a two-week crash course in escape and evasion, we're getting out.'

Buckingham inclined his head, but didn't reply. He wiped a strand of hair from his forehead, then turned and walked back towards the side of the road, where he sat down, clutching his knees with his arms and staring intently in Danny's direction. Danny felt a twinge of suspicion. Did the guy know something he wasn't letting on about?

But then he saw Jack walking back towards him. He was clutching the sat phone in his left hand, his M4 in his right. His expression was dark.

'What is it?' Danny said, though in his gut he knew what Jack was about to say.

'No pick-up,' he said, keeping his voice low so only Danny could hear. 'The op's still a green light. We continue into Homs.'

Danny glanced over at Buckingham and saw his gaze was fixed on the two Regiment men.

'Spud and Greg?' Danny said to Jack.

'They spun me some bullshit about diplomatic channels.'

Danny couldn't stop himself sneering. The Firm had made it quite clear this was deniable. Spud and Greg were on their own, at least for now.

'This stinks, mucker,' Jack said. 'They'll get Spud and Greg talking soon enough. We'll have half the fucking Syrian army on our tail. Plus the Russkies if they're in-country.'

He was right. The guys might hold out for a few hours, but it wouldn't be long before their captors started squeezing useful information out of them. Maybe Max Saunders had been right in holding back the details of his guys on the ground. What Spud and Greg didn't know, they couldn't reveal.

'We'd better get moving,' Danny said. 'Saunders' team are expecting us in Homs at dawn. I'm fucked if I'm going to be late for a bunch of mercenaries.' He nodded at the Renault. 'Take that one,' he told Jack. 'I'll look after our man. Hold back about half a klick. If we get into trouble . . .' He left it hanging.

Jack nodded his agreement. Then he squinted over Danny's shoulder down the road.

'What is it?' Danny asked. But as he turned round, he saw what Jack was looking at. Headlamps approaching down the straight road. A couple of klicks, if that.

'Move,' he said. Then he ran over to Buckingham, grabbed his arm and yanked him to his feet.

'What's happening?'

'You've got your wish, pal,' Danny said, one eye on the approaching headlamps. Fifteen hundred metres away? Certainly no more.

Buckingham stared anxiously at them too, even as Jack started the Renault. 'Who's that?' he said, his voice suddenly flat with dread.

'Let's not find out. Move.'

Buckingham didn't. He stared at the vehicle coming towards them.

Danny tugged hard on his arm. '*In the car!*' he hissed. '*Now!*'

ELEVEN

Danny was a good driver. He'd passed his advanced test before he even went up for selection, and since joining the Regiment he'd absorbed every last bit of know-how the members of mobility troop had fed him. He'd been up to the test tracks at MIRA, near Birmingham, where rally drivers had taught him how to handle different vehicles in icy and wet terrain. The ever-present instructors at Hereford had taught him J-turns and handbrake turns, and how to drive aggressively, using your car not just as a mode of transport but as a weapon. Right now, though, he wasn't interested in speed or technique behind the wheel. He needed to keep things steady. Unobtrusive. He was an ordinary guy driving an ordinary left-hand-drive car on ordinary business. At least, that was how he needed to appear. He accelerated to 50 kph and kept the needle there, hugging the side of the road.

Occasionally his eyes darted from left to right. The area seemed largely unpopulated, with the exception of an isolated farmhouse perhaps a klick to his right. Jack was hanging back 500 metres, just like Danny had told him to. Buckingham mercifully kept his trap shut, leaving Danny to concentrate on his driving.

And on the vehicle approaching from the opposite direction. Distance: 500 metres.

It took about forty-five seconds for the vehicles to pass each other. The other car's headlamps were on full beam. Dazzled,

Danny couldn't quite distinguish its make, but it had the shape of a Land Cruiser and he had a feeling the windows were blacked out. It whizzed past. Impossible to tell how fast it was travelling – 100 kph perhaps? That was suspicious in itself. This was a deserted part of the world and it was going nowhere in a hurry.

'It's passed,' Buckingham said.

'Thanks for the commentary.'

'No . . . I just mean, we're safe, aren't we?'

Danny didn't reply. He had one eye on the rear-view mirror, which he now adjusted slightly to give him a view of the other side of the road. He noticed the red tail lights glowing brighter. The car was coming to a halt. He cursed under his breath.

'What?' Buckingham said, twisting round in his seat to look back. 'Oh my God! It's turning round.'

'Do you still have my Sig?' Danny said. He gave the VW a bit more juice and the speedometer climbed to 80 kph.

'Your *what*?'

'My gun.'

Buckingham's eyes widened a little, but then he stretched out and opened the glove compartment in front of him. He gently removed the pistol with both hands.

'Hold on to it. I'll tell you when I need it.'

'What do you mean, "when"?'

Danny gave him a flinty stare. 'Just hold on to it.'

The VW was touching 100 kph now as they sped east away from the coast. Danny's attention was as much on the rear-view mirror as on the road ahead. The three vehicles were spread out. Jack was maintaining the 500-metre gap between them, which meant he had accelerated as well. Another 750 metres behind him, the headlamps of the other vehicle had come into view. Then, suddenly, they were extinguished.

'They've stopped,' Buckingham said, relief in his voice.

Danny shook his head.

'What do you mean? They've turned off their engine, haven't they?'

'They've turned off their *lights*,' Danny said. 'That way it's more difficult for me to judge how far away they are.' His face set, Danny flicked a switch on the right side of the wheel, extinguishing his own lights. Behind him, he saw Jack do the same.

'Hold tight,' he said.

Buckingham put the Sig in the footwell and clutched the sides of his seat as Danny floored the accelerator. At 130 kph the car began to judder noisily. Danny squinted, trying to make out potholes or obstructions in the darkness of the crappy road ahead. At this speed it would only take a dislodged stone in the wrong place to spin them out of control.

Three minutes. Danny checked the rear-view mirror. He could just make out Jack. He appeared to have closed the gap between them: 250 metres, maybe 200. That meant only one thing. The Land Cruiser was gaining on them. It was a faster vehicle. They couldn't hope to outrun it.

'Pass me my weapon,' Danny said.

Buckingham swallowed hard, but did as he was told. Danny took the weapon in his right hand and laid it on his lap.

'Recline your seat,' he said. Buckingham just stared at him. '*Recline your seat!*' Danny barked. '*As far as it'll go . . .*'

Breathing heavily, Buckingham did as he was told, awkwardly twisting the knob at the seat's base until the back was leaning against the rear seat.

'Stay down,' Danny told him.

The road had got worse. It was all Danny could do to keep the car straight. Jack was 100 metres back. Now fifty. Danny could make out the shape of the Land Cruiser a scant ten metres behind that. Jack was pulling out, as though overtaking on the outside.

Different scenarios spun through Danny's mind. Perhaps he should slam on the brakes right now, open up on the Land Cruiser while he had the advantage. He quickly dismissed that idea. He didn't know how many men were inside it. Entering into a contact was always the last resort, especially when you didn't know the nature of the threat. The tank was full, and this little VW was likely to have a better fuel consumption than the bigger Land Cruiser. But the Land Cruiser would have a much bigger tank. Could they outrun it? It wasn't something he'd like to bet on. And what if they hit a roadblock or checkpoint?

Sparks behind them. The side of Jack's Renault had just made contact with the Land Cruiser, which was now alongside him. Was he trying to muscle them from the road, or was it the other way round? Impossible to tell. The two cars were thirty metres behind.

And closing.

'What's happening?' Buckingham asked. He looked like he was trying to sit up.

'Stay down,' Danny shouted.

And it was a good thing he did.

More sparks. But these were not from a collision. They were from the barrel of a gun. Danny didn't hear the retort of the weapon over the shriek of the VW's maxed-out engine, but he sure as hell heard the crashing of its rear window as a burst of rounds spattered the glass. The entire panel shattered, and two bullet holes appeared on the right-hand side of the windscreen, directly in front of the passenger seat. If Buckingham had still been sitting up, Danny wouldn't have been looking at the spider-web of impact. He'd have been looking at the contents of his passenger's head.

Instinct took over. Danny slid lower in his seat as he swung left into the middle of the road and slammed his foot on the brake. So long as he was in front of the Land Cruiser, he was a target. He couldn't take a defensive option in that situation. His only hope was to attack. As the VW sharply decelerated, he rocked the steeering wheel left and right so that he didn't present a static target. The Land Cruiser – and Jack alongside it – caught up in a matter of seconds. All three vehicles were side by side, the Land Cruiser sandwiched in the middle. Danny felt for his weapon with his right hand and, with his left hand gripping the juddering wheel, discharged a single round across Buckingham's prone body and into the Land Cruiser's front-left window. The glass exploded, and the rush of air into the vehicle increased dramatically.

Danny was right alongside the Land Cruiser, and he had the shooter in plain view. He allowed himself a split second to take in some details. His target was leaning out of the rear passenger window. He wore a Kevlar helmet and carried what almost – but not quite – looked like an AK-47. Danny had it down as a Saiga-12 combat shotgun. Its owner was clearly surprised by Danny's sudden deceleration and was awkwardly swinging the weapon round ninety degrees so that he could aim at the VW.

Danny fired before he had the chance: three rounds in quick succession. Because of the speed of the vehicles, and the way they shuddered on the poor road surface, he couldn't tell how many of his 9mm rounds hit their target. At least one of them did the job, though. The Saiga-12 fell to the road and, through the darkness, Danny caught a glimpse of the trigger man's face, mashed by the full-on impact of a bullet.

He slowed down again. The tyres made a wincing screech as he fell in behind both Jack and the Land Cruiser at a distance of ten metres. His visibility was impaired by the network of cracks across the windscreen, but there was no way he could take out the glass while travelling at this speed – the shards would simply fly into his face. Instead he swung over to the other side of the road, hoping to lean out of his window and take out the Land Cruiser's tyres.

But he couldn't risk it.

Jack was still alongside the enemy vehicle, his right-side wheels just inches from the edge of the road. All of a sudden

148

they were playing dodgem cars. The vehicles collided once, twice, three times – with each collision there was a shower of sparks, and they careered all over the road. Danny was now ten metres behind the other two vehicles, which had both moved inward from the right-hand lane. But he didn't shoot. With moving targets like that, he had no way of being sure he would hit the Land Cruiser and not Jack.

The speedometer was still flickering around 130 kph. The road was still treacherous. If another vehicle came, there'd be a pile-up. Danny found himself shouting at Jack: 'Hold back! *HOLD BACK!*' All his mate needed to do was join Danny behind the Land Cruiser and they could open up on it together. But Jack, of course, couldn't hear him, and he remained locked in battle with the bigger car. A battle, it seemed to Danny, he couldn't hope to win.

'*What the bloody hell's happening?*' Buckingham shouted. Danny ignored him. If he lost his concentration, for even a moment, they were shafted.

It happened in the blink of an eye. It was the Land Cruiser that lost control. Maybe one of the front wheels had hit a pot-hole. Maybe the driver had lost his concentration. Whatever the reason, it swerved to the right, tilted on its right-side wheels and, still at speed, tumbled over on to the Renault, ploughing it off the road and on to the rough ground to the side. The dreadful crunching sound was audible even over the screeching VW and the inrush of air. Danny slammed on his brakes and skidded past the two vehicles.

Once more, instinct kicked in. Danny tried to bring the VW back under control, but, as he yanked the wheel down, the car spun violently. He heard two bangs in quick succession, and he knew his front tyres had gone. Within five seconds the car lurched to a halt. Buckingham, still lying back in the reclined seat, had his hands over his face. There was a dreadful silence. Danny twisted round to look back at the crash. All he could see was the undercarriage of the Land Cruiser, thirty metres away and at his five o'clock.

'Don't move,' he said. Sig in hand, Danny opened the driver's door and slipped out of the vehicle, keeping low, using the car for protection. He crept to the back, every sense on high alert. Heat pounded from the tyres. He could smell the burning rubber. Resting his weapon on his left forearm, he peered round the back of the VW.

He would almost have preferred the sound of gunfire to the silence that surrounded him – a silence that made dread seep through him like icy water. There was neither the sight nor the sound of movement from the crash site. Danny's eyes scanned the upturned Land Cruiser, ready to fire at the first sign of a threat. But there was none. Just that silence, which made the thumping of his pulse sound all the louder.

Sweat poured from him as he made his approach. He covered the stretch of open road in about twenty seconds, moving slowly with his pistol engaged so he was ready to react to the minutest sign of movement. There was none. When he reached the Land Cruiser, he crouched low, before creeping round the front of the vehicle to assess the damage to it, and to see what kind of state Jack was in.

The answer was bad. On all counts.

Jack had managed to keep all four wheels of the Renault on the ground. The roof, however, had been pushed in by the Land Cruiser upturning on it. The windscreen had smashed and crumpled like paper and Danny could quite clearly see a twisted, jagged shard of metal that had thrust itself into the flesh near Jack's jugular. The rest of his body was lost in the darkness of the crushed Renault, giving him the unnerving appearance of a disembodied head upon an ugly, improvised spike. His eyes were still open, bulging in their sockets. Blood frothed from his mouth.

A groan. Very faint. Jesus, the poor bastard was still alive.

He wouldn't be for long.

Another noise. A human voice. Danny turned his attention to the Land Cruiser. Miraculously, its windscreen was still whole. A sharp jab with the heel of his boot quickly rectified that. As the glass shattered, Danny aimed his Sig into the car, ready to fire at even the faintest hint of a threat.

The driver was clearly dead. The impact of the crash seemed to have broken his neck – his head was hanging gruesomely to his side at an unnatural angle. Like the shooter Danny had taken out, he was wearing a Kevlar helmet. Also, body armour. No question that these were pros. It was the guy in the front passenger seat making the noise. His eyes were closed, his face bloody from a severe gash along his forehead, but his lips were moving. His voice was very weak, and Danny couldn't understand what he was saying. But he thought he recognised the accent. If this guy wasn't speaking Russian, it was something very close to it.

Without hesitation, Danny fired a round into the whispering man's head. His body slammed back violently as his skull erupted like a cracked egg. He slotted the driver too, just to be sure, before climbing up on to the side of the Land Cruiser and discharging a couple of rounds into the rear passenger window. There were two bodies there. One of them Danny had already shot in the face. Both were now out of play.

Which left Jack.

The only indication that his mate was still alive were the bubbles of blood and phlegm that appeared around his lips as his dying lungs exhaled. Could he feel anything? Danny doubted it. His nervous system would have shut down by now. His brain would barely be functioning. Even so, Danny didn't want to think of him in pain. Jack had a mouth on him, but he'd been a good soldier and he deserved a quicker way out than this.

Danny raised his Sig once more, holding the end of the barrel an inch from Jack's forehead. His mate's eyes flicked open. He nodded, very faintly, then more foam spewed from his mouth.

'Goodnight, mucker,' Danny whispered.

And then he fired.

Danny's hands and the front of his clothes were covered in blood. Buckingham looked ill as he stared at him.

'I heard shots.'

They were standing by the VW. Danny said nothing. He was scanning up and down the road, checking for lights, movement. All clear for now, but that wouldn't last.

Time check: 02.10 hrs. Less than three hours till dawn, but the night sky was very clear, the moon bright.

'What about Jack?' Buckingham asked.

'Dead.'

'What? *How?*'

'Leaking head,' Danny said flatly. No point telling him any more. He strode to the boot of the VW and opened it. His pack was inside, his M4 beside it. He removed both items, shouldered the bergen and slung the assault rifle across his body.

'Who were the men in the other vehicle?' said Buckingham.

Danny didn't reply. He closed the boot quietly, to avoid attracting attention.

He needn't have bothered, because suddenly Buckingham slammed his fist noisily on the roof of the car. Danny felt his nerves snapping, and he turned to give him a bollocking. The expression on Buckingham's face stopped him. There was fury in his eyes, and his diffident expression had gone, to be replaced by a contemptuous sneer.

'Who,' he repeated, his voice much quieter, 'were the men in the other vehicle?'

Danny squared up to him. 'Bad guys.'

'I will *not*,' Buckingham said, 'be patronised by a *bloody* soldier. Is that understood?'

Silence. The two men stared at each other. Danny could see a vein pulsing in Buckingham's neck.

'Fine,' Danny said eventually. Now was not the time or place. 'Russian. Spetznaz would be my guess. Russian special forces. They were wearing body armour and Kevlar, and they were using Saiga-12s.'

'What the hell's a Saiga-12?'

'A very big gun,' Danny said, as though talking to a child. 'My guess is that our fixer is behind it,' he continued with a shrug. 'But that's only a guess.'

'How many were there?' Buckingham asked. His face and voice had softened a little.

'Four.'

'I heard five shots.'

'Then there's nothing wrong with your hearing. We need to get away from here, and we need to do it quickly. Understand?'

Buckingham drew a deep breath. 'I'm sorry about your friend.'

But there was no time to kiss and make up. Danny was already scanning the surrounding country. He knew, from his previous study of the terrain, that this road continued in a straight line for 100 kilometres east towards Homs. It cut through a mountain range on its way – the Homs Gap. Whatever their next move – whether they continued inland or retreated back to the coast – they needed to stay close to the road because it led directly to both destinations. He tried to think calmly. Tactically. If he was being tracked, what would his pursuers *expect* him to do? Retreat? Or get as far from the road as possible? One of the two.

Would they expect him to continue after losing three men? Probably not.

He looked east. He reckoned he could just make out, in the distance, the craggy outline of the mountain range. He had no intention of climbing it with Buckingham in tow. If they were to continue, the road was their only option. As options went, it stank.

Danny nodded in a northerly direction. 'Follow me,' he said.

The two men ran twenty metres off the road. At a word from Danny, they stopped. He turned and aimed his rifle back at the vehicles, discharging five rounds at the Land Cruiser. The spent cartridges fell at his feet.

'What are you doing?' Buckingham asked.

Danny lowered his weapon. 'They'll see gunfire came from this direction and assume we made our escape this way.'

'Who's "they"?'

'I don't know.'

He ran north for another twenty metres, then fired three more rounds. That was enough. He'd laid their false trail. They had to get out of there. They ran back to the road and over to the other side, passing five metres to the east of the crash. Danny sensed Buckingham slowing down as he caught sight of Jack's butchered head. But he didn't stop or speak.

Danny checked the time. 02.58 hrs. They had roughly two hours of night cover left. On his own and at a push, he could cover a good ten klicks in that time, but he knew Buckingham had nothing like his fitness and he wasn't sure he could beast him that far. Already the MI6 man was ten metres behind him, and they'd barely tabbed fifty metres from the road. They'd be lucky to cover seven klicks before the sun came up. He lessened his pace. Ten seconds later Buckingham caught up with him. 'We'll head south, staying a couple of kilometres from the road,' Danny said. 'After that we turn east again. They won't expect us to be heading to Homs, not after all that.'

'What happens when it gets light?'

'We find a lying-up point.' Danny didn't elaborate on where that might be. The terrain all around them was sparse, flat and open. At sunrise they'd be visible to anyone with binoculars. And Spetznaz, if it really was them they were dodging, would have a lot more than that. 'And then we make some decisions.'

'There's no decision to make,' Buckingham said quietly. 'We have to get to Homs. We've a job to do.'

Danny didn't reply. He was looking east along the main road. About three kilometres away, he could see the lights of a chopper, flying low along the direction of the highway. And on the road itself, more lights, perhaps three pairs.

'The Syrians might have something to say about that,' Danny said at last. 'Or the Russians.'

'Just tell me what to do.'

'Move.'

Buckingham didn't need telling twice.

TWELVE

06.00 hrs.

Clara Macleod's plans, such as they were, had failed to take one thing into consideration.

Her fear.

Huddled in the corner of the looted shop, she had just one objective in mind: to get to the Médecins Sans Frontières camp on the eastern side of the city. She didn't know where she was, or which way was east. She had no phone and no money. Her French was passable, her Arabic non-existent.

Her plan had been to wait until nightfall before leaving her hideout. Perhaps then she might keep to the shadows and have a chance of avoiding the violent government forces who had already killed both her boyfriend and the little girl she'd been tending. The thought of running into them made her limbs feel empty with dread. That plan had been a mistake.

As soon as night had fallen, the bombing had started again. So she had crouched in a dark corner of the shop, weeping with terror and indecision: was she safer inside, out of sight and mind, or on the street, where the building couldn't collapse on her? The impossible choice had paralysed her. As the city shook around her, the rumbling artillery punctuated by snatches of sniper fire, she'd remained where she was, wishing with a furious intensity that she could turn back time and not make the reckless, stupid decision to travel from the MSF base into Homs. She even prayed, and she hadn't done that since she was a child of eight.

The bombing had subsided an hour or so before dawn. The silence was almost soothing and, curled up on the hard floor, Clara had drowsed for perhaps forty-five minutes before waking with a sudden, horrible jolt as she realised where she was, shivering with cold, her throat rough with thirst. It was slowly growing lighter outside, and the new day brought her a new sense of determination. She could *not* suffer another night like that. She *had* to leave this place. She *had* to get back to the camp. Today.

Clara urinated in the corner of the shop and, ignoring the stabs of hunger in her belly, ventured outside.

The stars were still out, burning brightly in the indigo sky. A strange thought crossed Clara's mind: that her parents might be looking at the same stars from the window of their comfortable Wiltshire home, while she was surrounded by the rubble and shattered ruins of a bombed city. One look across the road told her how close she'd come to dying last night. A three-storey building that had been largely intact looked on the point of caving in. The render had fallen from its façade to reveal the shoddy brickwork underneath, and a lightning-shaped crack ran the entire height of the building. Clara couldn't tell if there was anybody inside. The street itself was almost deserted. A cat stood guard over the bags of rubbish fifteen metres away, its eyes glinting in the darkness. Twenty metres to the right, a man was loading a grey van with personal belongings. He had a furtive, hunted expression as he tried to stuff the end of a rolled-up carpet into the already crammed vehicle. A local inhabitant, collecting his gatherings and deserting his home. Clara ran to him. '*S'il-vous plait, vous pouvez m'aider?*' she said.

The man shook his head and slammed the rear doors of the van shut. Clara desperately grabbed hold of him, but he shook her off. Seconds later he was driving away, the tyres screeching on the rough road as he left Clara staring after him.

The familiar feeling of paralysis gripped her. She knew she had to move, she *had* to get back to the camp, but she didn't know which direction to go. It felt like an impossible choice, as if one direction led to freedom, the other to death. How could she know which one to choose? For a full thirty seconds she remained as motionless as the cat, but then the curious stillness around her was broken by a piercing, wailing voice.

'*Allahu Akbar . . . Allahu Akbar . . . Ash-hadu an-la ilaha illa illa . . .*'

The call to prayer.

The feral cat, disturbed by the noise, scampered away. Clara blinked. She turned left, in the direction of the voice, and an idea came to her. All mosques faced towards Mecca in Saudi Arabia. All Muslims prayed in that direction. She scrunched up her eyes and pieced together a hazy mental map of the Middle East. Mecca was almost directly south of Homs, she was sure of it. That meant she need only find the mosque if she wanted to orientate herself.

Suddenly released from her paralysis, she ran, her footsteps echoing against the shell-damaged buildings that lined this empty street. She didn't try to keep track of her location, but followed the muezzin's voice calling the faithful to prayer. As she turned right at the end of the street, she found herself in a wider one. Like everywhere else it bore the scars of the bombing. In front of a building on the far side was a pile of debris, three metres high and ten long. It contained old boilers and white goods, tyres and pieces of broken furniture, the accumulated detritus of homes that no longer existed. The street itself, although far from busy, was not deserted. Here and there, local people – all men, Clara noticed – hurried with their heads down and their collars up, in the direction of the voice. Nobody spoke. They didn't even look at each other, although Clara did feel the occasional curious glance as she joined these men on their way to the mosque.

Three minutes passed. The muezzin had fallen silent but Clara was now able to follow the little crowd. At a corner of this main street she saw a boy no more than ten years old sitting in a purple plastic chair. He had short black hair and a stripy jumper. On one side of him, sitting on the pavement, was his little brother. On the other side, propped up on a stool, a tray of cigarettes and lighters for sale. The eyes of both little boys followed the curious sight of this Western woman hurrying to the mosque with the men.

The men turned left off the main street into a smaller one that led to a large, open square about sixty metres by sixty, lined with trees and with an area of greenery that seemed quite out of place in this war-torn town. On the far side of the square was the mosque, low, sprawling and ornate, with a minaret on either side. The sun was just rising behind the mosque and its beams stabbed Clara's eyes, which had seen only darkness for nearly twenty-four hours. Her hands remained over her face for ten seconds as the dazzle subsided. Then, keeping her head down – as much to avoid attracting attention as to protect her vision – she moved forwards. For the first time since the horrific events of yesterday, she felt a twinge of hope. The sun was rising from the east, the direction in which the mosque was pointing. She knew which way to go. She had a chance of getting back to the camp. To safety, or something like it.

She stopped.

Fifteen metres to her right, a woman was crying. Clara turned to look at her. She was dressed in a black robe and looked poor. She had a child in her arms, little more than a toddler – Clara couldn't say whether male or female. The reason for the woman's distress was obvious: the child's face was covered with blood. He or she was conscious, but clearly in shock, silently trembling in the woman's arms. She kept approaching men on the way to the mosque, babbling at them through her tears, clearly asking them for help. None of them stopped. None of them even looked at her. Her distress grew worse.

The sun was a little higher over the mosque now, beckoning Clara eastwards, back to the MSF base. But the child needed her help. She froze for a moment, torn between fear and duty.

She tried to smile as she approached the woman, who at first backed away nervously – perhaps because Clara was obviously not Syrian. 'Doctor,' Clara said, before repeating herself with one of her few words of Arabic: '*Tabib.*' She opened her backpack of medical supplies and pulled out a fistful of swabs, crumpled but still in their sterilised packing. The sight of them seemed to calm the woman, and she allowed Clara to take her gently by one arm and lead her to the shelter of one of the trees that surrounded the square.

The woman sat cross-legged on the ground, still cradling the child. Clara softly used a moist wipe to clean the blood from her patient's face – she saw now that it was a little boy – until she came to the source of the bleeding. The wound was not nearly so bad as it appeared. There was a gash, about an inch long, in the fleshy part just under the child's left eye. Clara wiped it carefully and flushed it with an antiseptic spray, all the while making gentle cooing noises to keep the boy calm. When the wound was as clean as she could make it, she closed it up with three thin lengths of Steri-Strip. She even found a forgotten piece of chocolate at the bottom of her bag, which the boy gratefully accepted and wolfed down as though he hadn't eaten in days. Then he stood up of his own accord.

As Clara gathered her soiled medical equipment into a separate compartment of her rucksack, she felt the woman's tear-filled eyes on her. For the first time, Clara looked properly at her. She was young, maybe not even twenty. Clara had assumed she was the boy's mother, but perhaps not. Tentatively, the woman pulled at the foreigner's sleeve and said something in Arabic. When Clara gave her a helpless look, she tried again in French. '*Venez avec moi . . .*' Come with me.

At first Clara shook her head. Tending to the boy had been a distraction, but now the fear had returned. The sun was fully above the mosque and more people had ventured out of their battered houses. She could only assume that more people meant a higher chance of troops, and she didn't want to come face to face with anyone else bearing arms. But this woman was dogged, tugging at Clara's sleeve with a look of forlorn desperation. Then the child started crying, and Clara crumbled. She could always find the mosque again, she decided, so she zipped up her rucksack, looked anxiously around and nodded.

The woman went first. Clara and the little boy followed. She held his hand. He was as unsteady on his feet as a newborn foal. They made slow progress. The woman led them away from the mosque and through a network of streets even more war-torn than those Clara had already seen. She saw gunshot pockmarks all over what remained of the walls of certain houses. Everywhere there was an overpowering smell of sewage. On the corner of one street, a group of men were feeding rubbish into a burning iron barrel. The familiar chill of fear slid down her spine. Even though she wanted to run, the touch of the child's hand stopped her. Every thirty seconds or so, the woman looked back over her shoulder to check they were still following, before beckoning them on with a curled finger.

They hadn't walked for more than five minutes when the woman stopped outside the entrance to a narrow alleyway between two rows of shelled buildings. A large satellite dish hung precariously from the wall above, looking like it would fall at any moment. The woman looked around nervously, as though checking that nobody was paying them any attention, before slipping down the alleyway. Clara followed with the child. The smell of sewage was even stronger here. Clara had to hold her breath to stop herself retching, though it didn't seem to bother her companions. Twenty metres along, on the right-hand side, there was an iron door about five feet tall. The woman pushed it open – it was unlocked – and curling her finger once more she whispered, '*Venez . . . venez . . .*'

Clara swallowed nervously. She looked in both directions along the alleyway, then gently encouraged the little boy to enter, bent down low and followed him in.

It took a few seconds for her eyes to adjust to the darkness inside. They were at the top of a flight of narrow, winding stone steps. Sudden panic spilled over her. What was she doing? She should turn back now, find the mosque again, head east. This was madness. But then the little boy looked up at her, his big eyes imploring, and before she knew what was happening she had started to descend the steps. She trod carefully as she followed her companions down into the basement of the building. After five steps she felt the air temperature drop slightly. After ten steps a foul smell hit her nose. A few steps more and she was in the basement.

It was a large room, about fifteen metres by fifteen. The only source of light was a flickering, wind-up torch suspended from the ceiling by a short piece of wire. As Clara entered the basement, the light failed. A moment of silence, and then she heard the grind of someone winding it up again. Its feeble glow returned and Clara was able to look around.

There were twelve people down here, six of them children. The adults were all female. Their faces were as frightened as they were dirty. The foul stench came from a wooden box in one corner that Clara assumed was a makeshift toilet. Certainly none of the occupants of this squalid basement sat within five metres of it. They were huddled on the ground. At least three of the children were crying quietly, and two were coughing – a hoarse, croupy bark.

The downtrodden women were scared of her, that much was clear. They didn't know who she was, or what she was here for. In a strange way, it gave her strength to realise she was not the most terrified person in the city. And she suddenly understood why the woman had brought her here. These women and children clearly needed medical attention.

The woman Clara had followed started babbling Arabic at her. Clara held up her hands. 'English,' she said. 'I'm sorry, I don't understand.'

As she spoke, another woman stood up and walked towards her. She was older, forty maybe, with streaks of grey in her black hair. 'You are a doctor?' she said. Her voice was dry and weak.

Clara nodded.

'*Allahu Akbar*,' the woman said softly. 'My name is Miriam. We need a doctor very badly. Our children are sick. So are we. You can help us?'

Clara looked around the room. 'Where are your husbands?' she asked.

Miriam smiled sadly. 'All dead,' she said.

Instantly, an image of Bradley rose in Clara's mind. She hadn't even loved him, and the pain of his death was still raw. Imagine what these widows and orphans must be feeling. If she'd had any tears left in her, Clara might have cried.

'How?' she asked.

Miriam shrugged. 'The war, of course. The men die, the women are left . . .'

'Your homes?'

'Destroyed.'

'I'm sorry,' Clara said. It felt like a completely inadequate thing to say. 'But you *can't* stay here,' she said.

'We can't leave.'

Clara shook her head. She pointed out the makeshift toilet in the corner of the room. 'That will kill you,' she said. 'The germs . . .'

Miriam's expression was helpless. 'We have nowhere else—' she started to say, but she was cut short by the renewed coughing of one of the children. It sounded terrible. The child needed strong antibiotics, which was more than Clara's shoulder bag of medical supplies could provide. And that was just the start. Clara dreaded to think what assortment of illnesses were festering down here. She approached another of the kids and bent down to listen to his breathing. Heavy, laboured. The child had a chest infection at the very least. Another – a little girl – had bloodshot eyes and some sort of fungal infection on the inside of her mouth that had caused several suppurating white sores the size of ten-pence pieces over her inner cheek and tongue. Some of the occupants of the cellar – both child and adult – smelled as though they had wet themselves rather than use the disgusting toilet.

Most of the children at least had someone to cuddle. There was one who was alone, a boy with curly dark hair, huddled up against the wall. His wide eyes followed Clara's every move. She knelt down before him and took his hands. There were angry welts around his wrists, and his face was dotted with burns.

'What happened?' asked Clara.

Miriam was standing behind her. 'They tortured him,' she said in a flat, emotionless voice.

'Tortured him? But he's only—'

'Twelve, yes. The men came to his school. They put a hundred children in one classroom, and took them out one by one to question them.'

'What about?'

'Their parents . . . their friends . . .' Miriam's voice grew quieter. 'They tortured Hassam – his name is Hassam – worse than the others.'

'Why?'

'They found him playing at being a rebel fighter, using a stick for a machine gun. So they tied plastic cords around his wrists and hung him from the ceiling with his feet off the ground. Then they beat him. Most people last an hour hanging like that before they pass out. Hang for two hours and you are dead. Hassam passed out from the pain of the beating, so they woke him with cold water. Then they burned the skin on his face with cigarettes. They did this every day for five days. They wanted him to confess to something, but he had nothing to confess. His parents were already dead.'

Clara brushed the back of her hand against the child's cheek before standing up again.

'You see,' Miriam said, 'why we would rather stay down here?'

Clara barely knew what to say. With her limited supplies, there was very little she could do for them.

Unless . . .

She took Miriam by the hand. 'The streets are quiet,' she said. 'I know somewhere we can go, where my friends are. East of the city. There are lots of doctors there, and medicine. Do you understand? Medicine?' As she spoke she tried to block out the sound of scurrying from the toilet corner. Whatever rodents were attracted by the excrement, they were sufficiently brave not to be put off by the presence of humans. '*Medicine?*' Clara repeated.

Miriam nodded, but her face was uncertain. She turned to the others and addressed them in Arabic. As they spoke, the women seemed to shrink back against the walls. They started to mutter and it was clear that Clara's suggestion was unpopular.

'They will not come,' Miriam said. 'They are scared. The government men have guns . . .'

'If they stay here, they're dead. Hassam, all of them.' Clara felt the old fire in her veins. She wanted to help these people, but she couldn't if they refused to help themselves. 'I mean it, Miriam – two days, maybe three, the children will start dying, and that's if your building isn't bombed tonight. Do you understand?'

Miriam nodded, but she did not translate.

'Once you have one dead body in here,' Clara persisted, 'you'll be overrun with rats . . . bacteria . . . you'll have to leave anyway. Better to do it now, at the right time . . .'

Miriam relayed this to the others, who were silent.

'I'm going to where the doctors are. I'll take you all, if you like, but we have to go now. If we wait, the children will be too weak, and . . .' She shrugged. 'I'll wait for you upstairs.'

Clara turned her back on the women and children and climbed up from the basement. Out in the alleyway, she realised she was shivering, even though it wasn't cold. Was she doing the right thing? She had no idea. In the past forty-eight hours it had become impossible to tell any more.

She waited for two minutes that seemed a lot longer. Nearby, she heard the sound of vehicles. It was strangely comforting – a normal city noise, not the dreadful crash of bombing from above. She felt a glimmer of hope that she *could*, in fact, lead these women and children to the MSF camp, if only they would agree to come. She hadn't been exaggerating. Stuck down there in the medieval filth and darkness, it wouldn't be long before one of the kids succumbed to an infection, and it would spread. But it could be easily treated with the proper drugs.

If only they would agree to come.

Just when Clara thought the women had decided to remain where they were and she was to be faced with the impossible decision of going back down or leaving them to their fate, the little iron door opened. The face of the child she had tended at the mosque appeared. She smiled at him and held out her hand, helping him out into the alleyway. Miriam came next, before, one by one, each of the women and children filed out. Thirty seconds later they had congregated in the alleyway and were waiting silently, their expectant eyes fully on Clara, waiting for her to tell them what to do, and where to go.

Danny had to hand it to Buckingham. His fitness levels were crap, but he was willing to push himself. In the two hours between leaving the crash site and the imminent rising of the sun, they'd managed to cover about seven kilometres, travelling eastward and parallel to the Homs road, two klicks away. Now they were flat on the ground, Buckingham gasping for breath, Danny scanning the surrounding countryside through his night-sight.

There were mountains to the east – not jagged peaks but high, rolling hills through which the Homs road twisted and turned. The crash site, to the west, was out of sight now, but Danny counted three military vehicles travelling west and he didn't have much doubt about where they were headed. The road was busier now that dawn was approaching – a vehicle in one direction or the other every thirty seconds. The traffic was only going to increase as the sun rose. It was time to get out of sight.

The terrain – flat, dry grassland – afforded no camouflage. On foot, the hills were a good two hours away. Danny's trained eye, however, was picking out other options. Roughly a kilometre away, between his two and three o'clock and set back about fifty metres from the road, was a single-storey house with a couple of outbuildings. Danny didn't doubt that he could find a place there to hide, but it wasn't a good option. Too obvious. If enemy troops performed a search of this area, they *would* come knocking on that door. No question about it. He continued to pan around, looking for an alternative. Twenty seconds later he found one.

It would have been easy to miss it, which made it ideal as a lying-up point. To his one o'clock, the road started to slope gently upwards. Zooming in with his night-sight, and keeping his hand very steady because of the dramatically reduced field of view, he picked out the upper rim of a small, circular opening, perhaps a metre and a half in diameter. The rest of the opening was covered with foliage. It was a culvert, and would give them somewhere to wait out the day.

'Can you move?' he asked Buckingham.

'If I need to.'

'You need to.'

Danny helped Buckingham to his feet.

'Listen carefully. We're going to approach the road again.'

'Is that wise?'

'Wise doesn't come into it. It's the only option I can see. If you've got a better idea, spit it out.'

Buckingham looked around. His eyes fell on the house and its outbuildings. 'Over there,' he said. 'We could ask them for shelter.'

Danny gave him a look. Buckingham blushed.

'The closer we get to the road,' Danny continued, 'the more chance we have of being seen. I want you to walk ten metres behind me.'

'Why?'

'Because the closer we are together, the easier it is for a gunman to put us down with a single burst. This way, if one of us gets hit, the other can go to ground.'

Buckingham looked sick.

'I've spotted a culvert.'

'A what?'

'It's a big pipe that directs water under the road. It'll keep us out of sight while the sun's up.'

'You want to us to stay there all day?'

'We can't just thumb a lift, mate. Someone knows we're out here. They'll be looking for us. We've only got a few minutes of darkness left. Come on.'

Without waiting for any more questions, Danny headed for the road.

They reached it in approximately twelve minutes, and not before time. The sun hadn't yet broken above the horizon, but the sky was already a shade lighter. Thirty metres from the road, Danny went to ground, looking back over his shoulder to verify that Buckingham had done the same. A military truck covered in cam netting trundled west. Danny waited until it was fifty metres from their position before raising his left hand and jumping up to run forwards, with Buckingham close behind.

The culvert did not look like an inviting place to spend a day, but it sure as hell beat trying to stay inconspicuous on open ground. The winter rains had filled it with silt, through which thorny plants Danny didn't recognise crept towards the light at either end. The concrete inside was covered in lichen, patches of which were still damp, and there was a stench of animal shit, though the tiny droppings at the opening of the culvert told Jamie that they'd only need to worry about rodents rather than anything bigger disturbing them – unless the occasional snake found its way in there. Danny left the rough scrub at the opening undisturbed: messing with natural vegetation was a sure-fire way of making a hideout more obvious to anyone who knew what they were looking for. 'Get inside,' he told Buckingham. 'Halfway in. I'm leaving my bergen with you. I'll be back in five.'

Buckingham crawled awkwardly along the pipe while Danny pushed his pack after him, before reversing out. Keeping low, he ran fifty metres eastwards along the road to where there was a thicket of low brush. He cut an armful of this, taking just a little from various spots to reduce the visual impact of his plundering, and carried it back to the culvert. Pulling out his bergen, he whispered to Buckingham to come back out. The MI6 man did as he was told. 'Push this stuff in,' Danny said, giving him half of the brush. 'It will hide you from anyone looking in at the other end.'

Once Buckingham had inserted himself, Danny pushed the bergen back into the pipe, then pulled the remaining foliage in behind him and joined Buckingham. Passing him his Sig, he said, 'We'll sit back to back. If you see anything that looks like a face at the end of the culvert, don't shoot. If you see someone crawling inside, open up.' He knew that Buckingham was unlikely to score a hit, but it might buy them a crucial few seconds if they were discovered.

Danny removed his water bottle from his pack, offered Buckingham a mouthful and took some himself. Then he shook a little on to the dry silt that covered the floor of the culvert, mixing water into it to form a muddy paste. 'Face me,' he said. Using his second and third fingers, he pasted stripes and patches of mud over the other man's face.

'What are you doing?' Buckingham asked.

'Making you invisible. The markings break up the natural shape of your face, make you less conspicuous.' When he'd finished with Buckingham, he repeated the process on himself. Then he poked the barrel of his M4 through the foliage on his side and arranged it to give him an unobstructed view through his sight. 'Hope you're comfy,' he said.

'Not really,' Buckingham said.

'Well, we're here for the duration. Get used to it.'

Danny pulled a couple of foil-packed MREs from his pack. He handed one to Buckingham with a single word – 'Breakfast' – before wolfing down his cold meal and then settling down back to back with his companion.

It was pretty dark in the culvert, but the daylight filtering in was increasing all the time. Danny tried to clear his head, to decide on the best course of action. He'd been shocked when Jack had been denied a pick-up, but he'd had barely a moment to think through the implications. Now he did.

'You want to tell me what's really going on?' he asked.

His back felt Buckingham stiffen. 'What do you mean?'

'Normally we'd have been extracted as it was clear we'd been bumped. Standard operating procedure. What's so important about a few Syrian rebels that—?'

'Can you still get us to Homs?' Buckingham cut in, his voice very soft.

A moment of silence.

'It's too far on foot,' Danny said. 'We'd have to cross the mountain range with Russian SF and Syrian military searching for us. No offence, mate, but you're not cut out for it.'

'None taken,' Buckingham murmured.

Another pause.

'I need to get in touch with base again. Persuade them to let us extract.'

'Well, they won't allow that. You – we – have our orders. There must be a way for us to get to Homs.'

Danny hesitated. He didn't want to suggest it. It was like an admission of failure. But he told himself to remove his wounded pride from the equation. 'Saunders gave me a number for his private-sector guys,' he said. 'They'll know the state of the ground much better than I do. I could get in touch . . .'

'Do it.'

Though he bristled at Buckingham's instruction, Danny had to admit to himself that it was the right call. If he was alone, he could go to ground for days, even weeks. But Buckingham wasn't up to it. He just didn't have the fitness, the endurance or the skills. They needed reinforcements. They needed to call in the cavalry.

Danny rummaged in his pack for his Iridium sat phone, his GPS unit and the scrap of paper on which Saunders had written the contact number. For the sat phone and the GPS to work, he needed line of sight with the sky, so he shuffled to the end of the culvert, pushed the camouflage out and poked the handset's antenna into the open air. He switched on the sat phone, waited for a connection, then dialled the number.

A ringing tone: a one-second pulse followed by two seconds of silence.

It repeated. Eight times.

Nine.

A click.

A pause.

A voice. Dry. Unfriendly. Cockney accent.

'Who the fuck is this?'

Danny felt his jaw set. Everything about this voice raised his hackles. He tried not to let it sound in his response.

'Call sign Kilo Alpha Six Four.' Danny kept it terse.

There was no acknowledgement from the other end.

'Repeat, call sign Kilo Alpha Six Four. Identify yourself.'

Again, a long pause.

'*Identify yourself,*' Danny hissed. Was it his imagination, or had he just heard a snort from the man at the other end of the phone?

Something was wrong. If this was one of Saunders' men, why was he being so damn shady? Or maybe he was being shady *because* he was one of Saunders' men. Freelance. Cynical. Out for what he could get.

'*Identify yourself,*' Danny said for a third time. He was on the point of hanging up when the other guy spoke.

'I'm Skinner,' he said. 'Where the *fuck* are you?'

THIRTEEN

'We've been bumped,' Danny explained. 'I'm three men down.'

'Is the spook still alive?'

'Roger that.'

'Pity.'

Another long silence.

'We've got eyes searching for us. I need backup.'

Skinner, whoever he was, once more let his silence do the talking.

'Do you copy?' Danny asked.

'Loud and fucking clear, sunshine. What's your location?'

Danny consulted his GPS and relayed his precise lat and long. 'You want to read that back to me?' he asked.

But the voice at the other end had gone.

Danny stared at the phone. 'Nice talking with you, pal,' he muttered, before shuffling back to the centre of the culvert, dragging the foliage with him, to where Buckingham was resting against the side of the pipe, his eyes closed.

'Wake up,' Danny said, poking him in the ribs with the phone's antenna. Buckingham's eyes shot open. 'You can sleep when we're safe.'

'Did you get through?'

Danny nodded.

'And?'

'And we wait. They know where we are.'

'How long?'

Danny rearranged his M4 among the camouflage.

'As long as it takes.'

'How do you know nobody else will find us first?'

'I don't.'

Clara walked nervously through the streets of Homs. With every step she felt an earthquake might hit. Or a shake of some kind, perhaps caused by ordnance from above. Like a terrified Pied Piper, she led the ragged band of women and children, if not to safety, then at least away from their horrific, self-imposed imprisonment.

Miriam walked by her side. She had a slight limp, Clara noticed, and winced every time she put pressure on her right leg. But she didn't complain. None of this sorry little group complained, and they had been walking for less than ten minutes when Clara understood why. They came upon a building so utterly destroyed that its foundations appeared to have been ripped from the earth. Miriam looked at it sadly. 'We are the lucky ones,' she said.

They attracted stares. Some of them were from other children. She saw one little boy proudly displaying the metal casing of a spent shell to his mates, who crowded round and tried to grab it. Almost all the adults on foot were male. They looked at these women and children, and especially at Clara with her pale Western skin, with suspicion. Nobody asked if they were OK, let alone offered help. Weirdly – uncharacteristically – Clara didn't blame them. She understood that they had their own problems. And most likely their own families.

Whereas Clara had nobody.

When they reached the mosque, she saw that the open area in front of it was more crowded, despite early-morning prayers having finished. Perhaps a hundred men had gathered. They stood in little groups, some of them smoking, most of them casting occasional nervous looks around them and up into the sky. Clara and Miriam stood at the edge of the square, the women and children huddled behind them.

'We should avoid this place,' Miriam said.

'Why? It's a mosque. Isn't it safer . . . ?'

Miriam shook her head. 'People who defy the government meet here. They think they are safe, that the soldiers will not kill them in front of the mosque. But look.' She pointed to a far corner of the square. A small group of five or six soldiers, all armed, were loitering there, just watching. 'When these people leave the square, many of them will be questioned.'

'We don't have anything to hide,' Clara said, the old defiance rising up in her.

Miriam smiled weakly. 'In Syria,' she said, '*everybody* has something to hide. At least, that is how the government treats us. Come, I know a way round the square. We can continue east once we have passed the mosque.'

Clara nodded. As Miriam explained to the others what they were doing, Clara found her eyes lingering on the soldiers. She remembered Bradley, and the brutal way that the soldier had kicked the little girl. And was it her imagination, or did one of the troops – a young, bearded man with a sour expression on his face – look very like one of the soldiers who had assaulted her the previous day, then run away when their little game had turned sour?

And did his gaze follow Clara and Miriam as they led the others out of sight?

11.00 hrs.

Danny and Buckingham had sat in silence since dawn. The culvert was uncomfortable. Cramped. Hard. No problem for Danny, but Buckingham was getting twitchy. As the morning had worn on, the traffic passing overhead had increased a lot. Now there was no doubt that they had taken refuge under a major daytime thoroughfare. Night couldn't come soon enough.

175

'I could do with some more food,' Buckingham said.

'Sorry, pal. Hard rations. We need to make it last.'

'I thought you said they were on their way.' There was irritation in Buckingham's voice. Danny gave him a dangerous look. Wisely, he buttoned it.

The children were slowing down. It was hardly surprising. They were hungry and sick. The little boy with croup had not stopped hacking for the past hour. His mother had tried to carry him, but she was too weak. The child was too frightened to come to anyone else, and so he was forced to walk and cough, sounding sicker and sicker by the minute.

'You're sure we're heading east?' Clara asked Miriam for what felt like the hundredth time.

Miriam gave a half-nod, half-shrug that didn't inspire confidence. But the sun was high now, too high for Clara's rudimentary navigation. She had no choice but to trust her new companion. She wondered how far they had walked. She was rubbish at distances. A mile? Maybe a bit more? They found themselves in a part of Homs that bore fewer scars of war. The differences were subtle. In the area near the mosque she had seen street kids selling petrol from blue canisters that reminded her of camping holidays when she was a kid. She supposed that it must be a precious commodity in this city where electricity was scarce. She had seen men sawing up trees and telegraph poles to burn as fuel. They had passed the occasional street stall where kids who should have been in school were selling shoes. The one thing Clara had not seen was any food.

Here it was different. The area looked slightly more prosperous. The buildings were not unscathed – many of them were riddled with bullet holes – but on the other side of the road there was a woman with two dozen eggs on display. A few metres beyond her, a man cradled what seemed to be a bowl of hummus. And, a little farther on, two sheep's carcasses hung from metal hooks outside a concrete building. A man stood guard over them and Clara couldn't help noticing that he carried a gun. The meat he had for sale was his livelihood, so he clearly wasn't going to take any chances. The women and children looked with undisguised hunger at the food on display, and Clara herself felt her stomach groaning for sustenance. She hadn't eaten or drunk for, what, twenty-four hours? But none of them had any money, so she tried to think of other things. Should she find this change in their surroundings reassuring or unsettling? Did it mean this was a district more heavily populated by those loyal to the government? Certainly none of the men they passed had quite the same look of animal fear. Suspicion, yes, but that was different.

When the soldiers appeared in the street twenty metres ahead of Clara, she stopped.

There were eight of them, all armed. The young bearded soldier from yesterday was among them, and he stared at Clara with an arrogant sneer. The two groups faced each other for ten seconds, before the soldiers strode towards the women and children, their step oozing self-importance and aggression.

Clara felt her hands shaking, but her instinct, instilled in her from years of medical training, was to look after her patients. She walked forwards to confront the soldiers, not quite knowing what she would say even if they spoke English. The soldiers came to a halt two metres away, headed by a tall, thin guy with pockmarks and a pointed nose.

Suddenly Clara found herself being nudged out of the way by Miriam, who started babbling at these younger men like the matriarch she was, wagging her finger. Only the ones at the back seemed to be paying attention. Their leader, however, had no time for Miriam's remonstrations. Even before she had finished speaking, he had raised the stock of his rifle. With a sudden, solid blow, he cracked it down on the side of Miriam's head. She fell to the ground, clutching her head and rolling around in pain.

The soldier ignored her, but he didn't ignore Clara. He grabbed her by the front of her top and looked over his shoulder at the young bearded man, whom he asked a question. The young man nodded.

To Clara's surprise, her new captor spoke English to her. Broken and heavily accented, but English all the same. 'You are spy,' he said.

Clara shook her head. 'No,' she said. 'I'm a doctor. I'm just trying to help these people.'

Her captor spoke in Arabic over his shoulder again, and the others laughed. When he turned back to Clara, though, he was not smiling.

'You will come with us.'

'*No!* These people need help. Medical attention. Do you understand?'

She tried to wriggle from his grasp. It earned her a stinging slap across the face and she sensed the women and children edging back.

'Please,' Clara said, speaking softly now. 'I'm a doctor, that's all.'

'Identification?' the soldier demanded.

Clara looked at him helplessly. She had lost her ID the previous day. The bearded soldier had discarded it himself, but he would never admit that.

'You will be questioned in Damascus,' the soldiers' leader told Clara. Then he barked at Miriam, who, still holding her head, shuffled over to join the other women and children.

It was sheer frustration that made Clara do it. She swiped her free hand against the soldier's face, clawing at his eyes with what remained of her dirty, brittle nails. His response was to throw her to the ground and kick her hard in her side. She felt his boot connect harshly with her bottom rib and was aware of the women and children scattering. The soldier delivered another instruction in Arabic. His young, bearded colleague bent down, yanked Clara's arms behind her back and bound her wrists so tightly with plasticuffs that she cried out in pain. He grabbed a handful of her hair and pulled her, screaming, to her feet. The women and children had disappeared – all except the little boy Hassam with the cigarette burns on his face. He ran towards the soldiers and in his feeble way started kicking at the shins of Clara's bearded tormentor. The soldier spat in the kid's face, then pushed him away so harshly that the child was lifted off his feet before falling hard on the ground two or three metres away. Clara tried to run to him, but the soldier grabbed her hair again and yanked her in the opposite direction.

Over the next two minutes, Clara screamed three times. The first two screams earned her two brutal punches in the stomach, the third an agonising blow to her left breast. The pain was so bad that she couldn't bring herself to scream any more in case they did it again.

The soldiers dragged her roughly through the streets, where to she had no idea.

17.30 hrs.

Danny's muscles ached. His mind was drifting. He kept seeing the look on Jack's face before he delivered the round that finished him off. He knew he had to keep sentiment out of it while he was still effectively behind enemy lines. But he did wonder if he'd ever forget that face.

He was tugged back to reality by the sound of a helicopter. He listened carefully. It was circling overhead, and lingered in the area for three or four minutes before heading off to the west.

Coincidence?

He didn't think so.

'How much longer till it gets dark?' Buckingham asked.

'Two hours. Maybe a little more.'

'Where the bloody hell *are* they?'

'Waiting for nightfall, most likely.'

'What if they've been delayed?'

'Then they've been delayed.'

'What if . . . ?'

'I could do without the "what ifs", pal.'

'But—'

'Quiet!' Danny had heard a rustling at his end of the culvert. Slowly he lowered himself down to his M4.

Then he froze.

A snake was coiled half a metre from the culvert. About 150 centimetres long. Yellow, with brown cross bands. Difficult to tell from a distance but Danny had it down as an Egyptian cobra. Highly neurotoxic. Aggressive if provoked. Its head swung lazily towards the pipe, its tongue flicking.

Danny kept very still.

The snake moved very suddenly. Something – Danny couldn't tell what – had caught its attention outside the culvert, and it slithered away.

Danny exhaled slowly.

'What is it?' Buckingham whispered.

'Nothing,' Danny said. 'Just keep watching.'

The building to which the soldiers took Clara had once been a school. At first glance it looked to her like just another bombed, looted, trashed building. There were no tables or chairs, no blackboards or computers. But there were, among the rubble of masonry that covered the floor, hundreds of loose-leaf papers and exercise books. And even, hanging by one corner from a wall, an old, laminated map of the world. Clara found herself staring longingly at the tiny outline of Great Britain. What would she give to be back home?

This former school had been turned into a kind of holding area. A temporary prison for anybody who the government forces patrolling this part of town thought was a threat. There were six other prisoners aside from Clara. Two of the prisoners were women, each with a beaten face and a split lip. Both wept quietly in the corner. One of them was clutching her lower belly. Clara suspected that whatever torment they'd endured had been sexual as well as physical. The four male prisoners were cuffed in the same way as Clara. Three appeared too exhausted even to lift their chins from their chests. The fourth had more life in him. Even though he was missing several teeth, and had a cut across his left cheek that looked almost gangrenous, he was yelling non-stop at the guards, a ferocious babble of Arabic that pounded in Clara's aching head. At first the guards seemed to find him amusing. About twenty minutes after Clara's arrival, however, the novelty wore off.

Clara could scarcely bring herself to watch the beating he endured. It even crossed her mind that it would have been kinder of the guards simply to shoot him dead. Two of them grabbed him by the arms while the third kicked him repeatedly in the genitals. After five minutes of this, he was in too much pain even to shout. The guards let him drop. He lay on his back and one of the soldiers stamped on his face, grinding the heel of his boot into his broken nose. Clara found herself shouting at them to stop, but they ignored her.

The silence that followed the beating was terrible. The three soldiers lit cigarettes and stood around chatting as if nothing had happened. Their victim was unconscious on the ground. It was only the faint rise and fall of his chest that told Clara he was still alive.

She tried to guess what time it was. Mid-afternoon? She'd been here for at least two hours. And try though she might to protest her innocence, to explain who she was, her words had gone unheard. She was hungry and bursting to use the lavatory. She was in anguish for the women and children she'd led from the basement. But more than that, she was desperately afraid.

The sporadic gunfire outside only intensified that fear.

As soon as she heard the first burst she felt her body shrink back, like a badly treated dog shown a raised hand. Nobody else in the room even appeared to flinch. Clearly it was a noise they were used to. Even the soldiers barely glanced in the direction of the street as they finished their cigarettes and stubbed the butts with their heels.

It was only when they heard shouting in the corridors outside that they looked at each other with first bewilderment and then alarm. By the time the door burst inwards they had started to raise their weapons, but it was too late.

The men who entered – five of them – had their faces covered. Four had swathed their heads in keffiyehs, while the fifth had a black balaclava with two holes cut out for his eyes. They all wore camouflage trousers, military vests and webbing. They had a military air to them, but it was obvious that they were *not* military. All five men were shouting hoarsely – Clara had no idea what they were saying, but it was aggressive enough to shock the soldiers into a moment of hesitation. One of the soldiers dropped his weapon and seemed to be about to raise his arms in surrender, evidently overawed by these new arrivals. But the gunmen were not in the business of dispensing mercy. Only bullets.

Clara had no love for her captors, but the ruthlessness with which these newcomers dispatched them sickened her. All five men fired bursts of rounds and, in the ten seconds that followed, the schoolroom became a maelstrom of gore. The bullets knocked all three soldiers back a good four metres, ripping seams in their bellies, which spurted fountains of blood as they fell. One of them hit the ground just a metre from where Clara was crouched, and she felt a disgustingly warm spatter cover her, and nearly vomited when she saw the state of the dead man. Two bursts of fire had hit him. The first had practically split him up the middle and a reservoir of blood oozed out of his chest, pooling quickly on the ground around him. The second had hit him in the face. His features were now just a mash of raw meat, and one round had exited through the top of his head, bringing with it a shard of skull and a gush of blood. Always surprising, how much blood a human body contains.

The other two soldiers were in a similar condition, but their killers stepped over them as if they weren't even there. Two of them pulled knives and cut the plasticuffs that bound the male prisoners' hands. A third went to help the two women – the ones Clara assumed had been raped – to their feet. It was the man in the balaclava who turned to Clara. He inclined his head, obviously mystified to see a Western woman here. He spoke harshly to her in Arabic.

'Do you speak any English?' Clara whispered.

A pause.

'Who are you?' the man said, his voice muffled through the balaclava.

'Oh, thank God. I'm just a doctor . . . they wanted to take me to Damascus . . . I need to get back to the Médecins Sans Frontières camp . . . *Please* can you help me?'

The man hesitated. Clara was aware of her fellow prisoners being hustled out of the room to freedom. But nobody had cut her plasticuffs yet, and the man with the balaclava didn't appear in any hurry to do it. He bent down, grabbed her by the top of her arm and pulled her to her feet. One of his feet slapped in the pool of blood oozing from one of the murdered men as he dragged Clara towards the door.

'Where are we going?' she demanded. 'Where are you taking me?'

'To see Sorgen,' said the man. 'He can decide what to do with you.'

18.45 hrs.

A milky moon was rising in the west. They only had another half-hour of daylight. Even though they needed to stay put, Danny would feel safer when it got dark.

Buckingham was dozing fitfully, and Danny could feel him jolt each time he woke up. He decided to talk to him, just to keep his eyes open.

'You got family back home?' he asked.

'Why do you ask?'

'Just making conversation, pal.'

'Right, I see. Actually, no. Only child, you know. Parents gone on. You?'

'My dad's still around,' Danny said. 'Not my mum.'

'Ah, yes. I remember from your file. Tragic.'

Danny didn't reply.

'Must have been very hard for your brother,' Buckingham added, 'to see your mother shot like that.'

A pause.

'What are you talking about?' Danny growled.

There was an awkward silence.

'My mum died in childbirth,' said Danny. 'My dad was shot in Northern Ireland.'

'Of course. My mistake. I must have misremembered.'

'Damn right you must have done.'

But Danny was not convinced. He twisted round to face Buckingham. The man looked alarmed, as though he was desperately trying to think of a way out of this conversation. 'What else did my file say?' Danny asked, his voice deceptively level.

But almost as soon as he'd spoken, he held up one hand to stop Buckingham answering.

'You hear that?' he whispered.

Buckingham shook his head. 'No. Hear what? I can't hear anything.'

'Exactly. No cars.'

It was true. The sound of vehicles overhead, which had been constant since early morning, had stopped.

'Maybe it's just because it's getting dark . . .'

Danny shook his head, then jabbed one finger towards the other end of the culvert, indicating that Buckingham should keep stag on it. He twisted back to face his end, pushing himself prone into the firing position, M4 at the ready, and surveying the opening through the scope on his rifle. The terrain outside came into sharp focus, the atmosphere wavering in the heat. Danny noticed himself holding his breath as his forefinger lay lightly on the trigger of his M4.

Suddenly his field of view was filled with a pair of boots. He moved his eye away from the lens. A man was standing no more than five metres from the end of the culvert – eight metres in all from Danny's position. Above a boot, he could see about a foot of trouser leg. Military khaki. The tip of a rifle barrel came into view for about a second, then disappeared.

A voice shouted something in the distance. It sounded like it came from the road above, but not close – thirty or forty metres. The man near the culvert called back in Arabic. He sounded bored. He muttered something and shuffled his feet.

Walk away quietly, pal – that'll be best for both of us, was Danny's first thought. His forefinger remained in firm contact with the trigger.

But the soldier was walking the five metres towards the culvert. He stopped just by it and there was a gushing sound. It lasted for a good thirty seconds, not including the ten seconds he took to shake himself off and fasten his zip.

Then he bent down.

The soldier had a round face and fat lips. He peered into the culvert, squinting slightly. Then he crouched, spat on the ground and lit a cigarette. The smell of the tobacco drifted into the pipe, but he was clearly an enthusiastic smoker and he finished the cigarette in three drags, before peering into the culvert again.

His eyes narrowed. Had he seen something?

The soldier stood. When his face reappeared a couple of seconds later, he had a torch, which he shone along the length of the pipe.

His eyes narrowed once more.

He crouched lower and wormed his way into the culvert.

The guy was an amateur. He didn't even have his personal weapon engaged as he crawled two metres inside the pipe. Had he even thought what might happen to him if he actually found what he was looking for?

Slowly, Danny loosened his grip on the M4. Firing it to take out this particular target would immediately alert the other guy, and any others in the area, to their location. If the enemy was effectively unarmed, however, there was no need to discharge a round. Not when he had a silent weapon: his hands.

The soldier stopped a metre from the foliage.

He held the torch a little higher. Directly at Danny's face. Five seconds passed before the intruder realised what he was looking at. His eyes widened. He dropped the torch and started scrambling for his weapon.

Danny thrust himself forwards, bursting through the camouflage like it wasn't there, ignoring the thorns on the branches that scraped his skin. He swiped one big hand on to the back of the soldier's head, grinding his face hard into the curved bottom of the culvert. There was a crack as the nose shattered, and a muffled grunt from the intruder. Already Danny had scrambled on to his back. He twisted himself around so that he was facing in the same direction as his prone victim, then he gripped his throat and squeezed with a brutal, relentless strength. As he strangled the soldier, he shifted his body weight on to the man's upper back, expelling any remnants of oxygen from his lungs and compressing his chest so he was unable to inhale even the slightest breath of air.

It was quick. The man's legs flailed, but only weakly, kicking the bottom of the culvert with a dull thud. Danny maintained his stranglehold for thirty seconds after the kicking had stopped – he didn't want the corpse doing a Lazarus on him – then gently rested the limp head on the concrete.

The struggle hadn't lasted more than a minute. Buckingham gaped at the sudden burst of brutality and its fatal aftermath. But Danny had already eased himself off the dead man. Picking up the M4, he said, 'We have to leave.'

'What? I thought they were meeting us here.'

'Change of plan. This fella's cronies are going to come looking for him. I don't reckon they're more than about forty metres away. They'll be swarming round this place like flies before you know it.'

'But if we leave, they'll see us.'

'We'll have to risk it. I can't defend this position against more than one person, two at the most.'

'What if—?'

'Quiet!' Danny had stopped to listen. He could faintly hear a helicopter again. Somewhere off to the north – impossible to tell how far from this underground location, but close enough if they knew what they were looking for. They needed to leave by the south end of the culvert, which meant climbing over the body. Danny scrambled over the still-warm corpse on all fours – he felt the kneecap dislocate as he pressed his palm against it – then hissed at Buckingham to follow.

They emerged into a dwindling twilight. There were not yet any stars in the darkening sky, but the moon was rising. Danny took five seconds to check their situation. From the roadside the ground ran downhill, forming a steep bank about two metres high. If they kept to the line of the road, they could follow the bank without being skylined. Climb too high and they would present a silhouette; wander too far into open ground to the south and they'd be visible from the road.

'You still got the Sig?' Danny asked.

Buckingham held it up.

'Good. Keep down. I'm going to recce.'

Keeping his head low and moving as silently as possible, Danny crawled up the bank until he was level with the road and he was quickly able to evaluate the situation. All the activity was off to the west in the direction of the coast: a roadblock, fifty metres from the culvert, with four civilian cars waiting to pass. A chopper with a searchlight was circling about 500 metres north of the road – an indication that whoever was searching for them had swallowed their false trail.

To the east, nothing except the single-storey house and outbuildings he'd already seen about a kilometre up the road, which he'd dismissed as an LUP before deciding on the culvert. A couple of cars heading in their direction, and the twinkling lights of settlements in the hills up ahead. They were beyond the enemy troops' cordon. But as soon as someone found the body in the culvert, that advantage would be lost.

Danny turned his attention back to the house. The situation had changed. They needed somewhere nearby to wait for the PMCs. The house was out of the current search area, it gave a view on to the road and it was defensible. He decided quickly. Sliding back down the bank, he didn't waste time explaining his thinking to Buckingham. He just jabbed one finger in an easterly direction. 'Make for the house. Keep low, don't stop running. I'll be ten metres behind you at all times.'

'I thought you said the house was—'

'*Go!*'

The difficult thing was moving slowly enough to keep a safe distance from Buckingham. In the end, Danny resorted to allowing him to move ahead by twenty metres while he checked the ground behind them for threats through the sights on his M4, before catching up, stopping and checking again. Moving like this, it took some ten minutes to come within fifty metres of the house. Danny caught up with Buckingham and hissed at him to stop. They went to ground, and while Buckingham regained his breath, Danny withdrew his night-sight and examined the location. Single-storey. Flat roof. Two outbuildings, both tumble-down. The building looked old — as though it had been there before the highway was constructed — but it was definitely occupied. Light shone from a window on the facing side, and a motorbike was propped up against a wooden barn about twenty metres from the house.

It was fully dark. Danny judged that they could risk a sprint across open ground to the barn. They reached it in thirty seconds, by which time Buckingham was completely out of breath again. The barn had an open front and a quick look inside told Danny it was empty apart from a few old tools shrouded in cobwebs. 'Wait in here,' he said.

'Where are you going?'

'I need to keep an eye on the road.'

'What if someone comes?'

'I'll be keeping an eye on you too.' Danny pointed to a dark corner. 'Crouch down there. Don't move and don't put the gun down.'

'I don't bloody like it.'

'You don't bloody have to.'

Danny left the barn. Crouching low, he ran twenty-five metres west before going to ground. From here he had a clear view of the entrance of the barn, but also of the road. If the PMCs approached the culvert, he'd have eyes on. If the owner of the house, which appeared to be occupied, looked like he might discover Buckingham, Danny could be there in seconds.

He hugged the ground, covered by a blanket of darkness, and kept watch.

Fifteen minutes passed.

Half an hour.

To the west, a glow in the night sky told him that the search was still on. Every thirty seconds he checked the area around the culvert. So far nobody had approached it.

Maybe their luck would hold.

It didn't.

The vehicles came in convoy from the east: two standard military trucks, not unlike the technical Danny had encountered in Libya, only the rears were covered with tied-down webbing rather than displaying .50-cals. Danny estimated that they were travelling at a steady 50 kph. For a tense moment he thought they were slowing down as they passed the house and its outbuildings – which put them just fifty metres away – but they carried on in the direction of the roadblock, clearly reinforcement troops on the way to either relieve or bolster those already in situ. A hundred metres from the roadblock and fifty from the culvert, they slowed down.

They stopped almost exactly above the pipe containing the dead soldier.

Danny remained absolutely still, barely breathing, his nightsight magnifying the two trucks.

Doors opened. Men emerged. Eight in total. No, nine – a final figure appeared between the two trucks. He was bearded and dark-skinned. He wore the standard camouflage gear of the Syrian military. Assault rifle slung across his chest.

Danny focused in on the rest of the men. They were all dressed the same.

'*Shit!*'

The soldiers conferred for a moment. Danny tried to zero in on their faces but they were moving around and blurry. It soon became clear, though, that they'd decided to investigate the culvert. Three of them slid down the bank. One disappeared from Danny's line of sight.

Sixty seconds later he reappeared, dragging something from the culvert.

The three men rejoined the others on the road. Danny couldn't make out the corpse, which meant they'd probably left it outside the pipe. They started looking round. West towards the roadblock. North and south across open ground.

East, towards the house.

Danny wasn't sure which of these nine Syrian soldiers gave the order. All he knew was that the order was given. Within thirty seconds, they had all returned to their vehicles. The trucks U-turned across the road and started heading back the opposite way, their headlamps flooding the road in front of them.

Danny's veins had turned hot with adrenalin. He sprinted back to the barn. Buckingham was where he had left him, crouching in the dark corner, clutching the Sig.

'We've got company,' he whispered.

Buckingham's frightened eyes glinted in the darkness. 'Where?'

'On their way. We've got about three minutes.'

'What do we do?'

'Fight,' Danny said.

Buckingham said nothing.

'The house has a flat roof. If we can get up there, we're likely to have the advantage of height. I can lay down rounds from above and we can withdraw to avoid incoming fire. Whatever happens when we get up there, keep down. The moment you raise your head, you become a target. Understood?'

Buckingham nodded.

'Follow me. Stay close.'

Distance to the main house: twenty metres. An exterior staircase led up the back wall. Danny sent Buckingham up first, covering him until he reached the penultimate step, at which point he himself raced up. Once they were both on the flat roof – it was fifteen metres square and made of rough concrete – Danny dragged Buckingham to the centre and in one swift movement pushed him down on to his belly.

'Don't move,' he said.

Distance to the edge of the roof: five metres. Danny crawled it. By the time he had a vista on the road, fifty metres away, the two-vehicle convoy had already turned off it and was heading for the house.

Why? Had they been spotted?

Danny removed the two fragmentation grenades he had stashed in his chest rig and laid them next to him. Then he allowed the barrel of his M4 to protrude a couple of metres proud of the roof, set the weapon to automatic, closed his left eye and followed them with his right through the scope.

Use the element of surprise, he said to himself. Hit them hard and fast as soon as they stop. Put them down before they even know what's happening, let alone have a chance to fire back.

Forty metres.

Thirty.

The convoy stopped.

The headlamps stayed on. Danny waited for the doors to open and the passengers to disembark.

They didn't.

Instead the convoy moved on. Faster than before.

Twenty metres.

Ten.

For a moment Danny thought they were going to smash into the house. At the last second, however, the vehicles skidded through ninety degrees, coming to a halt parallel with the front of the house and so close to it that his advantage of height had suddenly been neutralised. Now he couldn't see the vehicles, far less fire on them.

He looked briefly over his shoulder. Buckingham was where he had left him, face down with his hands covering the back of his head. Voices and the slamming of doors returned Danny's attention to the front of the house. Activity. The soldiers were barking instructions at each other in Arabic. Danny made a quick call. A frag grenade – maybe two – would kill or wound a good number of them, and certainly confuse the others.

Suddenly Buckingham was beside him, tugging at his sleeve. 'What the hell's happening? We can't stay here . . .' He'd crawled over but looked like he was about to stand up.

'Get *down!*' Danny hissed, pulling him down again.

Twenty seconds passed before Danny looked up again and prepared to throw the frag. His location would be blown, but right now that was the lesser of two evils.

He was just stretching out his left hand to pick up one of the grenades when it happened.

A boot appeared to his left. With a deft tap worthy of Lionel Messi, it nudged both frags away before Danny could get his hand on one.

More than anything else, he felt a surge of anger with himself. Buckingham had made him take his eye off the ball. Somebody had crept up on them. But, lying prone as he was, there was nothing Danny could do. A strong arm reached down and yanked him to his feet as though he weighed nothing. He started to struggle, ready to use brute force to overcome this surprise assailant.

In the seconds that followed Danny noticed three things.

Buckingham, still pressed against the concrete, with a burly soldier in Syrian military camouflage hulking over him.

The military camouflage of his assailant's uniform.

The elaborate tattoo on the man's powerful forearm.

And nothing else. Because, right then, he felt a stunning blow to the back of his head. There was just time for him to feel his legs turn to water before the world turned black.

Danny awoke a minute later, or an hour, or even a day – he had no way of knowing. The back of his head was throbbing. His gut ached with nausea. It was dark. He was lying on a metal floor that was vibrating. His confused mind picked out the sound of an engine. He resisted the urge to sit up, preferring to pretend for a few more moments that he was still unconscious while he accumulated more information about his situation.

He was in the back of a truck. He could vaguely distinguish the outline of other figures crouched on the floor with him.

Two? Maybe three? They were moving at a constant speed and it was only by chance that he managed to establish their direction. There was a small gap between the canvas covering of the truck and its tailgate. Just an inch or so, but enough for him to catch a glimpse of the moon. It had been rising in the west, he remembered. That meant they were heading east.

Danny still had his personal weapon. He couldn't believe that his captors had been so stupid as not to confiscate it. That said, firing inside a moving vehicle was a risk. Rounds could ricochet. It was easy to lose control.

Movement. One of the figures was crouching over him. Broad-shouldered. Tall, even by Danny's standards. Danny closed his eyes again to feign unconsciousness, but almost immediately felt a rough thumb yank his left eye open.

He was able, just vaguely, to make out a face in the darkness. The man spoke.

'You did almost everything right, kiddo,' he said. 'You hid. When you couldn't hide, you ran. When you couldn't run, you fought. Just like I always taught you.'

Danny's grogginess fell away. He scrambled up into a sitting position, dumbstruck. The man didn't stop him.

'There was just one thing you did wrong. You didn't put yourself in the mind of your enemy. You didn't realise I'd know exactly what you were thinking, and how you were going to react. But I suppose we can forgive that.'

Danny stared. The man grinned.

'After all, you didn't know it was me who was coming to get you,' said Taff.

FOURTEEN

Danny wondered for a moment if he was suffering concussion from the blow to his head. He closed his eyes and tested himself. Seventy-three plus twenty-six: ninety-nine. Capital of the DRC: Kinshasa. Last known location: a hundred klicks west of Homs, Syria. His mental faculties seemed to be in order, even if he did feel like puking his stomach out.

Even so, maybe he'd been mistaken. It was dark. Faces were easy to confuse. Perhaps he was still in the mental no-man's-land between consciousness and unconsciousness.

'Looks like our boy soldier's woken up,' said an unfriendly voice.

'Shut the fuck up, Skinner.' A pause. 'I told him to go easy on you. No reason to knock you out.'

It was Taff's voice, no doubt about it. Danny would know it anywhere. It was as familiar to him as his father's or his brother's.

'Boyo lets things run away with him a bit sometimes. Him and Hector sometimes think they're still in the French Foreign Legion. Isn't that right, Skinner?'

'Right,' Skinner snorted. 'I'm very, very sorry, boy soldier. Next time I'll be more gentle.'

'What are you doing here, Taff?' Danny groaned. But he was already putting a few things together in his thumping head. He'd always known that Taff freelanced the military skills he'd learned in Regiment before Danny was even born.

It made some kind of sense that he'd be getting work from Saunders.

'Earning a crust, kiddo,' Taff said. 'Same as you. What the hell's been happening? We were expecting four of you, plus the spook.'

'Compromised,' Danny said. 'Two of our guys got captured. Taken away in a chopper.' He clenched his eyes as the full magnitude of how fucked up this operation had become hit him afresh. 'We need to track them down,' he said, his voice hoarse.

'Forget it. The Syrians will have taken them to Damascus. If they're not dead already, they're probably wishing they were.'

'We spoke to base. They said they'd go through diplomatic channels—'

One look from Taff cut him short. A look that said: you know better than that, kiddo.

'What about your third guy?' Taff asked.

'KIA.'

Taff didn't look remotely surprised. 'How?' he asked.

Danny paused for just a fraction of a second but it was long enough for Taff, who knew him so well, to notice and throw him a sharp look. 'Enemy fire,' Danny said. Taff made no play of disbelieving him. 'Where's Buckingham?' Danny asked suddenly.

'In the other truck,' Taff said. 'Don't want to put all our eggs in the same basket, do we, kiddo?' he added, answering a question Danny hadn't asked. 'Not now our Syrian friends have smashed most of them.'

Danny forced himself to sit up. He peered through the darkness at his old friend. It always surprised Danny that Taff no longer looked the way he did in his memory. The moustache he'd always worn with a certain pride had been replaced by a face full of scratchy stubble; the hair was no longer long, dark and scraggly, but short and gunmetal grey. His leathery skin had more lines around the eyes than Danny remembered. He was dressed in the standard camouflage of the Syrian military.

'Let's us move around more freely,' Taff explained, almost as if he'd been reading Danny's mind. He had a habit of doing that. 'We've paid a few disgruntled squaddies to drive us. They should be able to get us through any roadblocks between here and Homs.'

'How long have I been out?'

'Ten minutes. It'll take us a couple of hours to get there, assuming we don't run into any trouble.'

'Where, exactly?'

'Our digs. Not much, but keeps the rain out. If there was any rain, that is.'

'You sure you can trust the drivers?'

'As much as we can trust anyone around here, kiddo. But on balance, yes. Money talks out here.'

'Money talks everywhere,' said Skinner.

'True enough, my friend,' said Taff. 'True enough.' He smiled. 'It's good to see you, Danny.'

'You too,' Danny replied. They shook hands. It felt weird. Too formal. Taff obviously agreed, because he grabbed Danny in a rough bear hug.

'How's your dad?' he asked. He spoke quietly so Skinner couldn't hear.

'About the same.'

'Kyle?'

Danny shrugged. 'They let him out.'

'You should cut him some slack, kiddo. He'll find his way in the end.'

Danny didn't reply.

They travelled in silence while Danny tried to assimilate everything that had happened. Losing the guys. Meeting Taff. He'd been on edge ever since they'd stepped on to Syrian soil – hardly surprising, given what had happened – but now he felt himself relax slightly. To have his old friend and mentor beside him was encouraging. Taff was like a chunk of rock, solid and indestructible. The kind of guy you always wanted on your side.

And yes, Danny admitted to himself as he felt the truck start on a winding uphill course across the mountain range that separated Homs from the sea, Kyle's words back in Hereford had rung true. Having Taff here was a bit like having a father figure beside him. It made him feel a little bit safer.

The same couldn't be said for Skinner. Danny felt the hard eyes of Taff's companion boring into him as he suppressed the nausea caused by the man's ferocious blow to his head. The guy had a psychotic aura, and even though Danny had only spoken to him on the phone, he'd gleaned everything he needed to know about the man. He'd encountered a few like him back in Hereford: quiet, ruthless, violent men you wouldn't want to be stuck in a lift with. You didn't have to like these people, you just had to work with them. In that respect, being in the Regiment was no different to being a plumber or a teacher. You got on with your colleagues and did your job to the best of your ability. Nobody expected two plumbers to be best mates after a day of cleaning shit out of waste pipes. Same went for two soldiers. You left your dirty job and dirty colleagues at work. You had to, otherwise you'd go mad. And so, even though Danny wanted to ask Taff if he knew the full reason for his and Buckingham's presence in-country, he held back. Somehow he didn't want to be having that conversation in front of Skinner.

Forty-five minutes passed without a word. The truck twisted and turned and Danny felt his ears popping as they gained altitude. Occasionally a sliver of moonlight made its way into the back of the truck, lighting up Taff's face, and also Skinner's. Both men looked serious. Taut. They were quiet because they were in a state of readiness.

And they needed to be.

Danny estimated that they had just started their descent, which would put them about forty klicks from Homs, when they started to slow down. At first, he assumed they must be approaching a hairpin, but the truck did not turn as it slowed. Seconds later it stopped. Shuffling noises in the back as Taff and Skinner arranged their weapons. Danny did the same.

'Are we leading the convoy?' he asked.

Taff nodded. 'The others will be a klick behind. They'll cover us if we get into a contact. We'll do the same for them if we need to.'

'Who's got Buckingham?'

'Hector and De Fries. Good men. You can trust them.'

Coming from Taff, that was good enough for Danny.

Voices outside the truck. Arabic. From where he was sitting, Danny was able to distinguish between the soldiers speaking in the cab and those outside. The voices outside were muffled but the tone was unmistakable. They were arguing.

Taff and Skinner exchanged a look. Taff nodded. Very slowly, Skinner – who was sitting at the rear of the truck – drew a handgun. It was a double-action revolver with a barrel some-where around ten inches long. Hardly standard issue. Danny recognised it as a Smith & Wesson 500. With its .500 cartridge, it was more suited to hunting game than for military purposes. One shot from that weapon could take out a large animal at a couple of hundred metres. Danny could only imagine what it would do to a human at point-blank range.

'Bit excessive?' Danny said.

'Dead's dead,' Skinner replied, without looking at him. 'Doesn't matter how you get there.'

Taff turned to Danny. 'Hard and fast, kiddo,' he said. 'We give these fellas a chance to see our faces, they'll shoot first, ask questions later.'

Danny nodded and raised his rifle.

Footsteps. They were walking along the length of the truck, from the cab to the rear. Danny listened hard, trying to work out how many pairs of feet. Three, he reckoned. Taff obviously agreed: he'd held up three fingers himself.

A tapping on the wall of the cab. Seven quiet knocks.

'That means there's seven in all,' Taff said. 'Four more if we down these three.'

'Not much of a roadblock,' Danny said as he raised his rifle.

'Not much of a road,' Taff replied.

'What about the others?'

'They know to hang back. It'll be over by the time they get here,' Taff said, just as the canvas was pulled open.

It was like shooting fish in a barrel. The roadblock guards were dead the moment they decided to look in the back of the truck instead of just waving it through. There was a metallic clunking sound as someone rattled the tailgate. Then the latch clicked and the tailgate dropped down.

Skinner was the first to fire – a single .500 round straight into the face of the unfortunate Syrian soldier who had opened the back of the truck. It was almost as though a flashbang had exploded at the rear of the vehicle. There was a deafening noise and what looked almost like a burst of flame from the area around Skinner's firing hand, which was thrown upwards slightly by the ferocity of the recoil. The flame momentarily lit up the target's head, and for a split second Danny saw the devastating result of the impact: the high-calibre round had hit the target square in the face and the head had practically disintegrated, as though the skull was made of porcelain. He heard the thump of corpse hitting ground before his eyes picked out the outline of two figures standing a metre from the back of the truck. They weren't standing for long. Taff and Danny fired single rounds at precisely the same time, each hitting one of the targets squarely in the chest, though the retort of their weapons was puny after the thunder of Skinner's S&W. The three Syrians were dead less than five seconds after they'd opened the truck.

There was no time to waste. With four more targets outside, they had to move fast to maintain their shock and awe. Skinner fired two rounds in quick succession into the night to discourage anyone from approaching, then Danny and Taff ran to the back of the truck and jumped out.

The roadblock was pitifully inadequate. Three metal barriers, each of them about a metre long, stood side by side across the road, which was itself no more than ten metres wide. The truck had stopped five metres in front of them and at the same distance on the other side, parked up against a steep bank, was a dilapidated military Land Rover. One soldier was sitting behind the wheel. Two others were standing by the bonnet in the process of dropping their cigarettes and readying their weapons. The fourth was running, taking shelter behind the Land Rover.

Danny found himself working with Taff like a seamless unit. While Danny downed the two guys in front of the vehicle – they were only ten metres away – with a single swiping burst, Taff aimed his rifle at the windscreen, shattering the glass with a drilling of rounds and nailing the astonished driver. Which left just the escaping soldier. Skinner fired another shot from his Model 500. The round ricocheted with stunning force off the back corner of the Land Rover, making it shudder and a shower of sparks fly off the vehicle. There was a moment of silence, but then all three men heard the unmistakable sound of their terrified target scrambling up the bank beside the road. Danny took a step forwards, making to capture him. But suddenly he felt a heavy palm pushing him in the chest. It was Skinner and his eyes were wild.

'He's mine,' Skinner said. Handgun at the ready, he stalked towards the bank. Danny started to follow, but Taff grabbed him by the arm and pulled him back.

'He needs backup,' Danny hissed. 'The target's armed.'

Taff shook his head. 'Leave him, kiddo,' he said with a calmness that surprised Danny, given the situation. 'Skinner knows what he's doing. He won't thank you for getting involved.'

If it had been anybody else, Danny would have ignored them. It was one of the first things you learned in the Regiment: never try to do anything by yourself if you don't have to. But Danny had learned more from Taff than from any Regiment training officer. He held back.

It was like watching a cat toying with a mouse. Even down to the squeaking. The terrified Syrian soldier was whimpering as he tried to escape – he'd managed to climb about fifteen metres up the bank, which put him twenty-five from Danny's position – but it must have been obvious to him that it was hopeless. Hence the piteous noises. In his panic, the soldier didn't even think of defending himself with his weapon, so Skinner was able to take his time hunting him down. He stood at the bottom of the bank. The soldier was on all fours, now perhaps twelve metres from Skinner, making far less progress than his flailing limbs might have suggested. Skinner watched him for perhaps five seconds, before striding easily up the bank and standing over his petrified quarry.

A moment of stillness. Skinner aimed his enormous handgun, not at the soldier's head or chest, but at the area around his groin.

Another flash of orange light. Another deafening retort, which morphed horribly into the soldier's agonised scream.

The second truck – the one containing Buckingham – screeched up to the roadblock. Two more armed men, both dressed in Syrian army camouflage gear, burst out of the back, weapons at the ready. But there was nobody for them to engage. Taff held up one hand and, like obedient dogs, they immediately stood down.

The shot soldier was still screaming. Skinner was still looking down at him, his head inclined to one side. Danny could just make out a sneer of absolute contempt on his face. Having counted the number of shots Skinner had taken, he knew that the five-round barrel still contained a single bullet. But Skinner was prolonging the man's agony, and Danny had not the least doubt he was deriving some kind of sadistic pleasure from it.

He broke away from Taff. Skinner might be a sicko, but the soldier's screams were loud, a beacon to anyone who might be in the area. He had to be silenced. Danny ran towards, and up, the bank. He was only a couple of metres from him when Skinner, still engrossed in the results of his handiwork, realised he was there. 'Get the fuck out of it,' he said, turning to face Danny with his S&W.

Danny ignored him. He raised his M4 and discharged a single round into the soldier's head. The screaming stopped.

Then Danny confronted the shaven-headed mercenary. The guy's face was unreadable, but there was a sudden tension in the air that Danny could almost taste. He heard Taff, his voice low and urgent, shout, '*Hector!*' and was then aware that one of Buckingham's guards was running up towards them.

He was short and squat but broad-shouldered, and had a mop of blond hair. He didn't acknowledge Danny, but inserted himself between the two men. 'Leave it, mate,' he said. 'We need some distance behind us before some fucker finds these stiffs.'

For a moment Skinner didn't respond. But then, with a final narrowing of his eyes in Danny's direction, he turned and slowly descended the bank.

Hector gave Danny a withering look. 'Word to the wise, mucker,' he said as he made his own M16 safe. 'If you want to piss one of us off, don't make it Skinner.'

'I'll try to remember that,' Danny said, doing his utmost to sound even-tempered.

'Best you do, sunshine,' Hector said. 'Best you do.'

The remainder of their journey was uneventful, but uncomfortable.

They moved the bloody corpses off the road. Taff pointed to some gorse bushes on the bank twenty metres back and they stashed them there, out of sight. They wouldn't stay hidden for long – at the very least, wild animals and birds would start feeding on the flesh before long, and as soon as the sun warmed the corpses, the stench would be noticeable from thirty or more metres, depending on the heat and the direction of the wind. But by that time the convoy would be long gone. Buckingham watched them go about their gruesome work with a nauseous look on his face, though Danny noticed that he resolutely forced himself to witness what they were doing.

It was only once the road was clear, and all signs of the roadblock were gone, that Danny gave himself a few seconds to take in some more of his surroundings. The road, he estimated, was about a thousand feet above sea level. It overlooked a city which, Danny knew from his mental geography of the place, was Homs. As the crow flew, it was about twenty kilometres away, but the road itself wound down the hillside in a series of hairpin bends, so by car it was at least twice that distance, maybe three times. Homs glowed in the night, but it was not the intense, illuminated sprawl most cities resembled from the air. Vast areas of it – easily three-quarters – were in darkness. Clearly there were extensive power outages.

There were, however, other illuminations.

To the north of the city, Danny could see the orange glow of a fire. It looked tiny from up here, but that was a trick of the distance. Danny estimated that it covered at least an area of fifty metres by fifty. A lot of houses were burning down tonight. His eyes were drawn to five helicopters. Separated by height – although they were all a good 500 metres lower in altitude than Danny's position – they circled the city with their spotlights cutting through the night, lighting up even its darkest corners.

And then there was the tracer fire.

Danny counted three bursts in twenty seconds. Four-to-one tracer, he reckoned, covering a distance of about 500 metres. He assumed the firing was from a heavy machine gun, directed by the tracer into a small pocket of the down without electricity. From this distance he couldn't hear the noise of the weapon, and the tracer looked curiously like fireworks.

He had no doubt, though, that down on the ground the effect was brutal.

Buckingham joined him. He was silent for a moment. When he finally spoke, his voice was hoarse. 'Looks bloody grim down there,' he said weakly.

'Your choice, pal,' Danny replied.

'Was it necessary to kill all those people?'

Danny looked over to where Taff and Skinner were standing by the Land Rover that had carried them here. 'Buckingham stays with me,' he called out.

Skinner snorted dismissively. 'In your fucking dreams,' he said.

Danny ignored him. 'I mean it, Taff. He's my problem, not yours.'

'Thanks very much,' Buckingham murmured.

Taff spoke quietly to Skinner, who shook his head like he was dealing with a bunch of children, before stomping away. He jerked a thumb in the direction of the Land Rover and Danny nodded. 'Get in,' he told Buckingham. 'We need to move.'

They set off again, with Buckingham sitting next to Danny. Taff was silent. He didn't seem to have any problem with Skinner's behaviour and Danny found himself wondering if he'd overreacted. He was on edge and it had, after all, been a long couple of days. Skinner again sat at the rear of the truck, where he rolled and smoked a succession of cigarettes. Each time he inhaled, the glow from his roll-up lit his face. Each time, Danny saw the man's eyes on him, cold and unfriendly.

After another forty-five minutes, Danny felt the vehicle heading off the road. 'What's happening?' he asked Taff sharply.

'We'll wait till dawn to enter the city,' Taff replied. 'It's a quieter time. Night-time bombardments have finished, and snipers are still sleeping because there's not so many targets in the street. We should be able to move around without too much trouble.'

Danny nodded. The strategy made sense. When the truck came to a halt, Danny joined Taff and Skinner in checking their location. Their drivers had parked in an abandoned stone barn about fifty metres north of the road. The vehicles were well hidden, and they appeared not to have left any tracks in the hard-baked ground. It was a good place to stop.

'Get some kip, kiddo,' Taff said. 'You too,' he added, nodding at Buckingham. 'You both look like you could use it. We'll keep stag.'

Buckingham looked uncertainly at Danny. He clearly didn't trust these men, but Danny knew that his old friend was right: they couldn't function properly without sleep. Minutes later Danny was on his back in the truck, his weapon by his side and his bergen a makeshift pillow. Buckingham curled up nearby. Both men were asleep in seconds.

When Danny awoke, it was with a start. His limbs were heavy with fatigue and it took a few seconds for him to remember where he was. He could tell that the grey dawn of his second day in Syria had arrived. There was nobody else in the back of the truck, so he pulled aside the canvas to see what was happening outside.

The others had congregated in two groups. The four Syrian drivers were crouched on the ground in the five metres between the two trucks, while Taff, Buckingham, Skinner, Hector and the man they'd referred to as De Fries stood by the entrance to the barn. They were deep in a murmured conversation. Danny couldn't hear what they were saying, but Buckingham seemed unusually animated. The conversation continued for a good minute, until Skinner happened to look over his shoulder and noticed that Danny was watching them. He nudged Taff, who glanced quickly in Danny's direction. A smile spread across Taff's face as he walked towards his old mate. 'Good sleep, kiddo?' he asked.

Danny looked past him. The others had split up. Skinner was rolling a fag. Buckingham looked awkward as usual.

'What were you talking about?' Danny asked.

'Our route into the city.'

'Buckingham have a lot to contribute?'

'Not really,' said Taff. 'We've arranged an RV with your mate Asu at 12.00 hrs. We'll go to our digs first. You two boys can wash that mud off your faces.'

'Where are your digs?'

'An area to the north-west that's so far avoided most of the bombing. Rebel areas on the north, west and south sides, though. Hard to get through. But if you want to approach from the east you have to go round the houses.' He shrugged. 'Or what's left of them.'

'I thought you said dawn was a quiet time.'

'A quiet*er* time,' Taff corrected. 'No such thing as a quiet time in that dump. This Buckingham fella's a bit of a drip. Can't understand why you didn't drop the fucker when you hit land, and report back that he'd been hit by enemy fire.'

Danny blinked. 'I've got a job to do, Taff,' he said.

'Ah, you get paid all the same, kiddo, no matter what happens to the spook.' He suddenly grinned. 'I'm fucking with you, Danny. Come on, let's move. The sooner we get you into the city, the sooner you can both sod off home again. Trust me – Homs isn't a place you want to stick around for too long.' Another grin. 'Bit like Hereford, come to think of it,' he said.

FIFTEEN

Taff was right. It was strangely quiet for a war zone. Somehow that didn't make it feel safer. More like everyone was holding their breath, waiting to see what would happen next.

Danny didn't like being stuck in the back of this vehicle, unable to see what was going on around him, to identify threats and stamp on them before they got the better of them. But he had to admit that Taff's idea of having disgruntled Syrian soldiers drive them was a good one. Classic Taff. Better to avoid a fight than start one. They entered the city without hindrance. Even though they were travelling through high-risk areas, it sounded calm outside.

It wasn't calm in Danny's head, though. Far from it. In the hours that had passed since he and Buckingham had left the culvert, he'd been too busy trying to keep them both alive to reflect hard on their situation. Now the stark reality came crashing home. Three men down, within hours of entering the country. He winced as he thought of the look on Jack's face before he plugged him, and horrific images passed through his mind of the indignities the others would be suffering – if they were still alive. The Syrian secret police were known to administer beatings that many of their victims didn't survive. He frowned. It was one of the first rules of the Regiment: you look after your mates. He'd failed to do that. Not a good feeling.

But there was something else bothering him too. The conversation he'd had with Buckingham just before the Syrian soldier had disturbed them in the culvert was a shadow in a corner of his mind. He couldn't get it out of his head. What was it Buckingham had said? 'Must have been very hard for your brother, to see your mother shot like that.' But his mother *hadn't* been shot. She'd died in childbirth, shortly after his arrival. At least, that was what he'd always been told.

Or had he?

He tried to think back. Of course, those exact conversations were now gone from his memory. But he knew this: whenever the subject of his mum had come up, his dad had always – *always* – changed the subject. Danny thought he understood why. He knew his dad remembered nothing of his life before he was wounded in action.

He glanced over at Taff, whose back was against the wall of the truck, his eyes closed. Taff never changed, and as Danny stared at him he felt a familiar feeling of affection. As he stared, a long-forgotten memory rose in his mind. Danny couldn't have been more than ten, and Taff was making one of his irregular visits to their little house in Hereford. He was deeply tanned and had mentioned he'd just come back from Africa. Dad had taken himself off to the toilet – a half-hour operation at the best of times – and Danny had walked into the sitting room to find Taff holding the framed picture of his mum that always sat on the TV. He'd watched Taff for about thirty seconds before Taff noticed him and returned the picture to its place.

'Beautiful woman, your mum, kiddo,' he'd said. 'Beautiful woman.' There had been a bitter, self-mocking look in his eyes, and even as a young boy Danny had realised something: that Taff's feelings for his mum ran deeper than he could ever say. In the years that followed, Danny had tried to question Taff about her on the frequent occasions when they'd been alone together. But, like his dad, Taff had always found a way to change the subject.

A noise shook Danny from his thoughts. Gunfire. A single round. Not too close, but probably within 100 metres of their position. Taff's eyes sprung open, and Skinner suddenly looked more alert.

'Sniper fire,' Taff said, seeing Danny's quizzical look. 'Grows worse as the day gets on.'

'Who is it?'

'Hard to say. Government forces sometimes, picking off anybody they think looks suspicious. It could just be a regular Homs citizen, if that's what you want to call them. Not many of them left, but there are some people who actually like the civil war as it gives them a chance to go looting. Or it could be one of the organised rebel factions. Some of them are OK, some of them are total cunts.'

'What about this Asu guy, the one you've been supplying the training package to?'

Taff snorted. 'He's the worst of them, kiddo. Thinks he's Che Gue-fucking-vara. If I wasn't being paid to help the fucker, I'd be more than happy to give him one behind the ear.' He glanced at Buckingham, who just stared straight ahead as though he hadn't heard any of the conversation.

'Why, what's wrong with him?'

'Thinks he's the cat's fucking pyjamas. You'll see this afternoon. He's expecting us at his current HQ.'

'What about his brother Sorgen? You know him?'

'Only by reputation. I do know that Asu would start shitting rocks if he knew you were planning to make contact. Fucking hate each other. No brotherly love lost there. Something you'd know about, I suppose, kiddo.'

'I don't hate Kyle.'

'Course not,' Taff said blandly.

Before Danny could reply, the vehicle came to a halt. There was a knocking on the cab. 'We're here,' said Taff. 'Let's get out.'

Skinner – who hadn't spoken since they left the barn – opened the back of the truck and jumped out without a word. Taff went next, then Danny, then Buckingham.

They found themselves in a rectangular compound, about thirty metres by twenty, surrounded by a solid stone wall five metres high and topped with barbed wire. As Danny looked around, he was aware of Skinner, Hector and De Fries disappearing into the adjoining house. The gate through which the two trucks had driven was a thick sheet of metal attached to runners on the wall to one side. A Syrian kid – he looked about seventeen – was hurriedly sliding the gate shut. It clanged to, and he used a thick chain and a sturdy padlock to fasten it. Taff nodded in the kid's direction. 'Local,' he said. 'We throw them a few scraps to cook our meals, do our washing. It's peanuts, but more than they'd get anywhere else.'

The trucks had parked in the centre of the compound. Next to them were two Land Rovers. Along the right-hand wall were three battered old saloon cars. Another Syrian kid was sitting in the driver's seat of one of them, pumping the accelerator. 'We turn them over twice a day,' Taff said, 'to make sure they're running properly. If the bombardment hits this part of town, they're our ticket out of here. They're not up to much, but you can only shit with the arse you've got. Talking of which . . .'

Buckingham was approaching. He looked at them suspiciously, as if he thought they'd been talking about him.

'Come on, pretty boy,' Taff said. 'I'll show you round.'

Facing the compound was a two-storey house built of grey concrete. Although Taff had said they'd managed to avoid the worst of the bombardment, the building was not entirely unscathed. A deep crack ran up the front, and the left side was caked in thick soot.

'Fire?' Danny asked.

'Before we got here. That's why it was deserted.'

'What if the people who own it come back?' Buckingham asked.

'Trust me. Whoever used to live here, they've left for good. Took everything. They'll have buggered off to Turkey or

Lebanon by now, like half of Homs. Or they'll be stuck in one of those IDP camps up near the coast. Come on.' He led them through the main door into a large, open-plan room that seemed to take up half of the ground floor. In one corner of the room was an old CRT television, with a portable aerial hanging from the wall behind it. Al-Jazeera news was on, but the sound was down. The concrete floor was covered with enormous carpets that had no doubt once been brightly coloured but were now dull and dusty. The fire had not damaged this room, but everything in it seemed ingrained with an overpowering stench of smoke.

Along one wall was a wooden rack about two metres wide. Hanging from it was a selection of weapons. Five AKs, two Colt Commandos, even a couple of MP5s. On the floor beneath this armoury were three thin mattresses, all occupied by sleeping Syrians – Taff's cheap labour, Danny assumed. Against the far wall were two windows, both of them boarded up with thick planks of wood bolted to the concrete on either side. Consequently there was very little light in here, but Danny did notice that in each window there was a gap of about an inch between two of the planks – wide enough to accommodate the barrels of any of the weapons on the wall. Murder holes.

Under the windows were more mattresses, and more sleeping Syrians in dirty jeans and sleeveless vests. The carpet nearest them was littered with cigarette packets and empty Pepsi bottles. The young men were clearly dog-tired – they didn't even stir as Taff, Danny and Buckingham passed through. It crossed Danny's mind that Taff was getting his money's worth out of these locals.

Along the left-hand wall was a door, also boarded up. Taff pointed at it. 'Best to keep out of there. That half of the building's structurally unsound because of the fire.' Beyond the door was an open staircase, and they followed Taff up it.

They came to a corridor with five doors off it. The first led to a bathroom, of sorts. The door was open, and as they passed

212

Danny saw – and smelled – that it wasn't somewhere you would want to spend much time. Taff led them through the second door, into a long room some eight metres by five. In the far wall was a big window, two metres wide and a bit taller. There was no glass in the pane, but there were iron bars on the inside and thick wire mesh on the outside. At the bottom right, two of the iron bars had been cut and bent up and the mesh folded back. Pointing through this gap was the barrel of a GPMG, its body propped up by a bipod on the floor. Next to the gimpy were two ancient air-con units; their fans made a grating, grinding noise as they turned. They were powered by an old generator in the centre of the room, from which power cables spread out like spider legs, several leading out of the room to other parts of the house. The generator added a low hum to the noise of the air-con, and a fug of burning fuel. Bizarrely, to the right of the door was a chintzy old armchair, upholstered in a threadbare fabric with a red and beige floral pattern. Hector was slouched in the armchair, his M16 propped up next to him, eating cold Heinz baked beans from the tin. He barely acknowledged the others as they entered the room.

'It's not much,' Taff said dryly, 'but it's home.'

The windows of the adjoining room were boarded up like the ones downstairs. Morning light blazed through the murder hole, slicing across the darkness of the room. By this light, Danny could make out a couple of stained, thin mattresses below the window and, hanging at an angle on the wall, a photograph of what was presumably some local religious figure with a pink garland round his neck. 'You can bunk down here,' Taff told them. 'Make yourself at home.'

'I need to see the rest of the gaff,' Danny said. 'Work out the layout, in case we come under attack.'

Taff smiled. 'Cautious as ever,' he said. 'Help yourself. I'll be outside.' He looked at his watch. 'It's 09.00 hrs,' he said. 'Asu's expecting us at midday. We leave in two hours.'

He left them to it.

Buckingham was silent. Danny could practically feel the waves of anxiety pumping off the guy. He walked farther into the room and pulled the mattresses away from the wall. 'What are you doing?' asked Buckingham.

'A few planks of wood won't be much protection against mortar fire,' Danny said. 'Stay in here. Get some kip if you want. Just don't go near the window.'

'But it's quiet outside.'

'Fine,' Danny said. '*Go* near the window. I'll post the bits of you back home.'

'I don't much like your tone, old sport.'

'Just get some sleep. Don't move without checking with me.'

Danny left the room and walked back down the corridor towards the stairs, passing the room with the generator and the gimpy on the right. Hector was no longer sitting in the floral armchair, but was standing by one of the air-con units, his trousers flapping slightly in the breeze from its fan. Skinner had joined him. He had his back to Danny, who could make out more tattooed skin at the nape of his neck. Hector was handing him something, but froze when, looking over Skinner's shoulder, he saw Danny in the doorway. Slowly, Skinner turned to look at Danny, who saw what was in his hands: a wad of notes, perhaps half an inch thick. Dirty, crumpled, used notes. US dollars, by the look of them. Skinner made no attempt to hide the money. Instead he casually shoved the notes into the back pocket of his camouflage trousers. He shot Danny a hostile look. Hector did the same. There were a few seconds of tense stand-off, then Danny shrugged. 'Catch you later, lads,' he said, before turning his back on them and making for the stairs. What was it Saunders had said to him? 'There's always the chance to earn a little extra while you're out there.' Looked like Hector and Skinner had some little sideline going. Fine. That was their business. Besides, he had other things on his mind.

He found Taff sitting with his back to the house, his legs crossed, stripping down one of his Colt Commandos. Danny had never been in a war zone with Taff. With his craggy, weather-worn face, he looked more at home here than Danny had ever seen him. Part of the furniture. As Danny sat down beside him on the dirty ground, Taff nodded briefly before turning back to his weapon. The sun was already hot, and made Danny's skin smart. He removed his Sig from his chest rig and went through the motions of releasing the magazine and stripping down the handgun. But his thoughts weren't really on the weapon. There were questions in his head that he didn't quite know how to ask.

'What's eating you, kiddo?' Taff said without looking up from the Colt.

Nothing, Danny almost replied. No point hiding anything from Taff, though. He could always tell when something was wrong.

'I lost the guys,' he said. 'They were my responsibility and I lost them. Guess I'll just have to live with it.'

Taff lowered his weapon and looked across the compound. 'Did I ever tell you about Belfast?' he asked.

Danny shook his head.

'That sounds about right. I don't tell many people.' He picked up the assault rifle again and resumed working on it. 'We had this tout, gave us the address of a Provo safe house. I headed up a unit to raid the fuckers. We had a Rupert in the car, supposed to stay there. Decided not to. Fuck knows why. M60 shot him dead from a bedroom window as he was running down the street. Perhaps I could have stopped it happening. Perhaps not.'

There was a pause. 'Do you still think about him?' Danny asked.

Taff shrugged. 'Sure. But he was SAS. He knew what he was doing.' He sniffed. 'I'm sorry he bought it. I watched them plant him, and I shook his family's hands, said all the things you're supposed to say. But I don't feel responsible.' He gave Danny a piercing look. 'Nor should you. You're a good kid, Danny, but you think about things too much. What was the name of the lad who died?'

'Jack.'

'Well, if Jack was here now and it was you who'd been killed, do you reckon he'd be sitting having a DMC with me?'

Danny shook his head. Somehow Taff always knew the right thing to say. Danny leaned his head back against the wall and closed his eyes. 'There's something else,' he said.

'Fire away, kiddo.' Taff sounded amused, like he was indulging a favourite nephew.

'When we were dug in,' Danny said, 'in that culvert, Buckingham let something slip. Something about my mum. I reckon he'd seen some file or something. I don't know.'

Taff didn't look up. He removed the magazine from his personal weapon. 'What about her?' Suddenly he didn't sound quite so light-hearted. Tense, almost. Danny opened his eyes and looked at him. Taff failed to meet his gaze.

'Something about her being shot.'

Taff's face remained calm, but Danny, who knew it so well, detected a slight tightening around the eyes. Taff remained silent for a full thirty seconds. 'Not going to lie to you, kiddo,' he said eventually. 'You better be sure you want to know the answers, before you start asking the questions.'

'Jesus, Taff . . .'

A clunk from the Colt as Taff clicked the butt stock from the main body. Taff showed no outward sign of emotion as he spoke, his voice almost monotone.

'Your ma was Northern Irish. Her family didn't have time for sectarianism, but your dad was British Army. Parachute Regiment, to make matters worse. They always knew they were a target. Had to be careful.'

'But what—?'

Taff held up one hand to silence Danny. He appeared to be gathering his thoughts before speaking again. 'It happened the day you were born. You were just a couple of hours old. An IRA gunman got into the hospital dressed as a porter. Shot your mum. Tried to kill your dad.' He shrugged, as if that was all he had to say.

Danny felt his guts tighten. 'Who was it?' he asked.

'If I knew that,' Taff said, 'he'd be dead. I tried to find out. Started going through the Regiment's list of known Provo operatives. Chased them down, made them squeal. No one knew anything. Done three of them before the Regiment stopped me. Awarded me with an RTU for trying to find out who did it. Suppose I don't blame them.'

Taff stared into the distance. Danny sat in shocked silence, trying to absorb this information, this rewriting of the story of his life.

A minute passed.

'Why didn't he finish my dad off?' Danny asked quietly.

'He got disturbed by the hospital staff. Spooked, I guess. And then I turned up. Your dad was in a bad way. I didn't think he'd make it. As for your mum—' Taff broke off, a pained look on his face. 'Perhaps it was just as well he lost his memory. It wasn't a sight you want to remember.' For the first time since the conversation had started, he gave Danny a direct look. 'Your brother wasn't so lucky. He saw it all. He doesn't remember the details, but . . .'

'But what?'

'Next time you wonder why he went off the rails, remember what he went through. No kid should have to see that.'

'No kid should attack his father.'

'He's fucked up, Danny. Nobody's saying he isn't.'

'Why did you never *tell* me?' Danny's shock was rapidly turning to hot anger.

'It was your dad's decision. He saw what was happening to Kyle. He didn't want you to get messed up in the head too.' Taff sniffed. 'There's other reasons, of course.'

'Like what?'

'Special Branch kept names out of it. Just a random sectarian killing.'

'Plus they looked like fucking idiots not having caught the bastard,' Danny retorted.

'RUC found his scrubs on the hospital perimeter,' Taff said. 'Bloodstained.'

'Great,' Danny snapped. 'Give them a medal.'

'They did their best, kiddo. Whoever did the hit just vanished.'

Silence returned. It was broken by a sniper round somewhere in the distance. The Syrian kids in the compound – three of them – spun round in alarm. Danny didn't even flinch. He was sweating profusely, and not just because of the sun. His mind was a riot of emotions. Part of him was furious with Taff for never having told him any of this. Part of him understood. And part of him – by far the greater part – felt weighed down by a grim determination.

'I'll find him,' he told Taff. 'I don't care what it takes.'

Taff reassembled the remaining pieces of the rifle, minus the magazine. He cocked and fired it several times to check all the moving parts were working, then reinserted a full mag, cocked it and engaged the safety switch.

'Tell me when you do,' he said. 'I'll be right there.' He looked at Danny. 'I always knew you'd find out one day, kiddo. But it was never the right time to tell you. I'm sorry.'

He stood up and made to carry the Colt back inside.

'Taff,' Danny called him back.

His old friend stopped and turned to look at him.

'What was she like?' Danny asked. 'My mum.'

Taff paused. A strange look crossed his face – the same expression Danny had seen all those years ago when he'd caught Taff gazing at his mother's photograph. 'She was the best lass I ever knew,' Taff said quietly.

He turned once more and strode indoors, leaving Danny alone with his troubled thoughts.

SIXTEEN

They were due to leave at 11.00 hrs. Taff and his team started making preparations a good forty-five minutes before that.

Hector checked over the Land Rovers. They might be relying on Syrian nationals to drive them, but he obviously didn't intend to leave the maintenance to anybody else: their vehicles were too important for that. Then he lugged extra jerrycans of fuel into the backs of the Land Rovers and topped up the water levels from a plastic bottle. Skinner and De Fries took care of the weaponry. They loaded up the Colt Commandos and MP5s, along with extra ammo packs. It occurred to Danny that he hadn't heard De Fries utter a single word since they'd met. Taff had told him that he'd been in the Dutch SF, as if that explained his silence. He had a flat nose and a deeply cleft chin – ugly bastard, but he wasn't being hired for his looks. Taff himself crouched in the corner of the compound with a map of Homs spread out in front of him, their two Syrian drivers by his side. He was quietly explaining the route they would take and – Danny had no doubt – a couple of alternatives in case things went to shit. Danny would acquaint himself with their routes once they were finalised. Meanwhile he went up to find Buckingham.

Danny was pleased they were about to move. It gave him something else to think about after his conversation with Taff. He was glad to have the opportunity to focus on what he was here to do. As he crossed the ground-floor room he saw that the Syrian kids who'd previously been sleeping had woken up. They watched him with bleary-eyed suspicion, but none of them spoke as he headed for the stairs. He found Buckingham where he'd left him. He had undone his shirt to reveal a smooth-skinned torso and, to Danny's surprise, a leather pouch strapped round his waist. He'd unzipped the pouch and was pulling a mobile phone and a lozenge-shaped device from it as Danny entered the room.

'You should have told me you had a phone,' Danny said.

'No SIM card,' he said, with no hint of his previous peevishness. 'Just a few numbers in the momory, in case of emergency, you know.'

'You can still be tracked.'

Buckingham waved away the objection. 'Wanted to have a word before we left. I'll be talking to Asu privately when we get there. No need for you to be in attendance.'

'Don't be an idiot, Buckingham. He's not your fucking granddad. I've met people like him. He'd stick a knife in you without even thinking about it.'

'I'll take my chances, old sport. Make yourself scarce when I give you the nod, eh?'

Danny felt a sudden rush of anger. He'd lost three men and now this twat was playing games. He found himself bearing down on the spook, grabbing him by the neck and thrusting him up against the wall. 'What the hell's going on with you, Buckingham?' he hissed. 'What aren't you telling me?'

'For God's sake, let go of me.'

'Not till I know what you're hiding. Why don't you want me in on the RV?'

Buckingham's face was turning red, and Danny could feel the blood in his neck pumping a little harder. He tightened his grip.

'If I'm to persuade him to open a line of communication with Sorgen,' Buckingham croaked, 'I'll need to be extremely diplomatic. I hardly think a heavily armed SAS man at my shoulder will send quite the right signals, do you?'

The two men stared at each other, Danny's eyes narrow,

Buckingham's bulging. They stayed like that for five seconds, before Danny released him in disgust.

'What the hell are you playing at?' Buckingham hissed.

'Forget it,' Danny told him. Maybe the guy's explanation made sense. Maybe.

'I need to give you this,' Buckingham said. He handed over the lozenge-shaped device. It was no bigger than a thumbnail and resembled a three-volt battery. He noticed Danny's dangerous look and raised both palms in a gesture that approached – but was not quite – an apology. 'Should have mentioned it before. They call it an infinity device, apparently. I'm a bit of a duffer when it comes to all this.'

'You're right,' Danny replied. 'You *should* have mentioned it before.' He examined the device a little closer. 'What does it do?'

'Records conversations. Voice activated. Clever thing is, it contains a powered micro-SIM, which means one can call into it from any phone in the world and listen to what it's recorded. Rather like a portable answering machine.'

Danny looked at the device, then at Buckingham. For a self-proclaimed duffer, he seemed to know a lot about it. 'And?'

'Once I've finished my conversation with Asu, I'd like you to plant it on his rifle. I'm told he carries it everywhere. Can't be too careful, and it would be jolly good to know what he's saying behind our backs.'

Danny examined the infinity device again. 'It's dangerous,' he said. 'If he's any kind of soldier at all he won't let me in spitting distance of his personal weapon.'

'Then you'll just have to be inventive, won't you?'

'I still don't like it.'

'I didn't ask you to like it,' Buckingham said, closing his eyes to indicate that Danny was trying his patience. 'I asked you to *do* it. Be a good chap and stop looking for problems, would you?' He pointedly rubbed his neck where Danny had grabbed it. 'Shall we go?'

He pushed past Danny, out into the corridor. Danny touched the device against the strap of his watch. Highly magnetic. A cinch to secrete, but why hadn't Buckingham mentioned it before? What else was he keeping from him? He took a quick inventory of his gear. M4, Sig, extra rounds, grenades, med pack. Everything was in order. Except, of course, it wasn't. He was three men down. He was also acutely aware that his and Buckingham's safety depended on Taff, his men and a bunch of Syrian locals he didn't know from Adam. He'd trust Taff with his life, but he wouldn't trust Skinner, Hector or De Fries with the steam off his piss. He shook his head, put the infinity device in his pocket and headed back downstairs.

The Land Rovers' engines were running and the Syrian drivers were ready to move off. Taff shouted a word in Arabic and one of the local kids scurried over to open the gate. Squinting through the sunlight, Danny caught sight of the road outside – potholed and rubble-strewn. A couple of kids kicking a ball about stopped to look in through the gate. Danny kept one eye on them as he ushered Buckingham into the back of one of the Land Rovers. Maybe it was a throwback from Afghan, but just because they were kids, it didn't mean they were harmless. They just continued to stare, though, and seconds later they were moving away.

Even though they couldn't see outside, it was clear that the streets they were travelling were in very poor repair. The drivers took it slowly, veering occasionally to avoid particularly large obstacles and sometimes having to take a detour. Danny assumed these were roads they had expected to be clear but which had turned out to be blocked. He didn't like being in the dark and he sat like a coiled spring, gripping his M4, his senses alert to the sounds outside and the unseen, unknown atmospherics on the streets of Homs. He could tell that Taff and Skinner, both squeezed into the front with the driver, were on high alert as well, weapons ready, heads cocked as they listened carefully.

They were ten minutes out when Buckingham started to babble nervously. 'Where *are* we? How much *longer*? Don't they know which way they're supposed to be going?'

Skinner turned round and gave him a nasty look.

'Asu's compound is in the south of the city,' said Taff, changing the subject. 'He keeps himself separate from his commanders and tends to avoid the parts of the city that are openly held by the rebels, since they get bombed to shit every night. It means moving around fairly often – every week or so – before word of his location leaks out to the authorities. The current gaff isn't the greatest, tactically speaking, but I don't think word of where he is has spread yet. Though there's always a chance of being hit by government forces wherever you are in this dog turd of a town.'

'What he's saying,' Skinner added, 'is keep your fucking wits about you and don't be a twat.'

They trundled on.

It took a little more than an hour, by Danny's reckoning, before they came to a halt. Buckingham started to get up, but Skinner pushed him back with a single thrust of one hand. For once, Danny agreed with Taff's sour-faced comrade.

Five seconds passed.

There was the noise of the door on Buckingham's side being opened. Danny peered across him, squinting as light flooded in. Whoever had opened the door, and now stood silhouetted there, couldn't have been five feet tall. Then Danny saw that it was a child. No ordinary child, though: this kid had a bandolier strapped round his shoulders and was carrying a Kalashnikov with unstudied ease. If Taff or Skinner were surprised, they didn't show it. The tension in the Land Rover palpably eased as they climbed out in silence.

They had travelled from one house and compound to another. This compound was a little larger than the last – the walls were a good four metres high, and the rough ground they enclosed measured about thirty metres by thirty. The three-storey house had been white, but the paint was now grimy and black, peeling in places to reveal the building's breeze-block skeleton. Its windows were simple openings with metal bars.

In the centre of the compound a fire burned in a rusty iron drum, and children were sitting around it. When the gates of the compound had closed behind him, Danny took a closer look at the kids. There were four of them, all boys, all dressed in jeans, T-shirts and trainers, and all of them wearing khaki ammo vests. Their eyes had dark rings below them and their meagre shoulders were slumped like old men's. Each boy had an AK-47 lying next to him. Resting on one of the weapons was a half-eaten bag of boiled sweets. Treasure, in a place and at a time like this.

One of the kids stood out from the others. The left sleeve of his dirty green Adidas T-shirt was torn and poking out from beneath the strap of his ammo vest was the stump of a clumsily amputated arm. It was harshly scarred, as though it had been inexpertly cauterised. It seemed to have a life of its own, rolling in its socket even when the rest of the boy's body was still, but if the kid was experiencing any pain, it didn't show on his face.

Another oil drum had been split in half lengthways. The two halves were lying up against the left-hand wall of the compound and were full of ash – clearly a makeshift barbecue for preparing hot food in the absence of electricity. Set back a couple of feet from each of the three walls was a table. To one side of each of these tables a murder hole was punched into the wall at the level of the tabletop. A sniper lay on each table, the barrel of his rifle a foot or so from the hole, carefully scanning the outside through the sight. One of these guys, the gunman covering the left-hand wall, was, Danny could see, too close to the murder hole. A couple of inches away at most. He needed to move back a bit, to give him more cover in the event of incoming. Taff saw this too, and walked briskly over to him and put him right. He winked at the gunman in the same way he used to wink at Danny when he was kid.

The compound was surrounded by taller buildings – grim-looking blocks of flats, seven or eight storeys high, dotted with satellite dishes and with laundry hanging from some of the windows. Strange to think of people washing their clothes in the middle of a war zone, Danny decided, but he was less concerned about the neighbours' hygienic arrangements than about the obvious fact that the compound was overlooked. He narrowed his eyes and looked up and down one of the blocks. It didn't take him long to pick out three windows – one open, two broken – each with a few telltale inches of a sniper's rifle barrel protruding. The sort of thing you wouldn't even see if you weren't looking for it. Asu's men, he assumed, keeping watch over the rebel leader's current location. Hardly reassuring, though: enemy snipers could install themselves in any of the other windows. Tactically speaking, it was . . .

'A fucking dog's dinner. You don't need to tell me that, kiddo.' Once more Taff had read Danny's thoughts accurately. 'Asu's a stubborn son of a bitch. Saunders had to agree to pay the guys double time when they saw this place. They hadn't even made the murder holes when we got here. De Fries had to knock them through with a pickaxe. Asu's not a total idiot, though. He changes his base every ten days or so and keeps his highest-ranking commanders at separate locations around the city. Moves them around every week. That way the government can't keep a handle on where they all are at any one time, and they can't all be taken out in a single hit. The rebels can survive the loss of one commander, but not all of them.'

Danny pointed at the kids sitting round the fire. 'What about them? Tell me this Asu creep doesn't stick them on the front line.'

Taff shrugged. 'If they want to fight, let them. It's only a matter of time anyway.'

'They're child soldiers, Taff. Most people find that a bit dodgy.'

'Most people find war a bit dodgy, kiddo. This one's worse than most. Those kids have lost their parents, their homes. They'd be starving on the streets or rotting in an IDP camp if they weren't here. Or dead already.'

'And Asu gets a nice cheap fighting force into the bargain.'

'Grow up, Danny,' Taff told him bluntly. 'You know how the world works. At least you should by now.'

'You give them weapons training?'

'Of course. You think I'd let them walk around with AKs if they didn't know how to make them safe? We do it out in the desert, along with the adult rebels. Fucking nightmare teaching them to suppress the recoil. Seem to remember it took *you* a while to deal with it, back in the day.' Taff glanced up at the flats again. 'Come on,' he said, 'let's get your man inside. Asu will be waiting. Fucker starts throwing his toys out of his pram if you give him the chance.'

Buckingham was loitering a little nervously by the Land Rovers. Danny marched over to him, took him by the arm and led him into the house. It was a dark, gloomy warren of rooms. Joined by Taff, Danny and Buckingham checked them out. The gaff had clearly been looted at some point in the recent past. There were no furnishings or items of comfort. There were holes in the wall where light fittings had once been, and someone had even removed sections of floorboard here and there, probably to use for firewood. There were more boy soldiers holed up in here, all dressed similarly, like an army of clones. Most of them were asleep on the bare floor. Those few who were awake stared at the newcomers with the same dull curiosity Danny had seen in the eyes of the kids outside.

There were adults too, mostly men but also some women. Danny clocked the men's aggressive stares. Some of them sat and smoked. Others played games of dice or cards. One man was smoothing a nick out of his knife with a flat stone. The guy next to him was threading a greasy rag through the detached barrel of a rifle. A couple of radios were playing quietly in different rooms. One was tuned to scratchy Syrian pop. From the other came the insistent voice of a man speaking Arabic. Danny wondered if it was a rebel propaganda channel. It had that sound.

The women sat talking in groups of three or four. One sat with a child soldier at her feet, stroking his hair as the kid stroked his Kalashnikov. She was a distinctive-looking woman – long, black hair with a lock of snowy white at her forehead. She seemed curiously young and old at the same time, and as she returned Danny's stare, he sensed bitterness: here was a woman let down by life, and who didn't expect anything to change. 'Asu's daughter-in-law, Basheba,' Taff said quietly. 'Her husband – Asu's son – ended up in a Damascus jail. Presumed dead. That's her son sitting at her feet. You saw the kid outside minus an arm?' Danny nodded. 'Older brother. Asu only just tolerates her, and I've seen him give the kids a kicking too. They're shit-scared of him. Like I say, lovely fella. Pleasure to do business with.'

All in all, on the ground floor of the house, there were about thirty people and although they were quiet, Danny didn't sense that they were all despondent. It was more like they were waiting for something to happen. The first floor was more sparsely occupied. Danny found himself in some kind of antechamber, where two armed men stood guard by a closed door. There were a couple of chairs against one wall and a barred window looking out on to the compound. Danny glanced through it to see the kids still sitting round the fire. It nauseated him that children so young should be sent into battle, but he supposed Taff was right: that was the way the world worked. Deal with it. He dragged his attention back to the two armed guards. MP5s. Body armour. These guys were better equipped than half the

British Army. They clearly recognised Taff. One of them nodded a reluctant greeting at him. 'Been keeping that weapon in shape, boyo?' Taff asked.

The soldier frowned. He clearly didn't like the implication that he needed any help.

'Your man hadn't zeroed his rifle,' Taff explained to Danny. 'No wonder he kept missing.' He turned back to the guard. 'He's expecting us,' he said.

The guard nodded and opened the door. Taff led them through it. They found themselves in a larger room, ten metres by fifteen, occupied by just three men. One of them, dressed in camouflage trousers and a black T-shirt, stood by a barred window looking down on to the street. The second, similarly dressed, was examining a map of the city stuck to the wall with strips of gaffer tape. The third, sitting on a wooden chair at the far end of the room, to his side a table with three mobiles and a sat phone on it, was Asu.

Danny recognised the rebel leader's features from the briefing back at Hereford, but the photo he'd seen then failed fully to capture just what an unpleasant-looking man Asu was. He had a sallow face like candle wax, sunken eyes and a thin, ratty moustache. His greasy hair had a centre parting and was flecked with grey. In addition to the rifle slung over the back of the chair, he wore two pearl-handled Colt M1911s on his belt. He sat with one leg hooked over the arm of his chair, picking at his teeth with a tiny sliver of wood. Was this really the basket in which the British government was putting all its eggs?

The door closed behind them. Danny immediately checked the room for other exits. With the exception of a hatch in the roof, there were none. The windows were all barred and there were no other doors. For a high-value target, Asu had installed himself in a shoddy hideout that would be almost impossible to escape from if government troops came calling. Taff was clearly aware of this. His first move was to step over to the barred windows and look carefully out, alert for any signs of imminent danger.

'He thinks I am a stupid fool, this Mr Taff,' Asu said in a thin, reedy voice to no one in particular. His accent was curiously posh, and Danny remembered that he'd spent a lot of time in London. 'But show me a safe house in this city.'

'I'll show you plenty of safer ones than this, pal,' Taff said.

Asu ignored him. His attention was all on Buckingham, who now walked towards him.

'Let me guess,' Asu said. 'The British government sends me its very best wishes?' His glistening lips quivered with barely concealed amusement. He oozed the confidence of a soldier who thought he was close to victory.

Buckingham stopped a couple of metres in front of him and spoke a greeting in Arabic. Asu's expression changed – he was clearly impressed by this newcomer's facility with the language – and he responded in kind before reverting to English. 'Mr Taff and his men, they teach us wonderful new ways to kill people!' He said it with a smile. 'I have tanks and even helicopters at my disposal, but nothing helps us like men with guns.'

Every inch the diplomat, Buckingham inclined his head and spoke quietly but clearly. 'Her Majesty's government hopes the gentlemen from International Solutions are of some help in your endeavours.'

For some reason Asu found this uproariously funny. 'Yes!' he roared. 'Yes! They *are* of some help in my endeavours! I have children here who are better shots than most of the government soldiers. They pretend to be begging for bread and then . . .' He mimed firing a rifle, before dissolving into laughter again. Either he didn't notice or he didn't care that nobody else seemed to find this as funny as he did. He gave a long belly laugh while Buckingham stood patiently in front of him. He allowed his mirth to subside before speaking again. 'You've brought me another soldier?' he asked, pointing at Danny.

Buckingham glanced in his direction. Danny sensed in him a flicker of annoyance that he'd been brought into the conversation.

'Looks to me like you've got plenty of soldiers already, mate,' Danny said. 'Little ones.'

Moving very slowly, Asu got to his feet. He unhooked his rifle from the back of his chair, slung it over his shoulder and walked towards Danny. It felt like everyone in the room was holding their breath. Now the rebel leader's mouth was just a few inches from Danny's right ear. He carried with him a putrid stench of body odour and tobacco.

'You've seen the pretty children?' he breathed, so only Danny could hear him. 'Perhaps you would like to take a couple home with you?'

Danny turned to face Asu square on. 'Last lot I came across using kids to do their dirty work were called the Taliban,' he said equally softly, but making no effort to hide his disgust. 'Want to know what happened to them when we bumped into each other?'

But before Asu could reply, Buckingham was there. His eyes flashed nervously, and he cleared his throat to interrupt the whispered exchange. 'I've brought my own close protection, as you can see,' he said, nodding in Danny's direction. 'Please pretend he's not here.'

Asu inclined his head. 'Did you hear that?' he said to Danny. 'You're not here.' When he looked back at Buckingham, all the humour had left his face. 'Mr Buckingham, you do not really expect me to believe that you have been sent all the way here to keep an eye on our four mercenaries – I hope the word does not offend you, Mr Taff . . .'

'Takes a lot more than that to offend me,' Taff murmured. He too was looking intently at Danny.

'To check that our four mercenaries are doing their work properly?'

'You are even more insightful than I've been led to believe.'

Buckingham's flattery was outrageous, but it hit the mark. Asu spread his palms out in a show of false modesty. Danny had to hand it to Buckingham: he had the measure of this twat. 'I wonder if we might talk in private?' the MI6 man suggested.

Asu clapped his hands together, the revolvers swinging on his belt as he did so. 'Of course,' he announced. He nodded curtly at the two other Syrians, who immediately understood the instruction and silently left the room. Buckingham turned and made a similar gesture to Danny, who had the impression he was pathetically trying to mimic Asu's authority. Reluctantly, Danny stepped backwards towards the door. Taff stayed where he was. Danny shot him an enquiring glance, but Taff simply winked at him the way he used to when he was a kid. Clearly he was to be party to this private conversation, and Buckingham seemed to have no problem with that.

Danny closed the door as he left the room. The two guards who had shown them in were still in the antechamber, but now they were sitting on the seats by the wall, smoking roll-up cigarettes. Danny took up position by the door, which gave him a clear view through the window that looked out on to the compound. The armed kids were no longer sitting around the fire. They were standing in a line, as if on parade. Skinner was facing them, a couple of metres away, surveying them like some sergeant fucking major. Dickhead. In another time and another place, Danny would have given him a piece of his mind, not to mention a piece of his fist.

One of the guards stood up. Danny made a show of gripping his firearm. The guard threw his cigarette to the floor, stubbed it out with his right foot, then glared at Danny. Danny glared back.

Ten tense seconds passed.

The second guard stood up. Danny jutted his chin in his direction. The guard stepped over to his mate and muttered something in Arabic. The first guard sneered but seemed to take it on board. He sat down again, removed a pouch of tobacco from his ammo vest and started rolling another cigarette. Good decision. He didn't take his unfriendly gaze from Danny, but that was fine by him. They could stare all they wanted. Just so long as they didn't twig that Danny's mind was as much on eavesdropping as it was on close protection. He couldn't work out why Taff was still in there. He strained his ears, cursing silently that the moment of bravado had caused him to miss the opening gambits of Buckingham and Asu's private discussion. He carefully tuned in to the muted voices on the other side of the door.

Buckingham was speaking. He sounded like someone reciting a rehearsed speech. 'There's no doubt, sir,' he said, 'that Sorgen will understand you are stronger united than divided.'

'Sorgen is a stupid fool,' Asu retorted.

'Sorgen is a politician, if I may say so, to the tips of his toes. I know him well . . .'

'He is *my* brother!'

'But he is not your *friend*. We were close, years ago. I know I can persuade him.'

There was a pause. Danny heard footsteps and pictured Asu pacing the room. From the corner of his eye he was aware of movement outside. The kids weren't in a line any more. Two of them had gone. Skinner was talking to the other two. One of them was the kid with the amputated arm – Asu's grandson. He was holding something. Cylindrical. Perhaps a metre long. It looked like an RPG launcher. Jesus! Skinner was a wanker, but was he *really* going to teach these kids to mess around with weapons like that, in an enclosed space like this?

'The festival of Eid al-Fitr is tomorrow night,' Buckingham said, his tone now more urgent. 'A time for Muslims to present a show of unity. Sorgen is devout. He will accept this olive branch, if only to respect the memory of your father.'

More pacing in the room. Outside, Skinner had handed the rocket launcher to the able-bodied child and was showing him how to position it over his right shoulder. Danny squinted. The kid's right hand was forward on the launcher. It was resting on the fucking rocket. If he fired it like that, he'd lose his hand.

Danny was still focused on the conversation in the next room. 'I will tell Sorgen that the British government will match any offer the French have made him,' Buckingham said. 'Money, weapons, anything. Asylum, if things go badly for you, sir. He can't fail to see the advantages. And then, when we have him on side, we'll be in a position to . . . to do what we discussed.'

'What we discussed?' What *had* they discussed?

'What the *fuck*?' Danny hissed. He'd been listening hard for Asu's response, but his concentration was divided by what he saw outside. Hector had come into view. While Skinner continued to position the rocket launcher, Hector had taken the amputee kid with the green Adidas T-shirt by the shoulders and placed him no more than a metre behind his friend. What were they *playing* at? The back-blast from one of those things would kill the kid in seconds. Cursing under his breath, Danny abandoned his post. He ran from the antechamber and hurtled down the stairs. Seconds later he burst into the compound and sprinted towards where Hector and Skinner were giving their half-arsed lesson. They'd stepped back a couple of metres from the kids now, and wore the ugly grin of the playground bully. 'Nice one, Abdul,' Hector barked. 'You make very good soldier! Next time you fire it, stand like that!' He burst into laughter.

Danny was still running when the kid with the launcher turned around. The boy looked confused. He obviously knew that the two Brits were laughing at him, but he didn't know why. His face – pale for a Syrian – reddened and he looked like he was about to cry. As for his amputee friend, he seemed completely bewildered.

And then Danny was there. Barging past Hector, he shouldered the stocky mercenary out of the way, before marching up to the kid with the launcher and removing it from his shoulder. The two boys clearly had no idea what was happening. They scurried away to a corner, and Danny turned to face the two men.

'What the fuck do you think you're doing?' he shouted.

'Training,' Skinner said, his voice emotionless, his eyes dead. 'So be a good boy and get back to your babysitting.'

'Why's his hand on the fucking grenade?' Danny turned to Hector. 'And what are you playing at, sticking the kid in the back-blast zone?'

'Fuckin' Ada, mate,' Hector said. 'Lighten up. We were just having a laugh.'

'They didn't fucking know that. What if they'd followed your instructions in a combat situation?'

Skinner stepped up to Danny. 'Then we'd have a raghead without a hand and one without a face,' he said. 'Who gives a shit?'

'Feels good, does it, Skinner? Killing kids?'

'Dead's dead. I told you that before.'

Danny moved even closer to Skinner, so that their faces were less than a hand's breadth apart. 'Do that again, sunshine,' he said, 'I'll give you a chance to find out what dead feels like.'

Skinner didn't even flinch. 'You'd better make sure you do it right first time. You wouldn't get a second chance.'

'I wouldn't fucking need one, pal.'

Danny turned his back on Skinner and Hector and walked over to the corner where the two kids were standing. The able-bodied child was still holding the RPG launcher. It took no more than a gesture from Danny for him to hand it over. 'Never stand behind it,' Danny said. The kids looked at him, plainly not understanding. Danny held up the weapon and positioned the amputee child behind it again, before wagging his finger. 'Don't stand behind it,' he repeated slowly. As the light of understanding dawned on their faces, he made another gesture – a clenched fist opening up to indicate an explosion.

'Makes a big bang,' he said. 'Very big bang. You understand?'

The child copied Danny's charade. 'Big bang?' he repeated hesitantly.

He grinned.

Danny grinned back.

They were still smiling when the ground shook, and the air around them seemed to explode.

SEVENTEEN

Fast air thundered low over the rebel compound.

The roar of the jet engines was so extreme that Danny threw the kids to the ground as a matter of reflex. A split second after the aircraft had passed, there was a second explosion as some kind of ordnance hit the neighbourhood. Impossible to say how big the bomb was, or how close, but it was large enough and near enough to make the walls of the compound shudder. Danny heard Hector shout, 'Fucking air strike!' and was aware of the two men running towards one of the Land Rovers. His own instinct was to sprint in the opposite direction, back towards the house. If they were coming under attack, he needed to get Buckingham the hell out of here. Right now. First, though, he found himself dealing with the kids. They were crouched in a corner of the compound, covering their heads with their hands. The boys' instinct was obviously to shelter there, but if the wall collapsed it would crush them in a second. They'd be safer in open ground.

Danny grabbed each of them by one arm and dragged them five metres from the corner. 'Stay away from the wall!' he barked, just as a second explosion ripped through the air. He looked up. One of the tower blocks had been hit. The top three storeys were shrouded in a vast balloon of smoke. Orange flames were just visible halfway up it. As Danny sprinted towards the rebels' house, his face stung from the impact of the dust and debris. Chunks of rubble slammed into the ground around him. He upped his speed and covered the final ten metres to the entrance without being seriously hit.

The ground floor was in total confusion. The screams of women. The bark of male voices. The kids looked the most frightened, but that didn't stop them standing and strapping their weapons to their chests. Danny fought his way through the chaos and stormed up the stairs.

Taff had already evacuated Asu and Buckingham as far as the antechamber. When the shock waves of a third explosion blasted through the air, Buckingham jolted as though he'd been hit. Asu pushed past him and hurried down the stairs. Buckingham stood by the door of the room they'd just left, his eyes wide.

'Get him out!' Taff roared, not that he needed to. Danny didn't pussyfoot around. A seam had appeared in the ceiling and fine dust was showering down into the antechamber. Danny grabbed Buckingham by the arm and dragged him across the room and down the stairs, with Taff following close behind. The rooms on the ground floor were empty, although the sound of kitsch Arabic pop still drifted bizarrely around the deserted building.

'Do they know Asu's here?' Danny shouted over his shoulder at Taff.

'Who knows? Might just be a random strike. Happens all the time.' He looked up at the ceiling. 'Let's not stick around.'

'Roger that,' Danny muttered. He turned to Buckingham. 'When we get outside, head straight for the Land Rover. We're out of here before we take a direct hit.'

Buckingham was whispering to himself, 'Oh my God . . . Oh my God . . .'

'*Move!*' Danny roared. They ran along the corridor. The exit was ten metres ahead, and the door was open, but visibility beyond it was poor because the air was thick with a choking cloud of dust from the stricken tower block. Danny thought he could hear the sound of Asu's voice, shouting words of defiance, but all of a sudden his attention was grabbed by what he saw in a room off to the left. Unlike the other rooms they had passed, this one was not empty. The woman Taff had pointed out – Asu's daughter-in-law Basheba, with the long, black hair with the single white streak – was in the far corner. Crouched on the floor was the son whose head she had been stroking. The boy was clearly terrified and his mother was trying to persuade him to leave the building. Her other son, the amputee, was by her side. He saw Danny and looked over at him, clearly wanting help to get his brother outside. Danny hesitated, torn between the need to evacuate Buckingham and the kid's unspoken request. After a couple of seconds he nodded at the boy and stepped inside the room.

It was then that the bomb hit.

The noise of the strike was like a thunderclap, and they were right inside it. Danny was thrown to the floor, rubble and dust all around him, obscuring his vision. He could rely only on his hearing, which told him that chunks of the ceiling were dropping down. He covered his head and lay curled up for ten seconds until the noise subsided.

When he looked up, a fog of dust still obscured everything more than a metre away. But at the far side of the room, five or six metres from him, a shaft of sunlight cut through the dust where the ceiling and the exterior wall above had collapsed. Danny saw two silhouettes in the light: a woman and a boy. He could see that both the kid's arms were intact. There was no sign of his brother.

Coughing – almost choking on the dust – Danny got to his feet and picked his way across the rubble-strewn floor. 'Get to the Land Rover!' he barked at Buckingham, but he kept his eyes on the silhouettes. As he came within a couple of metres of them, he saw their faces. Dirty, tear-stained, anguished. The woman pointed at the floor and Danny immediately saw what was wrong.

The son with one arm was in a bad way. Terminally bad. A piece of concrete the size of a football had fallen from the ceiling and landed on him. Jagged, rusting iron bars were sticking out of it, and one of these had pierced the kid's chest. Blood was gushing from his thoracic cavity, smearing the stump of his arm and pooling on the floor. His eyes were open and wild and although he was not screaming – Danny assumed he no longer had the lung capacity – the pain he was enduring was written all over his face. For a split second Danny's mind conjured up the gruesome image of Jack, pierced and bleeding, in the wrecked Renault. The kid had the same look of agony.

Agony on the brink of death.

A piercing scream brought Danny back to the present. The boy's mother, Basheba, was clutching her hair in horror as she stared down at his brutalised body. She collapsed heavily to her knees, into the puddle of blood from her son's body. Her desperate wailing and horrid shrieks were far worse than the noise of the shelling minutes before. They made the sinister silence that hung over the rest of the building even more intense. Danny looked around. Taff was a couple of metres away. Behind him, Buckingham, staring down at the injured boy, his face unreadable. 'Get in the Land Rover,' Danny said again, but less forcefully this time. He wasn't really surprised when Buckingham ignored him.

Danny crouched down to give the kid a closer look. The boy was a goner, for sure. If the shock didn't kill him, the loss of blood would. Even if there were such luxuries as doctors or hospitals in the middle of this war zone, it would have been a waste of everyone's time trying to move this dying child. His legs and head were shaking from the pain. But Christ, he was a tough little kid, clinging to life even as it oozed from him. At the same time, like Jack before him, his expression seemed to beg Danny to put him out of his agony.

Unlike Jack, he had an audience.

Danny quickly assessed his options. Leave the child there to die a horrifically painful death. Or help him on his way. Put like that, the choice made itself. No point explaining to anybody what he was about to do. Now wasn't the time to discuss the rights and wrongs of the situation. Sure, what he was about to do was illegal by any rules of engagement. But sometimes on the ground you had to make your own rules. Every soldier knew that.

He pulled his med pack from his chest rig. 'Move the woman,' he barked at Taff. 'I can't do anything while she's screaming in my ear.'

There was a scuffle as Taff pulled Basheba to her feet and dragged her, screaming, several metres from where her son lay bleeding.

Danny took out a shot of morphine from his med pack. It was in a brown, rectangular box, one end red, the other yellow. There was also a black marker pen in the med pack. Normally he would mark 'M' on the forehead of anybody he'd just given morphine, along with the dose and the time of administration. No need for that now. Without hesitation, he stabbed the red end of the injection through the coarse material of the kid's trousers and into his bony left thigh. He felt the needle puncture the skin. It took a few seconds for the drug to spread through the boy's bloodstream, but it hardly seemed to have any effect. He was still shaking. His eyes were still bulging.

Danny threw away the spent shot and pulled out another. He punctured the kid's trousers again. As the morphine eased into the boy, Danny looked over his shoulder. Taff was five metres behind him, holding back the child's mother. She was still screaming, and Danny tried to block out the noise. Taff had an intense look on his face. The mother seemed like a minor irritation as his strong arms held her back. All his focus was on Danny. His old friend knew what he was doing, and he wasn't about to stop him. Behind Taff, Danny could just make out

Buckingham's dust-covered outline. He appeared to be holding something up, but Danny couldn't make out what.

A groan from the dying boy. Danny took another shot from the med pack.

This third injection seemed to have some effect. The trembling didn't stop, but it began to subside as the opiate did its work smothering the pain. Three shots. More than you'd ever normally administer on the battlefield. But not enough for what Danny had in mind. He felt inside his med pack for the fourth and final shot that he carried with him. The shot that would put the kid out of his misery once and for all.

'That's a lethal dose, kiddo,' he heard Taff say behind him. 'You sure you know what you're doing?' No attempt to talk him out of it. Just a warning.

'He's dead anyway,' Danny said between gritted teeth as he prepared to administer the fatal injection. 'This just makes it easier for—'

He didn't finish the sentence. Perhaps the boy's mother understood what he and Taff were saying and had found new reserves of strength. Perhaps Taff had just taken his eye off the ball. Whatever the reason, Basheba had managed to escape his grasp. Now she hurled her whole body at Danny, knocking him sideways from his crouching position beside her son. '*You not kill him!*' she screeched. '*You not kill him!*'

The morphine injection had dropped from Danny's hand, and lay propped up against a pile of rubble. Danny grabbed it. The boy's mother was hugging him now, but in doing so she had knocked the concrete chunk and its deadly shard. The boy gasped, his white face once more a mask of agony. It was pitiful to see. Danny lunged forwards and, as the weeping mother clutched her child, drove the fourth injection into the boy's arm. Basheba let out one more desperate, piercing scream as he exhaled whatever breath was left in his dying lungs. He shuddered a final time, then lay still.

There was a moment of silence. The woman was staring at Danny in shocked disbelief. Looking round, he saw Taff and Buckingham standing five metres away. Taff was expressionless. Buckingham looked almost as shocked as the mother. Danny was vaguely aware that he had something in his hand and he thrust it into his pocket. The woman was shouting again, yelling at him in a frenzied mixture of Arabic and English. Those words Danny could understand left no room for doubt. '*You killed my son . . . you killed my son! Murderer!*'

She threw herself at him, pounding his face with her fists, which were smeared with her dead son's blood. Danny grabbed her wrists. 'He was dead anyway,' he tried to explain. 'All I did was take away the pain.' But his words had no effect. She was screaming even louder.

And then Taff was there, pulling her away, manhandling her out of the room. Danny bent down and pulled the lump of concrete from the boy's chest. It made a wet, sucking sound as it started to come away. He felt the metal rod catching on one of the boy's ribs and had to reinsert it a couple of inches into his chest before he could remove it properly. Casting the blood-spattered concrete to one side, he lifted the corpse. Somewhere above him, he heard a sinister creaking: the building's death throes. Basheba's other son had the presence of mind to scurry after his mother and Taff, but Buckingham was still in the door-way, staring horrified at Danny.

'*Move!*' Danny's bark seemed to snap Buckingham out of his trance. He ran from the room, along the corridor and out into the compound. Danny followed, the boy's limp, bleeding body in his arms.

He sized up the situation immediately. The murder holes had been abandoned, the gates opened, and the other occupants of the building had flooded out on to the streets beyond. The doors of the two Land Rovers were open, the engines running. Danny couldn't see Hector, Skinner or De Fries, but assumed two of them were behind the wheels, ready to move. Chances were that their Syrian drivers had fled. Asu himself was standing at the gates, looking into the sky, holding up his rifle in a gesture of defiance and shouting aggressively. His two bodyguards were standing on either side of him, but their expressions made clear that they wanted to get out of there, and quick. Danny looked up. No sign of fast air or choppers. That didn't mean the bombardment had stopped. They'd been lucky so far, but they needed to exfiltrate immediately.

He carried the body to the middle of the compound and laid it down gently. Only then did Taff release the mother. She shot towards Danny, a projectile from a catapult, and once more pummelled him in her grief and fury.

Asu hadn't seen Danny bring out the body. He began shouting at the woman in Arabic. She stopped beating Danny and turned to face her father-in-law. A torrent of rage spewed from her mouth. As she spoke, Asu listened, and his face grew darker with each word.

He strode over to Danny. 'Is it true,' he demanded, 'what she says? You killed Nadim? You killed my grandson?'

Danny shook his head. 'No.' He pointed at the building. 'The bombardment killed your grandson. And if we don't get out of here soon, it'll kill you too. They know you're here.'

In a sudden movement, Asu pointed his rifle at Danny. He wasn't fast enough. Danny knocked the barrel to one side with his left arm, and pulled his Sig from his chest rig with the right. The barrel of the pistol was no more than ten inches from the rebel leader's face. His two guards raised their weapons and pointed them at Danny. This seemed to give Asu more confidence, but then he couldn't see, as Danny could, that Hector and Skinner had silently exited the Land Rovers and were ready to shoot if it went noisy.

A tense silence fell. 'Basheba tells me young Nadim was alive,' Asu whispered.

'Barely,' Danny said.

'He is *murderer!*' the mother shrieked. '*Murderer of my son!*'

Asu didn't take his eyes from Danny. They were calculating. Danny sensed that he didn't mourn the loss of his grandson one bit. To lose face, though, was agony for him. 'Why shouldn't my men kill you right now?' he said.

Danny almost gave him an answer, but then Taff was beside them. Keeping his eyes on the rebel leader, he stretched out a hand and gently moved Danny's Sig to one side. There was nobody else on earth that Danny would allow to do that.

'Don't kill your friends, boyo,' he told Asu quietly. 'Concentrate on your enemies. Danny's a good lad and Basheba's mistaken. I saw it all. He tried to administer first aid. Look at the boy's body. You know he couldn't have survived that.'

Asu glanced for the first time at the dead child. His chest was a bleeding mass of flesh and bone.

'He's right,' Buckingham said. 'Best to think this through.'

Asu bowed his head. His guards lowered their guns.

Basheba's reaction was heart-wrenching. She staggered back, tears streaming down her face. Whispering in Arabic, she gestured to her other son, who was watching from the doorway of the building. He started towards her, but stopped suddenly as Asu snarled an instruction. The boy was clearly terrified of his grandfather.

Basheba, realising she could not influence her son, turned her anguished face first to Danny, giving him a look of hatred like he'd never seen before, and then to Asu. She spoke again, now in English. 'Will you punish him?' she asked, pointing at Danny.

'No,' Asu replied. 'I will not.'

A strange whimper left Basheba's lips. With a final, imploring look at her surviving son, she ran, weeping, through the gates and disappeared into the street.

A long silence followed.

'She is a stupid woman,' Asu said.

'Stupid enough to let the enemy know your location?' Taff asked, a world of violence implicit in his question.

Asu waved his hand dismissively. 'I have people patrolling the streets,' he said. 'They will find her.' He looked, without pity or any other discernible emotion, down at the body of his grandson, then prodded it with his foot. 'He must be buried before the setting of the sun. Government forces will be here soon. We must move on from this place.'

Buckingham jostled past Taff and Danny. 'My condolences,' he said.

'He had one arm and was of no use anyway.'

If Buckingham found this distasteful, he didn't let on.

'Do we have an agreement, sir?' he pressed.

Asu nodded his head slowly. 'We have an agreement,' he said. 'Tonight I meet with my commanders in my safe house near the central mosque. Taff knows the place. I will explain everything to them.'

'You must tell us where we can find Sorgen if we are to progress,' Buckingham said.

Asu looked away. 'I only hear rumours.'

'What rumours do you hear, sir?'

'He and his people stay away from the city. Like me, he keeps his commanders separate from each other. They occupy tents in the desert south-west of Homs. They are easy to move, and from the air look like simple Bedouin.'

'But where is Sorgen himself?'

'Follow the road to Al Qusayr. After thirty kilometres you will see a track leading off to the right into the hills. Follow this. If my information is correct, you will find my brother.' He spat out the word 'brother' as if he was swearing. He looked at Buckingham and Taff. Something seemed to pass between him and them. Then he turned and barked a single word at his bodyguards. He walked with them to the waiting people carrier, they climbed in and the vehicle drove off.

Taff looked down at the dead body, then at Buckingham. 'Get in the Land Rover,' he said.

'What about—?'

'Just fucking get in.'

Buckingham did as he was told, and as soon as he was out of earshot Taff grabbed Danny by the arm. 'You're not one of us, kiddo,' he said. 'You're still serving and you just killed a child in front of a fucking spook.'

'He was—'

'I don't care why you did it, lad. Just don't give that twat the rope to hang you with. You can't trust a fucking spook.'

'What did you talk about in there, Taff? When Buckingham sent me out of the room?'

For a moment, Taff looked like he was going to give Danny a straight answer. But then he shook his head. 'Business, kiddo,' he said. 'Just business. Come on, let's get the fuck out of it before those government cunts come back and dish out second helpings.'

EIGHTEEN

'What the bloody hell do you mean, you didn't plant the device?'

Back at Taff's base, Danny and Buckingham were alone in the bleak first-floor room that had been set aside for their use. Danny was peering through the gap in the wooden planks reinforcing the windows. In the street below, fifteen metres to his eleven o'clock, he could see a group of five young men huddled by a pile of garbage the size of a small car. He spotted a couple of rats among the waste, but they didn't seem to worry the men. They were talking intently. Maybe they were making plans to cause, or avoid, violence. Maybe they just wanted to know where their next meal was coming from. In any case, they didn't immediately appear to be armed. Danny looked back into the room, where Buckingham was standing with his arms folded. His face was grimy and covered in dust. He looked a lot less suave than when they'd first met.

'I said, what the *bloody hell* do you mean, Black, you didn't—?'

'I had my hands full. Maybe you noticed?'

'Oh, I noticed. I bloody *noticed*. Risking everything for some kid who was going to die anyway.'

'I'll remember that, next time you need my help.'

'A fat lot of use you'll be.'

'You're alive, aren't you?'

'Just!' Buckingham was raging now. 'Which is more than can be said for Jack and . . .'

'Go ahead and say it, mucker.'

For a moment, Danny thought Buckingham was going to finish by laying at Danny's feet the death of his mates. Perhaps he thought better of it. Perhaps Taff's appearance in the doorway quietened him. Buckingham seemed very wary of these PMCs. Deep down, Danny didn't blame him.

Taff's frame filled the doorway. He didn't need to say anything. 'All friends?' he asked delicately.

'Oh yes,' said Buckingham. 'I'd say it was all going absolutely swimmingly, wouldn't you, Black?'

'Danny?' said Taff.

'Hunky fucking dory. When do we go and see Sorgen?'

'First light tomorrow.'

'That's too late. I want to get this over and done with.'

'No can do, kiddo,' Taff said. 'If we start moving around after dark, chances are we'll be stopped by government troops. Or even worse, followed. Better to leave it till the morning.'

'In any case,' Buckingham put in, 'Eid al-Fitr starts tomorrow. Sorgen will be more receptive to our offer then.'

'So we just sit around here and wait for a MiG to dump its payload on us?'

'Relax, kiddo, we're in a safe part of town.'

'That's what Asu thought.'

'Yeah, well, I'm smarter than Asu. Why don't you head downstairs? De Fries's cooking – some disgusting Dutch shit, but it fills a hole and there isn't much else to do till dawn.'

Taff nodded at them and disappeared along the hallway.

03.20 hrs.

Sleep was impossible. Not with the sound of a midnight bombardment raging all around. Taff had been right: the air strikes were avoiding this part of town. But when ordnance is dropping from the sky, any part of town is close. Lying on the hard floor in the darkness, the recumbent form of Buckingham just a

249

couple of metres to the right, Danny could see him jerk every time a bomb hit. And, truth to tell, Danny was on edge too. This wasn't his idea of a secure LUP. But Taff was calling the shots and he didn't have Regiment SOPs to adhere to. Not any more. If he said this was where they were staying, then this was where they were staying.

Buckingham sat up suddenly as a particularly loud explosion somewhere in the distance hit their ears. He cursed under his breath before lying down again. Danny got to his feet.

'Where are you going?' Buckingham whispered, unable to keep the nervousness from his voice.

'I need a slash. Come if you want. Just don't expect me to hold yours like Nanny used to.'

He didn't need a slash, but his companion's constant twitching was getting on his nerves and he wanted some air. Treading silently, he left the room and padded along the corridor. The generator was still grinding in the room next door, and Danny could see the outlines of Taff's local workforce lying on the floor, and the silhouette of the gimpy by the window. He peered in for a moment, wondering if Taff was in there, asleep. Difficult to say, but he couldn't make him out. Perhaps he was keeping stag outside. Danny decided to go and have a look.

The compound was still. There was a full moon overhead, and the fire pit that De Fries had used to grill fatty hunks of some meat Danny didn't recognise – camel maybe? – was still glowing near the left-hand wall. The vehicles were parked in a row about five metres from the rear wall, all facing the gate in case they needed to evacuate quickly. And beyond them, right by the gate, were two figures. Danny couldn't see their faces, but he could tell they were Skinner and Hector from their outlines. He could also see that they were tooled up. Heavily. Not only a rifle each, but Skinner held some other tool which Danny couldn't quite make out.

It was instinct that made Danny hold back in the doorway of the house. He didn't want these two to see him and there was something about their body language that suggested they didn't want to be seen. Hector looked furtively over his shoulder before quietly unlocking the gate and sliding it open just wide enough for the two of them to slip outside. It closed without the slightest noise.

Something wasn't right. Where were these two going? Why the secrecy?

Looking back into the house, Danny thought about returning to his position by Buckingham's side. But Taff was around somewhere, and he could trust him to make sure Buckingham was OK if anything went wrong. Danny had an itch that needed scratching. What were those two up to? Something they didn't want Taff – or anyone – to know about? There was only one way to find out. Danny felt his fingers move to his chest rig, which he hadn't removed since arriving in Syria. The Sig was there.

He crept round the compound's perimeter wall, keeping out of the moonlight and staying in the shadows. The gate was still unlocked. He slid it open and crept out. As soon as he had shut the gate behind him, he pressed himself back against it. He could hear a chopper approaching from the north. Twenty seconds later it was passing overhead, its searchlight beaming down on the compound and the street outside. But then it veered westward and the sound of its rotors disappeared. Danny breathed again.

The street was deserted, the outlines of the concrete buildings strangely ghostly in the moonlight. Eerie, too, to be in a city with no one on the streets. The only trace of movement was thirty-five metres to his right. Two figures, also keeping to the shadows, turning left into a side street and disappearing.

Danny made next to no noise as he ran lightly on the balls of his feet. He could move through jungle undergrowth without making a sound, so remaining the grey man, invisible and inaudible, presented no problems here in the chaotic darkness. When he reached the corner of the street, he waited and peered ahead in each direction. He saw Hector and Skinner walking along with the swagger of men who didn't think they were being followed, or didn't care if they were. If it hadn't been for the signs of battle all around them – two burned-out vehicles, one behind the other fifteen metres from Danny's position, the dark bullet holes on moonlit buildings, the total absence of civilians – they could have passed for a couple of blokes sauntering home from the pub. Except that blokes sauntering home from the pub didn't normally have Colt Commandos strapped to them, and God only knew what other hardware these two were packing.

Danny followed the pair for fifteen minutes, staying thirty metres behind them – far enough that they wouldn't recognise him even if they noticed they had a trail. What were they after? What diversions could this fucked-up town offer them? Hookers, maybe. It seemed unlikely. Would they really risk venturing out just to lose their load in some rancid Homs brothel, full of clapped-out prostitutes servicing the needs of government forces and rebels alike? It occurred to Danny once more that perhaps they simply wanted to keep what they were doing below Taff's radar.

He kept careful track of his route, ticking off landmarks in his head: a small mosque on his left, one of whose minarets was crumbling and dilapidated, a school with elephants and zebras painted on the perimeter wall. Finally, Hector and Skinner stopped in a side street. From his vantage point on the corner, Danny could see that this little road had avoided the worst of the fighting. It was deserted, of course, and there was the ever-present smell of rubbish decaying as fast as Homs's failing infrastructure. But the buildings – modern, two-storey structures on either side – looked largely untouched. The pair stopped outside one of these buildings, twenty-five metres from where Danny stood watching in the shadows.

What Skinner was carrying, Danny could now see, was a set of bolt-cutters. Hector kept watch while Skinner got to work on what looked like a shopfront. Whatever he was cutting gave way in about twenty seconds. He bent down and effortlessly raised a metal shutter – Danny heard it rattle. The two checked their surroundings once more, their gaze passing over Danny like he wasn't there. A short tinkle of glass breaking, then they disappeared into the building.

Danny gave it forty-five seconds before stepping from the shadows. He pulled out his Sig and unlocked the safety switch as he moved stealthily up the street. From nowhere, an aircraft roared overhead. He threw himself against the wall and steeled himself for another explosion, but none came. It was a strafing run, he decided, intended to put the shits up the local populace. Not that that was at all necessary.

He took up a position opposite the building Hector and Skinner had entered. Although he couldn't read the Arabic sign on the window of the building, the image of a golden loaf of bread told him it was a bakery. A broken padlock lay on the ground in front of the shop. The metal shutters were up. The glass door was smashed in.

The place had been locked from the outside. That meant either there was nobody inside or there was another entrance. For a moment Danny considered trying to find it, but then decided to stay where he was. Just watch, he told himself. He might have been trained to go in hard and fast when the situation required it, but he also knew the benefits of patient surveillance. He remembered Taff's story of his mates in Northern Ireland. Yeah, he thought. Nothing to be gained from going in blind.

A minute passed. Everything remained dark and still. If he hadn't seen the evidence of Hector and Skinner's forced entry, he wouldn't have known they were inside. But then he saw a light – not on the ground floor, but in a window on the level above. The light was dim and directional. It moved. Somebody was using a torch up there.

As Danny watched, something clicked into place. He remembered being back in London, face to face with Max Saunders in his comfortable office in St James's. What had he said? 'There's always the chance to earn a little extra while you're out there.' And, just a few hours ago, these two cunts had been counting out a hefty wad of cash. Where do you get money like that in a place like this? A place where the only holes in the wall were made by ballistics, not Barclays. Danny was no bleeding heart – a few months in the squadron hangar at Hereford would soon knock that out of you – but thieving from some poor bastards whose own government was bombing the shit out of them struck him as low.

It took Hector and Skinner longer than Danny expected to ransack the bakery. Fifteen minutes, maybe twenty. The torch told the story of their movements. The bulk of that time was clearly spent on the first floor – this seemed to be where they expected to find the richest pickings. There was a lot of moving about: the place was being thoroughly ransacked. When the torchlight disappeared, however, there was a pause of only about a minute before the two men reappeared.

The money was in Hector's fist – a disorganised wad of notes, rather thin. His face showed his disappointment. 'Hardly fucking worth it,' he grunted. 'Should have stayed back at base, yanked myself off.'

Skinner shrugged. The flat expression of menace he normally wore was even more aggressive than usual.

Hector was tucking the crumpled notes into a pouch on the ammo vest he was wearing when Danny stepped out of the shadows. His left forearm was just below eye level, his right hand holding the Sig, resting on it. Hector and Skinner, alerted not by sound but by movement, spun round. Their hands reached for their weapons, but they were experienced enough soldiers to know at once that Danny had beaten them to it. They slowly dropped their hands, peering towards him as they tried to work out who he was.

Distance between them: six or seven metres, no more. Danny stepped into the moonlight. 'Looting, fellas?' he said. 'What's wrong? Taff not paying you enough?'

Almost identical looks of disgust tinged with relief fell across their faces. 'Fuck you, kid,' Skinner said. He turned to Hector. 'Let's go.'

'You take a single step, Skinner, I'll plug you without even thinking about it.'

Skinner froze momentarily. Then he turned back to Danny, a dangerous look in his eyes.

'We're going back in there,' Danny said. 'You're going to show me what you've been up to.'

Skinner's eyes tightened. 'In your dreams.'

'I already warned you, Skinner. Don't tell me anyone's going to shed a tear over your carcass rotting in the gutter. I'm happy to do the world a favour and stick one in you.'

Skinner sneered. 'Bullshit,' he said. He moved, not away down the street but towards Danny. He made no attempt to step out of his line of fire, and stopped only when his face was half a metre from the Sig's barrel. 'You're stupid,' he said quietly. 'Even Taff knows that. But you're not *that* stupid.'

Danny didn't move. He just kept the gun pointing resolutely at Skinner's forehead. Somewhere in the distance, a bomb fell.

'What's the matter, kid?' Skinner taunted. 'Trigger finger not working? Or are you just scared that Uncle Taff will give you a bollocking when you get home?' His sneer grew even more pronounced. 'You think you're the dog's bollocks, you Regiment cunts. You wouldn't last two weeks in the Legion.' For the first time ever, Danny saw Skinner smile – a mirthless expression. He noticed something else too. A small smear, just above his left eyebrow. Blood? There was no sign of a cut. If it *was* blood, it was somebody else's. He glanced towards the bakery, an uneasy feeling rising in his gut, then looked back at Skinner.

'Get out of my sight,' Danny said. He glanced over at Hector, who, like his friend, was grinning unpleasantly. 'You too.'

Tilting his head sardonically, Skinner turned and started to walk away. He began to whistle. It was a tuneless sound, but Danny recognised it and remembered the words of the nursery rhyme it went with. The insult was perfectly clear. Skinner was right. He was never going to pull the trigger. Like it or not, they were on the same side, even if Danny was having trouble establishing just which side that was. He kept his weapon at the ready, however, as Hector and Skinner sauntered back along the street, neither man looking back until they reached the nearest corner. They disappeared from sight.

The looted building beckoned to Danny. He crossed the street and stepped inside. The ground floor, as he expected, had hardly been touched. There was a counter, and behind it some racks on the wall. Beyond a door in the back wall a staircase led up to the right. Danny stood holding his breath, listening. There was total silence.

Ominous silence.

He made for the stairs. The treads were wooden and rickety. Impossible to climb without announcing your presence. His weapon still engaged, he stopped halfway up and listened again.

Nothing.

He pulled a thin torch from his chest rig and held it parallel to the side of his head so it lit up the sight at the end of his Sig as well as the stairs ahead. He could see a half-open door at the top. Slowly, he ascended. He gently kicked the door open and panned the torch around.

It took every ounce of self-control to suppress his nausea.

This one room, about ten metres square, took up the entire first floor of the building. To his right, Danny saw the window through which he had watched Hector and Skinner's torch moving around. He lit up the middle of the room. A single glance told him that it served as a living area and bedroom for a family. He counted them – two adults, two children – dead in their beds and on the floor.

The kids' faces looked like they were sleeping. It was their bodies that told the full story of their horrific death. They were lying in a small double bed, covered by a single sheet so heavily saturated with blood that thick red gobbets dropped, mucus-like, from its edge on to the floor. Hard to believe that such small bodies could produce such quantities of fluid. Each child lay beneath a knife hole in the sheet. Danny figured they had been murdered in their sleep. Certainly they appeared calm – unaware of how the last few seconds of their short lives had passed. But he couldn't tell, at first, if he was looking at two boys, two girls, or one of each. Then he noticed that in one of the children's hair was a clip. Cheap, plastic and pink. The girl had probably been very proud of it.

The father lay on his back, naked on the floor. He was a stout man, and his belly spread out on either side like a jelly that was not stiff enough to hold its shape. His skin was smeared with blood. Its source was a deep, dreadful gash across his throat. Blood was no longer pumping from the wound, but the puddle that surrounded his head – a gruesome red halo – continued to spread slowly outwards. As he passed the torch over him, Danny thought he caught a glimpse of the man's severed, glistening trachea. His dead eyes were wide open, his mouth locked in a rictus grimace of agony.

But it was the sight of the mother that turned Danny's stomach.

He was no stranger to death. He had dished it out on more occasions than he could count, and the human anatomy held few secrets for him. But some sights should never be seen. This was one.

The woman was – had been – pregnant. Heavily. She lay, naked and exposed, on a second double bed. Her swollen belly had been cut: a long incision from an inch above her pubic hair, along her navel, bisecting her ribs and stopping just shy of her swollen breasts. A catastrophic amount of blood had spilled on either side of the incision. But although the woman was clearly dead, there was movement inside her stomach, a faint, slimy quivering. Danny stared at it, awed by the foulness of this atrocity, for perhaps twenty seconds. Then the movement stopped. The woman's belly was still. The final, youngest member of this little family had expired.

Sickened to his core, Danny switched off the torch and stood for a moment in darkness. In his mind he saw Hector greedily rummaging through his handful of worn notes. 'It was hardly fucking worth it,' he had said.

What *would* have been worth it? Danny wondered. A hundred dollars? A thousand? What price the medieval butchery of an innocent family?

And what kind of people had Taff surrounded himself with? His old friend needed to know. To understand.

It needed to happen now.

It took Danny fifteen minutes to get back to the base. This time he kept to the shadows more from habit than necessity, following the landmarks carefully as he tried to expel the image of the murdered family from his mind. Easier said than done.

As soon as he turned into the street where the base was located, he saw that there were lights on in the compound. By the time he was fifteen metres away he could hear the sound of a vehicle's engine turning over. He glanced at his watch. 04.39 hrs. The guys must be getting ready to leave. The gate was shut and locked from the inside. He pounded his fist against it and waited about thirty seconds before anyone answered. 'Who?' one of the Syrian kids shouted.

'Tell Taff it's Danny,' he called back.

There was a pause of about fifteen seconds before the gate slid open. Taff was there. He looked furious. 'Where the *fuck* have you been?' he demanded. 'Buckingham's spitting blood and I don't blame him.'

'We need to talk,' Danny said as he stepped into the compound.

'Damn right we need to talk,' Taff retorted. There was a clang as he slammed the gate shut and secured it. Danny looked around. One of the Land Rovers had its bonnet up, while the other's engine was running. Skinner sat behind the wheel, slowly revving the engine. The headlamps were shining straight at Danny, so he could only make out the outline of Skinner's head. Hector appeared in front of the bonnet of the second Land Rover. He didn't acknowledge Danny, but went about his business of topping up the vehicle's oil.

'You've got a problem,' Danny told Taff. 'Two problems.' He pointed at Hector and Skinner. 'One, two.'

Immediately he spoke, the engine of Skinner's Land Rover cut out. The headlamps died, leaving spots of colour dancing in front of Danny's eyes. A door slammed. Skinner was approaching. And now Hector. With his back to the gate, Danny found himself hemmed in: Taff two metres directly in front of him, Hector to his right, Skinner to his left.

'What's going on?' said Taff.

'Ask Skinner,' replied Danny. And then, when Skinner didn't comment, he continued. 'Your two boys here have just had a little night-time walkabout.'

Taff seemed to relax. 'They're big boys, kiddo. They're allowed out after midnight.'

'Not to break into houses and steal from the local population.'

A strange thing happened then. A flicker of annoyance crossed Taff's brow, but his lips also displayed the ghost of a smile. He looked left and right at the two men. 'This true, fellas?' he asked.

Skinner stepped forwards. 'You know what the trouble is dealing with kids?' he said. 'You have to put up with their fucking stupidity.' He looked at Taff. 'He's going to tell you next that we murdered a family and stole all their money.'

Taff's smile grew a little more pronounced. '*Is* that what you're going to tell me, kiddo?'

'Not so much murdered as butchered. They're out of control, Taff. Both of them. You need to stand them down. They're a liability.'

'You hear that, boyos? You're a liability.'

'I saw what they did—' Danny started to say, but he was interrupted by Hector.

'For fuck's sake. There's a baker's shop a few blocks away, all right? One of the kids back at Asu's told us there was a rumour the family had been killed by government forces. Happens all the bloody time, right? We went to investigate and yeah, they were properly fucked up. Some cunt had taken a knife to them. Taken anything of value too. We found a few lousy notes hidden under a mattress so we took them. It's not like they were going to spend it on anything, and trust me, the place will be looted within twenty-four hours anyway.'

'They're lying,' Danny said. 'I saw the bodies, they were—'

'Tell you what, fellas,' Taff addressed Hector and Skinner. 'How about you both get ready? We leave in ten minutes. Me and Danny'll sort this out.'

'Fine,' Hector said. 'I could do with a dump anyway.' He wandered back into the house. Skinner gave a look of triumph that only Danny caught, before joining De Fries back by the vehicles. Taff manoeuvred Danny away from the gate and across the compound. 'You want to be careful, kiddo,' he said, as the engines of both Land Rovers coughed into life. 'Hector and Skinner are good soldiers, but you don't want them pissed with you.'

'They're not soldiers at all,' Danny snapped. 'What they did was—'

'What they did was totally normal, kiddo.' Taff's voice was full of authority. 'They're not here because they like Middle

Eastern skirt. They're here for the money. They're mercenaries, for fuck's sake, and there isn't a mercenary in the world who doesn't go out of their way to earn a little extra if they see the chance.'

'And killing those people? What was that, a bit of fun?'

Taff shook his head. 'They didn't kill *anyone*, Danny. Didn't you hear what Hector said? You think that sort of atrocity is rare out here? It's two a penny. Why do you think your paymasters are helping the rebels? Because they think Asu's St Francis of fucking Assisi? Or because he's the best of a bad bunch? These government forces can do what the hell they want. There's no one to stop them. Plugging a local shopkeeper and his family isn't the half of it . . .'

'They used a knife.'

'What?'

'They didn't plug them. They used a knife. And they did it recently.'

'*Danny!*' Taff's voice was sharp. Almost like a schoolteacher. Or an irritated parent. He stretched out one arm to indicate the city around them. 'You're in the middle of a fucking war zone. Do yourself a favour and remember who your friends are.'

They stared at each other.

'I expected more of you, lad,' Taff went on. 'You're losing your grip out here. You're seeing things that aren't there. If you can't stand the fucking heat, you know what to do.'

He turned away and strode back to the Land Rovers, where he struck up a conversation with Skinner and De Fries. Danny watched them for a moment, then stormed over to the house. He paused outside the door that led to the fire-damaged part. He drew a couple of deep breaths and tried to calm himself. To clear his head and get things straight. Was Taff right? *Was* he losing it? He'd heard of such things happening. Maybe the loss of his three mates had affected him more than he knew. It wouldn't be the first time, he realised with a sick feeling, that a

Regiment guy had lost the plot in the middle of an op. He thought back to the bakery. Had he really seen what he thought he'd seen? It had been dark, and he'd been expecting the worst. Maybe Hector's explanation added up. If so, stealing a handful of notes was of a different order to massacring an entire family. There were plenty of guys back at Hereford who'd have done the same. It didn't make them monsters, did it?

But then the memory of the pregnant woman's quivering stomach returned. Those people were freshly dead. There was no doubt about it. Taff was being blind. He was a stubborn bastard – always had been, if Danny was honest with himself – and he clearly wasn't going to accept Danny's word for it that he'd teamed up with a couple of psychos. So what would it take? How could Danny convince him? What kind of evidence could he find that Taff couldn't dismiss so easily?

The idea came to him in an instant. Danny slipped his hand into his pocket. The small, magnetic infinity device that he was supposed to have planted on Asu was still there.

He flipped it around in his fingers for a few seconds as he looked up the stairs.

He checked over his shoulder to see if anyone was watching him from the doorway. Nobody was.

He went up.

At the top of the stairs, he listened. The sound of Hector straining on the throne emerged from the filthy bathroom. Danny stepped quietly away and into the generator room. As usual, Hector's M16 was propped up against the chintzy armchair. Danny bent down and pressed the magazine-release button on the side of the weapon. The mag clicked easily out.

He had to work quickly. Hector could walk back in at any moment. The mag was packed with 5.56s. Danny tipped them out and laid them on the armchair before turning back to the magazine itself. At the closed end of the mag was a detachable slide. He opened it to reveal the bottom of the spring action that fed the rounds up from the mag into the chamber of the weapon. He looked around the room. He needed something to push the bottom of the spring upwards. A splint of wood would do it. Removing his knife, the one Taff had given him all those years ago, he sliced off what he needed from the corner of the window frame. Nobody would notice, and even if they did they'd never guess why the wood had been cut. He stuffed the splint into the mag, raising the spring mechanism by about half an inch. Then he carefully placed the infinity device in the newly created cavity and refitted the slide on to the bottom of the mag.

A noise from next door: the sluicing of water down the pan.

Danny fumbled for the rounds on the armchair and started plugging them, one by one, into the doctored magazine. He'd reduced the capacity of the mag. By the time it was full, he still had five rounds left over. He shoved these in his pocket as he heard the bathroom door open and close.

Footsteps along the corridor.

He clicked the magazine back into place.

'What the *fuck* are you doing?'

Danny spun round to see Hector standing in the doorway, looking darkly from Danny to the M16 by his side.

'Looking for you,' Danny replied. He picked up the M16 and carried it to Hector, who warily accepted it. He didn't move from the doorway, though.

'If it wasn't for Taff, knobwad,' he whispered, 'I'd stick one in you right now. Or even let Skinner do it. He'd love to get to work on you.'

'You could even nick my wallet while you're at it,' Danny replied. 'Or maybe – what was it you said? – maybe it would be hardly fucking worth it.'

They stood, half a metre apart, eye to eye.

'I need to get past,' Danny said.

Hector's face oozed menace, but he stepped aside. Danny waited until Taff's colleague had headed back down the stairs before he continued along the corridor and into the room he shared with Buckingham. The MI6 man was standing waiting for him, obviously ready to go, obviously pissed off. 'Where the *bloody hell* . . . ?'

'Leave it, pal,' Danny said, grabbing him by the arm and pushing him out of the door. 'We've got an RV to make and I'm really, *really* not in the mood.'

NINETEEN

Clara had no idea where she was.

The soldiers who had rescued her from the awful makeshift prison had been less brutal than the government forces who had kept her there, but only slightly. They had blindfolded her and tied her hands behind her back. Clara had managed to stay composed as they'd bundled her into the back of a van, but when the doors slammed shut and it started to move off, panic had taken over. Her screams were piercing, and the effort of making them tore at her throat. An unseen companion had stuffed a rag into her mouth to shut her up. It had made her want to gag, and she'd had no option but to try to remain calm in order to avoid choking on her own vomit.

They had travelled for an hour, perhaps a little more, before stopping. The door had slammed again, and there had been the noise of voices and movement outside. Clara had been left, frightened and alone, for another hour, too scared to move and not even knowing what to do if she could.

When the door had opened again, she'd felt strong arms pull her out and drag her perhaps fifty paces. She had tried to work out where she was from the sounds and smell of the place. It was much quieter here, and the unpleasant mixture of odours in Homs — dust, rotting waste, sewage — had given way to something more wholesome but which she could not quite identify. She had stumbled a couple of times, but her captor had kept her upright, and then she sensed the air around her change. It grew warmer and she recognised the faintly musty smell of being under canvas.

Her captor had said something in Arabic. Another man had replied. He had a deep, resonant voice. On his command, she had felt the blindfold being ripped from her face. She'd blinked heavily as the sudden flood of light stung her eyes. Then she'd looked around.

She was indeed in a tent, but it was very different to those in which she had endured miserable childhood holidays. It was much bigger, circular and about twenty-five metres in diameter. A pole in the middle extended five or six metres into the air to prop up the roof, which spread down in billowing folds. The sand-coloured canvas was tough, utilitarian, and there was no hint of ornament inside the tent. Simply tables with maps and portable communications systems on them, guns, boxes of ammunition, and, Clara had immediately noticed, two flight cases marked with a red cross – medical supplies.

And men. Six, not including Clara's captor. Five of them were almost indistinguishable from each other: camouflage trousers, khaki T-shirts, ammo vests and black keffiyehs. They'd appeared hard at work, studying maps and issuing instructions into crackling radios, and barely bothered to notice her arrival. The sixth man, however, had stood out. He was huge, and wore a white *dishdash* with embroidered hems. His skin was dark, his hair – of which there was plenty – brilliant white. He had an enormous, bushy moustache, also white, which he'd stroked proudly as he stood in the centre of the tent, his small brown eyes twinkling.

He had looked at Clara for a moment before extending his arms. 'Welcome to our home,' he had announced in immaculate English. 'It's not much of a home, and I can't guarantee we will not have to strike camp at any minute and move elsewhere. But you are welcome to it anyway.'

'Thank you,' Clara had whispered, confused by his politeness and not entirely trusting it.

'My name is Sorgen.' The man had slapped his forehead with the palm of his hand in a strangely melodramatic gesture. 'Forgive me.' He'd clicked his fingers and barked a quick instruction in Arabic. Clara's captor had removed a flick knife from his pocket and opened it to reveal a wickedly sharp blade. Clara had stepped backwards, but he'd grabbed her arm. She'd opened her mouth to scream, but the scream had died on her lips as he cut the tape binding her wrists, releasing her arms.

'Excellent!' Sorgen had announced. 'And I have the pleasure to be addressing . . . ?'

It had occurred to Clara that she should lie, but her tired brain wasn't quick enough. She'd mumbled her real name.

'And what brings you to our poor, divided country, Miss Clara?' Sorgen's voice had been friendly, but his eyes were suddenly searching.

'I'm a doctor with Médecins Sans Frontières. I got separated from my friend . . . they killed him . . . I was trying to get back to my colleagues . . .' Amazing how she could mention Bradley's death without crying. Had she really become numb to it already?

'A doctor?' Sorgen had sounded impressed. 'Doctors are as rare as diamonds here. These days we have one doctor for fifty thousand people.' He'd nodded, to emphasise his statistic. 'That is what our government has done to us. It is not enough, especially in a time of war.'

'That's why we came,' Clara had whispered. She was on the edge of tears again.

'You said that you were trying to get back to your colleagues. Where is that?'

'A camp on the east side of Homs.' Sorgen had nodded, but Clara could tell he was deciding whether or not to believe her story. 'I'm afraid I don't quite know the exact location,' she'd added weakly.

Sorgen had raised his hand. He seemed to have come to a decision. 'That doesn't matter,' he'd said. 'We will find it.

You are, of course, free to go. I will ask one of my men to accompany you. You will not be offended if I ask you to wear a blindfold? It is for your own safety. We move around a great deal, and the government would dearly love to know our current location. What you don't know, they can't torture out of you.'

'Torture? Why—?'

Sorgen had smiled a rueful smile. 'There are places in Damascus, Miss Clara,' he said quietly, 'that a young lady like you wouldn't want to see. Like I said, you are free to go. But I have injured men, women and children here, and my troops are fighters, not medics. Perhaps I could ask you to look at them?'

Clara had never declined to help someone who needed her expertise. It was not in her nature. But on this occasion she had hesitated. All she wanted to do was get back to safety. This place and these people, wherever it was and whoever they were, were *not* safe. Would it be so bad, she had wondered, to think of herself for once?

She'd been on the point of asking to be taken away when something had stopped her. What was she *thinking*? Did she really intend to climb, willingly blindfolded, into a strange car with a strange man? Had her experience taught her that men like this could be trusted? The familiar hot, sick feeling of anxiety had crashed over her. She had found herself nodding her agreement and being led out of the tent, this enormous, strangely jovial man by her side.

Clara had seen, immediately, the advantage of the tent's colour. They were in the middle of the desert. The sand was hard and stony – not the rolling, Lawrence of Arabia waves she had always pictured as a child, but a harsh, weather-beaten landscape of crags and ditches. The tent was pitched against a sandstone cliff face about fifteen metres high. In the minutes after Clara's arrival, the sun had started to set and the cliff had cast a shadow over the tent. She had worked out that she must be facing roughly east. A track wound off in a roughly easterly direction, disappearing over the brow of a small hill perhaps a couple of kilometres away. Clara had found her gaze fixed on that track as she wondered if she dared walk it alone.

Around the tent, at a distance of about ten metres and fanned out in a semicircle, were armed men. They were lying on their fronts, rifles engaged, scanning the surrounding desert. Clara noticed that their clothes, headdresses and even weapons were the same colour as the tents. From a distance – or from above – they would blend easily into the landscape. Four trucks were parked at the camp. These too were camouflaged. Two were open-topped. One carried a satellite dish, from which long cables led into the tent. The other had a large machine gun of some kind mounted on the back. Clara knew nothing of guns, but she had observed that it was pointed skywards, and she'd had to suppress a shudder as she remembered the bombardments in Homs. Five metres ahead of them, she noticed the remains of a fire smouldering in a pit. A man had been busy shovelling sand on to it. 'We allow ourselves a fire during the day,' Sorgen had explained, 'but we must put it out at night.'

'Why?' Clara had asked.

'So we cannot be seen from the sky.'

Clara had nodded.

Immediately to the right of the round tent was a second one, half the size and set up as a field hospital. But basic. Very basic. Thin mattresses on the floor for beds. Nothing but a dim, red-filtered torch to see by once the light failed – and that, Sorgen had explained, was to be used sparingly. A beaten-up 4x4 parked by the entrance served as a medical supply store, but its stocks had dwindled to two boxes of clean dressings, a box of painkillers and some sterile wipes. Hardly enough to treat the four women with shrapnel wounds, the two men with suppurating gunshot wounds and the little boy with no physical symptoms but an alarmingly high temperature and acute delirium. No antibiotics. No saline. Scarce clean water that had to be taken from a large plastic drum outside. It was only a quarter full.

Clara had been here for two nights now, unable to practise medicine as such. All she could do was keep her patients comfortable, their wounds clean. They had been long nights. She'd hardly dared to use the red torch, fearful that she would make her own little tent 'visible from the air' as Sorgen had put it. She did not dare leave the tent, unless it was to use the camp toilet twenty metres away, which was little more than a hole in the ground and a bucket of sand to cover whatever waste ended in there. Food was brought to her before sunrise and after sunset – bland fare that she ate ravenously. Between periods of fitful sleep and tending to the sick as best she could, Clara had sat in the darkness, trying to work out who these people were that she'd fallen in with. Clearly they were not on the side of the Syrian government forces. She could only assume that Sorgen led one of the rebel groups the government were so keen on obliterating. It seemed such a ludicrously basic set-up from which to run a rebellion, but then she had witnessed at first hand the brute force with which the government was attempting to crush those who opposed it. There was very little activity here, but she sensed that everyone was on constant high alert. She figured that it was some sort of centre of operations, but one that could be easily dismantled and moved elsewhere if word of it reached the wrong ears.

Now the dawn of her second morning at the camp was arriving. Her patients were all asleep. She found herself at the front flap of the medical tent once more, watching the sun rise over the desert. The sky was a riot of pinks and oranges, and everything seemed very still. As usual, four armed men stood watch in a semicircle around the camp, the glow of their cigarettes as

270

they moved them to their lips the only sign of movement Clara could see. Beyond them, the bleak, unending desert. She again found her eyes following the track that wound off to the east, wondering where it led and what would happen to her if she escaped and tried to walk it alone.

She squinted. It was probably just a trick of the early-morning light, but she thought she could see a figure approaching over the brow of the small hill. She closed her eyes, rubbed them, then looked again. There was no doubt about it: it was a thin silhouette. Clara watched for several minutes. As the figure grew nearer, she could see that the person's gait was strange, as though he or she was limping. And only when she – it was definitely a woman, she could tell now – was fifty metres away did Clara notice how intently the guards were watching. They all had their weapons trained on her, and though no shot had been fired, Clara knew that eventuality was only a trigger squeeze away.

She was a bedraggled woman whose long, black hair, strikingly, had a white streak at the front. The closer she came, the more evident was her limp. Her face was dirty, her eyes haunted. She looked like a ghost. Clara could tell she was in a bad way.

Five metres from the guards, the woman stopped and raised her face. 'Sorgen,' she cried in a weak, broken voice. '*Sorgen!*'

Then she collapsed.

Clara started to run towards the woman, but one of the guards turned and waved his rifle at her. Suddenly terrified, she hurried back into the tent, where she bent over and tried to catch her breath. She heard a commotion outside, but didn't dare to peep through the flap again. Ten minutes passed before it opened. Sorgen walked in. It was the first time Clara had seen him since she arrived. He was with the woman, who had one arm round his shoulder and a dazed expression.

'This is Basheba,' Sorgen announced. 'My niece.'

Clara offered her hand, but Basheba shrank away.

'Please,' Sorgen said. His voice was thick with emotion. 'Take care of her. She has been through a lot.' And with no other explanation, he took his leave.

Clara's other patients were sleeping, which meant she could give this new arrival all her attention. She handed Basheba a cup of water, which she snatched and gulped down. Clara pointed at her right leg. 'Your foot,' she said, miming clumsily. 'Let me see it.'

'I understand English,' Basheba replied. She had a deep voice, very hoarse. She found the one remaining mattress, towards the back of the tent, and limped over to it. Sitting down, she removed her worn leather sandals. No wonder she was limping. The sole of her right foot was a mess of blood where blisters had burst, then formed again and the epidermis had deteriorated. Having fetched a sterile wipe from her meagre supplies, Clara gently dabbed at the damaged skin, trying to remove the dirt and sand which had accumulated on the open flesh. Basheba winced at each touch, but clearly understood that this was necessary. An infection now could lead to blood poisoning, and that could be fatal.

When the wounded sole was cleaned, Clara dressed it with a bandage. The two women had not said a word to each other since the operation began, but now Basheba spoke. 'Thank you,' was all she said.

Clara smiled at her. 'I shouldn't really be here.'

'Nor I,' Basheba admitted, 'but my uncle Sorgen is a good man.' The woman looked down. 'Better than my father-in-law.' She saw that Clara was confused. 'Asu is Sorgen's brother.' And then, with surprising suddenness, she started to weep. Not ordinary tears, but racking sobs that seemed to shake her whole body. Clara caught a few words of distraught Arabic before the woman whispered in English, 'My sons.'

Clara took her by the hand. 'Where are they?' she asked, dreading the answer.

'One is too scared to leave Asu. The other is dead.' And then a fire in her eyes. 'Killed by a British soldier.'

'*What?*' Clara was startled. 'Basheba, I think you must have made a mistake. There *are* no British soldiers in Syria.'

'And who told you that? Your government?' Basheba's expression clearly revealed what she thought of governments in general. 'I watched him do it. My son was wounded by the bombs. You' – she jabbed a finger at Clara – '*you* could have saved him with your skill.'

'I don't know . . . I . . .'

'The soldier didn't even *try* to save him. I watched him *kill* my son.'

'How?' Clara said.

'With . . .' Basheba hunted around for the word, before miming an injection into her arm.

'Basheba, it was probably just morphine. If he was wounded . . .'

'Morphine, yes,' Basheba spat. 'Four injections.'

Clara blinked. 'Four? Are you sure?' That was enough to kill an adult, let alone a wounded child.

'You think I would make it up?'

Looking at her, Clara thought nothing of the sort. 'I'm sorry,' she said. It seemed so inadequate.

'Asu refused to punish him,' Basheba said. 'So I ran away. They say he will be the leader of Syria one day. Perhaps very soon. But how can you be a leader if you do not punish the guilty ones?' She stared at her hands. 'If he knew I had come to Sorgen, he would be angry. Very angry. They hate each other. But Sorgen is kind. He did not turn me away.' She frowned. 'My father-in-law, he makes the children fight for him. They are too young to use guns, to kill men, but that is what they must do for him. I have seen eight-year-olds commit killings. And I have seen them killed, too. Losing their friends. Sorgen looks after the children in his care. He does not make them fight.' She smiled. 'You are kind, too. Thank you again

273

for . . .' She indicated the bandage, before trying to push herself upright.

'You must rest,' Clara told her. 'You'll hurt your foot even more if you—'

But Basheba was already walking, painfully yet steadily, towards the front of the tent. Clara joined her, ostensibly to continue their conversation, but really so that she could be there if the woman fell. Together they left the tent and stood just outside it looking across the desert.

The sun was a little higher in the sky now, a fierce white ball, the pinks and oranges of dawn having burned away. Clara wished she had sunglasses as she looked out across the desert.

'Someone is coming,' Basheba said quietly.

Clara shielded her eyes and squinted. Basheba was right. Coming along the winding track she had followed were two vehicles, the sun glinting blindingly off them, amid the dust they kicked up.

'Who is it?' asked Clara, not really expecting an answer. Why would Basheba know any better than she did? It hadn't escaped Clara's attention, however, that Sorgen's men had noticed these new arrivals and evidently weren't expecting them. Five men had emerged from the large tent and two of them were kneeling in the firing position with their rifles. A third ran to the open-backed truck with the machine gun and trained the weapon's sight on the approaching vehicles.

'We should get back inside,' said Clara.

But Basheba didn't move. She appeared transfixed, and Clara felt as if she was stuck to the Syrian woman's side. 'I recognise those cars,' said Basheba. Clara found that she was holding her breath.

The two vehicles, both Land Rovers, stopped side by side about fifty metres from the camp. For perhaps a minute there was no movement. Then the rear door of one of them opened and a figure stepped out. Still shielding her eyes from the sun,

Clara peered towards him. He had a slight frame, floppy brown hair, sloping shoulders and a somewhat diffident gait. He seemed to shimmer in the heat as he walked slowly but steadily towards the camp, his palms raised to indicate that he was unarmed.

When the man was ten metres from the Land Rover, a second emerged. This one made no attempt to pretend that he was unarmed. A rifle was slung across his front, and he gripped it with both hands as he followed the first man at a respectful distance.

Basheba inhaled sharply, then hissed.

Clara turned to her. 'What is it?' She was alarmed to see the look on her face.

'It's him,' Basheba whispered.

Clara was confused. 'Who?' she asked.

'The man who killed my son.'

'*Basheba! No!*'

But she was too late to grab her new friend. Basheba was running towards the newcomers, faster than Clara would have thought her injured foot would allow. She was screaming at them in Arabic, her hair flowing in the wind and her face filled with hatred.

At first, Danny didn't recognise her. All he saw was a wild-eyed woman sprinting in Buckingham's direction. His first instinct was to raise his M4 ready to protect him from this crazy apparition. But she ran past Buckingham towards Danny himself. He realised who she was at the same moment that she pulled a knife from under her robe. She couldn't have been more than three metres away, and it was a five-inch blade, broad and sharp, that glinted in the morning sun. She held it inexpertly – not low, as Danny would have done, but level with her head, ready to stab. She was screeching like a mad woman.

It only took a swipe of his left arm for Danny to knock her from her stride. She fell. It looked more alarming than it was, but suddenly everything was kicking off. The four armed men guarding the camp were shouting, engaging their weapons. Danny sprinted forwards and wrestled Buckingham to the ground. He was aware of Taff, Hector, Skinner and De Fries piling out of the vehicles behind him. He checked out the Syrian rebel gunmen. Distance: ten metres. Any contact would be short and ugly. Danny and Buckingham would be caught in the crossfire. Chances of survival: close to zero. Danny knew how to choose battles. Question was, did Skinner and Hector?

He saw that the rebels were hesitating. Had they made a similar analysis of the situation?

'*Hold your fire!*' Danny shouted, fully aware that there were members of his party who would enter into a contact without any encouragement whatsoever. '*Hold your fire!*'

'*Do as he says!*' Taff's voice lent weight to Danny's instruction.

A moment of tense silence. The rebels' hands were shaking anxiously – never a good sign. At the flap of the smaller round tent, a Western-looking woman stood with her hands almost covering her face. Buckingham was breathing heavily, but he didn't move as Danny had him pinned to the ground.

Slowly, the flap of the large tent opened. A giant of a man appeared – at least as tall as Danny and considerably broader. He wore an embroidered *dishdash* and had a white moustache and a thick mane of white hair. He stood at the entrance of the tent, shrewd eyes surveying the scene.

'Let me go,' said Buckingham.

'Don't be stupid. This could go noisy any second.'

'For God's sake, man, let me go. That's Sorgen. He knows who I am. If he doesn't recognise one of us, they'll massacre us.'

He had a point. Danny released his grip, and both men got to their feet. He let his weapon hang loose from its halyard and raised his hands to show he wasn't about to reach for anything else. Buckingham dusted down his clothes.

'Hugo Buckingham,' the fat man announced in a rich but strangely monotone voice, and in excellent English. 'It's a long way from the Quartier Latin, is it not? A man might become suspicious of such a remarkable coincidence.'

'Sorgen. It's good to see you again.' Buckingham's voice quivered slightly.

'Tell your men to drop their weapons, Hugo. Let us avoid any tragic accidents. Dead bodies quickly become carrion in the desert, and I would not wish that upon any of you.'

'Your men too,' Danny butted in.

Sorgen smiled. 'Bilateral disarmament? I don't think so.' The sweat on his brow glistened. 'I see no reason why my men and I should not protect our territory.'

'Do as he says,' Buckingham called over his shoulder. Danny sensed the others' reluctance. He shared it. '*Do as he says!*'

Danny looked back and caught Taff's eye. They nodded reluctantly at each other. Taff lowered his rifle. The others, with an obvious lack of enthusiasm, followed suit.

Nobody moved. The wild woman was kneeling on the ground, weeping.

Sorgen's face was unreadable. His footsteps crunched on the dry earth as he walked towards Buckingham, stopping half a metre from him.

'And now,' he said quietly, 'I find you here. In the middle of the Homs desert. Surrounded by armed men. A representative of the British government that would install my brother to a position of power in Syria, and that would shed no tears over my own death.'

Danny felt his fingers creeping back to his M4. Could he take these guys? Was there time? The four armed men were each separated from the other by a distance of about five metres. Too far to take them out with a single burst. He had a fragmentation grenade in his ops vest. If he hurled it in their direction, would they scatter? Or would they fire first and run later?

Buckingham looked nervous now. The assured look he had displayed as he approached the encampment had disappeared. He stuttered like a man who had made a colossal miscalculation. 'Sorgen . . . I . . .'

But Sorgen's arms were outstretched and his face had suddenly broken into a grin. 'Old friend,' he said. 'You are very welcome, today of all days, on the festival of Eid al-Fitr.' He wrapped his enormous arms round Buckingham's slight frame. He looked back at his soldiers and shouted a single order in Arabic. They lowered their weapons with obvious relief.

'What brings you here, my friend?' Sorgen boomed. 'No! Wait! Do not tell me! I have a feeling I will not like the answer! Let us have a few minutes, at least, to talk about the old days before the arguments start. Come! We are forced to live like nomads, and our surroundings are poor. But you are most welcome, Hugo. Your friends too. You are most, most welcome.'

With one arm still around Buckingham's shoulders, Sorgen accompanied him to the tent. Danny followed three or four metres behind, ignoring the hard stares of the rebel gunmen as he passed them. As they entered the big tent, Danny was aware of the Western woman running up to the distraught mother who had tried to attack him. She helped her to her feet and back towards the smaller tent. Both women stared at him with expressions sharper than the knife one of them had just used to try to kill him.

The festival of Eid al-Fitr marks the end of Ramadan, the holy month of fasting. It is forbidden to fast on the day of Eid, and Muslims often celebrate the festival by eating a small breakfast of something sweet.

As they had crossed the desert searching for Sorgen's encampment, Buckingham had explained to the others what they could expect from the rebel leader. So far, it looked like he knew what he was talking about.

Sorgen and Buckingham sat together on a carpet in the middle of the big tent, a small plate of crystallised dates between them. He remembered Buckingham saying that Sorgen was a devout man, and could only assume this was true: who else would remember the essentials for this small ritual among the comms systems and ammo boxes that filled this makeshift ops centre? Danny, though, was more concerned with breakouts than breakfast. There was only one way in or out of this tent, but the canvas walls would be no match for either of his knives. A guard was positioned on either side of the flap, while Danny stood three metres from the carpet. Taff and his crew had been invited into the tent but had been directed to a spot ten metres away. Danny felt Skinner's dead eyes on him. Fine. At the moment he had other things to worry about, like keeping Buckingham safe. These two might be playing happy families, but happy families could easily turn sour.

'*Eid mubarak*,' Buckingham said, accepting a date from the plate.

'*Eid mubarak*,' Sorgen replied. 'Hugo, do you remember the last time I saw you?'

Buckingham smiled. 'The Café des Amis in Châtelet. You drank coffee, I drank something a little stronger.'

'You heard about my father?'

Buckingham nodded. 'My condolences, Sorgen. I know how close you were.'

'He was killed outside that very café. I have friends high up in the French government, but none of them can tell me why this Algerian boy would want to kill my father.'

It was a very strange thing, but at that moment Danny had Hector and Skinner in his sights. They looked at each other. It was nothing more than a glance, but it was full of meaning. He even saw a flicker of a smile on Skinner's lips, before the moment passed as quickly as it had come.

But then he heard Taff's voice in his head: *You're losing your grip out here. You're seeing things that aren't there* . . . He dragged himself back to the main attraction. 'It's hard sometimes to understand the mind of a terrorist,' Buckingham was saying.

'There are some who would say that *I* am the terrorist, my friend,' Sorgen replied. 'Your government would gladly award me that label if Asu came to power. Which, I have to concede, looks ever more likely. And as soon as I have that label, there will be many people eager to help me on my journey to Paradise.' He took a date and chewed it thoughtfully. 'Which rather begs the question, my dear Hugo, of why I have this very unexpected pleasure.'

Buckingham took a moment before replying. Danny had the impression that he was choosing his words very carefully.

'Yesterday,' Buckingham said, 'I met with your brother in the city.'

Sorgen's face immediately darkened, but he said nothing.

'I explained to him that the British government would do anything in its power to effect a reconciliation between the two of you.'

'At which point, I am sure, my dear brother asked you to leave.'

'No,' Buckingham said simply. 'He didn't.'

Sorgen blinked heavily. 'That is a surprise,' he conceded. 'He must have had good reason.'

'Perhaps,' Buckingham said. He stood up and turned his back on Sorgen. Danny could see the fierce concentration on his face. This discussion was, after all, the whole reason he had come to Syria. 'I'm here with a proposal,' he said. 'My government understands your loyalty to the French. They looked after your father in exile, and they support you now with funds and arms, just as the British support Asu and the Russians support the current administration.' He started to pace slowly up and down the tent. 'I'll be honest with you, Sorgen. My superiors wanted me to lie to you. To tell you that we have Syria's best interests at heart. I told them I wouldn't insult your intelligence, that you fully understand diplomacy is about self-interest. It is in Britain's interest to have a mutually advantageous relationship with the new Syria when it arrives. I told them you would understand that.'

Sorgen tipped his head to one side and made a little hand gesture, as if to say: go on.

'You and Asu are stronger united than you are divided. You know that and he knows that. I'm here to ask you to consider joining forces with him to ensure that it is your family and not one of the other rebel factions that comes to power. And I'm here to offer you whatever it is you need to achieve that. However much the French are funding you, we are prepared to double it. Whatever weapons the French are supplying you with, we will improve upon it. We will make you the best-equipped fighting force in the Middle East.' Buckingham paused, then turned to look directly at his old friend. 'We will win this war for you, Sorgen. Think of the lives that could be saved. Think of the Syria that you and Asu could rebuild together, with our help.'

Sorgen stood to give his reply. 'I thank you for your offer. I fear, however, that the rift between myself and Asu is too deep to heal. And I feel – forgive me for saying it – a certain loyalty to the French that I do not feel towards the British.' He gave a knowing little smile. 'With the exception of the present company, of course.'

Buckingham nodded, as if what Sorgen had just said was entirely reasonable. But he had a response ready and waiting.

'Would your loyalty to the French be quite so fierce, my friend, if you knew that it was under their instruction that your father was assassinated?'

A silence fell upon the tent.

'You are my guest, Hugo,' Sorgen said in a dreadfully quiet voice. 'But if you take my father's name in vain—'

'Four weeks ago,' Buckingham interrupted, 'the Algerian suicide bomber met in Paris with his handler, a member of the GIA terrorist group. We know beyond question that this handler was an undercover member of the French security services. MI6 has more evidence, frankly, than you would wish to see. There's no doubt about it, and I'm sorry. But the French killed your father.'

Alarm bells rang in Danny's head. He thought back to the briefing Buckingham's boss – Carrington, wasn't it? – had given them at the vehicle pool back in west London. He'd mentioned none of this. On the contrary, he'd said that Sorgen's father was a valuable French asset. Either he'd been lying, or Buckingham was now.

None of these thoughts appeared to occur to Sorgen. It was as if a cloud had descended over the tent. The rebel leader's face barely moved. Buckingham was watching his face intently, clearly trying to tell what effect his bombshell was having. And the effect was plain to see. Sorgen's eyes grew watery. He dried them with the hem of his *dishdash*.

'If I learn that you have been lying to me, Hugo . . .'

'It's the truth, Sorgen. As sure as I'm standing here.'

Another pause.

'Asu has agreed to this – this reconciliation?' Sorgen asked.

'Absolutely. He is eager for it.'

More silence.

'I do not lead this army in isolation,' Sorgen said. 'You must understand that I cannot make a decision of this magnitude without first discussing it with my commanders. We meet tonight, here, to celebrate the festival of Eid.' His eyes narrowed. 'But of course, Hugo, you already knew that.'

'I suspected it. I remember your Eid celebrations of old. You will put it to your commanders tonight? I'm sure they'll see the wisdom of my suggestion.'

'Perhaps. Perhaps not. I can only suggest it.'

'That's all I ask, Sorgen. That's all I ask.'

'Come back tomorrow at dawn. I will have an answer for you, and for Asu.' Sorgen's face grew pensive. 'You are here, Hugo Buckingham, because we have a bond of friendship. Such things are important to me. I trust you will not betray that bond.'

'You have my word.'

'That is all I require. Until tomorrow, Hugo.'

'Until tomorrow.' Buckingham looked at Danny. 'We can go now,' he said curtly, as though to a servant.

'You come with quite a retinue,' Sorgen observed.

'Syria is a dangerous place, I've learned. One can't be too careful.'

'Indeed no.' Sorgen offered Buckingham his hand. Buckingham shook it. Danny, who was watching them both very carefully, observed that neither man would look the other in the eye. And he knew for certain that there was more happening here than their conversation had revealed. Both men were hiding something. He didn't know what. But as he escorted Buckingham from the tent and out into the sunlight, another anomaly presented itself. Why had Buckingham been so keen to exclude him from the RV with Asu, while not even blinking at his presence in Sorgen's tent? It made no sense. Outside the tent, his eyes scanned the desert, looking for any movement, any threat. There was none – just a haze of heat – so he started to lead Buckingham back to the Land Rovers, shimmering in the sun. They had gone only a few paces, however, when he saw the Western woman standing in front of the smaller tent. Her eyes were following him. It struck him again how strange it was to see this woman in such an unlikely place. He walked over to her. 'English?' he asked.

She nodded reluctantly.

'Everything all right?'

'You make me sick,' the woman hissed.

'What?'

'You heard me,' she said. 'I know what you've done. I have a grieving mother in here. Don't you think this country has enough misery without people like you adding to it?' She grabbed his hands and held them up. They were stained red. 'Blood on your hands,' she hissed. 'Actual blood on your actual hands.'

She turned round and stormed back into the tent.

For the briefest of moments Danny considered running in after her. Explaining that she didn't know what she was talking about. But in the end he just walked away. Let people believe what they wanted to. Danny knew he'd done the right thing, and that was all that mattered.

And besides, he had plenty of other worries on his mind. Like who was telling him the truth, and who was not.

TWENTY

Max Saunders straightened his tie and tucked in his shirt. Anastasia had just left. The scent of her perfume – Coco Chanel, seventy-five bloody quid a bottle and she went through it at such a rate he sometimes wondered if she was flogging it to her friends – hung in the air. No doubt it hung around his person too. When he got home tonight, his wife would pretend not to notice. Why would she rock the boat when she had her platinum Amex and the run of Bond Street? As Saunders glanced through the window of his office down on to St James's Square, he allowed himself a rueful smile. It was true what they said. You always ended up paying for sex. Any man who pretended otherwise was kidding himself.

Anastasia walked back into the office without knocking. Her hair was slightly mussed, but she walked with the same rigid, aloof air she always adopted after a session. That was the trouble with these posh bints. Always pretending they weren't what they were. She hadn't been so damn hoity-toity twenty minutes ago when he'd had her bent over the same desk in front of which she now stood primly. 'Yes, my dear?' he said.

'Three messages while we were . . . while you were engaged,' she replied without catching his eye. 'Oliver Carrington – he's the man from MI6—'

'Thank you, Anastasia. I know who Carrington is.'

Her lips thinned. 'Oliver Carrington would like a call back. Ditto a Monsieur Grandier from the Ministère des Affaires étrangères et européennes.' Bless her, she never missed a chance to show off her French accent. Saunders rather liked it. 'Something to do with the Syrian situation?'

Saunders nodded.

Anastasia turned to leave.

'Three messages,' he reminded her.

Anastasia's face coloured. She didn't like anyone to see a moment of inefficiency. 'Sorry,' she muttered.

'Please,' Saunders smiled at her. 'You've had a busy morning, my dear.'

'The third message was from Taff Davies. You probably don't remember, but he's embedded in—'

'Just give me the message, there's a good girl.'

Anastasia's lips looked like they might disappear. She read from her clipboard, and the military terminology sounded very out of place in her posh accent. 'Operation Domino is a go for this evening,' she repeated. 'That's all he said.'

'Good. Excellent.' He thought for a moment. 'Get Grandier on the phone, would you?'

'And Carrington?'

Saunders shook his head. 'I think not. I'll wait until tomorrow for that particular call. Be a good girl and get me that French chappie, then you and I'll pop out for a spot of lunch. And you could probably do with some more of that delightful perfume. We can nip into Harvey Nicks, if you like. What would you say to that?'

Even Anastasia was unable to stop a little flicker of pleasure cross her lips. 'Of course, Max,' she said, suddenly kittenish. 'That would be lovely.'

She left the office, quietly shutting the door behind her.

'What you doing, kiddo?'

Evening was falling. Danny had found a plastic bucket and filled it with water. He was now rubbing his palms with

286

handfuls of moistened dust, hoping that the abrasive sludge would remove some of the blood from his skin. He felt like he'd seen enough of the red stuff to last him a good while yet. His makeshift soap wasn't working very well. He dipped his hands into the clean water, then wiped them dry on his clothes.

'Cleaning up,' he told Taff.

'Why bother? You'll only get dirty again.'

'Why didn't you listen to me?' Danny said. 'This morning, when I told you what Skinner and Hector had done. You know I wouldn't make that shit up.'

Taff didn't answer. He just fixed Danny with a steady gaze that made him feel uncomfortable.

'What about Asu?' Danny pressed. 'What did he and Buckingham talk about? How come you were in on the meet and I was sent outside?'

'Don't take it personally, kiddo. Asu's a wanker but he trusts me. End of.'

'So what *did* you talk about?' Danny could feel himself growing angry.

'I thought we could take a walk,' Taff stonewalled him. 'You can get stir crazy in this place. The locals seem to think the bombing will subside a bit tonight. Eid al . . . whatever the fuck it's called. Makes them come over all peaceful, at least that's what the locals say.'

The locals. Taff had told them all to go home when they'd returned from Sorgen's camp. 'National holiday,' he'd explained to Danny. But why would he want to get rid of them? 'Yeah, bleeding heart, me, too nice for my own good,' Taff had said when he'd confronted him. And that was no kind of answer at all.

Danny kicked the bucket of water so its contents spilled on the ground. 'I'll stay here,' he said, his tone resentful. 'I've got Buckingham to watch.'

Talking of which, where was Buckingham? Half an hour ago he'd been in the far corner of the compound. Now all Danny could see was Skinner, leaning nonchalantly against one of the Land Rovers, his dead eyes fixed on him and Taff.

'Where is he?'

'He's inside,' Taff said softly. 'Resting. The others can watch him. They're at least as good as you, you know? And we can take that walk. You look like you need to let off some steam.'

Taff was lightly touching his elbow, gently manoeuvring him towards the gate. As he did so, his eyes darted back to the house.

Danny suddenly felt ice in his guts.

'Where's Buckingham?' he asked again.

'I told you, kiddo. He's—'

But Danny broke away. Something was wrong. He didn't know what, but he could hear it in Taff's voice.

He sprinted across the compound and into the house. The ground floor was empty. He thundered up the stairs, three at a time, and ran along the corridor to the room he'd been sharing with Buckingham.

Empty.

That was enough to make him arm himself. He touched the Sig strapped to his chest, then grabbed the M4.

Why was it so fucking silent? What the hell was going on?

He moved slowly back along the corridor, weapon at the ready. He stopped for a couple of seconds by the door to the generator room, listening carefully.

No sound.

He swung round into the doorway.

The room was empty.

A sound, farther along the corridor. A gush of water. It sent a jolt through him. He turned again and aimed his rifle back towards the stairs. The door of the stinking bathroom opened.

Buckingham appeared.

He was still doing up his trousers, and his face was screwed up because of the offensive smell. When he saw Danny, he froze.

Then he swore.

Danny lowered his weapon. His hand, he realised, was trembling.

Buckingham was barking some bullshit at him, but Danny didn't hear a word. Maybe Taff was right. Maybe this place truly was getting on top of him.

His old friend appeared at the top of the stairs. He had an urgent look on his face. 'Do us all a favour, pal,' he said to Buckingham, who was still in full flow, 'and shut the fuck up.' Buckingham looked outraged, but he fell silent.

'Come with me,' Taff said. He turned and descended the stairs. Danny followed him. Taff didn't speak again until they reached the ground floor, and then only quietly. 'Here's the deal,' he said. 'You're being an arsehole. If you were anyone else, I'd have kicked you halfway back to the fucking Med.' Danny opened his mouth to argue, but Taff carried on – *'Don't . . . fucking . . . speak . . .'* – before drawing a deep, calming breath. 'You say my men are committing atrocities. Fine. Show me.'

Danny blinked at him.

'I mean it, kiddo. Show me the bodies and find me one single scrap of evidence that it was my men who killed them, or shut the fuck up and do your job. What's it to be?'

Danny looked back over his shoulder. He shouldn't leave Buckingham, he knew that. But somehow this was more important.

'OK,' he said. 'Let's go.'

The two men said nothing more as they walked across the compound. De Fries was waiting by the gate. His eyes followed them as they approached.

'Open up,' Taff told him. 'The spook doesn't leave, no matter what. Understood?'

The ever-silent De Fries simply nodded. Something seemed to pass between him and Taff and for a moment, Danny felt again the cold grip of paranoia.

The gate slid open and they exited the compound.

It was twilight. The semi-darkness softened the now-familiar sight of the war-torn buildings along the streets outside. Danny thought he could hear music not far off – the thin, monotone wail of a woman's voice singing some traditional song.

'All right, kiddo,' Taff said, keeping his voice low. 'Lead the way.'

Danny still gripping his M4, they started walking to the right, taking the route Hector and Skinner had followed the previous night, staying close to the buildings on their left as they gave a little more shadow. Danny had a moment of déjà vu. He was ten years old, walking through a wood with Taff, who was teaching him how to tread without making a sound. But there were no trees here in the Syrian night. Just slabs of shattered concrete. No piles of autumnal leaves. Just heaps of rubble.

And soldiers.

Fifty metres ahead.

Danny raised his free hand instinctively. Both men stopped and pressed their backs against the empty window of a shop. Danny peered into the gloom ahead. Eight men. Government forces – Danny could tell that as much by their swagger as by their uniforms. They were blocking the road about fifteen metres beyond the side street he and Taff needed to take. It meant getting too close to . . .

A shot rang out. Impossible to be sure where it came from, but Danny sensed that it was from above. One of the soldiers fell to the ground.

'Sniper fire,' Taff hissed. 'Don't fucking move.'

Danny didn't need telling. The soldiers, on the other hand, were thrown into chaos. They started barking instructions at one another, losing formation and bunching up – the worst thing they could do. There was a second shot – a second direct hit. The remaining soldiers scattered.

'Go!' Taff whispered. But Danny was already moving, keeping to the shadows, taking advantage of the soldiers' bad luck. Twenty seconds later they had turned off that street and were standing in a slightly narrower one. Danny scanned ahead. There was a small fire on the side of the road about sixty metres distant. Five silhouettes around it. If they'd heard the sniper fire, they didn't seem to pay it any mind. There was no sound of artillery. If you closed your eyes, you'd never know you were in a city at war. Somehow it made Danny more tense. If he was a Syrian government strategist, he knew when he would strike the hardest: during a religious festival, when the population and the rebels were least expecting it. But so far there had been no fast air and no ordnance.

He pointed to a side street about twenty-five metres ahead and nodded to Taff. They continued to move confidently through the shadows. In less than five minutes they were standing outside the bakery.

It looked just as it had when Danny had left it: the padlock broken, the heavy chain coiled snake-like on the ground, the window smashed. Astonishingly, there was no sign of any further looting, though it occurred to Danny that there weren't many people with the stomach to stick around once they saw what secrets this building was hiding. He turned to Taff. 'Follow me,' he said.

'Lead the way, kiddo.' Taff's tone suggested that Danny was about to make a fool of himself. He stretched out one hand in an over-polite gesture.

Danny stepped into the shop.

He climbed the stairs.

He stopped at the door to the room and looked over his shoulder. Taff was right behind him.

It was the act of swinging the door open that displaced the air in the room and brought the stench to Danny's nose. He smelled the corpses before he saw them and it took only a single lungful of air for him to realise it was a stench he would never forget. Sixteen hours of putrefaction in an enclosed space in the Middle Eastern heat had done its work very well. The dead meat had started to turn.

Danny pulled his shirt over his nose and removed his torch as he stepped into the room. The two men's sudden arrival disturbed the flies that had settled on the bodies and the air seemed to move as he shone the torch around. He had to wave his hand in front of his face a couple of times to stop them settling on skin.

'It took them about ten minutes to do this,' he said quietly as he stepped into the room. 'No firearms that I could hear. Just knife work.'

He directed the beam at the children first. The skin around their eyes, noses and mouths glistened where fluid had discharged from these orifices and dried to a shiny crust in the heat. Their cheeks were already sunken. A fly crawled over the boy's left eyeball, its supper clearly too interesting for these intruders to disturb it. The little girl's pink hair clip glinted in the torchlight.

A second thin beam of light came from behind Danny as Taff turned his own torch on to the scene. The two beams crossed, like prison searchlights.

'They cut the father's throat,' Danny said in an emotionless voice as he shone his torch on the dead man. No sound from Taff behind him, so Danny continued. 'Guess they must have done the parents first. Take out the hardest targets before dealing with the kids.' The blood around the father's slit throat had congealed and even scabbed over in places. The shape of the incision looked strangely like a smile, a direct contrast to the grimace on his face.

And then there was the mother.

Danny had to force himself to shine a light on her. Some sights are best left in darkness. Her swollen belly had collapsed somewhat, and the fetid mixture of blood and amniotic fluid had dried on her skin and the sheet on which she lay. 'She was pregnant,' Danny said, the beam of his torch still trained on the decaying body. 'When I found her like this, the baby was still

292

moving. Only for a few seconds. So Hector's little story, that they found them like this? That's bullsh—'

The word caught in his throat.

Something was wrong.

The beam from Taff's torch was no longer moving around. It was pointing directly at Danny's back. He could see his shadow looming large against the far wall.

There was a click behind him.

'Drop the weapon and the torch, kiddo,' said Taff. His voice was deathly quiet.

Danny hesitated.

He started to turn.

'*Drop them, I said!*'

Danny let the rifle and the Maglite fall from his hands. They clattered on the floor, the torch shining at an angle across the room and lighting up the side of the dead man's belly.

'Hands in the air, lad. Turn round very slowly.' Danny detected a slight tremor in Taff's voice. He did as he was told, and winced slightly as the bright white beam from Taff's torch shone into his eyes. He couldn't see Taff's face, just the outline of his body, and the barrel of his pistol immediately next to the light source, held up at chest height.

Five metres separated the two men.

'What's going on, Taff?' Danny said quietly.

Silence.

'Why did they send you, kiddo?' Taff asked. 'Of all the Regiment grunts, you're the one that lands on my doorstep. Ever stop to think it might not be coincidence?'

'Taff, mate, put down the gun.'

'I'm going to do something now,' Taff said. 'You won't understand why. Not at first. But you will, kiddo. I promise, you will.'

He took one step forwards.

Danny felt his fingers twitching. He could pull out the Sig and shoot in under a second. If this had been anyone else, that's

293

what he'd have done. But not Taff. He knew how good his old mentor was. How fast. And anyway, why would he try to kill the man who'd been a father to him?

'Mate,' he said. 'If you're worried I'm going to talk about this . . .' He moved his hand to indicate the carnage around him.

'*Get your hands in the fucking air, boy!*'

Danny's hands snapped back to their original position.

'You're in the wrong game, Danny. The Regiment should never have sent you.'

'Hector and Skinner *did* this, Taff.'

'Of *course* they fucking did it,' Taff spat back. 'What do you think I need, an entourage of fucking Girl Guides? We're here to make a living, not win hearts and minds.'

Another step. Blue and red dots danced in front of Danny's dazzled eyes.

Three metres now between him and Taff.

Taff had something else in his left hand as well as his thin torch. Danny couldn't work out what it was. But he knew one thing. Taff wasn't about to shoot him. If he'd wanted him dead, he'd be on the ground with a bullet in the back of his skull. Whatever he wanted to do, he needed to be closer.

'Don't do anything stupid, kiddo,' Taff whispered.

'You're the one with the gun, Taff. Put it down. We can talk about this.'

Another step closer.

'Nothing to talk about, kiddo. Nothing to talk about.'

Danny made his move without another moment of hesitation. There was no point trying to swipe Taff's pistol away. He was as fast a shot as anyone in the Regiment, and in any case sudden movements could cause his old friend to make a mistake. Instead, Danny fell quickly and heavily to his knees, out of Taff's line of fire. He hurled himself at him, dragging him to the ground and steeling himself for the blow to the centre of his spine that he knew was coming when Taff thumped his fists down as he fell.

But he couldn't have prepared himself for its severity.

He knew instantly that Taff had Tasered him. An icy shock surged through his nervous system. It didn't last more than a second, but it was enough to paralyse his limbs. The two men hit the floor together with a dull bang. Danny felt himself being rolled over on to his back. Taff scrabbled around beside him for a couple of seconds as Danny tried, in vain, to activate his shocked arms. But then Taff was on top of him, one knee on his chest, the torch shining into his face again.

'Get out of Syria, kiddo,' Taff said. 'Turkish border is best. I'll leave you money. Don't bother with Buckingham. He won't be around to join you. Tell the Ruperts that Asu double-crossed you. The Firm don't have enough eyes and ears on the ground to know if it's true or not.'

'Taff, what the—?'

'Shut it, kiddo. This is for your own good.' A pause. 'You were only a baby, but I told you once you need to be ready for anything. Remember that.'

Danny had no chance to reply. Taff brought his hands down again, this time pressing the prongs of the Taser against his chest. There was a second agonising surge of electricity, more intense than the first, and longer. Taff had dropped his torch and Danny now caught sight of his face in the darkness. It was contorted. Agonised, almost. But it was also determined. The face of a man who wasn't going to be diverted from what he had to do.

And then it was gone, along with the pain, as Danny's world dissolved into darkness.

TWENTY-ONE

It was still dark when Danny woke up.

For the first few seconds of consciousness, he didn't know where he was. Hereford, maybe? But if he was in Hereford, why was he lying face down on a hard floor? What was that buzzing? And what was that disgusting smell?

Then he remembered.

He tried to stand, but he couldn't. His wrist was bound to something. Shaking his aching head, he peered around in the darkness. He was still in the same room. There was no sign of Taff. He was on the floor next to the bed on which the two dead children lay. A pair of sturdy metal handcuffs fastened him to the leg of the bed. He checked the time. 21.35. He couldn't have been out for more than twenty minutes, but twenty minutes had been enough for Taff to arrange things the way he wanted. In the middle of the floor, three metres away, just out of reach, were his M4 and his chest rig. No sat phone. He couldn't quite tell in the darkness, but it looked like Taff had left, as he'd said he would, a thin sheaf of currency with the rest of Danny's gear.

What the hell was Taff doing? Why had he left him here, cuffed to the bed in this bakery that had turned into a butcher's? He felt like he'd been sleepwalking for the past twenty-four hours, accepting Taff's word as gospel and not thinking for himself. Idiot. But he told himself to get his priorities right. Those questions had to wait. For now, he could concentrate on only one thing: getting out of here.

Taff had left him his weapons. That was significant. It meant he knew Danny would be able to escape, eventually. Fastening him to this bedpost was Taff's way of buying himself some time. Danny examined the post. It widened out at the bottom, so he couldn't just lift the bed and slide the cuffs down. The obvious answer was to use all his strength to upturn the bed itself, then make a start on destroying the frame with his bare hands. But it was a heavy, solidly built bed. Even if he managed to upturn it with the added weight of the dead children lying on top, breaking it down to the point where he could release himself would take a long time. A couple of hours. Maybe more. Danny didn't have that long. Not if he was going to find out what was happening.

There had to be another way.

With his free hand, he patted himself down. Perhaps there was something in one of his pockets he could use to pick the lock. He found nothing but the loose rounds he'd confiscated from the mag of Hector's M16. He slammed his fist on the ground in frustration. These cuffs were a piece of piss to pick if you had the right tool. A paper clip. Even a fucking hair clip.

A hair clip . . .

He twisted himself round and kneeled up. The bed was high – three foot or so – and he could just see over the edge of the mattress. The dead boy was lying closest to him. Danny swung his free hand and grabbed the kid's arm. Even through the sheet that covered it, he could tell it was icy cold and heavy. Rigor mortis had subsided, though, and the limb was easy to manoeuvre.

Danny pulled. The corpse shifted a couple of inches in his direction.

He pulled again. There was a splintering sound from the body as the shoulder joint cracked.

On the third pull, however, the boy's frame tumbled from under the sheet and over the side of the bed, collapsing in a heap at Danny's side. He wore just a pair of baggy underpants – they looked like he'd pissed himself with blood – and Danny could now clearly see the wound that had killed him. It was about four inches long, running up his stomach. A new odour hit Danny's senses: the rotting remains of the boy's last meal. He felt himself gagging, but managed to hold down the contents of his own stomach as he turned his attention to the dead girl.

She was on the far side of the bed and there was no way he could reach her. Instead he pulled gently on the lower sheet on which she lay. The body shifted gradually towards him with the movement of the sheet. He tugged a little harder, but quickly stopped when he felt the sheet slip between the body and the mattress. He pulled again, more gently. Then again. Finally the little girl's corpse was within his grasp.

As he pulled her over the side of the bed to join her brother, Danny saw that she had an almost identical wound in her little belly. A bubble of intestine the size of an orange protruded from the gruesome incision. Danny averted his eyes, and concentrated instead on her head.

He cursed. The plastic pink hair clip was no longer there.

It was thirty seconds later that he found it. It had dropped from the girl's hair as she fell off the bed and was now resting on the ground just a few inches from where Danny was sitting. He grabbed it with his free hand and examined it in the darkness. It was about four centimetres long, with a hinge at one end and a clasp at another. He squeezed the clasp and the clip opened, doubling in length. The pink plastic part was merely a fascia. The rest was made of soft metal. Easy to bend. He gently inserted the clip into the keyhole of his handcuffs, then bent it down, so that the few millimetres inserted into the hole were now at right angles to the rest of the clip. He tried to turn it.

Nothing doing. The mechanism was jammed.

He fiddled blindly with it. Another twist. Another failure.

Only on his third attempt at manoeuvring the clip within the keyhole did the cuffs click open.

Danny jumped to his feet. The sudden movement caused the flies to swarm up from around the corpses, but Danny ignored them as he strode towards his gear. He stuffed the money into his pocket, then strapped on his chest rig – Taff had left it fully stocked, as far as he could tell – and fitted the Maglite to his M4. Without another look at the horrific scene he was leaving behind, he left the room and hurried down the stairs.

He stopped before entering the shop on the ground floor. Listening. Looking. There was no sign or sound of anyone. He advanced to the door and out into the street.

He checked his watch. 22.03 hrs. He'd been out for a couple of hours.

The streets were still deserted, but he could hear noises elsewhere. Shouts. A small crowd, by the sound of it. And then one – no, two separate gunshots. Retaliation for the sniper fire that had just downed the two government soldiers? Likely, but it was impossible to be certain.

He moved quickly but cautiously, scanning ahead as he retraced his steps back towards the base. It took him ten minutes to reach the corner nearest to it. To his left – fifty metres away – there was activity. A mob, maybe thirty people, dressed in civvies, advancing on a group of five or six government soldiers. It was seconds away from getting very ugly, but at least their attention was on each other. Danny turned to the right. A minute later he was standing in front of the sliding gate. He couldn't tell from outside whether it was locked or not, and there was only one way to find out. He pressed his back against the exterior wall, double-checked his rifle, then gently pushed the gate with his right foot.

It slid open. No problem at all.

Danny swung round into the opening and dropped down on one knee in the firing position, checking out the compound through the sight of his rifle. It was empty. Totally empty. No Taff. No Hector. No Skinner. No De Fries even. And, crucially, no vehicles. The place showed every sign of having been abandoned.

Danny wasn't going to take that for granted. He trained the sight on the windows of the house, then on the door. Nothing, so he advanced carefully towards the entrance. It was very dark inside the building. Danny switched on the Maglite. A calculated risk: the beam would indicate his precise position, but he had to see what was ahead of him.

Or *who* was ahead of him.

The torch sliced a narrow beam across the dark room. The mattresses were empty. So was the wooden gun rack. The ground floor looked deserted. He trained his M4 on the staircase and moved towards it, past the door that led to the fire-damaged part of the house – even though Taff had pointed this out to him, it had gone completely unused. Better to check upstairs first. He realised he could hear his own pulse thumping as he edged up the stairs to the first floor.

The corridor came into view. The doors to the generator room and toilet were wide open. He checked them both. The generator was off, the air-con no longer whirring. The gimpy that had been by the window was no longer there. The toilet was unoccupied, but it still stank. He moved along the corridor to the room he had shared with Buckingham. Also empty.

A knocking sound.

Danny spun round, his M4 aimed back down the corridor. He paused and listened.

There it was again. Very faint, but just audible. Hard to tell which direction it came from, but he sensed it was downstairs. He trod carefully back to the staircase.

The knocking was a fraction louder.

Danny started to move back down the stairs.

He was halfway down when he saw what he had missed before. The door at the bottom, which led into the fire-damaged part of the house, was slightly ajar – just a couple of inches, but it was the first time he had seen it anything other than firmly shut. And as he reached it, he realised that the knocking sound was coming from the room beyond.

Danny was breathing very slowly now. He needed a constant flow of oxygen to keep his wits steady and his aim true, if it came to that. With the butt of the rifle pressed firmly into his shoulder, he kicked the door fully open. The scent of fire damage thumped his nostrils. He directed the narrow beam of the torch into the corners of the room, his trigger finger ready to squeeze at the sight of the slightest threat. The walls and ceiling were blackened with soot. Part of the ceiling in the far-left corner had collapsed, forming a pile of rubble on the ground. No windows. No other exits.

The beam travelled quickly across the right-hand wall. It illuminated a face.

Danny tracked back, ready to fire.

He saw a seated figure, tied to a high-backed chair. Several revolutions of duct tape masked the lower part of the head. Eyes wide in terror. Hair matted to the forehead with sweat.

Buckingham.

He was rocking backwards, banging the chair against the wall. A desperate moaning came from his throat, muffled by the tape. Dazzled by Danny's torch, he couldn't know who had just walked in. The rocking became more desperate. The banging louder. The moaning more frenzied.

There was something on the floor surrounding Buckingham's chair. Danny lowered the beam to light it up. He saw four blocks, about the same size as ordinary building bricks. Instantly he recognised the bright orange of Semtex plastic explosive. A wire led from one block to the other, the four of them forming a semicircle round the legs of the chair. Wired into one of the blocks was a small battery pack connected to a digital timer the size of cigarette packet. A detonator.

Taff's words flashed through Danny's mind. *Don't bother with Buckingham. He won't be around to join you.*

Instinct took over. Danny let the rifle fall and hang from his body as he strode the five metres between himself and Buckingham. The moans of terror grew more high-pitched – Buckingham sounded like a pig squealing before slaughter – but Danny ignored them as he lifted him, chair and all, out from among the explosives. Buckingham was heavier than his small frame suggested, and Danny's muscles were burning by the time he had hauled the man and the chair out into the compound.

They were five metres from the house when the explosion came.

Danny heard it first: a seismic crack that stung his ears. Then the shock wave hit, throwing him forwards a good two metres. Buckingham flew from his arms, landing with a dull thud and then a crack that Danny hoped was the sound of a chair leg breaking, not a bone. Looking back, he saw the left side of the building collapse in on itself, sending up a great cloud of dust. He crawled over to where Buckingham was lying on his side. His eyes were scrunched shut and he was trying to scream. Danny pulled out his knife and with two swift slashes cut through the ropes that bound him to the chair. Then, without any thought for the pain it might cause him, he pulled away the duct tape coiled round Buckingham's head. Clumps of his hair came off with the tape, and when his lips were finally exposed, his shrieks were shrill and womanish. Only when he realised it was Danny who had rescued him from the building did the screaming subside. But if Buckingham felt relief at seeing his SAS chaperone, Danny didn't intend to let it last for long. He grabbed him by the front of his shirt and yanked him to his feet.

'*Talk!*' he roared over the noise of the flames crackling behind him.

'I . . . I don't know what you mean . . .'

'You and Taff have been planning something. You'd better tell me what it is, Buckingham, otherwise you're not walking out of here.'

'You wouldn't dare!' Buckingham shouted.

Wouldn't he? With the anger surging through him now, Danny wasn't so sure. He swung Buckingham round so that he was facing the burning building and Danny was behind him. He wrapped his left arm around the man's neck, tightly enough for the air supply to be slightly restricted. He could feel the heat of the fire against his forearm, but the rest of him, including his face, was shielded by Buckingham's body.

Ten metres between them and the flames. Danny pushed him towards the blaze, halving that distance.

'What have you been planning?' he hissed in Buckingham's ear.

'Nothing,' Buckingham croaked. 'His men just tried to kill me . . . you saw . . . For God's sake, man, it's too hot . . .'

Danny pushed him another metre nearer the flames.

'You know what I think?' he said, sweat dripping from his body and his forearm scalding. 'I think Taff's double-crossed you in some way. He's made a fool of you just like he's made a fool of me. *Now tell me what you were planning.*'

When Buckingham didn't respond, he pushed him forward another metre.

Every man has a breaking point. Buckingham reached his sooner than most might have done. As the intense heat began to sear his face, the words tumbled from his mouth as though they were buckets of water trying to douse the pain. '*Sorgen!*' he shrieked. '*They're on their way to kill him!*'

Danny spun both himself and Buckingham round 180 degrees so that they were no longer facing the fire. With a tremendous effort that momentarily threw Danny off balance, Buckingham broke free and ran. Once he was ten metres from Danny, he fell to the ground and clutched at his face, screaming curses. Danny ignored them. 'Why?' he hissed.

'That's what this has all been about, you idiot!' Buckingham shouted back. 'Sorgen is Asu's only serious contender in this war. If he comes to power, the French will have Syria sewn up, and we can't afford that!' He took a few deep breaths. 'My job was to clear Sorgen's assassination with Asu, then make sure that Sorgen and his commanders would all be in one place at one time. Then Taff and his men could go in and eliminate them.'

'Jesus, Buckingham. I thought Sorgen was your friend.'

Buckingham shot him a poisonous look. 'I thought Jack was yours.'

With great difficulty, Danny kept his cool.

'Why did Taff try to kill you?'

'*I don't bloody well know!*' Buckingham shrieked. '*Because he's a lunatic, I suppose. Like all you fucking animals!*'

Danny started to pace up and down, trying to work out his next move. What was Taff up to? Was it really true that his old friend – his *oldest* friend – wasn't the man he'd thought he was at all?

And if he was about to carry out Buckingham's instructions to the letter, why had he felt the need to get him – not to mention Danny – out of the way?

Only one person could tell him that.

Taff.

Danny turned back to Buckingham.

'Get up,' he growled.

'Where are we going?'

'*Get up!*'

'Not until you tell me where we're going!'

Danny walked over and pulled Buckingham to his feet, holding him face to face as he spoke. 'You and me are going to steal a vehicle,' he said. 'Then we're going to locate Taff. And then we're going to find out exactly what kind of fucked-up scheme you've got us involved in. And trust me, you piece of shit: if I find out you've told me any more lies, you're going to wish you'd ended up being part of Taff's firework display after all. Got it?'

Buckingham stared at him in terror. 'It's too dangerous,' he whispered.

Danny had no time for the man's pathetic hesitation. He pushed him towards the gate, then followed close behind, his rifle pointing at his back. '*Move!*' he shouted. '*Now!*'

TWENTY-TWO

22.30 hrs.

They had started to arrive with the setting of the sun.

Clara had watched them from the entrance to her medical tent, and she hadn't liked what she'd seen. Each of the seven pick-up trucks that were now parked in no particular order about twenty metres east of the main tent was heavily armed with a machine gun that looked, to Clara's untrained eye, identical to the one that had been pointing at the sky since she'd arrived here. The men who emerged from the pick-ups looked no less threatening, with their assault rifles on show and heaven only knew what other weaponry. Without exception, each man wore a black scarf wound around his head to hide his features, with just his eyes and nose visible. Some of the pick-ups had brought two people, some three. In each instance, however, there was one man who was clearly of a higher rank than the others. As each vehicle arrived, Sorgen appeared at the entrance to his tent and greeted this man with a solemn embrace, before leading him inside.

'Sorgen's commanders,' Basheba explained as she joined the watchful Clara. 'It is rare for them all to be together. That is the last of them, I think.'

Now, all Clara could see was the big tent glowing faintly in the darkness from the lights that were on inside, and the dark outlines of the pick-up trucks and their evil-looking weapons against the increasingly inky desert sky.

And another vehicle approaching from the distance.

'Who is that?' Basheba breathed by her side. 'Who else is coming?'

But Clara, of course, couldn't answer that. She could only watch, and wait.

The vehicle – it was a Land Rover – came to a halt about ten metres beyond the pick-ups of Sorgen's commanders. Four men emerged. From this distance, Clara couldn't make out their features, but she could see that they were holding assault rifles at an angle across their chests, and that they walked with a certain wary purpose. Only when they were halfway between the pick-ups and the tent did she see that these were the same men who had been there that very morning.

She heard Basheba give a low hiss, and shot her hand out and grabbed her wrist. 'Stay where you are, Basheba. They're armed. And anyway, the younger man, the one you said did it – he isn't there.'

'These others are just as bad. They watched it happen. They defended him.'

'They're *armed*, Basheba, and there are four of them. They're going to watch out for each other. *Look!*'

Sure enough, two of them – the squat guy with shorter hair and the taller man with a shaved head and tattoos on his neck – had taken up position by the entrance to the tent while their companions entered. The guy with the shaved head looked over in their direction. A nasty leer crossed his face, so menacing that the two women almost involuntarily stepped inside the tent. Clara realised her pulse was raising, and a little voice in her head told her that their safety – hers and Basheba's – depended on what was going on in the main tent. She had to find out, she decided. She had to eavesdrop.

Clearly, walking closer to the big tent to listen in was impossible, not with those brutal-looking men standing watch. But the medical tent was, after all, just a tent. Clara looked towards the back wall. There was nothing stopping her from clambering under the canvas and approaching the other tent from behind. Basheba saw what she was looking at. 'What if they come?' she said. Clara gave her hands a reassuring squeeze and made for the rear of the tent.

It had been erected with care. The lower edge of the canvas was pegged tightly to a groundsheet. It took a minute or so for Clara to loosen it sufficiently to wriggle out, but, with a final look back at a clearly anxious Basheba, that's what she did.

The tent had been pitched close to the sandstone cliff. There was a gap of less than half a metre for Clara to squeeze along. It was dark, but the gentle glow of the main tent, fifteen metres away, gave her enough light to see her way. A minute later she was crouching by the back of the tent, straining hard to hear the conversation that was going on inside.

'Nothing happens,' said a voice – not Sorgen or any of his men, so Clara could only assume it was one of the newcomers – 'until we see the money.'

'Hugo Buckingham is dead?' asked Sorgen quietly.

'As a dodo. No bullets. If anyone finds his body, they'll just put it down to an explosion. One of the many.'

'Ah,' Sorgen replied sadly. 'He was once a good friend.'

'I'd hate to see how you treat your enemies, pal.'

Sorgen ignored the comment, asking, 'His bodyguard – the other young man?'

'It's dealt with, Sorgen. Where's the money?'

'Ah, the money,' Sorgen said quietly. 'I take it you have already levied a handsome charge on the British government for eliminating myself and my generals.'

'Upfront, Sorgen, luckily for you. If it had been cash on delivery, we wouldn't be having this little chat.'

'And now we pay another fee for you to double-cross them.'

'Why get paid once when you can get paid twice?'

'You would make an excellent politician,' said Sorgen with a rueful laugh. 'Still, 750,000 dollars. It is quite a price, for such a small thing.'

'It's loose change for your French paymasters, boyo.'

'They are *your* paymasters now.'

'Today maybe. Tomorrow, who knows? Anyway, if it's such a small thing, you should do it yourself.'

'Delegation is the first rule of leadership, Mr Taff. A strange name, "Taff". Where did you come by it?'

'The money. Unless you want us to carry out the British government's instructions and not the French.'

There was a significant pause. 'Not yet,' Sorgen said, and his bantering tone had changed to something more serious.

'Don't start messing me around, Sorgen,' Taff replied, his voice low and menacing. 'You'll find that's bad for your health.'

'If I was quite so badly outnumbered as you, Mr Taff, I would be worried. But if your intention is to wipe out me and my men, I think you've rather – what is that delightful phrase? – missed the boat. However, I can assure you that I have every intention of letting you walk away with your suitcase of cash. But you must concede that, by your own admission, you are not entirely to be trusted. We are paying you a great deal of money to wipe that animal Asu and his commanders from the face of the earth. I'd be foolish to let you leave here without some kind of guarantee that you're not simply going to disappear.'

Another pause.

'What kind of guarantee,' Taff said, 'did you have in mind?'

'Do you believe in fate?' Sorgen asked. There was no reply from Taff. 'Well, if she exists, she has smiled upon us. Two days ago Asu's daughter-in-law Basheba appeared at our humble camp.'

'I know her,' Taff said.

'Then you know what a tiresome woman she is, and will have no problem helping her on her way to Paradise. You look shocked, Mr Taff. Don't be. If Basheba had stayed with Asu, you would be eliminating her along with the others. I'm sure you understand, though, that if I have footage of you, or one of your men – I'm not an unreasonable man, you may delegate this convenient execution if you want – I have at least some small assurance that your loyalties do not really lie with my brother.'

Clara felt all the strength drain from her body. Her brain shrieked at her to run back to the other tent, to grab Basheba and help her escape. But her limbs wouldn't obey those instructions.

'Fine,' Taff said. 'Bring her here.'

'Just one minute,' Sorgen said. 'We have another issue. Our French backers require some sort of evidence that your loyalty to them is not limited to taking their money and then carrying out the wishes of the British government regardless.'

Clara felt dizzy with nausea.

'As luck would have it, fate has deposited a young British doctor on our doorstep. Perhaps you noticed her this morning. A pretty little thing. If we had more time, I'd be happy to allow you to have your way with her. As it is, I must insist that you also kill her for the camera.'

Clara pressed her hands to her lips, then turned and started stumbling back to the medical tent. She knew she had only seconds to get herself and the Syrian woman out of there, but it seemed to take an age to scramble back under the canvas wall, like she was stuck in a nightmare where she couldn't escape some faceless pursuer.

'*Basheba!*' she hissed once she was inside. One of the wounded male patients had woken up, and Basheba was kneeling down beside him, one hand on his forehead. Clara ran towards her and pulled the surprised woman to her feet. She limped as Clara tugged her back towards the rear of the tent.

'What are you doing?' Basheba asked, clearly startled by Clara's urgent behaviour.

'They're coming for us. We have to get out of here *now* . . .'

Clara glanced towards the flap at the front of the tent. She thought she saw the canvas ripple as somebody touched it. She pushed Basheba down to the gap at the bottom of the tent, looking anxiously over her shoulder as the Syrian woman wriggled awkwardly beneath the canvas wall. She was startled as she saw a hand begin to draw the flap to one side, and she hurled herself through her emergency exit, into the tiny space between the tent and the cliff face.

And then she screamed.

Basheba was on her feet. Behind her, a foot taller, was the man with the shaved head and tattoos on his upper chest and throat. In one hand he held a clump of Basheba's hair. In the other was a knife, with cruel-looking hooks pointing back towards the handle. The wickedly sharp point was pressed to the soft flesh of Basheba's neck, and a thin bead of blood dribbled down her dark skin.

The man sneered. 'Sorgen said you were worth having,' he said. 'Suppose a raghead like that would give his left nut for a taste of a white girl. Maybe I'd do you too, if there was nothing else on the menu.' Clara took a terrified step backwards, but stopped and screamed again as the man yanked Basheba's head back and made as if to slice through her throat. 'Get to the front of the tents, bitch,' he said. 'If I get the feeling you're about to run, I'll start doing some halal butchery right now. Got it?'

Clara stared at him.

'*Got it?*'

She nodded frantically and started retracing her steps towards the main tent. She turned left to follow the narrow passage between the two tents, Basheba and the man with the knife following her. Twenty seconds later they emerged in front of the main tent. The short, blond-haired man was there. He appraised himself of the situation at a glance. 'Nice one, Skinner,' he said, before pointing to the entrance to the tent. 'In you go, ladies,' he said. 'They're waiting for you.'

'*Please*,' Clara begged. 'Let us go. I'll do anything.'

The man called Skinner barked a short, ugly laugh. 'Hear that, Hector? What's it worth? A desert freebie?'

'Only if you take the raghead,' Hector said. And then, as if he'd been asked to explain himself, 'Don't wipe their fucking arses properly, do they?'

'Looks like you're out of luck, ladies,' said Skinner. He nodded at Hector, who grabbed Clara by the hair and pushed her towards the tent.

'Get in,' he said. 'Now.'

There was silence inside the tent. A sense of expectation. The light was dim, coming from a couple of red spotlights trained on to the centre of the tent. Sorgen stood in the middle, his robes and moustache bathed in the red light. A couple of metres behind him, lying on the ground, was a leather suit-case. His commanders, who still wore their scarves around their heads, were dotted about the tent's perimeter – fifteen or so of them – an audience watching the show unfold. Skinner and Hector nodded at a third Western man standing guard by the entrance as they forced the women into the tent. Standing next to Sorgen was the man Clara assumed must be Taff. He was older than the others, somewhere in his late fifties, with straggly grey stubble. He watched the women approach with a curious lack of expression.

Sorgen shouted something in Arabic. One of his command-ers stepped forwards. He was clutching a small, hand-held camcorder. The viewfinder was flipped open.

Basheba spoke angrily in Arabic. A sharp word from Sorgen did nothing to silence her, so Skinner, whose knife was still pressed against her neck, kneed her brutally in the small of the back. Her body went momentarily limp from the pain, and she appeared to be hanging by the fistful of hair Skinner was still clutching. Then he threw her to the ground.

Too terrified to scream again, and restrained by the strong

arms of the man called Hector, Clara could only watch the horror that unfolded.

It was an order from Taff that started it all. He nodded at Skinner and said, 'Do it.'

'Basheba first,' Sorgen said. Still bathed in red light, his eyes were filled with a kind of greed, as though he was about to feast on the sight of this poor woman's execution.

Skinner nodded. He was still holding the vicious knife. With the red light glinting off it, it looked as if it was already covered in blood. The guy with the camcorder held it at arm's length. Clara saw a light on the side switch from red to green.

Skinner walked up to the terrified woman, whose head was in her hands as she wept uncontrollably. Grabbing her hair again, he hauled her to her feet.

'What's your name, bitch?' he said.

Basheba couldn't answer. She just stared at him with undisguised horror.

Skinner raised the knife to her face. In full view of the camera, he sliced each cheek vertically. The blade was sharp, cutting through Basheba's flesh as though it was barely there. She screamed as blood leaked from each incision, smearing her cheeks and lips.

'What's your name?' Skinner repeated.

'B . . . Basheba,' she managed to say.

'To the camera.'

'*Basheba.*'

Skinner smiled then. It was an expression of such cold violence that Clara could barely look at him. Something, though, some kind of horrible magnetic force, kept her eyes glued to Skinner as he raised the knife again. He was standing behind Basheba now, his knife arm around her neck, the blade pointing at her throat.

He pressed it against the skin.

Clara closed her eyes as Basheba screamed.

But that scream was not the only sound that suddenly filled the tent.

There was a gunshot. It came from the front flap of the tent. The shock of the ear-splitting noise was enough to make Clara wonder, for just a fraction of a second, if she herself had been the target. Her eyes jerked open again, just in time to see Skinner go down. The bullet had hit him in the head, ripping a chunk from the skull and causing a gruesome shower of blood, bone and brain matter to rain down. The impact of the shot threw his body back a couple of metres. He hit the ground with a solid, terminal thump. His knife fell a metre from where he dropped.

Basheba screamed again. Her hands were covering her face, but blood was still seeping between her fingers. For some reason she ran towards Clara, as if Clara was in any position to protect her as Taff, Hector and the rest of Sorgen's commanders turned towards the front of the tent, their weapons ready.

In trepidation, Clara did the same.

She saw a figure at the entrance.

It was too dark to make out his features. She could tell that he was tall, that he had a rifle strapped across his body and a pistol in his outstretched right hand. His left hand was above his head, and it held something small and cylindrical.

'*Kill him!*' Sorgen roared. But at the same time, Taff shouted an instruction of his own.

'*Hold your fire!*'

Taff launched himself forwards. When he was five metres from the intruder he turned his back on him to address the rebel leader and his men. 'He's got a grenade. If you shoot him, he'll release the detonation lever. It'll kill us all. *Tell them to drop their weapons, Sorgen!*'

Sorgen looked unsure, but after a moment of deliberation he issued an instruction in Arabic. With obvious reluctance, his commanders lowered their weapons.

Taff turned back to the man with the grenade, who was standing motionless at the entrance to the tent. 'You shouldn't have come here tonight, kiddo,' he said quietly. 'I tried to warn you.'

No reply.

The only sound in the tent was Basheba's continued sobbing.

'*Damn it!*' The words seemed to explode from Taff's mouth. 'You don't understand what the hell's going on. You're still just a *fucking kid!*'

The intruder stepped farther into the tent.

Clara gasped as she recognised the grim features of the soldier Basheba had tried to kill that very morning. Gun still pointing at the rebels. Grenade clearly visible in his left hand.

'Not any more, Taff,' the soldier said quietly. 'But then I guess we all have to grow up some day, don't we?'

TWENTY-THREE

Danny turned to look at the English woman. 'Get outside,' he said. 'Take Basheba with you.' And when at first neither woman moved, he shouted, '*Now!*'

He waited for them to scramble past him and out of the tent before turning back to Taff. His old friend – if that was the word Danny still wanted to use – was standing five metres from him. Sorgen stood five metres beyond that, some of the self-satisfaction wiped from his smug face. Between them lay the bleeding body of Skinner. Hector and De Fries were edging towards the perimeter of the tent, where Sorgen's men were dotted at intervals of two or three metres. Every one of them, Syrian and mercenary alike, had their eyes on the frag, which they knew would cause a lot of damage in an enclosed space like this.

Except for Taff: his gaze was fully on Danny's face.

'You crept up quietly, kiddo,' he said. 'I'm impressed.'

'You taught me well.'

'Perhaps. Sometimes I think I didn't teach you enough.' A pause. 'You're so naive, Danny. I should have given you a crash course in how the world works while I could.'

'I'm learning pretty fast.'

'Maybe. Maybe not. Let's stick a pin in that frag, eh? Talk this through man to man.'

Silence. Danny didn't move.

'You can still run, kiddo,' Taff said. 'If I say the word, none of these cunts will follow you. It's your best call. Buckingham's dead. You've got no reason to stick around.'

Danny whistled. He could sense the flap opening behind him and didn't need to turn round to know that Buckingham had just entered. He could see that written on Taff's face.

'You'll bloody well answer for this . . .' Buckingham started to say.

'*Shut up!*' Danny and Taff gave the command in unison, but neither of them stopped staring at the other.

After ten seconds, Taff smiled. He turned round and waved his arms in the air to indicate everyone in the tent. 'Fine, kiddo,' he shouted. 'Take us all out. Great idea! But, before you do, ask yourself a question.' He faced his protégé once more, and even took a couple of steps towards him. 'When – if – they find your body rotting in the Syrian desert, what will the powers that be say about you back home? Do you think they'll remember your name in Whitehall? Do you think they'll be toasting you down at their fucking gentlemen's clubs? Or do you think you'll be swept under the carpet like all the other rubbish? Eh? Sorry, kiddo, can't hear you! Cat got your tongue?'

Silence.

'Here's the bottom line, Danny,' Taff continued, his voice a little quieter now. '*Nobody . . . gives . . . a . . . shit.* Do you really reckon anybody outside the squadron hangar gives a fuck that your mate Jack caught it? Do you think those twats at the MoD have made a single phone call to Damascus to get the other two off the hook?'

'I'm just a soldier, Taff,' Danny replied. 'I do what I'm told.'

'Oh, *please*,' Taff spat. 'Spare me the Queen and Country bullshit. You want to know what this is about? All this?' Without waiting for an answer, he stormed to the back of the tent, where a tatty leather suitcase lay on the ground. He picked it up and carried it back to the centre of the tent, stepping nonchalantly over Skinner as he returned. He opened the suitcase and let the contents fall to the floor: wads of notes, maybe fifty of them. Danny couldn't begin to guess how much money was there. 'Do you think the British, or the French, or the Russians would come anywhere near this place if there wasn't money to be made? How many mates did you lose in Iraq so that a bunch of Yanks could hold on to a few oil contracts? Half these Syrian rebels are propped up by Al Qaeda anyway, so don't give me that crap about patriotism. You and me are just tiny cogs in one great big fucked-up machine, and you know it.'

'All I know,' Danny said, doing his best to keep his voice level, 'is that you're out of control. Skinner was going to butcher that woman, just like he butchered the family back in Homs.'

Taff waved one hand, as if to say, let's not sweat the small stuff. It made the rage boil hotter in Danny's blood. 'I had a lot of respect for you once, Taff,' he said. 'Back in the day when I didn't realise you made your living killing defenceless women.'

'I make my living the same way you do, kiddo. The only difference is that you get paid in worthless medals and empty words, and I get paid in cash.' He bent down, picked up a wad of notes and casually flicked through them. 'US dollars,' he said. 'Used, non-sequential, untraceable.' His eyes brightened as if a very good idea had just struck him. He tossed the bundle of notes at Danny's feet. 'There you go,' he said. 'Skinner's not in a position to use his share. You take some of it. There's five grand there.'

For the first time, Danny's eyes left Taff as he glanced down at the money. Taff nodded knowingly. 'Feels like a good pay day, eh?' he said. 'Let me tell you, that's not the half of it.' He walked back to where Sorgen was standing, positioned himself behind the rebel leader and put both hands on his shoulders. Annoyance flickered over Sorgen's face, but he managed to suppress it and to stand silently. 'Take Sorgen,' Taff proclaimed. 'If he comes to power in Syria, the French are going to be pissing rainbows. I'll have influence, kiddo. Real influence. You've met that tosser

318

Max Saunders. You think I want to be working for him for the rest of my life? Do *you* want to be working for him the rest of *your* life? Because, believe me, that's what's in store for you when the Regiment finally sends you packing – if not with Saunders, then with some other Rupert happy to sit behind a desk and fuck his secretary while you risk all the bleeding. But the French? I just need to say the word and they'll set me up with my own private military contracts.'

He nodded again, then sauntered back towards Danny. 'I'll cut you in,' he said. Danny wasn't sure if he was trying to stop the others from hearing him. 'You and me, kiddo. We can sit behind a desk in Paris, count our money and fuck French tarts till our dicks bleed, while some other mug risks his life on the ground instead. You're not going to tell me that isn't better than a paltry army pension or an unmarked grave if you're KIA.'

Taff was again facing Danny, just a metre between them, and he dropped his voice once more. It was definitely a private conversation. 'You did the right thing, nailing Skinner,' he said, and for once Danny saw a bit of honesty in his eyes. 'You're right. He was out of control. I should have done something about it before. I owe you one.'

No reply. 'You can take his place. We'll let the women go. Sorgen won't do anything. He's too scared the Frogs will withdraw their support. We'll finish the job together – you, me, Hector, De Fries – and split the money.' He looked up at the grenade that Danny still held aloft. 'Let's be honest with each other, kiddo,' he said. 'I'm not going to hurt you, and you're not going to hurt me. Too much water under the bridge for that, right?'

Right.

Danny was aware of Buckingham stepping back outside the tent. Slowly, and without taking his eyes off Taff, he lowered his arm but kept his fingers tight around the grenade's detonation lever.

'Good lad,' said Taff. He bent down and picked up the wad of notes. 'Plenty more where this came from, Danny,' he said. 'You know what I'm thinking? I'm thinking you could do with it. Get your dad out of that shitty little bungalow. Pay for someone to come in twice a day, wipe his arse, cook his food.' Danny felt himself blushing at the reminder of his father's incapacity. 'He's only going to get worse, you know. You think you'll be able to help him out on a Regiment wage? Because it's not like Kyle's going to be there for him, right?'

Kyle. What was it he'd said, what seemed like an age ago back in the UK? 'Sometimes he thought you were more like Taff's son than his.' And now here he was, holding his own mentor at gunpoint, threatening to wound or kill them both with a fragmentation grenade.

Had he ever, he asked himself, truly believed that Taff made his living in a straightforward way? Was he being a twat, only pretending to have scruples about it now he had come face to face with the reality?

Taff took a step forwards, ignoring the grenade, ignoring the gun, ignoring everything but Danny himself.

'Tell Buckingham and the women to get out of here,' he said firmly. 'We'll finish the job off. Asu's a cunt anyway. Him and his commanders are all in one place tonight, just like I planned it. Easy target. Then we'll head home and sort your dad out. And *then* . . .' He waved the bundle of notes under Danny's nose.

And Danny had to admit it. He felt his resolve weakening. Maybe Taff was right. He always had been in the past. If his bosses cared about the lives of him and his men, they'd have pulled them out of Syria the moment they were compromised. If they'd done that, maybe Jack would still be alive.

He felt his weapon lowering.

Taff moved with incredible speed. His right hand shot out and his fingers curled round Danny's clenched fist, squeezing both his hand and the detonation lever. He had an immensely strong grip. At the same time, he pulled out his own pistol and pressed it against Danny's skull. Danny's gun was level with Taff's stomach. Stalemate. Danny's advantage with the grenade was neutralised. To get it back, he had to kill Taff, and they both knew he was never going to do that.

'So what do we do now, kiddo? Kill each other? Or let each other go?'

Danny had no answer.

Taff looked over at Hector and De Fries. 'Get Buckingham and the women.' The two men left the tent. Silence. Then the sound of a struggle outside. A minute later they marched the captives in at gunpoint.

The atmosphere in the tent had changed. Sorgen's men were no longer standing rigid and uncomfortable around the edge. Three of them had moved forwards a few steps, and they all held their weapons with a little more confidence.

'I know what you're doing, kiddo,' Taff said. 'You're estimating the distance to each target in the tent. You're thinking, should I take out Sorgen? He's only ten metres away, and unarmed. You're thinking, if I could get to my M4, I could take out his commanders in a few bursts. But you're holding your Sig, aren't you? You could take one shot, maybe two, before they disobey my instruction to hold their fire and put you down. You're thinking, how did this happen? I was on top, and now Taff's calling the shots.'

Danny didn't reply. Each one of these thoughts had passed through his mind. He didn't have an answer to any of them.

'Let me put you out of your misery, kiddo, and tell you exactly what's going to happen. You're going to very gently release your grip on that grenade. Then you're going to roll it into my hand so I can keep the detonation lever pressed. If I get the idea, even for a moment, that you're fucking me around, Hector here will take out each of his three prisoners in turn. First the raghead, then the blonde, then the spook. I'm going to count to five, and then we're going to do it.'

He looked over at Hector and gave him a nod to indicate that he wasn't joking. Hector raised his weapon to the trembling form of Basheba.

'One,' said Taff.

Distance between him and Hector: no more than four metres.

'Two.'

Danny's pistol was still pressed into Taff's belly. He could put Hector down with a single shot, but it would mean shooting Taff first.

'Three.'

He's not the guy you thought he was, Danny realised. You can't trust him. Think of the women. Hector will kill them without a second thought. Look what he and Skinner did in the bakery.

'Four.'

Do what you have to do, Danny told himself. He felt his finger exert a little bit more pressure on the trigger.

'Five, kiddo.'

He couldn't do it.

But he didn't need to.

The movement came from his left. Not from Hector, or even Buckingham, but from the British woman. She launched herself at Hector, knocking his rifle out of Basheba's way. There was a burst of fire as Hector accidentally sprayed rounds to Danny's left, ripping holes not only in the canvas of the tent but also in the belly of one of Sorgen's commanders. Danny didn't wait to see the guts burst from the guy's stomach. Instead he took advantage of the moment of distraction.

His hands were out of action, and so he used his head, jabbing it forwards as hard as possible so that his forehead cracked into Taff's nose. He felt the bone shatter and flatten. The barrel of Taff's gun slipped from Danny's head. The fist wrapped round his grenade hand loosened. Danny jabbed his Sig hand sharply upwards into Taff's ribcage, knocking the air from his lungs. Taff staggered backwards, but Danny was already focused on other threats.

There was panic in the tent. Basheba, her slashed face still bleeding, was screaming and Buckingham had already scurried for the exit. Sorgen was edging backwards, towards the rear of the tent, and a couple of his commanders were flanking him. Only one of the guys, however, had raised his weapon. He was standing seven metres to Danny's ten o'clock. Calmly, Danny fired a single round at his scarf-swathed face, instantly transforming the only part of his skin on view into a bloody mash of flesh before he fell backwards.

By now, however, Hector had regained his balance. If he hadn't hesitated for half a second, unable to decide whether he wanted to kill the British woman first or Danny, then Danny would have been dead on the ground. As it was, that moment of indecision gave Clara time to hurl herself at him, knocking him to the ground as once more he discharged a shot, this time harmlessly. She scrambled to her feet again.

Holding his grenade above his head again – a renewed warning to everyone else inside the tent what would happen if they slotted him – Danny turned to the two women. '*Get out of the tent!*' he roared. '*Now!*'

Clara grabbed Basheba and pulled her towards the flap. Danny, edging backwards, addressed Sorgen. 'Tell your men,' he said, 'that I'll shoot anyone I see outside the tent.' Sorgen hesitated, so Danny fired a single round in the air to concentrate his mind. '*Do it!*'

Sorgen issued his instructions in Arabic as Danny continued to step backwards. Three metres to the exit. Two metres. He glanced at Taff, who was crouched on the ground, blood streaming from his broken nose.

And then Danny was outside.

He turned sharply to his right and dashed along the front of the tent. Just as he expected, a flurry of gunfire burst through the canvas, but none of it in his direction. And nobody appeared bold enough to come after him. At least, not yet. Danny gave himself a couple of seconds to take stock.

Buckingham and the women were crouching by one of the seven open-topped technicals parked about twenty metres east of the main tent. These pick-ups were facing the desert, for a quick getaway if the situation required. That gave Danny to believe that the keys would be in the ignition of each of them. The beaten-up VW that he'd hot-wired in a street near the compound in Homs stood abandoned a kilometre from the rebel camp. He and Buckingham had silently covered that final stretch on foot. In any case, if they wanted a chance of getting out of here alive, they needed an upgrade.

Danny sprinted at a forty-five-degree angle to join Buckingham and the women. He was only a few strides from them, and maybe twenty metres from the main tent, when an armed, headscarfed figure stepped out of the tent. Danny was ready for him. He hurled the primed grenade in the man's direction. It landed a metre from the target and exploded a fraction of a second later. The noise filled the air, to be followed a moment later by the screams of the wounded rebel. Danny was happy for him to scream away. It meant the others were less likely to stick their noses out.

Danny forced Buckingham and the women to the comparative safety of the far side of the technical. To his relief, he saw that the key was in the ignition.

'We're taking this,' he said in a tone of voice that offered no possibility of argument. 'I'll man the weapon on the back and give us covering fire.' He looked at the British woman. 'What's your name?'

'Clara,' she replied. 'Look, I'm sorry I—'

'You can drive?'

She nodded.

'Take the wheel then.'

'Don't be so bloody ridiculous,' Buckingham cut in. 'I'm perfectly capable of—'

'You,' Danny said forcefully, 'are in the back with me where I can keep an eye on you.' He ignored the protests that followed and turned back to Clara. 'Don't stop at *all* unless I knock three times on the cab. Got it?'

Clara nodded. 'Where are we going?'

'Away from here.' That was as far as he'd got. He could work out a strategy once they'd found a place of safety.

'They are going to kill Asu?' Basheba asked.

Danny glanced towards the tent. Was that plan likely to be abandoned? He doubted it. There was money involved, and Danny now understood that, for Taff, money was everything. He nodded briefly at Basheba and prepared to mount the vehicle. But she grabbed his arm with surprising strength. 'My son is with Asu,' she said. 'They will kill him too.'

'I'm sorry.'

'I have already lost one son,' she whispered. 'You have to help me find the other. You *have* to.'

'Don't be so stupid,' Buckingham hissed. 'Black, I forbid you to do any such damn-fool thing. We need to get to the Czech Embassy in Damascus. It's the only safe place for us.'

Danny looked anxiously at the tent. They needed to move. Any second now, either Sorgen's men or Taff's were going to get brave.

Clara spoke. 'If you're going to abandon Basheba,' she said, 'abandon me too.' And her eyes challenged him: what kind of man would you be if you did that?

'Oh, for fuck's sake!' Buckingham said.

'Shut up, Buckingham.' The women had made Danny's mind up – he was damned if he was going to land on Buckingham's side of the fence. 'OK,' he said. 'Asu's surrounded by child soldiers.' He nodded at Basheba. 'Including her son. If Sorgen and Taff get their way, they'll be butchered. We're going to find him and warn him.'

'*I forbid it!*' Buckingham yelled.

Gunfire. A round ricocheted off the pick-up. Danny pulled his only remaining frag from his chest rig, readied it and lobbed it towards the four rebel fighters who had ventured outside and spread out.

A warning shout, then the explosion, followed by the agonised screams of two of the rebels.

'*Go! Now!*' Danny hissed. He grabbed Buckingham and dragged him round to the tailgate of the technical, which he opened, and then pushed him up on to the floor before climbing on board himself. 'Get down,' he said. Buckingham needed no more encouragement and lay flat and still as Danny took up position at the machine gun. A chain link of .50-cal rounds hung from the chamber, ready to fire. As the engine started, Danny swung the weapon round on its tripod and fired a thunderous burst at the rebels. The surviving two shuddered violently from the impact of the rounds, before dropping to the ground. '*Jesus!*' Buckingham cried out. The pick-up edged forwards.

Ideally, Danny would have disabled the other technicals before moving off, but the situation was far from ideal. His only option was to take them out on the run. Clara had barely driven ten metres before he trained the machine gun on each of the pick-ups in turn, concentrating his fire on the wheelbase. None of them would get far with blown-out tyres and a crumpled axle. In the event, the weapon did a lot more work than that. By the time they were forty metres east of the encampment, two of the vehicles were in flames. The remainder were a mess of bullet holes, shredded rubber and shattered glass.

Their own vehicle accelerated. Sixty metres. Eighty. More figures appeared in front of the tent and started to fire, but the rounds fell harmlessly some twenty metres short of them. It occurred to Danny that if Taff had been firing, there was no way he'd have missed them. Had he just allowed Danny to escape for a second time? With the thunder of the .50-cal ringing in his ears, Danny pulled his night-sight from his chest rig, put it to his eye and trained it on the camp. Men were swarming around the big tent, and when Sorgen appeared he looked faintly ridiculous in his white *dishdash*, shouting instructions while flapping his arms around. But Danny was only interested in picking out one man. Taff. He stood at the tent's entrance, seemingly unconcerned by his broken nose, his eyes following the pick-up as it headed off into the night. It could have been a trick of his imagination, but to Danny it seemed as if Taff was staring straight down the barrel of the night-sight, and into his mind.

Then he turned, stepped back into the tent and was gone.

TWENTY-FOUR

It was his prostate that caused it, Max Saunders had decided. Back in his army days he'd been able to piss thunderously before bed and again when he woke up. Now he was a three-times-a-nighter, squeezing out the remains of his St Émilion or Chivas Regal against the porcelain in his marble-clad en suite with all the vigour of a coffee percolator. He should get the old chap looked at, only he didn't like the idea of some turban-clad Indian doctor examining his dick, or worse still sticking a latex-clad finger up his arse. He put that thought from his mind with a shudder.

This was his second piss of the night, which meant it must be about midnight. All the more curious, therefore, that he should be disturbed by the sound of his mobile phone buzzing on the bedside table. He swore under his breath, shook himself off, and then padded naked back into the bedroom where his wife was asleep, or at least pretending to be. His mobile was still ringing – the vibrations had shifted it to the edge of his bedside table. He caught it just as it was falling to the floor, and accepted the call.

'Who the . . . ?'

'It's me. We've got a problem.'

Taff Davies. The line was bad, but that figured. Saunders stepped out of the bedroom and on to the dark landing.

'Is this line secure?' Taff asked.

'Of course it's fucking secure,' Saunders snapped. 'What's so important you need to get me out of bed?'

A pause. Saunders could feel Taff's own irritation coming down the line, but chose to ignore it.

'Skinner's dead,' Taff said.

'Well, boo-fucking-hoo, stick him in a hole. Seriously, Davies, this line's for emergencies, not gossip.'

'Buckingham walked in on our RV with Sorgen. He knows everything.'

Now it was Saunders' turn to fall silent.

'I thought Buckingham was dead,' he said eventually. 'Along with that fucking Regiment kid.'

'They got away.'

'Away from *where*? Jesus *Christ*, they shouldn't have been anywhere near your meet with Sorgen. Do I have to do everything myself? I tipped off the Syrians *and* the bastard Russians so they could thin down Buckingham's babysitters. All you had to do was take care of two guys, and you couldn't even do *that*?'

'You should haul your arse over here for a few days, Saunders. We'd give you a warm welcome.'

'Spare me,' Saunders spat, the officer in him coming to the fore. 'I pay you a lot of money to be out there. If you don't like it, fuck off and I'll find someone else. Cunts like you, Davies, are two a penny. Is Sorgen still alive?'

'Roger that.'

'Do you have the French money?'

'It's here.'

'I said, do you *have* it?'

'Sorgen will release the money when he knows Asu is dead. Not before.'

'Fuck it! Can't you just take it?'

'We're outnumbered, Saunders. Heavily.' An awkward, almost embarrassed pause. 'They've taken out our vehicles. I can't get to Asu to finish the job, not before morning. You're going to have to come up with something else.'

Saunders could no longer contain his fury. He paced up and down the landing, slapping the wall with his free hand. 'And Asu's current location? Tell me you know that, at least.'

'He has a safe house near the central mosque. Number 35, Fares Al Khaldoun. That's where he's meeting with his commanders.' Another pause. 'I think there's a good chance that Buckingham and Black are on their way there to warn him.'

'Jesus Christ!' Saunders muttered to himself. Taff Davies, normally so reliable, was presiding over this crowning glory of a clusterfuck. Saunders realised he was going to have to get involved directly if he was going to sort out this situation. 'Stay by your phone,' he instructed. '*And don't take your eyes off that fucking money!*'

He hung up, then stormed back into the bedroom and pulled on his kimono dressing gown, before hurrying downstairs to his basement office, where he locked the door behind him. He tried to straighten this all out in his head. He was taking money from the British government to provide a training package to Asu and to eliminate Sorgen. He was taking a larger sum of money from the French government to have Asu and his commanders assassinated. So long as everything went according to plan, he could be the servant of two masters. With Asu dead and Sorgen alive, he'd be the apple of the French government's eye, whereas the British would have to continue paying him anyway because they simply couldn't function abroad without the help of International Solutions and companies like it. But the strategy depended not only on Asu's death, but now also on the deaths of Hugo Buckingham and Danny Black. Nobody who had contact with the British authorities could know what Taff – and by extension Saunders – had been up to.

But he smiled to himself as he realised that if he moved quickly, and if it was true that Buckingham and Black were at this moment heading to Asu's safe house, he had a chance – not only to eliminate everybody who needed to be eliminated, but to earn himself a third paycheck too.

Contacts were everything in this business, and Saunders had them all. Sadiq Dahlamal ran a business importing Middle Eastern artefacts from his warehouse in Lots Road. He also happened to be a direct conduit to the Syrian administration. Dahlamal had been in the same boarding house – Fircroft – as Saunders at Uppingham. He'd been delighted to receive the tip-off that a British SAS unit had breached the Syrian border. Saunders was almost certain Dahlamal would take his call again, whatever the time of day or night.

He was right.

'Sadiq, old boy,' he said smoothly to the groggy-sounding Syrian merchant once he had him on the phone. 'Hope I didn't wake you. Probably worth your while if I did.'

'What the bloody hell you want, Saunders? I busy man.' They never had liked each other much.

'I'd like to give you the exact location for the next few hours of your government's good friend Asu and all his rebel commanders,' Saunders purred. 'For a small consideration, of course.'

That got Sadiq's attention. The grogginess left his voice. 'Where you come by this information?'

'Ways and means, old boy. Ways and means.'

'Where is he?'

Saunders found himself smiling. 'I hate to be vulgar, Sadiq, but let's get the money conversation out of the way first. Shall we say 750,000 dollars, cash?'

'Half a million.'

'I don't think so, Sadiq. Seven hundred and fifty thousand.'

A pause.

'Agreed. But we pay you only when Asu is dead.'

'Naturally. And I can't tell you what a relief it is to know that I trust you. It would be such a shame – and *such* an embarrassment – if word of your homosexual schoolboy dalliances leaked out, wouldn't it? And the pictures, Sadiq. Enough to make a

331

grown man faint. They cost me a considerable sum, but I'd like you to rest assured they're safe and sound, for the moment.'

Another pause.

'Where is he?' Sadiq said.

'Number 35, Fares Al Khaldoun.' Saunders repeated the location Taff had given him.

'That is heavily populated area,' Sadiq observed.

'Not my problem, old boy. Anyway, do a few more dead really make much difference?'

But Sadiq had already hung up.

Saunders put the phone down on his desk and inhaled deeply. He congratulated himself that this was turning out rather well. There was a certain pleasure to be drawn from dealing with regimes who feared that the end was close. They could be relied upon to act decisively.

The citizens of Homs, and anyone damn fool enough to join them, were in for a brutal few hours. Max Saunders consoled himself with that thought as he climbed back upstairs to the marital bed.

23.57 hrs.

Warm and muggy, considering it was nearly midnight. The stars were very bright overhead. Danny rapped three times on the cab of the pick-up. Clara pulled in at the side of the road.

They'd been travelling for fifteen minutes, and Danny estimated that they were just over thirty kilometres from Sorgen's encampment. He'd been scanning the darkness constantly through his night-sight, but had seen no sign of any tail. Another eight klicks, he reckoned, and they'd hit the outskirts of Homs. When that happened, a fucking great .50-cal on the back of the truck would draw more attention than he was comfortable with. He started to disassemble it.

'What are you doing?' Buckingham asked.

'Keeping a low profile,' Danny replied, lowering the machine gun from its tripod.

'Look,' Buckingham said, standing up awkwardly. 'I should have listened to you before, when you said we should extract. Hands held high, and all that. But really, is this necessary? If the women want to go on this ill-advised errand, let them. You and I can . . .' He jabbed one thumb over his shoulder.

Danny stared at him in disgust but Buckingham didn't seem to understand the look. 'Get me out of here,' he said, 'and I'll see to it that they'll be singing your name from the rooftops of the MoD. I can do that, you understand? I know people.'

'You're a piece of shit, Buckingham. If I leave anyone to fend for themselves, it'll be you.'

'Damn it, man . . .'

But Danny didn't want to hear it. He pushed Buckingham back down to the floor of the pick-up. 'Don't fucking move,' he said, before jumping down and walking round to the cab. He opened the driver's door. Clara was gripping the wheel and staring straight ahead. She looked like she didn't want to think about what she was doing. 'Less than ten kilometres, we'll be in the city,' he said. He looked over at Basheba. 'Can you direct Clara to Asu's safe house?'

The cuts on the Syrian woman's face were beginning to congeal. She nodded.

'If anyone stops you, try to talk your way past them,' said Danny.

'And if we can't?'

'I'll deal with it. We'll stay out of sight in the back. Once we've given Asu the tip-off, we'll get straight out of Homs and head for the Lebanese border. Do you have somewhere you can take your son if we find him?'

Basheba nodded. That was good enough for him.

'Let's go,' he said. And then, because Clara looked so frightened, he gave her a word of encouragement. 'You're doing well,' he said.

She nodded gratefully at him as he slammed the door.

In the back of the truck, Danny raised the tailgate, then lay on his front, M4 cocked and locked and pointing towards the rear of the vehicle. He found, alongside him, a sturdy crowbar. Could be useful. No need to tell Buckingham to keep his head down. He looked like he was trying to disappear into the corner. The two women in the front had more courage than him in their little fingers, he realised as the vehicle moved off again.

His stomach was turning over. The confrontation with Taff had upended his life for a second time in as many days. It seemed like every anchor he'd ever known was being cut away. Like he wasn't even the same person any more. He knew, however, that if he didn't keep focused, it would all be meaningless anyway. He'd never see home again. So he forced himself to stay alert, keep his ears sharp and his brain active. Asu was a loathsome bastard, but even if he wasn't lording it over an army of child soldiers who would be wiped out if his safe house was hit, Danny's duty was clear. The British government wanted him alive. That was all he needed to know.

The pick-up slowed down. It meant they were approaching a more built-up area. Danny looked up, above the side of the vehicle, and saw the occasional building looming overhead. A small mosque with its colourful minaret lit up in the darkness. The shell of a former department store, its windows smashed. He thought he could hear a helicopter nearby, but it wasn't directly above him so he couldn't see it, and a minute later the sound disappeared.

They'd been travelling for maybe twenty minutes when they came to a sudden, screeching halt. The .50-cal, lying lengthways, crashed to the back of the pick-up. Danny felt his body tense up. The engine was still turning over, but above its low rumble he could hear a male voice beside the cab. He was speaking Arabic and his tone was unfriendly. Basheba gave the odd short reply. Thirty seconds passed, then the man stopped speaking. Danny heard footsteps and saw the top of his head moving along the side of the pick-up. He wore a hat with the standard camo of the Syrian army.

How many men? He'd only heard one but there could be more. A gunshot would immediately alert any other soldiers to his presence. A silent kill, on the other hand, could give him a few extra precious seconds. He grabbed the crowbar and shuffled along to crouch behind the tailgate. Buckingham was breathing heavily. Bastard was going to give them away if he wasn't careful.

Movement on the other side of the tailgate. It opened.

The Syrian soldier only had a split second to be surprised at the sight of two men in the rear of the vehicle. He was carrying an AK-47 and immediately started to raise it. But Danny was too fast. The crowbar made a dull, wet thump as it connected with the soldier's skull, then the guy hit the ground.

Behind them, a street devoid of traffic but with two oil-drum fires burning, one on either side, about twenty-five and thirty metres away respectively. Piles of debris along both sides, and deserted, bomb-shelled buildings, a jungle of concrete and steel reinforcing rods. There were silhouettes around the fires, but Danny couldn't tell how many. They didn't appear to be an immediate threat. His rifle engaged, he looked round the side of the pick-up.

The road ahead was blocked by a fallen telephone pole.

He gestured to Buckingham to follow him, then moved round to the cab and opened the passenger door.

'Basheba,' he said, 'how far to the safe house?'

'It is close. Maybe 500 metres.'

'Get out of the truck. We'll do it on foot. You lead.'

'Her feet are bad,' Clara said. 'I'll have to help her.'

Danny nodded. 'You next, Buckingham. I'll take the rear. Stay close to each other. If you hear gunshot, hit the ground. If I get hit, take my firearms and make your own way.' They stared

335

at him as the implications of that scenario hit home. '*Move!*' he hissed.

The going was slow – Basheba limped along and it was clear there was no point hurrying her. Danny couldn't fret about that. He needed to keep a 360-degree lookout, which meant pointing his M4 forwards, backwards and from side to side every few seconds as they advanced through this ghost town. Basheba led them past fires that were burning but recently abandoned – but somewhere behind him Danny could hear vehicles and the sound of voices shouting. Reinforcements, he assumed, and they'd be mob-handed.

Up ahead was a roadblock. Fifty metres before it they took a right. They skirted round an abandoned tank, covered with Arabic graffiti and lying at right angles across the street, before taking a left twenty metres beyond it and continuing for another 100 metres.

'How much further?' Danny asked.

But he didn't have chance to hear Basheba's reply.

A MiG shot overhead. Its payload hit the city a couple of seconds later. The earth shook so violently that all four of them fell, and they were still on the ground when a second aircraft flew over, dropping a load of similar ferocity. Danny's eardrums thundered, but the immense noise didn't dissipate with the impact of the bombs. Straight ahead, he saw that ordnance had hit fifty metres along the road. The way was barred by a mini mushroom cloud of dust with orange flame at its heart. The cloud was being sucked along the street towards them, and seconds later they were engulfed. It was thick, black and choking. And hot – it smarted Danny's skin and singed his hair. It blocked out the moonlight and left them in total darkness. Danny could only tell where the others were by their hacking coughs. He thought he heard one of them vomit.

Fifteen seconds passed. The cloud was beginning to thin. Danny's stinging eyes made out the grey silhouettes of his companions lying, like him, on the ground. 'Everyone OK?' he rasped, before spitting out the dust that had entered his mouth when he spoke.

Buckingham was the first to get to his feet. 'This is madness,' he croaked. 'You're going to get us all killed. We need to get out of here.'

Danny had to admit that he was right. Had they been just a little farther along this road, they'd be dead.

Buckingham was off on one. 'This is *fucking* idiocy,' he ranted. 'I'm *ordering* you to get us out of here, Black. You hear that? I'm fucking *ordering* you.'

But then Basheba was there by Danny's side, tugging desperately at his arm. Her face was black with the dirt, and tears stained her cheeks. 'Don't leave me,' she said, her voice hoarse and choked. 'Help me get to my son. I'm begging you.'

'Leave her!' Buckingham shouted. 'We don't owe her anything.'

It was Clara who shut him up, slapping his face with a force that Danny would never have expected of her. When she turned to Danny, there was a fierceness in her eyes that meant she didn't even need to speak. It said, are you with us, or with him?

For Danny, the answer was clear. He pointed the rifle at Buckingham, then yanked it in the direction of the impact site. 'Move,' he said.

Buckingham looked at him with poison in his eyes. But he stumbled forwards, and the ragged group advanced – coughing, limping, yet strangely determined.

They reached a crater in the road where the bomb had hit. It was two metres deep, ten wide, a crucible of smouldering rubble. They edged round it, still choking from the dust. Fifteen metres beyond the crater, the sound of screaming drifted towards them. The buildings on either side were ramshackle concrete residential blocks, and as they pressed on, faces and figures emerged from the clouds of dust. People had left the flats and were running towards them. Many were limping. All of them ignored Danny and his companions, even though he was armed, as they fled the area as it came under ever fiercer attack. Flames spewed from the windows of a block on their left, along with plumes of black smoke. They pushed on past, and after another thirty metres the road opened out into a square of about sixty metres by sixty.

'I know this place,' Clara said breathlessly. 'I was here before.'

Danny took in his surroundings. Ordnance had clearly hit in the last few minutes. The green, tree-lined area in the centre of the square was smoking and four or five of the trees that were still standing were burning ferociously. On the far side of the square Danny could make out a mosque, one minaret still intact, the other half-destroyed and also smoking.

'Someone told me that this was where people who defy the government meet,' Clara said. 'Not any more, I guess . . .'

Basheba pointed to their eleven o'clock, where a low, sprawling, single-storey building was apparently untouched by the current bombardment. 'The safe house,' she shouted above the noise. 'That's Asu's safe house!'

Distance: twenty-five metres. A single door at the front, but Danny would have put money on there being further exits at the side or the back. Ten metres from the door lay an uprooted tree, and its sprawling branches would give decent cover if he used it as an OP for the door.

'Get to the tree!' he shouted. 'Move!' They started to cut across the square, sweating from the heat of the burning trees. From the corner of his eyes Danny was aware of figures retreating from the square. Within thirty seconds the four of them were crouching by the fallen tree. 'Listen,' Danny shouted. 'If they're still in there, they're going to be jumpy. Asu will be wondering if the government forces know where he is and if this aerial strike is aimed directly at him—'

'It probably bloody well is!' Buckingham hissed.

Danny ignored him. 'If his men see me armed, they'll get the wrong idea. Buckingham, Asu trusts you. You need to approach with the women. I'll cover you from here.'

'Oh,' Buckingham sneered. '*Very* fucking brave.'

Danny grabbed him by the throat. 'I'll have you in my sights, pal. Any crap, I'll drop you.' He turned to Clara. 'There's no reason for you to approach. You should stay here.'

She shook her head. 'Not until Basheba's found her boy.'

Danny shrugged. 'It's your choice.' He set himself up in the firing position, resting his M4 on the tree trunk and aiming it at the door. 'Go,' he instructed.

They made a strange trio, Basheba limping with her arm round Clara's neck, Buckingham creeping along just behind them, his head darting left and right like a frightened animal. It was Clara who banged on the door: three solid thumps with her fist, and three more when there was no response. Only after a minute or so did the door open. An armed figure appeared. Danny recognised him: one of Asu's personal guards. He felt a weird kind of relief. They could warn Asu, find the kid and then get out of here.

It was a feeling of relief that didn't last long.

The attack, when it came, was so swift that Danny instantly recognised the hallmark of special forces. If the burning trees around him had not been crackling so ferociously, he might have heard the chopper arrive from the direction of the mosque. As it was, the enormous black Mi8 only came into earshot when it was almost above him. Seconds later it was hovering six or seven metres above the safe house. Everything happened so quickly. Asu's bodyguard grabbed the women and pulled them into the safe house. Buckingham hesitated, but then he too was yanked inside. At the same time, four fast ropes fell from the chopper and black-clad commandos slid down them with the swift ease of well-practised soldiers. Russian, like the chopper? They looked too slick to be Syrian. Danny counted them: four, eight, twelve, sixteen. He could only watch. He'd have time to take out two, maybe three of them before the remainder laid down fire in his direction. There was no way he'd survive the onslaught of more than a dozen weapons.

But how did they know so precisely where Asu was? Danny's face hardened as the thought came to him: Taff.

Of the sixteen commandos, six were now by the front door, while the remainder had taken up positions out of sight, presumably at the rear and sides of the safe house. The helicopter remained hovering over the house, but it spun round so its tail was pointing in Danny's direction. A guy stood guard on each side of the front door. Two more, Danny realised, were carrying a pneumatic battering ram. They smashed through the door in seconds, dropped the battering ram and entered with the remaining two, all four with their weapons raised.

Danny took a second to examine the two soldiers guarding the door. Plate hangars. Kevlar helmets. If he was going to take them out, it would need shots to the face. Still shielded by the branches of the tree, he lined up the cross hairs with the face of the guy on the left. He fired. A single shot and he was down. At this range of ten metres, the round made a catastrophic mess of the soldier's face. The thunder of the chopper above the house masked the retort of the rifle, giving Danny an extra half second before the man on the right realised what was happening. By that time it was too late. Another shot. Another kill.

He climbed over the tree trunk and sprinted the ten metres to the safe house. The door was ajar. Weapon engaged, he pushed it open with his right foot and stepped inside. An entrance hall, twenty metres long. It seemed to extend the entire length of this single-storey building. There was a door at the far end, guarded by a black-clad soldier who raised his weapon the moment Danny appeared. It was the last thing he ever did. Another round from Danny's M4 and he lay dead on the floor.

There were four doors leading off the corridor, two on either side, and different sounds throbbed in the air: the chopper, the barking of voices in a language Danny instantly recognised as Russian, one gunshot, a second. More shouting, then screams. Danny kicked his way into the first room on the left. There were two soldiers in there, both with their backs to him. Against the far wall were between ten and fifteen of Asu's child soldiers. Some of them were armed but none were sufficiently brave to raise their weapons against these two black-clad commandos.

The Russian SF soldiers, however, were raising theirs.

It was obvious to Danny what was about to happen. These child soldiers, some of them no older than ten, were about to be massacred.

He wouldn't let that happen.

He shot the two soldiers from behind, pumping a single round into each man's back at point-blank range. Their weapons clattered on the ground as they fell, and the children stared at the scene of sudden violence with a weird lack of emotion, as if they were used to such sights. None of them moved until Danny shouted '*Go!*' and pointed at the door. As he stepped back into the corridor he was aware of the kids rushing towards the door, but he had to refocus his attention. There was movement at the far end of the house. Danny watched as two figures emerged from the second door on the right, about ten metres from his position. His finger was resting on the trigger of his M4, but he held his fire as he saw the scene unfold.

Clara and Buckingham had their hands on their heads and looked terrified. Danny expected one of Asu's men to be with them, but his stomach turned as he saw that they were being held at gunpoint not by the Syrian rebels, but by three Spetznaz soldiers.

One of whom had clocked him and was about to fire.

Danny couldn't risk a shot. The five figures at the far end of the corridor were all moving, and he was as likely to take out one of his companions as one of the enemy. He hit the ground just in time. A burst of rounds splintered into the wall just above him. There were screams from the child soldiers, but no casualties yet as they made their way out of the main door. One of the SF soldiers dropped to one knee in the firing position, clearly preparing to take Danny out. Staying still was his worst mistake. Danny already had his weapon trained on the target. The Russian went down before he could take a shot.

All the kids were out of the house. They were on their own now: there was nothing more Danny could do for them. All his concentration was on Buckingham and Clara. Of the two remaining soldiers, one was hustling them out of the rear door at the end of the corridor, the other was turning to fire on Danny. Danny took another shot, but this time his accuracy failed him. The round thudded into the back wall of the house, just inches from Clara. He rolled away, through the door of the first room – and just in time, because a burst of rounds thundered along the corridor. Had he still been in the line of fire, he'd have been mincemeat.

He jumped to his feet, desperately trying to work out his next play. These Russian commandos were here to eliminate the occupants of the safe house – that much was clear. That Clara and Buckingham were still alive could mean only one thing: somebody had decided that this stray British pair needed interrogating. And it wouldn't happen here. The chopper was still hovering above. They had the means of extracting their hostages with ease.

Danny took a deep breath and peered round the door frame.

The corridor was empty. Clara, Buckingham and their Spetznaz guard were gone.

The door at the end was swinging open.

Danny advanced. As he passed the remaining doors – two on the right, one on the left – he kicked them in to see what secrets they contained. Dead bodies. Ten, maybe more, in each room.

They were exclusively male, so far as he could see, and Danny assumed that these were Asu's commanders and entourage, though their bodies were so freshly butchered by Spetznaz rounds that it was difficult to tell for sure. He looked for Basheba, and Asu himself. It was difficult to be sure, but he didn't think they were among the dead.

He continued towards the back door. Ten metres. Five.

Something was happening outside. The noise of the Mi8 had grown louder. Closer. The door started swinging to and fro on its hinges. Each time it opened, Danny felt a rush of air against his face. When he was a metre from the door, he could feel the vibrations from the chopper's engines judder through him. It was landing. The Spetznaz team were leaving, and any hostages would be going with them . . .

He kicked at the door with the rifle butt still pressed hard into his shoulder, taking in his surroundings in an instant.

The area behind the safe house was a dilapidated wasteland. It had once been a large courtyard, about twenty metres square, but the chain-link fencing that had enclosed it now lay on the ground, the uprights broken or ripped out. Surrounding the courtyard were the skeletons of bombed buildings. In most cases the front had crumbled and the roof had caved in. Inside, the ceilings had collapsed, littering the floors with rubble. They were clearly deserted.

Unlike the courtyard itself.

The Mi8 had landed. It sat, a great, black, hulking beast in the centre of the courtyard, its tail pointing towards Danny, its nose away from the safe house. Its rotors were spinning fast, flattening down the air and kicking up dust all around, so that Danny had to half-close his eyes. He was too late to stop the Spetznaz soldiers loading Buckingham and Clara into the chopper. Then, to his two o'clock, he saw Asu. Terror was etched on his face, but he didn't look nearly so terrified as Basheba. The rebel leader had the crook of his left arm around her neck and was pressing a revolver to her right temple. A kid – Danny recognised him as Basheba's boy – was tugging at his mother's arm, screaming something that was totally drowned out by the aircraft's noise.

What the hell did Asu think he was doing? Did the sickening coward really imagine that threatening Basheba's life would stop these Spetznaz commandos from doing what they had come here to do? Did he really think they'd spare his life to save hers?

'*Let her go!*' Danny bellowed.

Too late.

It was the chopper's side-gunner who took them. Even the thunder of the rotors couldn't drown the sound of his Minigun, which was trained directly on all three Syrians from no more than six metres away. The short burst of 7.62mm killed them, of course, but it did more than that. At such close range the rebel leader, his daughter-in-law and her young son practically exploded on the spot. In a handful of seconds, once the nauseating flurry of guts had slapped down on to the ground, they didn't so much resemble humans as butchered animal carcasses, cut open and bleeding.

Incoming fire. One of the Spetznaz soldiers who had forced Buckingham and Clara into the chopper had spotted Danny and was firing at him from the side of the chopper, even as it started to rise. Danny had no other option. He dived backwards, through the swinging door, into the relative safety of the house, landing with a thump next to the body of the commando he'd downed. He felt like shouting with frustration, like thumping his fists on the floor. Everything had happened so quickly, and now Basheba and her son were dead, while Buckingham and Clara were in enemy hands. In the three or four minutes since the contact had started, everything had gone to shit. The air stank of gunfire, flames and death, and a little voice inside Danny told him it was a miracle he wasn't among the dead.

He stood. His intention was to get outside again, to see which way the helicopter was headed. But then he noticed movement at his feet.

The commando was still alive.

His face was creased with pain. Danny figured that the round from the M4 had hit his body armour and crushed a few ribs, knocking him out in the process. Now, though, he was coming round. Danny wasn't going to give him enough time to get his bearings. He dropped heavily on the soldier's chest, pressing his knees down hard on the plate hangars. The soldier's eyes widened in agony.

'OK, Dmitri,' Danny hissed. '*I* know you speak English, and *you* know I'm not going to fuck around. Where's the chopper headed? Where are they taking the prisoners?'

He didn't expect an immediate answer. If this guy had had SF training, he'd be practised in resistance to interrogation. It was up to Danny to make sure that resistance crumpled quickly. He pulled his knife from his chest rig and got to work.

In Libya he'd got a militant talking simply by piercing his hand. But this soldier was a tougher nut to crack. He held the guy's left wrist and with a single swipe made a swift incision down the webbed skin between his third and fourth fingers. The blade took him as far as the knuckle and it must have severed an artery, because the blood flow was sudden, explosive and pumped in time with the Russian's accelerated heartbeat. Danny stashed the bloodied knife in his chest rig, then grabbed the fingers on either side of the cut and wrenched them apart. The commando screamed as his flesh tore halfway up his hand, exposing tendons and thin bones. Blood poured over Danny's hands, but he ignored it. All he wanted was an answer.

'You've got ten seconds to tell me where they're going before I do the other hand. After that, it'll be your dick.'

That was all it needed. The soldier started gibbering, a

confused welter of words cloaked in a Russian accent, but Danny could discern a single place name: Damascus.

He pulled out the knife again and laid the tip against the soft underside of the man's right eye. 'Where in Damascus?'

His victim's breath was coming in short, sharp gasps. The hand was pissing blood. At this rate, the guy didn't have much consciousness left in him.

'*Where in Damascus?*' Danny gently pressed the knife, indenting the flesh. A tiny spot of blood appeared.

'*Mukhabarat,*' the soldier whispered, and Danny recognised the Arabic word. Syria's secret police.

'*Shit!*' Their headquarters would be just about the most heavily defended place in the whole stinking country. Danny knew how to choose his battles, and this was one he couldn't win by himself.

He needed help.

He stood up, re-sheathed his knife and replaced his Sig. But there was no way he could leave this man alive, not with the knowledge that Danny had a lead on Buckingham and Clara. Yet the guy was a soldier, just like him. He deserved a quick exit. Danny took out the Sig, extended his right arm and discharged a single round into the Russian's head. His whole body juddered and fell still, by which time Danny was already on the move. Grim-faced and purposeful, he strode back up the corridor to the front entrance and out into the square.

Dawn was coming. The trees were still burning. On the periphery of his vision, Danny could make out some of the kids he'd just released from the safe house, hiding on the corners of side streets or in doorways. Some ran off when they saw Danny appear. One little boy was hiding behind the fallen tree. He didn't move. His wide eyes were fixed on Danny, who approached him without hesitation. He pulled out some of the notes Taff had given him and handed them to the kid, who grabbed them greedily, his eyes riveted on Danny's bloody hands. Danny mimed driving a car, then offered the child another note but snatched it away before he could take it.

'Can you find me a car?' Danny said, miming the act of steering.

The little boy nodded. 'Car,' he repeated.

'Find me a car, I'll give you this,' Danny said, waving the note in front of the boy's face again.

It was all that was needed. The boy signed to Danny to follow him, then turned and scurried across the square, thin and ragged amid the smoke and the grey light of dawn.

TWENTY-FIVE

'This isn't nearly as bad as it seems,' Buckingham said. 'I have influence. I know people.' Clara hoped her look fully conveyed her contempt for him, and for the plain stupidity of what he'd just said.

They were crouched on the floor of a dirty, stinking helicopter. Their hands were tied behind their backs. Three black-clad commandos had them at gunpoint. One of their number had just butchered Basheba and her son. And Asu.

For several minutes now, Buckingham had been steeling himself for this moment. He jutted his chin out at one of the soldiers. 'I'm a representative of Her Majesty's government,' he said, speaking loudly and slowly. 'I demand that you explain who you are and where you are taking us.'

The craggy faces of the commandos didn't change.

'This is intolerable,' Buckingham went on. 'In the absence of a British consulate in Syria, I demand that you deliver us to an alternative embassy of a European Union state for consular protection. Do you understand what I'm telling you?'

He tried to stand up. Bad move. The commando he'd been addressing delivered a brutal blow to the side of Buckingham's head with the barrel of his assault rifle. It knocked all the bluster out of him, and he collapsed to the floor with his head in his hands and started to shake.

Clara felt strangely numb, as though she was so jaded by the horrors she had witnessed that there was little else anyone could do to shock her. But then the glimpse she had seen of Basheba and her little boy being shot replayed itself in her head. She leaned over to one side and vomited copiously.

Their captors just looked on.

It was growing light outside. Wiping flecks of vomit from the side of her mouth, Clara shivered, suddenly cold. She'd lost track of time, she realised, and so she had no way of judging how long they'd been in this foul helicopter before it started to lose height. All she knew was that the prospect of landing made the fear run through her veins again. Where were these men taking them? What was going to happen next?

The Mi8 had barely touched down when two soldiers hauled Clara and Buckingham to their feet and forced them out of the side door. The downdraught from the rotors threw grit into Clara's face. She closed her eyes as she felt an arm drag her away from the helicopter. Only when she was a good fifteen metres away could she open them and quickly take in her surroundings: a featureless patch of desert, not unlike the location of Sorgen's camp. A pale-brown military truck was waiting for them with its rear doors open. The commandos shoved them inside and the same three who had kept guard in the helicopter now took up positions in the back of the truck. The doors slammed shut, and the only light trickled in through letterbox-shaped peepholes on either side of the vehicle at about the height, Clara noticed, that a man would hold a gun. As the truck moved off, she reminded herself to try to keep better track of time.

It was an hour and a half, Clara estimated, before they came to a halt. They sat in silence for another minute before a sharp rap on the rear doors startled her. The doors opened and the guards pushed their hostages out. Clara landed heavily on her side, Buckingham right next to her. She cried out in pain, then silently cursed herself for displaying weakness like that. The streak of obstinacy that her father had tried so hard to quell in her was asserting itself again. She was damned if she was going to give these people the satisfaction of thinking they'd crushed her.

She pushed herself to her knees and found that she was in a yard at the rear of a nondescript three-storey building. The yard measured no more than ten metres by ten, but was surrounded by brick walls a good five metres high and topped with thick rolls of barbed wire. Just before a pair of metal gates clanged shut, Clara caught sight of a single armed guard outside. The sound of traffic reached her ears: she was in a busy town or city. Before she could take in anything else, two of the commandos pulled her and Buckingham to their feet and dragged them across a parking bay to a small door at the back of the building. It opened on to a flight of stone steps leading down into a dark basement. One of the commandos pushed Clara down the first couple of steps but she retained her balance. When they pushed Buckingham, however, she broke his fall and tumbled to the bottom. Still desperate not to show any emotion, she was then manhandled along a dark corridor by one of her brutal, silent captors. Buckingham was shouting something inane behind her, but she'd long since zoned out. The soldier flung her into a pitch-black room, and as he clanged the door to and locked it, it was almost a relief to realise she had been separated from her companion.

The relief lasted only as long as it took to inhale once. The air stank. Not an ordinary stink, but a disgusting fug that seemed to coat Clara's throat, making her want to retch. There was a smell of excrement, but also of something else she couldn't quite identify, and didn't want to: a rotten, gamey stench like meat that had festered for days. She knew there was something else in this room. Something in the centre. She didn't want to know what it was. Her body fought against the need to breathe, and she found herself squeezing her nostrils and gulping nervously at the air. Trying to keep her mind off whatever it was she was sharing this room with, she walked its perimeter to measure the space. Twelve paces by thirteen. Cold concrete walls and floor. She crouched down in a corner opposite the door, pulled her T-shirt up over her nose and put her hands over her head.

She'd been sitting still like that for about thirty seconds when she heard the rustling sound. Rats, she thought. Nearby. She shot to her feet and the sudden movement made the rustling stop, but only momentarily.

When it started again, Clara screamed. She couldn't help it. She didn't even know what it was that she was shouting, but it seemed to have an immediate effect. A key turned in the lock and the door opened. A silhouetted figure appeared in the doorway. By the scant light that seeped in from the corridor, Clara could see that this person, a man, was short – no taller than her – but broad. She also saw that there was indeed something in the middle of the room, but it was still indistinct. And by the time the newcomer closed the door behind him, Clara still had no idea what it was.

She didn't move. All she could hear was her own heartbeat and the strangely heavy breathing of the man who had just entered the room. She could see nothing.

'You are a spy, of course.' The voice was high-pitched, weaselly, but it had a certain precision and the accent was English. Relief flooded over Clara once again.

Once again it was short-lived.

'I know what you're thinking,' the voice continued. 'You're thinking that, through some diplomatic channel or another, the British government's representatives will have you out of here very soon. Allow me to assure you that this will *not* happen. *Nobody* knows you are here. As far as everybody else is concerned, you have disappeared. Which means I can do, really, whatever I want with you.'

Silence.

'I know what else you are thinking. That as long as you *know* something I *want* to know, I will be obliged to keep you alive. This is true, but do not allow that thought to comfort you. There will come a point at which you do not *want* to continue living. A point where the idea of continuing your pathetic existence will be quite intolerable. It's at that point that you'll tell me everything – who you are, what you know about the anti-government rebels, the names and locations of any other agents in our country. Then you'll beg me to kill you, and I'll oblige.'

'But I'm just a doctor, and—' Clara said.

'I should point out,' the voice continued, 'that reducing you to a state where you no longer wish to live will not be a great hardship for me. Quite the opposite. I rather enjoy my work. It gives me pleasure. I was born and bred in Kent, you know. Not much call for my skills in Tunbridge Wells, so I find myself here. The gentleman in the next room will crumble easily. I can sense it in him. In you, however, there is a little more strength. I'm pleased to note it, my dear, not just for myself but for my helpers. Good torturers – I mean those truly skilled in the application of pain, rather than brutes who use it as a blunt weapon – are harder to find than you might imagine, and they get bored easily.' He sighed dramatically. 'We are like addicts, you see. We soon forget our last fix, and think only of the next one.'

A pause.

The voice became little more than a whisper.

'Would you like to see your room mates?'

Clara shook her head in the darkness.

'Rebel sympathisers. One has to make an example of them.'

A sudden light. The man was holding up a torch. Its beam was very bright and pencil-thin. It stabbed at Clara's eyes and she clenched them shut.

'Look, my dear. Do look.'

She didn't want to, but somehow she couldn't help herself. Her eyes gradually opened and were drawn to the ceiling in the middle of the room, lit up by the torch.

There were two sturdy meat hooks. Hanging from each was a piece of rope, taut, thick and about half a metre in length. And hanging from each rope by their wrists was a naked corpse, one male, one female.

Clara saw their heads hanging heavily, open jaws resting against their chests, eyes wide with horror. She saw their pronounced ribs and concave stomachs. As she stared aghast at the cuts and bruises that covered them, and at the way a broken rib jutted out from the man's skin, her tormentor lowered the torch a little.

Clara bent double and started dry heaving. Where the genitals should have been, there was nothing. Just a gaping hole as though someone had eviscerated the area with a monstrously sharp scoop. Blood was smeared all over the corpses' inner thighs, and had dripped all the way down to their ankles. The exposed flesh appeared to move. In the fraction of a second before she averted her eyes, Clara saw that the wounded areas were infested with hundreds of tiny white maggots.

The torch moved down to the floor. Here were piles of excrement – while they were alive, the prisoners had clearly been forced to defecate where they hung – but there was something else too. Hunks of flesh were draped over the faeces, and encrusted with dried blood. The organs that had been ripped from the two bodies were not individually identifiable, but it was clear that they'd been left to rot where they fell. The flesh and faecal matter were likewise covered in maggots and appeared to move.

The torch hadn't been on for more than ten seconds, but it was ten seconds Clara wished she had never experienced. Now her tormenter turned it off. Darkness returned.

'I don't want you to think,' said the man, 'that I or any of my assistants would perform such surgery on you. Not at first, at least. You're female, after all, and Western, which is a great novelty for them. I'm not that way inclined myself, but I can't deny them *their* entertainment.'

'You've got it wrong,' Clara pleaded. 'I'm not a spy. I'm a—'

'Yes, yes, a doctor. A doctor who just *happened* to be hiding with the most wanted man in Syria. I think, my dear, I shall leave you for a while to contemplate just how preposterous your story is. Please don't worry your pretty head too much about the rats. They're much more likely to feed on the dead than the living. By the time they get to you, you won't be in a position to feel their sharp little teeth. In any case, there's really no point in screaming again. I'll come when I'm ready for you, and not before.'

The man turned and opened the door, locking it firmly behind him.

09.00 hrs.

To Danny's left, the rising sun had streamed into the car that the boy had led him to – a light-grey Peugeot with battered body-work and torn upholstery. It was old – the windows had manual winders – and the kid had even looked a little apologetic about the state of it. It was fine by Danny. Old models were a lot easier to hot-wire. Beneath the steering wheel, the wires spilled out like spaghetti. The engine was noisy as it turned over, but it worked.

There was not much traffic. Danny doubted he'd seen more than a hundred vehicles in the fifty-odd klicks between Homs and his current location. But about a quarter of them had been military, and each of those made him tense up. He couldn't get to Damascus quickly *and* stealthily. If anyone stopped him, his only possible response was violence. His M4 was on the passenger seat beside him, his Sig on his lap. The first soldier to tap on his window and ask him to wind it down wouldn't have time to regret it.

Danny couldn't decipher the Arabic road signs. He'd studied his mapping, however. Homs to Damascus: 160 kilometres. If nobody hindered him, he'd be there by midday.

But that was too much to hope for.

Thirty klicks from the Syrian capital, he saw a roadblock fifty metres ahead: barriers across the road, and a low concrete hut on the left-hand side. Three vehicles queuing to head north, four on Danny's side of the road heading south. Four armed guards, two at each barrier. And more inside the hut, Danny reckoned. Another two, maybe three.

One thing was certain: he couldn't talk his way through. The soldiers would search him as soon as they realised he was a foreign national. And when they found his assault rifle, pistol and ammo, he'd have no chance.

It only left him one option.

He checked his rear-view mirror. Two vehicles behind him, the first five metres away, the second about ten behind that. Then nothing for as far back as he could see, perhaps two kilometres. Current speed: 50 kph. He slammed on the brakes and the driver behind him sounded his horn before overtaking. Then he reduced his speed until the second car was forced to overtake, leaving him at the back of the little convoy as they approached the checkpoint, now only twenty metres away.

Ten metres. Five.

All three cars came to a halt.

There was only one car on the opposite side of the road now, and as the barrier rose for it, Danny briefly considered swinging over to the other side and breaking through. If he did that, he'd have half the Syrian army on his tail. No. If he was going to force his way through this checkpoint, he needed to make sure there were no witnesses left behind. He leaned over the passenger seat and wound down the window, before propping his M4 barrel downwards, the butt resting against the door just below the glass.

The barrier in front of him rose, and the first car moved through. Danny and the next car edged forwards.

Of the two guards on Danny's side of the road, one walked over to the driver's window of the car in front and rapped on it with the butt of his AK-47. The second walked round to the back of the car, eyeing it suspiciously. Fifteen metres to Danny's ten-thirty, the soldiers on the opposite side stood on the edge of the road, talking together.

The driver in front lowered his window. The guard bent down to talk to him. Forty-five seconds later the barrier opened and the car passed through.

Which left just Danny and the guards. He looked in the rear-view mirror. A vehicle was approaching about a klick back, shimmering in the heat. He'd have to work fast.

He edged forwards and stopped in front of the barrier.

The guards' routine was the same. One of them walked to the rear of the Peugeot. The other knocked on the window with his AK. Danny raised the Sig and lowered the window.

The guard bent down. His face appeared.

Danny fired.

There was blood, of course. But the force of the round as it pierced the guard's forehead knocked him backwards before Danny could see the full damage. He thrust the door open – its bottom edge scraped across the dead soldier – pushed the man's body aside and climbed out. It had all happened so quickly that the second guard, just two metres away, barely had time to register what was going on. Danny nailed him with a single chest shot, and the man slumped to the ground.

He had to keep up the momentum if he was going to retain the element of surprise. Using the Peugeot to shield him, he turned and rested his gun arm on its roof, the two soldiers on the other side of the road firmly in his sights. One of them was looking around for somewhere to run, the other was raising his rifle. Danny took out the potential gunman first, sending a round from the Sig straight in his stomach. The second guy was now sprinting away from the checkpoint. Danny aimed his shot fractionally in front of the fleeing guard. By the time bullet met flesh, it was on target. The soldier hit the ground.

The oncoming vehicle – Danny could now see it was a car – was 500 metres away. He looked over to the concrete hut. Were there more targets in there? Did they know what was happening? Reholstering his Sig, he hurried round the back of the Peugeot and then along its length, grabbing his M4 from the open passenger window as he passed. He released the safety switch as he strode towards the hut.

Distance to the door: fifteen metres. It began to open inwards. Danny didn't wait for an enemy target to show himself. He simply fired at the door itself – two short bursts that kicked up a flurry of splintered wood. Distance: ten metres. Despite the ferocity of the burst from the M4, the door was still only a few inches ajar. That told Danny something was blocking it on the other side. A corpse. Nobody was going to risk exiting from that direction now. He swerved to the left and upped his pace, dashing round to the back of the hut. Sure enough, he saw two figures emerging. Five seconds later they lay dead on the ground.

The approaching car was 250 metres from the checkpoint. Whoever was driving, Danny didn't want him to be able to give a detailed description of himself or the Peugeot. He hit the ground and trained the rifle to a position twenty metres in front of the car. He fired a final burst and the car headed straight into the stream of rounds. Its tyres exploded and it skidded round 180 degrees before coming to a noisy halt. By that time Danny was already running back to the Peugeot. Seconds later he was pressing down on the counterweight that raised the barrier. And seconds after that, he was away.

*   *   *

The door of Clara's prison opened again. In one way this was good: it allowed a small breath of less putrid air to circulate in the dark room. In another way it was bad: the short silhouette of her tormentor reappeared in the door frame.

'Mr Buckingham,' said the voice, 'is a gentleman.'

A pause.

'Yes, we know his name. He told us immediately. And yours too, Clara. Touchingly, he insists on sticking to the fiction that you and he have agreed. It won't last, of course – self-interest always prevails over honour – but I thought it might be instructive for you to watch how we do it.'

'He's telling the *truth*,' said Clara, sobbing.

The man didn't reply. He stepped aside to allow two others, much taller and broader than him, to enter the room. Clara cried out as they crossed the room, stepping around the corpses hanging from the ceiling before dragging her out into the corridor. Through her tears she could see that these men were Syrian. As for her tormentor, she saw him only from the back. He was a dumpy little man, wearing plain chinos and a beige shirt. He opened a door on the right. Clara was forced to follow.

She found herself in a room measuring about six metres by three. In the far wall was a large window, about three metres wide and two high, that looked on to another room roughly three times as big as this one. On the wall to the right of the window was a grey box with a speaker grille and a switch. The second room was brightly lit by ceiling-mounted spotlights that stung Clara's eyes as they had become used to constant darkness. A lean, naked man was hanging by his arms from a rope attached to a hook in the ceiling. It took perhaps thirty seconds for Clara's eyesight to adjust and confirm what she already suspected: it was Buckingham.

Her tormentor stood inches from the window, next to the grille, his back still to her. She could just make out the reflection of his face. Jowly. Sweaty. The eyes bright with expectation.

Buckingham was shouting. Clara knew this because his mouth was moving, but she couldn't hear his voice.

Another man entered the room beyond the glass. He was in his late thirties and had straggly, shoulder-length hair and thick-rimmed glasses. He was holding something that looked like a riding whip but consisted of several thin strips of leather about half a metre long. In his other hand he had a small, white plastic spray bottle, the sort of thing an old lady might use to water her houseplants.

The short man flicked the switch beneath the grille. Buckingham's voice flooded into the observation room, screaming and hoarse. '*Let me down . . . let me down!*' He was clearly in great pain. Another flick of the switch and his voice was silenced, though Clara could tell he was still shrieking.

And then his new companion got to work.

He was clearly well practised with the whip. He flicked lightly, and the leather strips licked against Buckingham's flat belly and his genitals. A number of thin red welts immediately appeared where the leather had struck, vertically up his belly and on his penis, as though the leather had been doused in red paint.

'I've always found this a very effective way of loosening a man's tongue,' the short man said quietly as Buckingham's jaw stretched open in a silent scream.

'I swear he's telling you the truth,' said Clara. 'I am a doctor. Médecins Sans Frontières will confirm it.'

Inside the room, Buckingham's torturer had raised the spray bottle.

'Salt water,' said the small man. 'Nothing more. I've found that the simplest methods are often the best. I think this might be worth listening to, don't you?'

He flicked the switch again as the torturer sprayed Buckingham's wounds. The sound that came from the grille was almost inhuman. More like an animal in pain. Clara felt her knees buckle. She wanted to beg this dreadful man beside her to make it stop, but she found that her terror had robbed her of the power even to speak.

Her tormentor turned, and for the first time she saw his face in the light. Piggy little eyes. Flared nostrils. Moist, sensuous lips.

'And now, my dear, I think it's time for us to start on you. Unless you'd like to stop your fiction and start telling us the truth?'

11.37 hrs.

Damascus. The capital city and nerve centre of the Syrian administration.

Danny had been briefed that there was no British embassy here. Like most states, the Brits had abandoned Damascus. But his intel was that the Czech Embassy was still active. As an EU member it was obliged to offer assistance to other member nations. Danny had noted its location on his map before leaving the UK.

The Czech Embassy was a plain, dark-brown building, situated at the intersection of two roads in a quiet part of the Abou Roumaneh district. It was surrounded by two-metre-high green metal railings, the top quarter bent outwards to make them more difficult to scale. Each of the three floors had a balcony – these were also protected by railings – and all the windows were barred. Danny hadn't spotted a trail in the time it had taken to get here, but that didn't mean there wasn't one, and he had no intention of staying out in the open any longer than was necessary. Two wheels of his vehicle were on the pavement as he jumped out. He fully expected there to be an armed presence in the building. Embassy protection in a war zone was bread and butter work for any country's special forces. Danny had done it himself, escorting the British ambassador in Kabul to *shuras* with warlords in the Afghan badlands. He let his rifle hang around his neck before entering, and walked through the main door with his hands clasped above his head.

The embassy's reception area looked deserted. There was a time when it would have been thronging with foreign nationals seeking visas or other consular assistance, but anyone in their right mind had now taken their government's advice and left Syria. It was a large room, some fifteen metres by twelve, and had seating areas along the two long sides and dog-eared posters of Prague and other Czech beauty spots on the walls. At one end of the room was a long reception desk, and it was only as he was stepping into the building that he noticed two armed guards lounging casually behind it. When they saw an armed man entering the building, they sprang up, raised their rifles and started barking at Danny in Czech. Within seconds he was face down on the floor and his hands were being plasticuffed behind his back. He didn't resist – not even when they pulled him back up to his feet and confiscated his M4 and his Sig, along with the wad of dollars Taff had given him. They then escorted him at gunpoint to a windowless, unfurnished basement room and locked him inside.

Danny knew the Czech ambassador would see him soon. A heavily armed Brit rocking up on his doorstep would have all the hallmarks of a potential diplomatic incident. This wasn't something he'd want to delegate.

He was right. After ten minutes the guards led him from the basement room and up an echoing flight of stairs behind the reception area to a room at the back of the first floor that looked on to an unlovely lightwell. Here a gaunt man with a bushy grey moustache sat behind a wooden desk, a nervous, pensive look on his face. Danny's weapons were on top of a low cupboard behind the ambassador. His money lay on the desk. The two armed guards stood menacingly by the door.

'You speak English?' Danny asked the ambassador.

The ambassador nodded. He made no attempt to stop him as Danny, still handcuffed, picked up his money and flicked through it.

'It's two thousand light,' he said.

The ambassador raised his hands in a gesture of apology, but Danny saw the greed and corruption in his eyes.

'I need a private room and a secure, encrypted connection to MI6 in London. Can you fix that?'

'Perhaps,' the ambassador said.

'Tell them you have a communication from call sign Kilo Alpha Six Four. And get your men to remove the grey Peugeot out front. The Syrian authorities will be looking for it.'

The ambassador thought about that for all of five seconds, then issued an instruction to the guards. One of them disappeared. The other uncuffed Danny before following his colleague.

'May I ask,' said the ambassador in excellent English, 'the nature of your business in Damascus?'

'No,' Danny replied.

'Do not misunderstand me, but the sooner you leave, the happier I will be.'

'Trust me, pal. I feel the same.'

The ambassador stood up. 'Please wait here. I apologise for the surroundings. My real office is in the front of the building. Less safe, they tell me. I will see to your communications.' He left the room, returning a couple of minutes later. 'Follow me,' he said.

He led Danny to a room directly opposite his temporary office. A young man sat at a laptop, which was connected by a short lead to a mobile sat phone. The noises coming from the computer sounded like an old-fashioned fax machine: the technician was clearly having trouble connecting. Ignoring him and the ambassador, Danny edged towards a barred window that looked down on to the street below, keeping out of sight by staying to one side of it. There were no pedestrians and very little traffic. A blue Citroën drove by. Four minutes and thirty seconds later it passed by again, going in the same direction. Coincidence? Unlikely.

The laptop fell silent. The young man said something to the ambassador after an image popped up on the screen: an empty room. A face appeared. Danny walked over and recognised it immediately. Carrington, Buckingham's boss. The spook who had sent them on this job.

He looked at the ambassador and the technician. 'I'll need the room,' he said.

The ambassador nodded rather reluctantly. The two men left.

The connection was poor. Carrington's face pixelated every few seconds and his voice had an almost robotic quality through the laptop's tinny speakers. As he spoke, the first part of his sentence broke up. '. . . to see you, Black. We were beginning to worry, and we certainly weren't expecting you to turn up in Damascus.'

'We've got problems.'

'So I understand. Let's hear it.'

Danny was used to debriefs. What was relevant, what was not. He recounted the bare bones of the past few days to Carrington in not much more than a minute.

A pause. Even though the connection was poor, Carrington's displeasure was unmistakable. 'This is regrettable,' he said.

'Might have turned out better if you'd been up front with me from the start.'

Carrington smiled indulgently, as though Danny was a petulant child. 'We couldn't tell you the real reason for the operation, Black,' he said. 'If you'd been captured and interrogated, the jolly old *entente cordiale* with the French would have been well and truly shafted. I'm sure you understand.'

'Not really,' Danny said. 'I'd have lasted a lot longer than Buckingham under interrogation.'

'Of course. Think of it as damage limitation. Buckingham is an insincere little toad, as you've no doubt observed.'

At least that was something they could agree upon. 'I can't take on the Damascus *Mukhabarat*,' Danny said. 'You have to get on to the Syrians. Put some pressure on to get Buckingham and Clara released.'

'We'll do what we can, of course,' Carrington said evasively. He smiled again. 'This business with Taff Davies is unfortunate.'

'You knew he was part of the private military team?' Danny said.

'Naturally.'

'Then why didn't you tell me?'

Carrington removed his glasses, inspected them at a distance of a few inches, then wiped them on his tie before putting them back on and continuing. 'I was hoping not to have this conversation with you, Black. Now it seems it's unavoidable. You're quite alone?'

Danny nodded.

'When Sorgen and Asu's father was killed in Paris three weeks ago, the family of the suicide bomber, an Algerian national, were also found dead. The working theory was that the bomber dealt with them before the hit, but there was a curious anomaly. French investigators found DNA traces that matched a former French Foreign Legion member called Liam Skinner. Does the name mean anything to you?'

'You know it does,' Danny said. 'If you want to speak to him, tough – he's fertilising the desert.'

'I think, on balance, that I'm pleased to hear it. His file doesn't make edifying reading. I'll spare you the details of how the Algerian's children died.'

Danny shrugged. There was nothing Carrington could say about Skinner that would surprise him.

'When we learned that one of Taff Davies' team may have been involved, certain alarm bells started ringing. It's not that we knew for sure that he was batting for the other side. We didn't even particularly suspect it, as these private military chaps go from one contract to another all the time. But we did feel the need for an insurance policy. And that insurance policy, of course, is you.'

'What the hell are you talking about?'

'Really, Black. You're meant to be the Regiment's finest. Are you telling me you didn't wonder why we plucked you straight from the battlefield to lead this patrol?'

Danny had no answer to that.

'Davies is a damn good soldier,' Carrington continued. 'Too good to be allowed to roam free if he's taken it upon himself to make a monkey of the British government. And it looks like he's done exactly that, so now it's time for us to cash in on our insurance. You know Davies better than anyone. You know his methods and his tradecraft. You're to locate him immediately, and eliminate him and the remainder of his team. When that's done, we'll get you out of there.'

Danny clenched his jaw and looked straight into the webcam.

'No,' he said.

'It's a direct order, Black.'

An image flashed in Danny's mind: Taff, standing outside Sorgen's tent. He could have stopped Danny, but he'd let him go.

'I won't do it.'

There was a silence, but despite the pixelation Danny could read a calculating look on the spook's face. Finally, after about ten seconds, Carrington spoke again.

'Remarkable thing, DNA,' he said. 'Imagine. Seven billion people on the earth, and we could identify Skinner's beyond any doubt whatsoever. It's certainly changed the way we do things. Not that you'd remember. You were still a child when profiling became routine. Shame really. It could have helped a lot when the RUC were investigating who shot your old man. And your mother, of course, God rest her soul.' Another pause. 'I take it Buckingham slipped that little nugget of information into the conversation at some point?'

Danny just stared.

'What did Taff Davies tell you when you asked him, Black? That an unknown IRA gunman entered the hospital where you were born and escaped after killing your mother and wounding your father? That the only evidence they ever found was the scrubs the gunman was wearing bundled up under a bush in the hospital's grounds?' Carrington nodded. 'That's all true,' he said. 'But there's something he *didn't* tell you, because he didn't know himself. A year or so after the shooting, Special Branch found themselves in a position to analyse those scrubs. They still contained DNA from your parents' blood, of course, but also an overwhelming amount from the man who'd worn them.'

A pause.

'We know who killed your parents, Danny. We've known since you were a child. I wouldn't be surprised if, somewhere deep down, you know too.'

Danny found himself holding his breath. Surely he wasn't about to be told what he *thought* he was about to be told.

Numbness. And then a strange kind of anticipated grief, reduced to a single point in his chest.

'I'm afraid there's no doubt about it, Black. Davies was the gunman. He killed your mother. He *tried* to kill your father. If you had a mind to, you could blame your brother's – how can we put it? – *difficulties* on him too. There's no doubt they stem from the trauma of what he witnessed that day.' Another smile. 'Listen to me. Quite the psychiatrist, eh?'

'I don't believe you,' said Danny.

'Ah, but I think you do, Danny. I really think you do. MI6 has sat on the knowledge all these years because it suited our purposes having Davies as a gun for hire, doing our dirty work through the agency of private military contracts. But I rather think he's past his sell-by date, don't you?'

Danny was shaking his head. It didn't make sense. Taff *loved* his mother. It was obvious. He'd always been there for his dad. And for him too. Jesus, Kyle had been right. He *had* been more like a father than a friend. 'Why would he do it?' he whispered, more to himself than to Carrington.

'Jolly good question,' Carrington said. 'Perhaps when you catch up with him, you can ask. We have a good idea where you can find him. It seems Buckingham's infinity device didn't end up quite where we expected it to.'

'I put it in Hector's weapon.'

'Ah,' Carrington replied, as if a mystery had been solved. 'We did wonder. Jolly useful, I must say. Kept us abreast of the situation. Would you care to hear the result of your efforts?'

Without waiting for a reply, Carrington looked like he was pressing a button on the table. A sound came over the line. It was muffled – that was to be expected from a listening device hidden in the magazine of an assault rifle – but it was clearly the noise of a vehicle in motion.

Then voices. Indistinct – Danny had to strain to pick up every word.

'Nothing happens until we see the money.' Taff's voice.

'Hugo Buckingham is dead?' Sorgen.

'As a dodo. No bullets. If anyone finds his body, they'll just put it down to an explosion. One of the many.'

A click. A gap. The recording played on.

'*Damn it!* You don't understand what the hell's going on. You're still just a *fucking kid.*'

'Not any more, Taff.' Danny heard his own voice. 'But then I guess we all have to grow up some day, don't we?'

A gap.

Gunfire.

A gap.

A vehicle's engine.

A gap.

Taff's voice. He sounded angry. 'Fuck you, Saunders. When you're out on the ground, then you can start criticising my decisions.'

A pause.

'I'm not a fucking delivery boy. Get someone else to do it.'

Danny realised that he was listening to a phone conversation. 'Hold back my money, Saunders, and you might get an unexpected visitor in the middle of the night. Got it?'

Silence.

'You're a piece of shit, you know that? . . . Yes, I've got the fucking address, 157 Al Kamada Street, Damascus, midnight. You'd better hope your new Syrian mates haven't flattened the place . . .'

Another pause. And then a clattering sound. Danny pictured Taff throwing his phone against the dashboard in rage. He carried on listening.

For a moment, nobody spoke. Then Danny heard Hector's voice.

'What does he want us to do?'

'Shut the fuck up and drive.'

The engine, however, slowed down. Then the sound disappeared entirely. Danny realised that the vehicle had come to a halt.

'What does he want us to do, Taff?' Hector's voice sounded dangerous. 'If you think me and De Fries are going to follow you without knowing what's happening, think again. You already fucked up once not killing that Regiment kid.'

'That "Regiment kid",' Taff spat, 'is a weak-arsed little cunt. If you're worried about him, you're in the wrong fucking game.'

'Just tell us the plan, Taff.'

'Fine. Saunders made a deal with the Syrians. He gave them Asu's location. They've bombed the shit out of him. He wants us to collect his payment from a contact in Damascus. Seven hundred and fifty thousand dollars, in cash. He doesn't want to leave a money trail. Happy?'

'Not really, mucker. You said it yourself. What are we, fucking FedEx?'

'Just shut up and drive.'

The recording ended.

'Charming,' said Carrington, staring directly into the webcam. 'Sixteen kilometres south of Damascus there is a crossroads where the M5 highway meets a road heading east–west along the brow of the hill. An Israeli helicopter with an Apache chaperone will be there to airlift you out of Syria at 01.30 hrs, by which time I expect Davies and his team to be dead. We'll do what we can to get Buckingham and the woman there in time, but don't hold your breath.'

'What about Spud and Greg? Have you done anything about them?'

'I would forget about your friends, Black. They won't be coming home. The most important thing is that Davies is eliminated. Is that understood?'

Danny gave him a dead look. The bastard clearly had no intention of seeing Clara and Buckingham released.

But Danny had other plans.

'Understood,' he said.

They had stripped Clara naked, groping her painfully as they did so. But that was by no means the end of her indignity.

She was in a third bland, concrete room, strapped to something that looked like a hospital bed. On the wall opposite there was a bright yellow hosepipe coiled round a couple of pegs, one end fitted to a tap. She couldn't imagine what it was for. There was a sheet beneath her. It was vile-smelling and covered in blood. Her arms were tied to her side and her legs had been forced apart and then secured that way, leaving her open and exposed. More groping. One of them had forcibly inserted a dry finger. Its fingernail had scraped her internally and she'd screamed. That had just made the two brutes manhandling her laugh as they left her on her own, a bright light dazzling her eyes from above, the only sounds she could hear the occasional scream from elsewhere in this awful place. She shivered with cold, but tears were burning her eyeballs.

What was to come? It didn't bear thinking about. She lay in terrified silence, dreading the moment when the door opened again.

TWENTY-SIX

'Do you know Al Kamada Street?'

Danny was back in the ambassador's temporary office. 'Of course,' the ambassador said. He pulled out a map from his desk and laid it out in front of him. 'It's in the Christian quarter, near Bab Touma. I suggest you avoid it.'

'Why?'

The ambassador shrugged. 'The government is paranoid about Western spies. They keep a close eye on it.' He grinned suddenly. 'But if you want a drink, it's the place to go.'

Danny looked the ambassador up and down. He decided that this was a man on the take. The guy had plundered his cash without even pretending to be embarrassed about it.

'I've got an offer for you,' Danny said. 'Do as I ask and you'll be several hundred thousand pounds sterling richer by tomorrow morning.'

The ambassador's eyes narrowed. 'Go on,' he said quietly.

'You have contacts inside the *Mukhabarat*?' It wasn't really a question.

The ambassador shrugged. 'Perhaps.'

'They have two British captives. If your contact gets them out of there to a safe RV at 01.00 hrs tonight, I'll pay you 100,000 for each of them. There are also two British SAS soldiers who were captured on the west coast a week ago. If they're still alive, same deal: 100 K apiece.'

'Forgive me,' said the ambassador, 'but you don't look like you have that sort of money to spare.'

'I know a man who does. I'll have it before the deadline. Do we have a deal?'

The ambassador nodded slowly. 'We have a deal.'

The door to Clara's room opened. The short man appeared, flanked by two of his goons.

Nobody spoke. Not even Clara, who wouldn't have known what to say even if her throat hadn't been constricted with fear at their sudden arrival. The short man issued an instruction in Arabic – the first time Clara had heard him speak the language – then closed the door behind him and stood in the corner of the room. The two Syrian guards approached Clara's bed. She felt herself trying to close her bound legs, but the straps held them firmly apart. But, to her momentary relief, the men didn't seem interested in that side of things. Instead they stood one on each side of her and adjusted the bed so she was lying at an incline of about twenty degrees, her feet higher than her head. That in itself made her feel dizzy. She heard the short man's footsteps. His face appeared above her, upside down. His nostrils flared slightly, then he stepped away.

Another instruction in Arabic. Clara heard the sound of water. She felt sick all over again. She'd heard of waterboarding, of course. She'd heard that most people lasted only a matter of seconds before crumpling utterly, the horrific sensation of drowning being more than anyone can bear. As the sound of the hose spurting on to the floor grew nearer, she let out an uncontrollable sob. It was the worst thing she could have done. It forced her to inhale deeply, and at that precise moment, the guard carrying the hose lifted it and allowed water to pour over her face.

It was icy cold as it gushed down her throat and nostrils, and although she was lying back, she felt it hit her oesophagus like an internal punch. Her gag reflex instantly kicked in, but fresh water was still flowing over her face, forcing the previous lot back down into her system. It didn't hurt, but the panic it induced was a hundred times worse than any pain the torturers could have inflicted. She wanted to cry out, but she couldn't. Her body arched. Her limbs strained against their bonds. Seconds felt like minutes. She would do anything, *anything*, to make it stop.

Suddenly water was no longer falling on her face. She continued to gag, aware now of the horrific, gurgling, guttural sound that came from her throat as she tried to force the water up out of her lungs while her body screamed at her to breathe in. Moments later she felt a brutal blow to her abdomen, which forced the water up through her nostrils. Finally she was able to suck in some precious oxygen.

And then he was there once more, looking down at her. 'What is your real name, and who are you working for?'

Clara's voice shook as she spoke. 'I promise you . . . *please* . . . I'm telling you the truth . . .'

A flicker of annoyance passed over the man's face. He soon mastered it and smiled his oily smile.

'It seems to me,' he said quietly, 'that we'll have to do it again.'

Clara's screaming only stopped when the water started to flow over her face once more.

19.45 hrs.

Danny watched from a first-floor window, waiting for the blue Citroën that had been circling the embassy all day to complete its drive-past. The ambassador had instructed his men to replenish Danny's ammunition, and had supplied him with a sat phone into which the number of the ambassador's equivalent handset was programmed. As he watched, his mind turned over. He thought of Taff and the mockery he'd made of his life. Maybe it wasn't true. Maybe Carrington was feeding him a stream of bullshit to force him to do the Firm's dirty work. That was clearly the way he did things. He thought back to the conversation about his mother's death he'd had with Taff back in Homs. There'd been no hint that Taff was lying to him then. Danny would only know the truth if he looked his mentor in the eye and asked the question.

And if he didn't like the answer? What then?

He thought of Buckingham and Clara. Of Greg and Spud. All of them suffering at the hands of the Syrian authorities. He'd learned enough about this country over the past week to realise that meant brutal treatment. Were they still alive? Was a hundred grand apiece enough to make some corrupt member of the secret police risk his own skin to get them to Danny's 01.00 RV? Could he trust the Czech ambassador not to double-cross him? Could he trust *anyone*? He didn't know the answer to these questions. All he could do was see where the evening took him. And hope that he was still alive to see the following sunrise.

The blue Citroën passed. He had four minutes and thirty seconds to get out of here.

One minute and thirty seconds later he was walking out of the embassy, his clothes covered by one of the ambassador's grey raincoats. And two minutes after that, he was in the Peugeot, negotiating the streets of night-time Damascus.

20.50 hrs.

One fifty-seven Al Kamada Street was a downmarket hotel – a three-storey prefab building with a glass frontage. It had a name, but the Arabic letters meant nothing to Danny. He pulled over about twenty metres from the entrance, and took a moment to recce it from the safety of his vehicle. He counted the windows of twelve rooms, four on each level, looking down on to the street. Opposite the hotel was a bar. This also had a glass frontage, tinted. A neon sign flickered the words 'Zodiac Lounge' in

English above the entrance. Would Taff be sitting in there? Doubtful. He'd want to keep a low profile.

Danny turned back to the hotel. Was Taff there, waiting to collect Saunders' cash? Danny would put money on it. He'd have arrived in very good time for the midnight RV and Danny felt certain he'd have a room overlooking the street. Even now he'd be at the window. Watching carefully. Assessing any threats. Waiting. And were Hector and De Fries with him? Or were they off looking for other amusements?

Danny looked at his watch. 21.00 hrs. Three hours. He assessed his options. Enter the hotel now and try to locate him? No way. If Taff sensed anything untoward happening before the appointed time, he'd react. If he had Hector and De Fries with him, they'd overpower Danny. Staying in the car wasn't an option – an occupied vehicle parking in the vicinity for three hours would scream a warning. Maybe he could walk into the hotel and pump the receptionist for info, but he quickly rejected that idea. Even if the receptionist spoke English, Taff would have already turned on the charm and offered them a few dollars to let him know if anyone came asking about him. So Danny turned his attention to the Zodiac Lounge. The tinted-glass window was an effective camouflage. Could he use that as an OP? He decided to try.

He left his M4 locked in the boot of the car. Turning up the collar of the raincoat, he walked along the street on the same side as the hotel, out of the line of sight of anybody watching from the windows. When he was alongside the entrance, he turned his back on it and crossed the street with the buzzing, flickering neon of the sign illuminating his face. Seconds later he was inside.

The place was dimly lit and surprisingly chintzy. Strange to think you could travel half a klick from here and see mortared football stadiums and craters in the streets. There was a low throb of dance music in the air, and maybe twenty-five customers were sitting at tables dotted around the floor. Along the back wall, fifteen metres from the entrance, was a gleaming metal-topped bar with an array of optics behind it, though Danny immediately noticed that several of the bottles were empty. Two women sat on bar stools – Middle Eastern, but decked out like Western women, all tits and arse. They watched Danny as he entered, another prospective client.

There was a table by the front window. Danny sat down and made a pretence of studying the laminated cocktail menu in front of him. In truth, his eyes were searching the windows of the hotel opposite. The flickering neon light reflected off the hotel's windows. It made it difficult to examine them, but Danny did so, starting at the top left of the building and moving slowly to the right before starting on the floor below. The windows were all closed, and it was impossible to see into any of them, especially with the neon dazzling his eyes.

Only when his eyes landed on the second window from the left on the first floor did he notice something odd. This window was open. Just a little – a gap of a few inches at the bottom – but definitely open. What did that tell him? It was a hot night, so why were all the others shut? Maybe they were just not occupied. Or maybe . . .

Suddenly aware of somebody standing over him, Danny started. As a reflex, his hand reached for his Sig. But then he stopped. It was a barmaid, standing by his table with a pad and looking rather bored.

'Speak English?' Danny asked.

She nodded.

He pointed to the street. 'That hotel,' he said. 'Does it have air-conditioning?'

The barmaid gave him an unfriendly look and glanced back at the two girls propping up the bar. Then she nodded.

'I'll have a beer,' he said. The barmaid went to get his order.

Danny turned back to the hotel, and to the window that was open. If the room had air-con, you'd keep it shut on a muggy night like this. Unless, of course, you were relying on your ears as well as your eyes to tell you what was going on outside. And Taff would, without question, be doing that.

His beer arrived. Danny took a pull on it, but he didn't take his eyes off the window. He knew where Taff was. All he had to do now was wait.

Three times they had poured the water over her face. Three times she had been engulfed by such panic she thought she would go mad. As the water gushed down her nose and throat for the third time, she tried to scream out that yes, she was a spy. She would say anything to make it stop. But then, just as her brain was telling her that she would surely drown if this torment continued, the water ceased and she felt the bed adjusting to its original angle.

Her tormentor was standing at the end of the bed, looking at her curiously, as though she was a specimen he had never encountered before. One of the Syrians had left the room. The remaining one was coiling the hose back on to its holder, his feet slapping on the wet floor as he moved. Once it was tidied away, the short man spoke a few words of Arabic, then he too left the room, leaving Clara alone with the Syrian. He was leering at her with an ugly, lascivious look, and with a burning sensation in her gut, Clara knew what was coming.

He walked round to her right side and slowly moved his vile lips towards hers. She could smell his breath – a stench of cigarettes, coffee and decay. As he pressed his mouth against hers, he tried to force his dry tongue through her lips. She gritted her teeth, but although he was unable to penetrate them, she felt his disgusting tongue massage their front before forcing its way into the hollow of her cheek. She tried to dislodge it by shaking her head, but he grabbed a clump of her hair with one hand to keep it still. She felt the other wandering down to her breasts, which he squeezed painfully, the nails digging into her flesh, before moving down across her belly to between her legs, where the painful groping continued for another half-minute.

Suddenly he stepped back. His expression was contemptuous and hungry. The features of a man who both loathed her and wanted her. He walked round to the front of the bed and started to unbuckle his belt.

Clara looked away, clamping her eyes shut. She heard the man unzip his trousers, then the shuffling sound as they dropped to the floor. She did not want to look, but somehow she couldn't stop herself. Through half-closed eyes she saw him standing there, trousers and underpants around his ankles, his penis erect. He was shuffling towards her, at once ridiculous and terrifying. With a whimper, she shut her eyes again, but she could already feel the heat of his body and smell that foul breath.

He was inches away.

There was nothing she could do to stop him.

21.30 hrs.

Danny had been sitting here for thirty minutes and his beer was already warm. He'd drunk only three mouthfuls. As she had done all evening, the waitress was loitering, making the point that his meagre consumption didn't warrant his prime spot by the window.

The bar was fuller now, standing room only as Westerners and locals alike arrived to get some respite from the reality of their lives in the midst of a civil war. None of them passed the threshold without an analytical glance from Danny. He was principally on the lookout for Hector or De Fries, but none of them seemed to be anything other than punters, out for a good time. Perhaps Taff's cronies were in the hotel room with him. Perhaps they'd found other diversions. He'd know soon enough.

The hotel was doing a far less brisk trade than the bar. Danny had seen one person go in, at 21.05 hrs. The guy had swiped a card to open the front door. That could be a problem.

Danny sipped his beer. By the bar, the waitress was talking to a Middle Eastern man in a suit. They were looking in his direction. Twenty seconds later the guy was walking towards him. He had shining black hair and an obsequious expression. Danny noticed a gold signet ring on one finger, and a spot of food on his tie.

'I'm very sorry, sir,' the man said, bowing slightly. 'This table is reserved.'

Danny looked back out of the window. 'Who for?'

A pause.

'Paying guests, sir.'

Without looking at him, Danny plunged his hand into his coat and pulled out the wad of banknotes. He tossed two 100-dollar bills on to the table and continued looking across at the hotel.

The man grabbed the money. 'Will sir require anything else?' he asked.

Danny shook his head, but then an idea struck him. 'Wait,' he said. He looked back towards the bar where the two hookers were still sitting, waiting for a john. 'I want some female company,' he said. 'Someone who speaks English.'

The man dipped his head politely. 'Of course.' He walked back to the bar and spoke briefly to one of the girls, who immediately got down from her stool and tottered across to where Danny was seated.

'Sit down,' he said, his attention back on the hotel.

She sat. Halter-neck top that didn't cover much. Plunging neckline. A necklace of cheap beads.

A minute passed in silence. Danny could feel the heat of her stare become increasingly surly. It occurred to him that he might not smell that fresh.

'I like champagne,' she said finally.

'We'll need a room,' Danny said. He pointed across the street. 'There.'

The woman shrugged. Danny laid another 100-dollar bill on the table. 'Go and book it. Then come back here and you'll get your champagne.'

She scooped up the note in a way that told Danny he was vastly overpaying for the room. He didn't care. He watched as the woman left, walked across the street to the hotel and rang an entrance buzzer. The door clicked open. Three minutes later she returned. If Taff was watching, he'd have clocked her, but that was OK. There was nothing so anonymous as a hooker in a bar. She sat down again and gave Danny an expectant look.

'Give me the key card,' he said.

She removed it from her clutch bag and placed it on the table. Danny took it and dropped a 100-dollar bill in its place. 'Have the rest of the evening off,' he muttered.

She didn't move for about ten seconds. Then, with a disgruntled little snort, she took the money and strode back to the bar, seemingly offended that she'd had such an easy trick.

Danny continued to watch.

23.56 hrs.

Four minutes till Taff's RV. The bar was throbbing now, but nobody disturbed Danny. His money was good.

He spotted him immediately. A young Syrian lad who carried a worn Nike sports bag and had a furtive look about him. He approached from the north end of the street, walking a little more quickly than any of the other passers-by and looking over his shoulder every few seconds. He stopped outside the hotel, bathed in the flickering neon light from the bar, and swiped a card. Two seconds later he was inside.

Even though the clock was ticking – he still needed to get to his 01.00 RV with the ambassador – Danny didn't stand up immediately. He gave it a full four minutes. Time enough, he estimated, for the kid to make his presence known and get to Taff's room. Right now, Danny reckoned, Taff would be frisking him thoroughly. And that probably meant his eyes wouldn't be on the street.

Danny stood up and slipped out of the bar. He didn't cross the road directly, but walked thirty metres up the street before getting to the other side and retracing his steps. Ninety seconds later he was swiping the card. The door clicked open. He entered.

The hotel's reception area was bland and antiseptic. Pale ceramic tiles on the floor, fake plastic pot plants, faux-leather chairs. On the counter there was a brass bell, but the receptionist was nowhere to be seen. Behind the counter, a door led to another room, where Danny could hear someone whistling. He leaned over the counter and quickly examined the contents of the desk behind it: an old computer terminal, a packet of cigarettes, an empty can of Coke and a key ring with a single swipe card attached.

The whistling stopped. Danny heard footsteps. He grabbed the key ring and hurried to his right, where a door led to a flight of stairs going up. In a corner of his brain he wondered how long he had before the receptionist realised his card was missing. Ten minutes?

That would be enough.

Danny emerged on the first-floor corridor. The same ceramic tiles. Four identical doors along the right-hand side, each with a card slot. He edged silently towards the second door. Once outside, he put his ear to it, and listened.

'. . . sure you're a nice enough fella, but humour me and empty the money out on to the bed. I don't want any nasty surprises.'

Taff's voice. He was in there.

The messenger boy didn't say anything, but there was a light shuffling sound inside the room.

A minute passed.

'OK, son. Looks like it's all there. Be a good lad and pack it all back in while I go for a slash. Do it nicely, there'll be a dollar or two in it for you. Hurry up before my friends come back. They're not as generous as me.'

Danny felt his jaw setting. The idea that Taff would disappear for a slash at a time like this was ludicrous. If he was heading into the bathroom, it was for some other reason. Danny's instinct told him that whatever he was up to, it would end badly for the messenger.

But Taff's words suggested there was no Hector or De Fries. It would just be him, Taff and the Syrian kid.

He rested the card in the slot.

'Make sure it's all packed neatly, son,' Taff called, and Danny could hear that he had changed position.

He slid the card down and there was a faint click.

'I don't want to have to do it again myself.'

Danny drew his Sig, then opened the door very slowly, very quietly.

The room was maybe eight by five metres. Garish bright orange carpet tiles on the floor. Double bed, dressing table, wardrobe. The air-con hummed gently. The window was still slightly ajar. A bedside lamp burned dimly. A door led from the left-hand wall into an en suite. There was a light on in there, and Taff's elongated shadow stretched out from the doorway. The messenger boy was leaning over the bed, packing bundles of notes into the Nike bag.

Distance: two metres. Danny advanced quickly but silently and slammed the butt of his Sig against the kid's neck. He slumped into a heap, the soft bed cushioning his fall. A couple of wads of dollar bills jumped from the mattress on to the floor.

Danny raised his Sig and aimed it firmly at the bathroom door.

The toilet flushed. There had been no sound of piss against the porcelain. Danny knew Taff would reappear with a weapon of some sort.

He kept his hand steady.

The shadow started to move.

Taff appeared in the doorway.

He froze.

Danny's mentor was carrying a rope about three-quarters of a metre long. A good length for strangling someone. He had clearly intended the messenger's death to be silent.

Now, though, his mind was on other things.

Danny could see in Taff's face the many minute calculations he would be making. Where were his exits? Could he draw his own weapon before Danny had the opportunity to fire? Was the messenger truly out cold, or might he wake up and cause a distraction? All these mental processes occurred without him taking his eyes off Danny.

'Good to see you, kiddo,' Taff said eventually, his voice breaking slightly. His nose was still flattened from their previous tussle.

Danny didn't respond.

'Fuck me, son, put the gun down. We've been through this. You're not going to use it.'

'That was then,' Danny said. 'This is now.'

'So what's changed?'

'Everything,' said Danny.

Then a strange thing happened. Taff's brow creased and Danny saw something in his expression that he'd never seen before. Doubt. And weariness too. Taff looked old. His skin looked grey in the flickering neon. Deeply lined. Careworn.

He bowed his head. 'You know?'

Danny nodded.

'How?'

'The Firm.'

Taff was making no attempt to deny it. He sounded almost relieved.

It was true.

'I always knew you'd find out,' said Taff. 'One day.' He looked around. 'I didn't think it would be in a place like this.' He closed his eyes. 'I did what I could to make it up to you, Danny. So finish it quickly. You owe me that.'

'I don't owe you anything.'

Silence. Ten seconds passed. Taff opened his eyes again.

'Why?' Danny asked.

'What does it matter?'

'It matters to me.'

Taff stared blankly. 'Money,' he said. 'I told you already: it always comes down to that.' For a moment he looked as if that was all the explanation he was going to give. But Danny didn't move, and after thirty seconds he continued to speak. 'Back in the Province,' he said, 'the Regiment had access to good intel on the whereabouts of high-value IRA targets. There was money to be made selling that intel to loyalist paramilitaries. I took advantage of that. End result was the same. One behind the ear. What did it matter if it was the Regiment nailed those scumbags, or some Michael Stone wannabe?'

'Dead's dead?'

Taff managed a sneer. 'You're the same as your dad.'

'What's that supposed to mean?'

'He found out what I was doing. Threatened to shop me. Couldn't let it happen, kiddo. Simple as that. When I heard your mum was giving birth in Dundonald, I knew where to find him. Dressed myself as a hospital orderly, got into their room. Piece of piss.'

A glazed look passed over his face. A pained look.

'I didn't want to do it, kiddo, but your dad gave me no choice. It was only ever meant to be him, though. Not your mum. Never your mum.'

The neon flickered. Taff's eyes looked watery in his grizzled face.

'She threw herself at me. Knocked my aim. The round grazed your dad's skull. When we hit the ground the weapon went off by accident. She died quickly.' There was something about the way he said it that made Danny feel he was trying to persuade himself on that count. 'I lost my head,' Taff continued. 'Escaped through the window, dumped the scrubs under a bush. Then I returned to the hospital.'

'To finish the job?' Danny asked.

'I don't know, kiddo. I was in a state of shock. But when the doctors told me that your dad was likely to lose his memory, I knew I didn't have to . . . to finish what I started.' He closed his eyes again and drew a deep breath. 'I never meant anything to happen to your mum. I loved her.'

'You had a strange way of showing it.'

'I did what I could,' Taff snapped. 'I looked after you, didn't I? Kept my eye on you. Taught you things. You think you'd be where you are now if I'd left you to your fucking vegetable of a father? Jesus, kiddo – I *was* your father, or as good as.'

Danny felt his brow creasing. 'No,' he said. 'You weren't.'

Taff winced at this.

'Was it worth it, Taff? To shoot your friend for money?'

'We all shoot people for the money,' Taff spat. 'You as well as me.'

Danny shook his head. 'You're wrong,' he said.

'Bullshit.' Taff nodded at the bundles of banknotes on the bed. 'Try and tell me you won't pocket that lot when you leave here tonight.'

Danny didn't look at the money. He kept his gun arm straight, his gaze firmly fixed on Taff.

'*Fucking do it!*' Taff shouted. '*End it!*'

It required a blow. Nothing else would release the anger building up in Danny's blood, certainly not the cowardly squeeze of a trigger. He lunged forwards, covering the three metres between them in a fraction of a second. He struck Taff on the side of the face – the blow half fist, half gun metal – and his bulk slammed into Taff's body, knocking them both to the ground with a solid thump. He felt Taff's cheekbone crack, but he knew in an instant he'd made the wrong move. There was a flurry of arms and legs, of bones against muscle. Taff was more than thirty years older than Danny, but his strength had never deserted him. Danny felt his gun hand being slammed against the floor. He managed to keep hold of the weapon, but when Taff attacked his wrist for a second time his fingers opened and the weapon fell from his fist on to the thin carpet.

Taff's weapon, however, the rope with which he'd clearly intended to eliminate the messenger boy, was still firmly in his grasp.

Danny tried to drive his fist into Taff's already broken nose, but Taff caught his arm in time and, with a titanic effort that caused him to grunt from the exertion, rolled Danny over on to his front. Danny felt a knee against his spine. And then a rope around his neck.

His arms flailed, but although he could reach Taff, who was kneeling on his back, he couldn't hurt him. He could feel the rope constricting his airway. Taff was twisting the loose ends together, tightening the noose. Within seconds Danny couldn't speak.

Couldn't breathe.

He moved his arms up, but his fingers could get no purchase between the rope and his skin.

He started to feel dizzy. Light-headed. He heard Taff's voice. Whispering. Hissing. Like he was talking to himself, and not to Danny. 'I gave you a fucking chance. More than one. It's not my fault if you were too stupid to take it . . .'

The rope grew tighter.

Tighter.

'I didn't want to do this. I never wanted to do this. You've been like a son to me, but you've forced me into it.'

Danny's lungs were burning from a build-up of carbon dioxide. He could feel his system shutting down.

'Your mum was too good for the both of you . . .'

In the darkness clouding his mind, Danny saw his father, alone in his wheelchair, staring at the photograph that sat on the TV in his tiny home. Saw the look in his eyes. Saw Kyle, half pissed and fully fucked, just another piece of collateral damage in the battle of Taff's greed.

Danny's hands fell from his neck. With his final scrap of strength he wormed his hands down his body, feeling for his chest rig, his fingers edging towards the knife Taff had given him all those years ago.

'A man always has need of a good knife, kiddo.' The memory flashed through his mind.

His fingers slipped from the hilt. He tried to grab it again, this time with more success. It slid out. His fist closed round the hilt.

He knew he only had one chance. That if he didn't strike in the next few seconds, the last thing he would ever see would be an extreme close-up of the bright orange carpet in this hotel room.

It was a single movement. Danny yanked the knife out from under him and swung his arm randomly back in towards Taff's body. He felt the blade puncture the coarse material of Taff's trousers and plunge deeply into the flesh of his left thigh. Taff roared in pain. He released his grip on the rope. Danny gasped as he inhaled deeply. With a supreme effort, he twisted his body around and threw Taff sideways on to the floor.

There was a distance of two metres between them. The Sig lay on the ground in the middle. The two men lunged for it at the same time.

Danny got there first.

And now Taff was lying on his back, the knife still sticking out of his thigh and blood pissing over the carpet. He had stopped howling, but his face was white with pain. Danny was kneeling, and although rage and confusion surged through him, his gun hand – fully extended, the weapon pointing at Taff's head – was steady.

'You think I'm going to kill you, Taff?' he said. 'I'm not.'

Hope flashed across Taff's face.

'At least, not quickly. I'm going to let you know what it was like when my dad took that bullet to the head.'

'I've regretted that all my life,' Taff said.

'Not enough,' Danny told him. 'Not nearly enough.'

In one swift movement he changed the trajectory of his hand, so now the gun was pointing across Taff's forehead.

He fired. He knew it would be noisy, but he didn't care.

The round only skimmed Taff's frontal lobe before slamming into the wall of the hotel room. It was sufficient, though, to take a couple of centimetres' depth of skull with it. A shard of bone flew across the room, and Danny caught a brief glimpse of brain matter before a curtain of blood slid down over Taff's face. His eyes widened, and then all his limbs started to shake and judder as the signals from his brain became confused and degraded and he lost control of his body. A gurgling sound came from his throat, like he was trying to say something. But even if the power of speech had not deserted him, Danny wouldn't have listened.

The shaking grew more violent, more grotesque. Danny stood up and turned his back on his long-time mentor. He saw that the messenger boy was still unconscious. He approached the bed and started collecting up the bundles of notes and stuffing them into the bag. No time to count them, but he was sure Taff would have done his sums properly. When he was done, he looked over at his old friend. The shaking was beginning to subside, but his face was still a mask of blood and his tongue was lolling from the side of his mouth as if he was having an epileptic fit. He looked helpless. Like a child.

Danny turned. Without looking back he walked out of the room and back down the corridor, allowing the door to close quietly on the dying man behind him.

TWENTY-SEVEN

01.03 hrs.

Someone was waiting for him.

The RV point was not of Danny's choosing. The ambassador had suggested it. It made him nervous. It was a T-junction on the M5 heading south. The road itself was surrounded by bleak, flat desert as far as was visible in the moonlight, and although there was no other traffic, it was out in the open and entirely indefensible. There were two cars parked side by side off the highway, five metres between them. Danny estimated that they were ten metres in front of the T-junction. They were alongside the right-hand southbound carriageway, but heading north, clearly ready to move quickly if necessary. Headlamps were off. Danny pulled over at a distance of seventy-five metres, parking the car at right angles to the road so he could at least use the vehicle for some sort of cover. He used his night-sight to zoom in on the two cars. They were certainly occupied, but he couldn't make out any faces.

He pulled out the sat phone he'd taken from the embassy and dialled the ambassador's number, still keeping an eye on the interior of the two cars. He saw a glow inside the one on the right, just as the ambassador's phone was ringing.

It rang eight times. Why the delay? What was the ambassador waiting for? What was he discussing?

'Hello?'

The Czech sounded wary.

'Do you have them?' Danny asked.

'Do *you* have the money?'

'That wasn't the question.'

A nervous pause.

'Three men, one woman. They have been badly beaten.'

'I want to see them. Tell them to get out one by one and walk round to the far side of the vehicles.'

'I want to see the money first.'

'Forget it, pal. Buyer's market. You're not seeing shit until I know you've got them.'

Another pause. And then the passenger door of the left-hand car opened. A figure emerged.

Even through the green haze of the night-sight, Danny could make out the bruises on Buckingham's face. His cheeks were swollen, his eyes puffy. He limped as he walked and his body twitched nervously. Whatever had happened to him at the hands of the *Mukhabarat* had been severe.

Clara came next. Her face was not so swollen, but she walked in such a way that suggested her tortures, though less visible, had been more violent. Sexually violent. She seemed to be doing what she could to hold her head up high as she joined Buckingham.

When the next figure appeared, Danny felt a strange mixture of horror and relief. It was Spud, or at least a version of him. His hair had been shaved off, his nose was clearly broken, his lips split. His left arm hung at an angle from his shoulder, smashed and left untreated. Hard to imagine the pain he must be in. He limped as he walked round to join the others, though Danny noticed how, despite everything, his eyes were scanning the surrounding area, looking for threats. How much did he know about what was happening? Not a lot, Danny figured by the look of suspicion he cast in the direction of his vehicle.

And then Greg. Jesus, the poor bastard couldn't even walk. Two Syrian men – Danny could only assume that these were the ambassador's *Mukhabarat* contacts – had to carry him with one arm around each of their shoulders. His head – also shaved – lolled, and Danny wasn't sure that he was even conscious.

But at least he had four positive IDs.

He spoke into the sat phone again. 'Get out of the car,' he told the ambassador. 'Tell your secret-police mates to stand twenty metres back from the hostages. Then I want to see you standing ten metres in front of the vehicles with the sat phone to your ear. If I get the impression your buddies are listening, the deal's off.'

'This is not what we agreed. They will not do that.'

'Fine. Nice knowing you, pal.'

'*Wait!*'

Ten seconds passed before the ambassador stepped out of his car. He walked towards the others and spoke to them for perhaps thirty seconds. Danny watched as the two Syrians stepped back, as he had instructed, then the ambassador paced nervously northwards in Danny's direction, the phone pressed to his ear, before coming to a halt out of range of the vehicles.

'If you want your money, you have to do exactly as I say,' Danny told him over the handset. 'Are you carrying a weapon?'

'Of course.'

'A handgun?'

'Yes.'

'Give it to the man called Spud, along with your phone. Then get back in your car and drive towards me. I'll have a weapon trained on you all the time. Don't switch your lights on. If you exceed twenty kilometres an hour, or if I see that there's anyone else in the car with you, I'll open fire. Stop ten metres from my vehicle and stay behind the wheel. Understood?'

A silence.

'Understood.'

Danny watched him walk round to where the hostages were waiting. He handed something to Spud, then hurried back to his car. Seconds later it moved off.

'Spud, can you hear me?'

'Who the fuck's that?' His voice sounded rough.

'Danny.'

A pause.

'Took your fucking time, mucker.'

'RV at 01.30 hrs at a crossroads five klicks south of here. Can you overpower the goons?'

Another pause.

'We're in a bad way, mate. I didn't think Greg was going to make it through another night.'

'We need them to get us through any roadblocks. We don't have time to fight our way through. I'll deal with the ambassador first.'

Danny returned his attention to the approaching car. It had stopped exactly where he had instructed.

Taff's bag of money was resting on the passenger seat of the vehicle. Danny leaned in and grabbed a fistful of notes. He didn't know how much it was, but neither did he expect the ambassador to sit around counting it. Money in one hand, unlocked Sig in the other, he walked towards the car.

The ambassador lowered his window as Danny approached. By the time he was alongside, pistol fully on view, the Czech had his hands resting on the top of the steering wheel. Sweat dripped from his brow, he licked his lips nervously and his eyes darted towards Danny.

Danny chucked the bundle of notes on to the ambassador's lap.

'Go. Now.'

Immediately the ambassador veered off the side of the road and crossed to the correct lane. His tyres screeched as he accelerated and he'd already travelled thirty metres before he remembered to switch on his lights. In the distance, Danny saw that another car was approaching. It was maybe two kilometres away. Most likely just another civilian, but he didn't want to make assumptions. He jumped back behind the wheel and drove towards the others.

As he pulled up ten metres from the remaining vehicles, he could see that Spud had already taken control of the situation. Although his broken arm was still hanging uselessly by his side, he had the ambassador's pistol aimed at the two Syrians, who had raised their hands in the air and looked very frightened. Danny raised his own weapon in their direction, then edged over to where the others were standing. Buckingham and Clara were holding Greg up now. Buckingham had the thousand-yard stare and was shivering. At least it meant he kept quiet.

No time for pleasantries. Just instructions.

'We need both vehicles,' Danny said. 'Too many of us crammed into one will just raise suspicion if we're stopped.'

'Leave *her*,' Buckingham interrupted.

Clara turned to him and, quite coolly, slapped his bruised face. Buckingham squealed with pain.

'I've been wanting to do that for days,' Danny muttered, before turning back to Spud. 'We'll take one of these Syrian fuckers each in case of roadblocks. They'll—'

'Danny . . .' Clara interrupted. She tugged at his sleeve and pointed back along the road.

Danny turned. Another vehicle had parked almost exactly where he himself had stopped. The headlamps were on full beam and the driver's door was opening. Danny raised his scope, wincing slightly as the close-up of the headlamps burned his retina. The figure emerging was short and squat. He carried an assault rifle.

Danny recognised the face.

Hector. Bastard must have seen him leaving Al Kamada Street and followed him. Must be here for the money . . .

'*Get down!*' he yelled.

He pulled Clara to the ground. Greg and Buckingham fell with them. Spud dived of his own accord. A burst of gunfire rang out, and suddenly the air was filled with inhuman screaming. One of the secret police had been hit.

Danny made his way to the front of the *Mukhabarat*'s vehicle, where he got line of sight with Hector. He saw that De Fries was sitting in the passenger seat. Distance: seventy-five metres. Danny loosed a round. It ricocheted with a spark off the open driver's door, causing Hector to seek cover in the vehicle.

'I know this cunt,' Danny shouted over his shoulder to Spud. 'We don't want him after us. I can distract him. You need to get the others to the 01.30 RV with the chopper.'

'Roger that!'

The wounded Syrian was still screaming. Movement from the direction of Hector's car. He was emerging again . . .

There was ten metres of open ground between Danny and his own vehicle. If he didn't move quickly, Hector wouldn't give him the chance to cover it. He jumped to his feet, raised his Sig and, arm outstretched, released another round as he ran to the car. It took him five seconds to get there, in which time he released another three rounds. The windscreen of Hector's car shattered to reveal De Fries still in the passenger seat. Hector dived back in.

As Danny hurled himself into his own vehicle, it crossed his mind to grab his M4 from the passenger seat and open up. He quickly rejected that idea. Two against one. Even if Danny made it through those odds, he couldn't be sure that his companions wouldn't be wounded in the crossfire.

So he didn't grab his rifle. He grabbed Taff's bag of money instead. He held it out of his window, in full view of Hector, for three seconds. His message was clear. You want it – come and get it.

Then he slung the bag back on to the passenger seat, slammed his foot on the accelerator and sped west into open country.

The beaten-up Peugeot bounced over the stony desert floor. Immediately Danny started driving in a random, zigzag pattern. He knew he was going to draw fire and he needed to make himself as difficult to hit as possible. Screeching up through the gears, he checked his rear-view mirror. Hector was already chasing him, but Danny was accelerating faster. The distance between them was thirty metres and increasing. They'd pick up speed soon, but at the moment he had the edge. Back by the road, he caught a quick glimpse of the others. Spud was forcing the remaining secret policeman at gunpoint into the driver's seat of their vehicle. That was all Danny needed to know. The others were in Spud's hands now. The responsibility of getting them to the RV was his.

The Peugeot's ancient engine screeched as Danny forced the speedo up past 90 kph. It rattled its way across the uneven desert. When he was 150 metres from the road he yanked the steering wheel to the left so that he was heading south. Five seconds later the first round hit.

The Peugeot's rear windscreen shattered and the noise of the protesting engine was joined by a sudden, deafening rush of air. Danny checked his mirrors. There was forty metres between them and the gap seemed constant. They were moving at the same speed. Which was bad news, because if Danny had to continue to zigzag to avoid being hit – and he did – it meant covering more ground. And that meant Hector would catch up.

With his right hand still on the wheel, he used his left to point the Sig over his shoulder. He couldn't aim, of course, but perhaps a couple of loose rounds would make his pursuers think twice about getting too close.

He let one go, almost deafening himself in the process. It flew harmlessly through the desert air. His second shot was more successful, smashing into Hector's left headlamp. He zigzagged again, and noted that the gap still remained constant. They'd slowed down. For now.

No more rounds from behind. Had they spent their ammo? More likely they were saving it for when they had a better chance of a kill. Danny set his eyes on the landscape ahead. The terrain had become more undulating, so he could no longer see the road to his left and every few seconds the vehicle behind him disappeared in a dip.

He tried to analyse his options. They really wanted this money. Perhaps he should just stop and throw it at them.

No. They'd still move in for the kill.

Time check: 01.17 hrs. Thirteen minutes till RV. He reckoned it was about three klicks to the crossroads. He realised he still hadn't disconnected the sat phone, so he grabbed it from the dashboard and yelled into it: '*Spud! Update me!*'

No answer. '*Shit!*'

But his only option was to keep going.

Incoming fire.

A round flew over his right shoulder, missing him by inches and slamming into the windscreen. The glass splintered but did not break. He couldn't see a thing. Even as his foot was pressed on the accelerator, he whacked the body of his Sig against the glass. It shattered and fell inwards, cutting open the back of his left hand. Blood and glass were suddenly everywhere. He ignored it and fired another round behind him. It went astray.

'*Fuck!*' They'd closed the gap. Twenty-five metres max. The threat of Danny's loose rounds was no longer slowing them down.

With the force of the wind in his face, it was difficult to see up ahead, but was the gradient increasing? Could he see the brow of a hill silhouetted against the inky night sky?

He could. What was more, he could make out the lights of a vehicle moving along that brow from west to east. That meant the crossroads was somewhere up there. The RV point was close. No more than a klick and a half.

'*Spud!*' he roared into the sat phone. '*Where the fuck are you?*'

Still no reply, but as he raced on he caught sight of the road a couple of hundred metres to his left. A vehicle was speeding along it, roughly adjacent to Danny's own position. Was it them? He had to hope so.

He moved the steering wheel a few degrees counterclockwise, aligning his bearing to where the road met the brow of the hill. A sharp pain stung through his cut hand. The blood loss was heavy, but he had to ignore it. He could see De Fries leaning out of the passenger window rifle in hand, preparing to fire. He swerved to the left, and just in time. The rounds destroyed his right-hand wing mirror, and for a moment he lost control of the vehicle. But he brought himself back on to his bearing with another shot over his shoulder.

Time check: 01.27 hrs. Three minutes till RV. Distance to the brow of the hill: 500 metres. Danny saw the other vehicle disappear over the top. That figured: Spud would never halt on a ridge where he could be seen for several kilometres all around. He estimated that he was thirty seconds from the RV point. Could he defend it for two minutes while they waited for the pick-up?

He didn't get the chance to find out. There was a horrific explosion as a round from behind slammed into his rear left-hand tyre. The car spun out of control, turning two full circles at speed before coming to a sudden, jolting halt. In the confusion, Danny could hear the screeching of the other car's brakes. He knew he only had seconds before they opened up on him. Seconds in which to dive from the car, which was about to be showered with rounds. Grabbing his M4, Danny hurled himself out of the driver's door, landing with a thump on the hard ground. And just in time, because at that moment a furious barrage of rounds slammed into the trashed Peugeot – the only object now between Danny and the two mercenaries intent on killing him.

He was 100 metres from the top of the hill. Between the Peugeot and Hector's car was another twenty. Another burst of rounds slammed into the abandoned vehicle, and then everything fell silent.

Hector's voice rang across the desert.

'Throw us the money, kid. Maybe we'll let you go.'

Danny didn't answer. He knew that Hector had no intention of letting him walk free. If he moved, or replied, all he'd do was give away his exact position.

'That was quite a mess you made of Taff,' Hector taunted. 'Never had you down as the type. *Kiddo.*'

Danny fought the urge to defend himself. They're just goading you. Ignore it.

'You're fucked, kid. You know that. Make it easy on yourself, eh?'

A noise reached Danny's ears. Mechanical. He looked back towards the brow of the hill. There was a faint glow beyond it. He looked at his watch. 01.30 hrs.

Hector had clearly noticed it too. He didn't sound very worried. 'What you going to do, kid? Walk across open ground to your friends? I don't think so. Don't be a twat. We'll have you before you've gone five metres. It's over. Face it.'

But Danny wasn't going to face it. He reckoned he had one play left.

He felt for his night-sight and looked back towards the ridge of the hill. It took him only a couple of seconds to zoom in on Spud. He was lying on his front, and also had a scope held to his eye. As soon as he saw that Danny had clocked him, he held up five fingers of one hand.

Four fingers.

Danny hunkered down, his breath heavy, sweat pouring from his dirty face.

Three fingers.

'OK, kid. You had your chance. Say your fucking prayers.'

Two fingers.

One finger.

Rounds thundered against the Peugeot once more. But at exactly the same time newcomers joined the party. Two Apache helicopters, separated by a distance of no more than thirty metres, rose swiftly right above the hill. For a couple of seconds they seemed to hover at a height of about twenty metres.

And then, very fast, they advanced.

Within seconds, the thunder of the attack helicopters' rotors felt like it was going right through Danny. One was directly above him, at perhaps thirty-five metres, nose down, ready to strike.

The noise of its front-mounted Minigun was like the grinding of an immense chainsaw as it dispensed its 7.62mm rounds in the precise direction of Hector and De Fries.

Five seconds of fire.

Ten seconds.

Fifteen.

It stopped.

And then there was an explosion.

Danny didn't need to look towards Hector and De Fries's car to realise that its fuel tank had ignited. The sound of the explosion and the subsequent rain of debris told him everything. He covered his head for ten seconds, waiting for the shower to subside. Then he pushed himself to his feet again.

The Apaches had gained height. Seventy-five metres, maybe more. But now, above the brow of a hill, a third aircraft rose. Danny instantly recognised the silhouette of a Black Hawk as it hovered, dark against the horizon. Only as it flew in his direction did he find himself looking back into the remains of the Peugeot. The interior was lit up by the flames of Hector and De Fries's burning vehicle twenty metres away, and he saw the bag of money sitting there on the passenger seat. A small part of him thought about taking it. It crossed his mind that Taff would have expected him to do just that.

And so he left it. His days of following Taff's advice were gone.

As the Black Hawk touched down twenty-five metres south of his position, Danny strapped his M4 over his shoulder and nursed his bleeding hand as he ran towards it. The downdraught kicked dust up into the air. As it hit the blades it caused a halo of glowing sparks above the chopper. Danny kept his head down and ran to the side entrance.

A soldier was shouting at him to climb inside, holding out one hand to help him in. But Danny didn't need any help. He climbed inside the dark but spotless interior of the Black Hawk and immediately his eyes picked out those faces he recognised. There was no sign of the *Mukhabarat* officer Spud had taken in the car. No doubt, having outlived his usefulness, he was dead on the side of the hill. Greg was on his back, receiving medical treatment. Spud crouched anxiously by him, but looked over to Danny and gave him an understated nod before turning back to his mate. Buckingham was crouching in one corner, his terrified eyes glowing pale in the darkness, his floppy hair a straggly mess over his bruised face.

And there was Clara. As the Black Hawk took to the air, she stood up and moved towards Danny, before embracing him wordlessly.

He accepted the embrace, then disentangled himself and looked out of the chopper's side door. In the air above them, about fifty metres away, he could see one of the Apache chaperones keeping watch. And below, in the distance, the sprawling lights of Damascus. On the eastern edge of the city, tracer fire arced above the buildings, a glowing reminder that Buckingham and Carrington's ill-judged intervention had changed nothing in this war-torn country. The Syrians would keep on killing themselves. There was very little anyone on the outside could do about it.

Danny turned his back on the view. It wasn't his problem any more. He was going home.

EPILOGUE

London. Ten days later.

Hugo Buckingham winced as he stood up from his desk. His skin was still sore from the beating he had endured at the hands of the Damascus *Mukhabarat*, but he wore the scars with a kind of pride. Here, newly installed in the MI6 building with a fancy new job title and an even fancier new salary, he was surrounded by analysts and administrative staff who'd heard whispers of his bravery in Syria and looked at him with a certain respect.

He walked over to the door. Someone had just knocked and he knew who it would be. He fixed his face into a smile before opening up.

'Danny, old sport! Bloody good to see you!' He held out his hand. The SAS man didn't take it, but Buckingham shrugged off the insult. 'Come on in, come on in, have a seat.' He walked over to the window. His fifth-floor office looked straight over the entrance to the building and across the Thames. 'Bloody good view, eh? Must say it's good to see the London skyline after our little fracas in the Middle East . . .'

He turned back to Danny, who was standing on the other side of the desk, his face expressionless.

'Carrington told me about Taff. Turn-up for the books, eh?'

Silence.

'Perhaps for the best. Everyone's a little embarrassed about his role in the whole Syrian debacle. Drink? No? Don't mind if I do?'

He poured himself a nip of Scotch from a trolley by the window, and drank it in one hit.

'I was wondering if you'd seen Clara? Bloody good-looking girl that. Got a bit of guts – I like that in a woman. Thought I might ask her out for a spot of supper, see where it leads. No? Ah well, I'm sure I can track her down.' He waved one arm to indicate the building in general. 'Not like I don't have the resources, eh? Actually, that's what I wanted to talk to you about. Sure you won't have a seat?'

Danny didn't move.

'Truth is, old sport, you and I have rather come up smelling of roses. Wasn't quite the outcome we wanted in Syria, but everyone's impressed by the way we handled the situation when it all went wrong. Quite a team, you and I, wouldn't you say?'

Danny still didn't speak, but he couldn't prevent a look of deep contempt crossing his face.

'Thing is, in my new capacity here in the Service, there's every chance going forward that I'll need to call on someone resourceful for issues of a . . . a *sensitive* nature. I know I can rely on you.'

'There's plenty of men in Hereford, Buckingham,' Danny said after several seconds' silence. 'Ask one of them. You and me won't be working together again.'

'You think?' Buckingham replied with a little smile. 'You might be surprised, old sport. You might be surprised.'

'Is there anything else?'

'I don't think so. We'll speak again soon, I'm sure.'

'Not if I have anything to do with it.'

Buckingham smiled again. 'Well, there's the funny thing,' he said, a certain amount of steel entering his voice. 'You really don't.'

Danny started to leave the room. But when he reached the door he stopped and looked back. Buckingham was pleased to see a flicker of uncertainty cross his face. Then he turned and was gone.

Buckingham sat down at his desk. There was nothing but a laptop and a telephone on it, but from a drawer to one side he pulled out a small mobile phone. It looked rather beaten up, but that was only to be expected. He'd carried it all round Syria, after all. A miracle they hadn't taken it off him in Damascus, and a bloody good job too. He opened up the back and removed a 5GB SD card, which he inserted into a slot on the side of his laptop. A window popped up, containing a number of yellow folders. He clicked on the one labelled 'Video', then on one of the icons that appeared.

A moving image filled the screen and a chaotic noise burst from the speakers. Buckingham was instantly transported back to that terrifying afternoon in Asu's compound. His hand had been shaking as he covertly recorded the events, and the footage juddered. But even at a distance of several metres, and through the dust, he could quite clearly make out Danny Black, kneeling at the side of the child he was about to kill with an overdose of morphine. And the voices – Taff Davies, Black himself, the mother – were quite clear.

'That's a lethal dose, kiddo. You sure you know what you're doing?'

'He's dead anyway.'

'You killed my son! Murderer!'

What Black had done was illegal. A war crime. That piece of footage in itself was enough to see him behind bars. For a long time.

Which meant he had enough on Danny Black to ensure the kid came running whenever he called. His own personal Regiment operative, there to do his bidding whenever he wanted. A hundred times better than one of Max Saunders' untrustworthy private military contractors. Could be useful, he told himself. Very useful. The person who could control such a resource could go far.

He stood up again. Wincing, he walked back over to the window and looked out over the front of the SIS building. Black was there, trotting down the steps. And somebody was waiting for him. A woman. Bloody pretty. One arm in a crutch. Buckingham squinted, and he felt a certain pang when he realised who it was. And a bigger pang when they kissed.

'Little *bastard*,' he muttered to himself.

They spoke, and then Black looked up in the direction of Buckingham's window. For a moment, it felt as if he was staring directly at him. But then Buckingham reminded himself that it was impossible. The glass was mirrored. Nobody could see through it. He was hidden.

He watched Black and Clara walk away, hand in hand. Then he returned to his desk and removed the SD card from his computer. He needed to keep that safe, he told himself. Very safe.

He didn't know how soon he was going to need it.

CHRIS RYAN

IS BACK WITH HIS NEW NOVEL

HUNTER KILLER

SEPTEMBER 2014